EROSION

EROSION

A NOVEL

BY

S. A. HEMMINGS

And the moon swept down black water
Like an empty spotlight.

Joni Mitchell, *For The Roses*

To Liz
in very best wishes

[signature]

Christmas 2014

ISBN-13: 978-1495952463

For Cassius and Rudi

1967

They gave him the bed he'd had before, the one with the window behind it, and the fire escape zigzagging past like the skeleton of a giraffe's neck. He was pleased, it made him feel like a welcome guest. They left him to unpack his bag, telling him to find his way to the dining room when he'd finished. He knew where it was. They'd save something for him. Scrambled egg tonight, said Janet, licking her lips and making her eyes round, as though scrambled egg was the most delicious tea ever. And fruit salad, she added, waddling away down the dormitory, the soles of her fluffy mules slapping against the lino.

He wasn't hungry. His stomach had been knotted up ever since The Other Craig had turned up in their kitchen, wearing nothing but his y-fronts and frying bacon. Craig One, his mother introduced him as, propped in the doorway between kitchen and living room in her pink nylon negligee with the frills. *But I'm Craig One,* he'd felt like shouting, *you had me before you had him.* He'd said nothing, though. His mother would never listen when she was in this mood, her shining eyes fixed on The Other Craig as if she'd never seen anything as wonderful as a man cooking bacon in his y-fronts before. He'd known then what would happen next and he'd waited, curled up inside like a hedgehog in the road.

There was a pattern to life with his mother's boyfriends, as predictable as the pattern on the car tyres that would squash the hedgehog. For a week or two, sometimes as much as a month, it would be all happy families, him wedged between them on the sagging sofa while they watched *Coronation Street*, or running down to Just Call Me Patel's for a bottle of cooking sherry so Mum could make a trifle for Saturday tea, after the football. Then he'd begin to hear shouting and crying, sometimes a slap, through his bedroom walls. Thin as a tin. He'd pretend he was a tiny alien, living in his nan's Coronation biscuit tin that had stood in the middle of her mantelpiece before she'd died and taken with her everything clean and permanent in his life, the smell of furniture polish and violet creams and the deep bath that was always slightly gritty with Vim. He'd take his model of the Apollo spaceship off the bedside table and clutch it under the bed covers and tell himself he was going to the Moon. Even when he couldn't see it, he carried the Moon around inside him, round and gleaming like a new sixpence. It was his promise to himself.

He spent some time unpacking his things from the shopping bag Mum had stuffed them in, saying she and Craig One needed a bit of time to themselves to sort a few things out, that it'd only be for a week or two, then he could come home. 'Tell you what,' she said, ruffling his hair as they stood in the yawning stone porch of Appsley House and the laurel bushes dripped in the drive behind them, 'I'll get Craig to paint your room for you, shall I?'

'Thanks, Mum,' he'd replied, but glancing up at her sidelong, he'd seen something in his mother's expression that reminded him of the time he'd been in the front row at the circus, close enough to the clowns to read the expressions of desperation not quite hidden by their makeup.

He'd felt this overwhelming, embarrassing pity for them that stuck in his throat and made him throw up, so then Mum and whichever boyfriend it was then had a row about the extra lolly. He didn't think there was much chance of The Other Craig painting his room.

He was relieved when Janet answered the doorbell and Mum handed him over with one of her showy hugs, precariously content now to be alone in the dim yellow light from the bare bulb overhead as he folded his pyjamas and put them under the thin, flappy pillow. He set Apollo on top of the hardboard bedside cupboard, like the one Nan had had in hospital, but not painted white, and smelling of Dettol rather than lavender bags. Then he lay on his bed, on his front, chin cupped in his hands, looking out of the window and waiting for the Moon. He remembered that the Moon came up in this window, peering through the fire escape and the bars of the bedstead so it looked as if the Moon was in prison and he was free.

He knew he hadn't met Arthur Ingliss before, even though Arthur insisted he'd had the bed next to his for ever so long, as long as he could remember, since before England had won the World Cup anyway. He'd have remembered Arthur. He was a runty little kid, even though he insisted he was older than Craig. ('When're you eleven, then?' 'February 23rd.' 'Well I'm November 12th so there.') He had the kind of skin that always looked dirty, and thick, pale hair that stuck out all over his head, and a face Craig thought of as weasely even though he'd never, to his knowledge, seen a weasel. But he carried himself like a film star, with a moody slouch and his greenish eyes half closed and a hands-in-pockets swagger that made you believe he was wearing Levis rather than grey school shorts.

Not that he went to school all that often. On Craig's first day, Arthur mooched up to him in the breakfast queue and said, 'How about bunking off, then? We could go to the arcades.'

'I haven't any money.'

'We can get money.' The way he said it sent a little thrill through Craig.

'OK,' he said, and felt as though he'd stepped into *Brighton Rock*. He'd watched *Brighton Rock* one Sunday afternoon with Mum, the gas fire hissing and rain streaming down the windows, just the two of them, when she was between boyfriends. She'd been as excited as a girl when she discovered it was on, and told Craig she'd written an essay about it at school that had won a prize. 'Here we are,' she'd announced, after going through the boxes under the stairs. She'd put a heavy book in Craig's lap, its red cloth binding decorated with gold images of fairies and strange, twisted trees. 'See?' She opened the book. Inside the front cover was a label covered in the kind of writing you got on gravestones. Copperplate, Mum called it.

THE MRS. GASKELL PRIZE FOR LITERATURE
ELIZABETH BARNES
12TH JULY 1956

Then Mum sighed and looked sad, but when Craig asked, she told him there was nothing wrong and to pay attention to the film.

That day, the day it happened, they never got as far as the arcades. Afterwards Craig couldn't explain it, not to the police or the woman with dolls and drawing paper whose bosoms wobbling inside her cheesecloth smock terrified and fascinated him. Or in the courtroom, where he felt as if he'd been thrust on to the stage of a macabre pantomime and forgotten his lines.

The baby had looked so well cared for, so complacent, bundled under its jolly blanket of knitted squares, each square like a bright postcard bearing the message, 'Someone loves me'. He remembered its plump red cheeks and mittened hands boxing a string of blue and white horses stretched across the pushchair handles. He remembered a surge of emotion that picked him up, carried him across the road and kicked off the pushchair's brake. Later he found a bruise on his big toe which reminded him he'd only been wearing tennis shoes. But he couldn't say what the emotion was or why it had made him do what he did, so he kept quiet. Keeping quiet seemed less stupid than saying, 'I don't know.' He didn't want to be thought stupid, by the men in wigs or the woman with the bosoms, or Arthur, or Mum with her name in copperplate inside the cover of *Fairy Tales* by Hans Christian Andersen.

Besides, Mum was making enough noise for both of them, sitting in something called the public gallery, surrounded by men who kept looking at her then taking notes, just like the students he'd once seen on a school trip to the Graves, glancing at paintings then scribbling in drawing books. Except that the men looked seedy rather than cool, and Mum, he had to admit, with her mascara running and her mouth pulled out of shape by her loud sobbing, was no oil painting. He wished she hadn't come but she did, every day, and the seedy men's eyes lapped her up like she was some kind of film star, and his wishes were powerless.

He'd only meant to push the baby as far as the next shop, just far enough to cause a momentary panic, but Arthur said, 'What's the point of that?' Arthur's favourite question.

What's the point of school, of families, church on Sunday? 'What's the point of this friggin' home?' he'd bawl, after a beating from the house mother, splayed out face down on his bed so the others couldn't see he'd been crying. What *was* the point? Craig didn't know either, so he kept quiet.

1986

Silence. That's what it was, she decided, that's what had woken her up because it was so unusual. All she remembered was noise. Voices in different combinations, solo, duet, chorus of approval, snoring, roaring of engines, of the sea, something else she couldn't identify. Cats yowling in the throes of passion, mosquitoes whining. Screams. Silence. The silence was lovely, such a relief. She went back to sleep.

The next time she awoke it was because she was thirsty. She turned, reached out for the water glass on her bedside table, but there was something in the way. Her knuckles hit... stone? Concrete? Something resistant and rough edged. Instinctively she pulled her grazed knuckle back and put it in her mouth. Her mouth was full of dust. She really was very thirsty, suckling her knuckle like a baby at the breast, desperate for the taste of her own blood. With the other hand she felt about for Nathan. Nothing. He must have gone to the bathroom. She hoped he was OK, not done in by the seafood he'd insisted on for dinner. She called out, 'Bring me a glass of water, will you?'

She must have dropped off again. When she woke, she was still thirsty. Obviously he hadn't heard her. She'd have to get up and fetch the water herself. She tried to sit, and cracked her head hard against something that wasn't there before, in their hotel bedroom. Blood trickled down into the corner of her mouth and she lapped at it greedily. The crack on the head seemed to have shaken everything back into focus, a bit like hitting the top of the telly to stabilise the vertical hold. She remembered. They hadn't been in their room, they had been in the restaurant, arguing about the seafood. So what had happened?

She strained her eyes but it was pitch dark; more than that, the darkness seemed to have taken on physical form. It had sharp edges which dug into her back and ribs, and a point pressing into her leg like a large and very bony finger, and chunks which crumbled and sighed every time she tried to move. The dark air was thick with dust; it was like trying to breathe calamine lotion. But when she coughed, the dark rasped against her ribs, so she tried not to.

She felt as though she was on the verge of understanding what had happened. But she was watching the news in a foreign language, without subtitles, struggling to intuit the facts from facial expressions and tone of voice. What she understood was approximate, partial, with huge bits missing. All Greek to me, she thought, and started to laugh.

She became aware it was no longer so quiet. She could hear a low rumbling, like a train passing in the distance though less rhythmic, and struggled to remember how long ago she had first noticed it. Impossible, it could have been seconds, it could have been hours. It had always been there, but it was new, and seemed to be bringing with it other new sensations. Suddenly her darkness jolted, changed shape to the accompaniment of a series of sharp cracks and a metallic clang like a bell tolling. *Do not ask for whom the bell tolls...*she began, then she was falling, grateful for the distraction because she didn't know the rest of the line and telling herself she must look it up when she...*they* – got home. She came to rest lying on her back, looking up at a perfect night sky, God's starry cloth stretched across his heaven and a sharp-horned sliver of moon just waiting for a cow to jump over it.

Now

Day Zero

Someone's watching him. It's a Saturday night and the bar is crowded, a heaving mix of locals, sightseers and walkers straight off the hill. The place reeks of dog and wet socks and woodsmoke, and sounds like the Tower of Babel on day one, while they were all still yelling at each other, desperate to make themselves understood. He's a barman; tens of people are watching his every move, holding out their folded banknotes, smiling, shouting, jigging up and down, trying to catch his eye. But this is different. Someone is watching *him*. Not the tall, skinny Sassenach barman who doesn't smile much but him, Ian Slight.

Someone in the bar knows who he is.

Ian doesn't like people to know who he is. Who he is, is his business, no-one else's. He wonders, as he pulls at the Red Cuillin pump, waits for the ale to settle, pulls again, if it's time to move on.

'Two packets of pork scratchings with that, mate, and a glass of dry white.'

Ian reaches behind him for the pork scratchings without taking his eye off the beer. He knows his way around this bar too well, he tells himself, putting the pint and the scratchings in front of the customer then ducking down to the glass-fronted fridge for the dry white.

'Two pints of Guinness,' a man calls from further down the bar. Tosser. Can't he see Ian's serving? And a please would be nice. Repressing an urge to climb over the bar and punch the guy in the nose, Ian pours the wine.

As he moves down the bar to the till with a tenner from Mr. Pint, Pork Scratchings and a Glass of Dry White, Tara brushes past him on her way to serve Two Pints of Guinness. Tara's young and eager to please. Ian likes this in her, when her youth and eagerness are focused on him, but right now it's an irritant, it just makes the job harder. 'He's not next,' he tells her and she pauses, right behind him in the narrow space between the bar and the shelves where the hundred and fifty two different single malts are arrayed, her breast brushing the top of his arm. 'Don't let them bully you,' he adds more kindly. She has lovely tits, does Tara, firm and buoyant, like they had a life quite independent of the rest of her. 'If you serve people out of order we'll have a riot on our hands.'

'Like in a western?' Tara giggles. 'A saloon brawl.' She attempts a cowboy drawl. Ian thinks, Sloane Ranger, and is quite pleased with himself.

'Get on with you.' He pinches her arse and goes to give Pint, Pork Scratchings and a Glass of Dry White his change.

'We're running short of logs, Ian.' Colin, the bar manager. 'Bloody weather. It's more like January out there than June.'

'I'll get some in.' Ian wouldn't normally volunteer for anything, but is drawn by the chance to escape, however briefly, this sense of being watched, which makes the crowds and the noise and the suffocating smell seem more oppressive than usual. He goes out the back, by the kitchen, rather than trying to fight his way through the Saturday night drinkers. Sadie's plating up steak pie and chips as he passes, and he reaches over her shoulder to steal a chip. She smacks the back of his hand. 'Naughty boy,' she says, as if it was a compliment. He's in with a chance there, when he tires of Tara.

'Come out the back with me,' he whispers, biting her ear. She chuckles. A threesome? he wonders, and is glad of the blast of cold air from the hill as he steps outside. He has to keep his mind on the job. He'll move on when he's ready, not because they've sacked him.

The moon is up, a paler crescent against the pale sky of a June night in the Highlands. Not a cloud in sight, and the hill still hoarding the last of the day, the rock and grass, the patches of early heather and the sheep like white boulders, all faintly glowing. The beauty of it catches in his throat, like grief, making him feel stupid, childish, as though he'd been caught dipping toast soldiers in a boiled egg or crying in his sleep. Because he knows what grief is, and it isn't this.

He should settle down. He'll be fifty three next birthday, though everyone says he looks ten years younger, and he knows it's true, and he has nothing to show for his half century in the world, no wife, no children, not even a house. He sometimes dreams of being able to buy a pub of his own, or a little B and B in a seaside town where retired couples in per mapress clothes and rain ponchos take their grandchildren for days out. Donkeys, plastic windmills stuck in sandcastles, ice creams and fish and chips with mugs of bright orange tea. Somewhere other people pass through, but where he could stay. He could take Sadie with him. She could do the breakfasts. Not Tara. Tara's just passing through, earning money to 'go travelling'. Ian's been travelling; he has a longing, now, for smaller horizons, unchanging things.

What's that? A movement caught in the tail of his eye, a shadow detaching itself from the well of deep shade where the chalet block backs on to the foot of the hill. And there it is again, that sense of being watched; he can feel it on his skin like the drip of cold water. *Drip, drip, drip.* He knows what that can do to a man.

He has to fight a ridiculous instinct to take cover behind the log store. It's probably just a guest going between the chalets and the hotel, or one of the smokers who mill about the car park in all weathers since the ban. He hauls out one of the plastic baskets that are kept beside the log pile and begins to fill it with logs, whistling as he works to show whoever's watching him he knows and doesn't care. He goes back inside, through the front door this time; he isn't superstitious.

The relentless tide of drinkers breaking against the bar keeps him busy for the rest of the night, keeps his fear at bay. He expects it to go altogether as the bar empties out towards closing time, but it doesn't, it just gets worse, as though it has been diluted by the presence of all those eyes upon him, hopeful, impatient, relieved, and now, ultimately there's just one pair of eyes, the eyes on the advertising board, the last image he remembers before the cinema blew up. Correction. Before the bomb went off. An IED they'd call it today but bomb was good enough for them back then. Back there. He never has seen the rest of *The Great Gatsby*, never found out if Robert Redford got the girl.

'You coming to my chalet tonight, then?' he whispers to Tara as they clean the bar, the neck of her shirt swaying away from her cleavage as she bends down to load the glass washer. Normally he wouldn't ask. Too proud, he supposes, if he's honest, though he likes the uncertainty of it, the will-she-won't-she, the naughty thrill of her knock on the door and him answering it, her in the bathrobe that makes her look like a teddy bear with tits, him in his boxers, with his scars and his readiness. But tonight he definitely doesn't want to be alone.

'You sure?' she asks, straightening up, looking pleased as punch, her cheeks flushed and tiredness giving her eyes a smudgy, sexy expression. He's sure; he'd have her now, braced against the bar counter, if the others weren't still around, gossiping and eating bowls of leftover chilli while they mop tables and sweep the floor. He nods, holds her gaze just a fraction longer than usual, then she reaches up to touch his cheek and he rears back. Mistake. Not in public. She doesn't own him.

They go out together into the night, side by side but not touching, and walk across the car park towards the chalet block where several of the seasonal staff have rooms. The sky is still clear, but it's very cold, the moon veiled by a fine mist which makes the stars look small and myopic. As if the earth has breathed out and her breath is hanging on the cold air. A night that just misses being beautiful, even though Tara's smiling up at it in some kind of wonder, eyes wide, mouth open.

'Come on, it's freezing out here.' He drags at her arm like an impatient toddler.

'Arthur?'

He stops. Dead. He feels the letters of that name branded into his back with a cold fire that makes him shiver, then numb, but only the way anaesthetic numbs you, with the promise of pain to come, exquisite and possibly unendurable. He's waited a long time for this, it's been there, in the hackles on the back of his neck, in his knotted shoulder muscles, though he's hoped it would never happen, has even begun to relax a little as the years have rolled by and he has come to believe in Ian Slight.

'Go on, Tara,' he says, 'I'll be with you in a minute.'

'But...'

'This won't take long. Have a shower or something.'

'OK. I'll use that stuff you like.'

'That would be nice,' What was she talking about?

'Bit young for you, isn't she?' says the man who has called him Arthur. 'Doesn't look much older than my daughter.'

He knows that voice, knows it in his bones, even though he's never heard it before, well, not like this anyway, in the intense, transient intimacy of a dark car park, thick with the stale echoes of other greetings, other farewells. He turns to face the man, a simple movement that seems to take forever, because it will change everything. Fishing his cigarettes out of the pocket of his jeans, he flips open the pack and puts one in his mouth. A lighter is proffered. Gold. As he draws on his cigarette, he discerns in its glow the initials HT, etched on the lighter in plain, blocked capitals.

'How did you find me?' Ian cups his hand over his cigarette; he doesn't want the other man to see the point of light trembling.

'I need to talk to you, Arthur.'

He shudders. 'Don't call me that.'

'What should I call you?'

'Ian. My name's Ian.'

'Mine's...'

'Don't tell me, I don't want to know. I don't want to speak to you. Don't you know what the risks are?'

'...Harry Theobald,' he finishes, ignoring Ian's plea. The name is familiar to Ian, which fills him with a creeping anxiety until he remembers who Harry Theobald is. The GardenMart millionaire, one of those benevolent despots everyone knows, like Lord Sugar or Richard Branson; there's nothing weird about his knowing Harry Theobald's name. What's incomprehensible is how the man standing here could have become Harry Theobald.

'What the fuck are you doing here?' he asks. 'What do you want from me? As you can see, I haven't made a fortune. I did you the one favour you're going to get from me years ago. How the fuck did you even find me?'

Harry Theobald's tone remains smoothly sardonic, but a steel edge has crept into it when he speaks again. 'Let's get one thing straight, shall we, Arthur? Whatever you did, you did to save your own skin. I kept quiet, I kept my half of the bargain and I paid for it.'

'Yeah, sure you did. It must have been tough, piling up all those millions.'

'Yes,' he replies, 'it was.' His smile snaps shut, like someone turning off a light. 'You're very exposed in my position. You never know if...well, let's just say, you have to be on your guard.'

'Which brings me back to my original question. What *are* you doing here? It's a helluva risk. I mean, if I was going to blackmail you or something, I'd have done it years ago, wouldn't I?'

'I've been careful to keep my picture out of the papers. Every time some damn magazine wanted to do a piece on me, I'd see you in my mind's eye and tell them to piss off.'

'Me too.'

Theobald looks puzzled for a moment, before it dawns on him Ian is being sarcastic. He always was a bit dogged, a bit sincere. *Blood brothers, Craig, remember? Not a word, whatever happens.* They'd shaken hands, solemnly, the way he'd seen other men shake his father's hand at the funeral, and Craig hadn't said a word, ever.

'But now,' says Theobald, 'things have changed and I need to talk to you.'

The look he fixes on Ian works on his heart like a fist, squeezing. 'You've not...done it again, have you?'

'Christ, nothing like that!'

Ian breathes again.

'Is there somewhere we can go?' asks Theobald. 'A bit more private?'

Ian tosses his cigarette butt away across the car park, empty now except for the hotel minibus and a black Range Rover Sport he assumes belongs to Theobald. 'Us, Craig? There's nowhere we can go, you know that. Whatever you want to say, just get it over with and let me get back to my evening's entertainment.'

'OK,' says Theobald, then pauses, breathing deeply as if gathering his strength for some great feat of endurance.

'It's fucking freezing out here, just spit it out, will you?' says Ian.

'I think someone's on to me.'

'On to you? You mean..?'

'The bloke that runs my local. He's only been there about twelve months, and he asks a lot of questions. People say he's just being friendly, you know, taking an interest, doing what landlords of village pubs do. But he got my hackles up. I'm wary, obviously. So I did a bit of digging into his background and found out he used to be private dick. Working for the tabloids. It was a pay-off from one of them bought him the pub. He could have gone anywhere – nice little spot in the Cotswolds, Cornwall...But he ends up in my neck of the woods, in a village that's got nothing except a crumbling coastline and a caravan park...and an Arts and Crafts house I fell in love with. Something stinks, Arthur, something definitely stinks.'

'And you think if this bloke knows who you are, then he knows who I am. Nice of you to be concerned but no need. No-one knows who I am, Craig. I had my fifteen minutes of fame forty years ago, thanks to you, and I liked it so much

I've made sure I stayed incognito ever since. I don't even have a fucking bank account for Chrissake.'

'I found you,' says Craig quietly. 'It wasn't that difficult.'

'I'll go to probation. They'll fix me up with a new identity again.'

'You haven't been to probation for almost as long as me. You go to probation, they'll lock you up again and you know it. Don't waste your time bluffing.'

'What do you want?'

'I want you to keep quiet. The way I see it is this. As long as we stick to what we always said, or didn't, in my case, I can salvage something. Maybe not my reputation but at least my marriage. I love my wife very much, Arthur, and she loves me, but she's a tender-hearted woman, a good mum...You know what I'm saying? If she thought...well, she'd take the kids and run a mile and I doubt any lawyer would be able to make much of a case against her. On the other hand, I can see how you might be tempted to tell the truth to anyone that uncovered you.'

With a kind of irrational exhilaration at the discovery of how much even this mean, shrunken, hand-to-mouth life of his matters to him, Ian realises the threat of revelation is unthinkable. He hasn't set eyes on Craig for forty-one years, and every attempt he's made to recover since has failed. He realises he's always believed he'd have another chance, and now Craig is threatening to take even that away from him. He fumbles with shaking fingers for another cigarette. He snaps off the filter before lighting it and taking a deep draught of pure tobacco, which makes him at once dizzy and clear-headed. He glares at Craig, choked with rage and grief, his lips clamped around his cigarette. If he opens his mouth, his whole rotten existence will come out of it. He'll let it, he will, because it's what Craig deserves, to drown in that torrent of sewage, but he'll do it when he's ready, when the ache of regret has left him and he's strong enough.

'I can give you money, help you get away. Abroad if you like.' Theobald's voice has taken on an unpleasant, wheedling tone. He'll drown in his own bullshit, thinks Ian, still smoking furiously. He looks away, over the empty car park, the lowering hill with the chalets at its foot looking like POW huts in a war movie, the hotel, drab and unwelcoming now the lights are out. Everything is black and white and slightly out of focus in the hazy moonlight, and a drift of crisp packets and fag ends blows towards the log store in a sudden gust of wind. He shivers. How much money, he wonders. Enough for that B and B he'd been thinking about? Or a house on stilts on a white beach somewhere, like the ones on some website Tara had shown him while she was planning her travels? There isn't enough money, he realises, not enough money in the whole bloody Bank of England to pay for what Craig Barnes has done to him.

'Come on,' says Theobald, 'stop pissing me about. Whatever you want. This is my marriage we're talking about. My life.'

'And what about my fucking life, you smug bastard?' Something inside him ignites. He lunges for Craig, and before Craig can take evasive action, he has his hands around his solid, rich man's neck. He's screaming in Craig's handsome face, 'You wrecked my fucking life, you cunt, my whole fucking life! You've no idea, have you? What you've done? Shall I tell you?' He's shaking Craig like a terrier with a rat. Craig gargles. His face is turning a colour Ian doesn't have a word for. *Purple for violence, black for anger.* 'About Orla? I bought her a ring, one of them daft mood rings. Said she'd wear it for the rest of her life. Well she did, she fucking did.' *Red, in the cinema, for excitement. His fingers stroking her thigh.*

19

Her not looking at him but smiling like the Sphinx and the slow strobe of the projector flickering across her face. He's sobbing now, loud and hoarse.

Craig's eyebrows arch, in interrogation or appeal, he doesn't know. Doesn't care. His thumbs press against Craig's windpipe, but Craig's hands are clamped around his wrists, dragging him off. He can feel pulses throbbing and he doesn't know if they're his or Craig's. Power surges through him and he squeezes. Harder. His fingers reading all the intimate details under Craig's skin, the sinews and gristle, the vertebrae strung along his nerves. Craig's grip on his wrists begins to loosen, his face relaxes and his bloodshot eyes lose focus, roll up into his head.

Abruptly, Ian lets him go. Craig's legs buckle and he sinks sideways onto the tarmac, lying there with his knees drawn up as if he's asleep in bed.

'Come on, get up.' He kicks Craig in the ribs for good measure. Craig doesn't move. Shit. Panic balloons in Ian's head. His hands begin to ache, as if reminding him just how hard they were clamped against Craig's windpipe, his spine, his vagus nerve... If Craig's dead...he ought to check. He kneels, takes hold of one of Craig's wrists and feels for a pulse. He's supposed to know how to do this; they taught him in the army. But his fingers grope and slip; he can feel nothing. The army has confused his hands, he concludes, by training them both to kill and to seek for life.

Whether Craig's dead or not, he can't leave him here. Rolling him on to his back, he pats down his pockets until he finds the keys to the Range Rover. He doesn't look at his face. Still Craig doesn't move, but Ian fancies he can feel the shallow rise and fall of his ribs as he searches for the keys. He'll get him into the car and dump it somewhere, make it look like an accident. Now he has a plan, his panic subsides.

'Ian..?' Fuck, fuck, FUCK. Tara. 'What are you doing?' She is standing in the chalet doorway, in her teddy bear dressing gown, her curly hair and curvaceous form framed in dingy yellow light. He bites back his resurgent panic.

'Nothing. Get back inside. I'll be with you in a minute.'

'But...'

'Bloke's just dead drunk, that's all. I'll get him on to the back seat of his car and leave him to sober up.'

She steps forward. 'I'll help you.'

'No! No, it's fine, I can manage.' She hesitates, one slippered foot on the threshold, one on the tarmac. 'Babe, look, just get into bed, right? It's freezing out here and you're no good to me if you're freezing. I want you hot, yeah?' It works. She gives a naughty little giggle and retreats indoors.

'You bastard,' he mutters as he hauls Craig upright then over his shoulder. 'You rich, overfed bastard. She's the best lay I've had in ages...well, the most willing anyway,' he corrects himself as he staggers towards the Range Rover and pushes a button on the key fob to unlock it.

He opens the tailgate and off loads Craig like a sack of coal into the boot. Craig is profoundly unconscious, no resistance at all in his slack body. One leg is twisted under him, one crooked over an expensive-looking leather Gladstone bag. His face, in the moonlight, has the painted pallor of a ventriloquist's doll. Ian thinks it'll be a miracle if he wakes up, but if he does, at least there's a dog grille barring the space between the back seats and the roof, so he won't be able to get at Ian in the driver's seat. The thought gives Ian a wholly irrational sense of security and well being. As he starts the engine, suddenly light of heart, he turns on the CD player.

...Keep your 'lectric eye on me babe
Put your ray gun to my head...

David Bowie's voice, operatic sounding despite the nasal Mockney accent, soars above the bass line. They were still inside, thinks Ian, as he turns into the road through the glen, when this one came out. He wonders if Craig had come to it late, or if it was a part of his legend in which he had grown to believe.

DAY ONE

Ian's first thought had been to drive up into the hills, haul Craig into the driver's seat then push the Range Rover over into one of the many steep ravines carved out by the burns whose course the lanes followed. If Craig wasn't dead already, that would be enough to kill him, and even if Tara were to link him to the man in the wrecked Range Rover, he could simply persist in his story that Harry Theobald had been dead drunk and must have driven himself off the road. Besides, by the time anyone stumbled across the accident up here, he'd be long gone.

But once he noticed the Range Rover had an almost full tank, he changed his plan. He'd drive south, as far as he could before running out of petrol, and dump Craig and his fancy car as far from the Head of Etive as possible. If he headed for the M74 and M6, he could easily pick up a lift and lose himself wherever he ended up. As he drove, however, he became aware of a need growing in him, a nagging irritation to begin with but taking more concrete shape as the night gave way to dawn, almost as though it too, like the road signs, the lowering and softening hills, the solitary farms and huddles of villages and truck stops, was emerging into the light.

What Craig had said about the pub landlord kept spooling around in his head, just like *Ziggy Stardust*, which he hadn't changed because he didn't want to stop in order to rummage around in Harry Theobald's CD collection for something different. Harry Theobald's taste in music was an idle curiosity for less pressing times. What if the ex private dick was on to him as well? Bloody hell, he should have taken Craig up on the offer of a getaway instead of nearly breaking the guy's neck. But instead, here he is, in a stolen car, with a body, if not dead, as good as, in the boot. He's such a fucking cliché he might laugh, if he wasn't brought so low by his fear of the landlord of Harry Theobald's local and what he might know. He clicks open the glove compartment, thinking the car's log book might be in there, but his rummaging fingers reveal nothing but a clutter of sunglasses, sweet wrappers and petrol receipts.

He is on the M74, just south of Gretna, when the petrol warning light comes on. Pulling into the slow lane, among a growing stream of trucks and caravans, he hopes to god he hasn't left it too late and will find a service station before the gas runs out completely. A roadside rescue is exactly not what he wants. The signs for Southwaite Services begin as the road sweeps around Carlisle and turns into the M6. Twenty one miles. He limps along at a steady fifty, wrestling with an illogical intuition which urges him to drive faster, get there quicker, before the petrol finally runs out. He wonders if the Range Rover's gas guzzling reputation is justified, his gaze flicking repeatedly towards the gauge, which seems not to move for miles and then is suddenly, noticeably closer to empty than before. And then, just as the drizzle is turning to rain, the tail lights of the traffic in front of him blurred and bleeding their reflections on to the tarmac, the services slip road emerges into view like the highway to heaven.

He finds a discreet spot in the far corner of the car park and backs up right to the fence, so the Range Rover's tailgate is overhung by bushes growing in the wasteland on the other side of it. To his horror, when he switches off the engine, he hears a low groaning coming from behind the back seats. He realises he'd been assuming Craig was dead. He'd like Craig to be dead, but he'd like him to be dead all by himself. He feels oddly squeamish about killing Craig which, when he stops to think about the people he has killed, none of whom had done him half the damage Craig did him, is ridiculous.

Before opening the tailgate, he peers through the rear window. Craig isn't moving. His eyes are closed and his face, in the grey-green light of the dripping bushes, still shows the rigid pallor of the ventriloquist's dummy. He looks, Ian realises with a sudden shock of recognition, just like he did in court, his profile as unmoving as an Easter Island statue whenever Arthur stole a look at him in the dock, his features expressionless, closing in the silence with which he greeted every question put to him by the lawyers or the judge.

'Cunt,' mutters Ian, opening the door. 'Cunt,' he repeats, when he's finished catching his breath at the stench of urine coming off Craig, and punches Craig's jaw. Craig's head slams back against the wheel arch. The moaning stops. Ian goes through his pockets and removes his wallet, then hauls the Gladstone bag out from under his body and dumps its contents on top of him. One hand, strong, square, well-manicured and adorned with a gold signet ring on the pinkie, sticks out. Yanking the ring off, he stuffs the hand beneath the pile of clothes. Satisfied that an idle glance would show only a heap of clothes strewn in the back of the car, he wipes the steering wheel, gear lever and door handles as carefully as he can with his sleeve, locks the Range Rover and tosses the key over the fence into the bushes.

As soon as he has put some distance between himself and the Range Rover, he begins to relax. The car park is virtually deserted at this early hour, and he's certain no-one has noticed him. This is his milieu, this marginal, transient world. He feels the damp air, smelling faintly of petrol and burgers, settle around him like a cloak of invisibility.

Once inside the service station, he slips into the disabled toilet and sits on the lid while he goes through Theobald's wallet. Around two hundred in cash, which he pockets, some business cards, and a half dozen credit cards and store cards, over which he hesitates before depositing them in the sanitary bin. The business cards carry no personal details, nothing to help him find out where Harry Theobald lives, but his driving licence is more forthcoming. Wildwood House, Aylsburgh, and a Norwich postcode. Aylsburgh. So that's it, the village with nothing but a crumbling coastline and some fancy house where Craig Barnes could play at being Harry Theobald. Aylsburgh, near Norwich. He tears up the driving licence and the business cards and flushes them down the pan. The ring he keeps; it's heavy, solid, eighteen carat he guesses from its reddish hue, and how many signet rings are there bearing the initials HT? Must be thousands. It'll be easy to sell; everyone wants gold when money's worthless.

Hi, this is Harry. Leave a message or curiosity will kill this cat.
Alice clicks off her mobile. She must have speed dialled Harry half a dozen times on her way to The Dog's Head, and his voicemail message wasn't that funny the first time. Or the countless other times she has tried to call him from home in the past couple of hours. Where is he? He hadn't texted her last night, as he usually does every night when he's away from home, so she had tried to call him in the

morning but there seemed to be no signal. She had thought little of it, knowing he was on his way home. Now, though...

'I suppose I'll have to go to the coastal defence meeting,' she'd announced, banging down plates of chilli con carne in front of the children. 'God knows where your father is. You'll be alright, won't you? It'll only be for an hour or so.'

Polly, fifteen, cast a withering glance at her mother, speared a single red kidney bean with her fork and put it in her mouth.

'Eat properly,' snapped Alice, and immediately wished she hadn't. A girl from Polly's class had been admitted to the eating disorders clinic in Norwich last term. Was anorexia contagious, she wondered? Could it spread through the collective psychology of a class full of teenagers like the mediaeval dancing plagues she had once read about?

'We'll be fine, mum,' said Jesse, 'it's only at the pub and anyway, we've got Chas and Dave if we, like, need an adult.'

Chas and Dave, Stan and Ollie, and Jedward, the six security guards who work rotating shifts, holed up in the gatehouse with their CCTV screens, their dogs and endless cups of tea. Alice always has to look at their badges to remind herself of their real names, especially Jedward.

'Of course you will.' She ruffled Jesse's hair, grateful that, two years younger than his sister, he was still enough of a child to want to please her. He ducked his head and made a face.

'I'll take Daisy,' she said. 'She hasn't been out of the grounds for weeks.'

You don't need to take her out for walks, Harry had told her, when he'd brought the puppy home their first Christmas at Wildwood, we've got fifty acres here, that's more than enough for one Dalmatian. Maybe, Alice had thought, but had kept it to herself, as coastal erosion ate away at their land, they would have to have smaller and smaller dogs to satisfy Harry's insistence that she shouldn't go wandering about the countryside. Maybe, at some point in the future, when she and Harry were very old, it would be just them and a cat and the sea lapping at the terrace steps.

She smiles, now, at this image, as she waits for the security gates to swing open and nods a greeting to Chas and Dave as she and Daisy slip through into the outside world.

The Dog's Head is about fifteen minutes brisk walk from Wildwood's front gate, into the centre of the village, although you could do it in seconds by climbing the *magnolia denudata 'Fei Huang'* in the white garden and dropping over into the pub's back yard. But there are cameras trained on every point where it might be possible to circumvent the electric fencing. Harry had made sure of it, walking the entire perimeter of the gardens with the head of the security firm when he'd first employed them. Unobtrusive, he'd said, but foolproof.

Alice wants to shake him sometimes, to see what comes loose, what falls out. He runs garden centres. Yes, they've made him very rich, but where's the danger in garden centres? They agreed, didn't they, right at the beginning of their marriage, that they wouldn't hide away behind the barricades of privilege but live like ordinary people, send their kids to local schools, walk on the beach, go to the football, have Sunday lunch at the pub. Yet gradually, discreetly, almost without her noticing, Harry has chipped away at their agreement, and she wonders, sometimes, if he ever meant to keep to it or if it was just a story he allowed her to tell herself to reassure them both she hadn't married him for his money.

She doesn't ask, though, or shake him. She treats the guards with courtesy, and bakes them cakes, and might even scratch their Rottweilers' noses if she dared. She knows there has to be a place for privacy within a marriage.

Yet now, as the walk soothes her irritation, she cannot escape the nagging suspicion that perhaps Harry does have a good reason for his paranoia. This silence isn't like him; he knows what she thinks of the Coastal Defence Committee, he would have rung to apologise as soon as he realised he couldn't be back in time for the meeting. He would have rung anyway; punctuality is part of this need he has to be in control of his world.

Even though it's close to the middle of summer and not yet seven in the evening, the sky is dark as Alice walks up the lane between steep banks of cow parsley and wild garlic, and turns into the village square. The Co-op windows shine unnaturally bright and a gritty, gusting wind eddies bits of rubbish around the war memorial. A storm is coming. Appropriate, thinks Alice, as a backdrop to the monthly meeting of the coastal defence campaigners. A reminder, not only of what they're fighting for, but how futile it is. The beach below their crumbling cliff is littered with clumps of broken concrete and reinforcement wires, warped and rusting. It is as if a giant child had thrown a tantrum and hurled his toys everywhere. Standing on the cliff edge, looking down at the beach, Alice can feel the earth's scar tissue, ridged and inflamed beneath her feet, and knows in her bones there is nothing to be done by mere puny humans to avert the inevitable. But she won't say that this evening. She'll nod and smile and vote as Harry would, ever the loyal wife, for inside, she too is fighting erosion.

How many times had she awoken in the night, the bed vast and empty around her, and reached for her phone, and stared at the illuminated display until her eyes ached, as if wishing for a text alert might conjure one into being?

Finally, as dawn was beginning to pick out the furniture in the room, she had consoled herself with reading the text Harry had sent the night before. *Hey you. Caught a salmon this big earlier and just eaten it for dinner. So much tastier than once caught by someone else. Love you. Miss you. Sweet dreams. Big hugs. Hxxxxx*

'Daisy!' She yanks on the dog's lead as the dog lurches towards George, whose arrival at the pub coincides with her own.

'Evenin', missus,' says George, touching his cap. It is a tweed cap, frayed and greasy, and George wears it rain or shine. Alice isn't actually sure he has any hair other than the white bristles covering his neck and temples, which are all the cap leaves exposed. 'Harry not back, then?' She is 'missus' but Harry is always Harry. George had been a fixed star in Harry's firmament long before Alice met him. He had worked at the first ever GardenMart store and, after his retirement, had come to Wildwood to help Harry reclaim and develop its gardens. She thinks of him as if he were Harry's father.

'Hello, George,' she says, trying to keep the edge out of her voice; if she'd known George was coming, she needn't have bothered. George can speak for Harry better than she can. But she's here now, so she might as well go in. 'No,' she says, as George holds the door for her and a blast of stale beer, chip fat and furniture polish assails her nostrils, 'he's been delayed. So here I am.' She wishes pubs still smelled of tobacco, and turns in her tracks. 'Look, you go on in. I'm going to have a quick smoke.' She gives George a conspiratorial smile, but is by no means sure that's the way he takes it. 'Brace myself for Bernard.'

Bernard Higgs is the landlord of The Dog's Head, which seems to confer on him the necessary authority to chair the

Aylsburgh Coastal Defence Campaign. He has the apple cheeks and welcoming beam of the archetypal country pub host, but his large teeth are yellow as old piano keys. His shock of hair is white except for a jaundiced streak above his right eye left by years of rising pipe smoke.

Alice stubs out her cigarette and glances up at the sky. The wind has risen, driving a flock of small, grey clouds in front of purple stormheads. The pub sign, featuring the head of a Dalmatian, an acknowledgement of the Theobalds' presence in the village that Alice feels is somehow backhanded and unsatisfactory, sings a high, wild song as the wind slaps it back and forth. She fancies the first raindrops are flying around her as she enters the bar.

Dogs Head, reads Ian as he scrolls through Harry Theobald's phonebook over his second latte. Dog's Head. That must be it, the local, the pub with the nosy landlord. Swallowing the last of the coffee, he quits the cafe and goes in search of a phone box. The phone has been ringing interminably, and he is just about to give up when it is answered.

'Dog's Head,' says a man with a pronounced estuarine accent.

'Oh...yeah. I'm...er...I'm just calling for directions.'

There's a pause, a questioning hesitation, which seems to Ian to expose his intentions, but then the landlord asks, casually enough, 'Which direction are you coming from?'

'North.'

'Not much north of us except the North Sea, mate. D'you mean Kings Lynn?'

'Yes, sorry. I don't know the area all that well, see.'

'Well it's not difficult. You take the A148 to Cromer, then the coast road going east and Aylsburgh's about fifteen miles. We're right in the middle of the village, by the church. You can't miss it.'

'Thanks,' says Ian, replacing the receiver. Fifteen miles from Kings Lynn.

'Oh,' says Bernard, elbows planted on the bar, his ACDC teeshirt stretched over his gut; there is a bulge in the lettering which echoes the bulges in the cliff wall as the weight of the land presses down on its sea-hollowed base. 'No Harry this evening?'

'I'm afraid not,' says Alice, sliding on to a long settle beside Venetia Manning. The two women exchange brief smiles; they are not friends exactly, but moved to the village at around the same time and have daughters in the same class at school. Every winter they are thrown together by the village pantomime, which Venetia directs and for which Alice helps to build the sets.

'Is Polly going to this midsummer party thing?' whispers Venetia as Alice sits down and Daisy lies on her feet.

What party? 'I'm not sure,' Alice whispers back. 'When is it?'

'Friday night, I think. On the beach.' The wind snarls in the empty fireplace and rattles raindrops against the window behind them. It's a night for disasters, for upturned boats and waves that gobble up chunks of land like ogres, for disappearances and sudden deaths that smash into the surface of things like bricks hurled through windows. Premonition so concrete it feels like memory prickles along Alice's spine.

Bernard raps the bar with a small gavel and shouts, 'Order, order,' and the faces of everyone present turn to him as if they are naughty schoolchildren. Bernard holds a dramatic pause for several seconds, gavel in the air, then declares the meeting open and invites them all to pick up an agenda from the piles set out on the pub tables. He has just said, 'Item one, minutes of the last meeting,' and raised his parti-coloured eyebrows in the direction of the secretary, a retired solicitor whose face is familiar to Alice but to whom she cannot attach a name, when the door bangs open and Basil Keats comes in.

'Sorry I'm late,' says Basil, then adds, 'Shove up, old girl,' sliding on to the settle beside Alice, smelling of wet gabardine and lemon-scented aftershave. 'Frightful out there now. Be a few more chunks of the caravan park in the sea by tomorrow morning,' he adds, with a gallows grin, to the assembled meeting.

'Every cloud...' says someone.

Alice smiles, and shuffles along the smooth wooden seat, disentangling herself from the billows of Venetia's peasant skirt as she does so.

'Where's Harry?' mutters Basil. 'Not your sort of thing, this.'

She cannot answer. Instead she nods towards Bernard, who is frowning at Basil, and stares at her agenda, and wills the door to open again to admit Harry, rain sparkling in his tight, dark curls, wearing that smile of his that lights up a room and everyone in it.

The meeting passes. They progress from one agenda item to the next, but Alice is oblivious to what is agreed. Wedged between Venetia and Basil, she raises her hand when they do, and feels the warmth of their thighs pressed against hers, the force of their presence and of Harry's absence. Her thoughts yaw between wondering whether Polly should be allowed to go to the beach party and knowing she should not be forced into making up her mind about this alone. Suddenly, people whose company she usually enjoys have become an irritant to her. What would Harry decide about the party?

The phrase 'any other business' drifts through her consciousness, just as she is thinking Polly can go to the party as long as one of the security men accompanies her; after all, the only stretch of beach clear enough for it lies just below Wildwood's seaward boundary. She can easily see it from the windows of the former maids' dormitory in the attic.

No-one has any other business and the meeting draws to a hasty close. The storm is in full spate outside, the wind snarling around the pub walls and lightning bouncing blue and violet off the uncurtained windows. Everyone is anxious to get home.

'Lift, old girl?' asks Basil.

'Thanks, I wouldn't mind.' Alice gathers her belongings, rouses Daisy, and follows Basil to the door.

'I'll drop the minutes round for Harry tomorrow, shall I?' calls Bernard, his voice all but drowned out by a thunderclap that sets Daisy shivering. 'Where is he, then? Off plant hunting in the Himalayas or something? Alright for some, eh?'

Basil, holding the door for Alice, flashes her a glance of complicit sympathy, as clueless, she thinks, as Bernard's vulgarity. Harry was already very wealthy when she met him, and she has always regarded this as faintly absurd, like his immaculate and effortless good looks; neither was what attracted her to him. Neither really seems to be part of him.

'Bloody oaf,' says Basil as they get into his Jaguar, Daisy on the back seat despite Alice's attempts to keep her in the footwell. 'Cigarette?' He offers her a pack of Marlborough Lights but doesn't take one himself.

She shakes her head; she is monogamous where cigarettes are concerned, faithful to her full-strength Camels for the seedy loveliness of their pack. 'I'm expecting Harry back any time,' she says. As if saying the words will make them true.

'He's away, is he? Thought he might be ill or something.' He gives a snort of laughter. 'Bernard allergy, eh?'

'Fishing.'

'Be able to fish in these bloody potholes by morning,' says Basil as the car dips and sways its stately way across the car park.

Jesse has gone to bed by the time she arrives home.

'I wanted to watch *Vampire Diaries*,' explains Polly. 'It's only fair. I finished my essay and Jesse didn't do any homework so I was entitled, wasn't I?'

'Oh Polly, that is mean. Couldn't you find something you both wanted to watch?' Alice has always felt closest to her daughter, her firstborn, so sometimes she over corrects in her effort to navigate safely between her children. An only child herself, she is often perplexed by the ties between siblings which seem to be as precisely and precariously balanced as stones in an arch; remove the keystone and the whole structure collapses.

'He's got TV in his room. What's the big deal? Besides, he's supposed to be in bed before me, he's the youngest.'

'And you're supposed to be grown up. Or so you're always telling me.' She reaches out a hand to stroke Polly's hair but Polly ducks out of her reach. She skips backwards in front of her mother as Alice dumps her sodden mackintosh in the scullery and advances into the house. A vast silence lurks behind Polly's chatter.

'Was Mads' mum there? Did you talk to her about the party? Can I go?'

'I don't know... as long as dad agrees. And as long as you go to bed right now.'

'But...'

'Now, Polly, please.'

'But if dad says no, you'll persuade him, won't you?'

'Yes,' she lies, so Polly will go upstairs. So Harry will come home.

As she stands in the great staircase hall, listening to Polly's footsteps drum up the stairs and along the landing, the house phone rings. Although this is what she has been expecting, hoping for, willing for hours now, its sudden shrillness makes her jump. She fumbles as she picks up the handset and almost drops it.

'Hello?' she says, biting back the urge to utter Harry's name. What if it isn't him? What if..?

'Darling.'

'Isabella.'

'I know it's late but I simply had to call. Basil tells me Harry's disappeared.'

Alice forces a casual laugh but she isn't smiling. 'Hardly disappeared. He's just late back from a fishing trip, that's all. He's in Scotland.'

'Scotland?'

Something in Isabella's tone sends a cold drip of fear through Alice's body. She walks into the snug and stands staring at the empty fireplace; if Harry had been here, he would have put in a fire on a night like this, even though it's midsummer.

'Are you still there?' asks Isabella.

Silence. Alice struggles to fill it but the words won't come. What she has to face now has been wrapped in silence for too long.

'God, Alice,' says Isabella, 'what's happened? Has he left you? Rowena Harper's husband went to Scotland. With Betty Marsden. Apparently she'd always fancied crofting, whatever that may be. Sounds like some ghastly sexual perversion to me.' Isabella giggles and Alice cannot help joining her. Suddenly, she feels better. Wives are always being abandoned in Isabella's world, for younger women or Harley-Davidsons (and younger women in leathers) or mid-life gap years (and younger women with backpacks and long, brown legs). Isabella has a routine for them. First, she gets up a party to go to some expensive restaurant and drink it out of champagne, followed by a weekend of luxurious deprivation at a spa, a shopping expedition (before the errant husband stops the credit cards) and a subscription to an internet dating service. ('We're all cougars now, darling, just like Madonna.')

But Harry and Alice are not part of Isabella's world. Harry and Alice have their own world, bounded by Wildwood and the crumbling coast, from the fastness of which they can look upon the likes of Basil and Isabella with tender mockery. They joke that Alice is Harry's trophy wife because she is ten years younger than him. Some trophy wife, they laugh, in their indissoluble harmony, with her undyed hair and her face free of makeup or Botox, her working hands and shallow breasts.

Love you. Miss you. Sweet dreams. Big hugs. Hxxxxx

'No, of course he hasn't left me...I don't know,' she admits, because he could have done, and perhaps she deserves it, 'it's odd. He went away on Thursday, saying he was off for a long weekend's fishing in Scotland and would be back today, in time for the ACDC meeting. He knows I think those things are a waste of time so if he couldn't get back, I'd have expected him to ring, but he hasn't, and I can't get hold of him either.'

'I'm going to get Basil out of his bath and get him to try,' says Isabella with grim determination. 'If he uses his mobile, Harry'll never recognise it, so he'll pick up if it's just you he doesn't want to speak to. You just hang on.'

A tinny jumble of thuds, splashes and raised voices emerges from the phone. Alice sits back on her heels in front of the hearth and waits.

'No,' she hears Basil say, 'I'm not getting involved. It's nothing to do with me.' Suddenly mortified, Alice ends the call. She doesn't need this, to be tossed between Basil and Isabella as though she is something contaminated with failure. When the phone rings again, seeing the Keats' number, she doesn't pick up. She'll manage this alone, the way she always does, except that, until now, alone meant alone with Harry. The storm has worn itself out, but she can still hear rain smacking down on to the terrace beyond the curtained windows and the wind racketing around in the chimney. She thinks of the garden, lying low in the dark, of smashed peony heads and broken delphiniums and tree branches lashing out at the sky. Harry is out there somewhere. In the dark. Where the truth lies.

The drip of fear becomes an icy stream, snaking down her spine. The children. If he isn't coming back, he'll take the children; they'll be here, then gone. She must be vigilant; she knows how easily that can happen.

The one photo she has of Harry stands on the tenon and spindle coffee table, competing for space with TV remotes, gaming controls and a dog chew. It was taken on their wedding day. Harry and herself, nineteen years ago, smooth faced, not even a work in progress yet, at the beginning. Alice stands at Harry's right hand, her bouquet of chrysanthemums (all they could get at short notice, in November) clutched in front of her little tummy. On Harry's left, trussed into a sensible tweed suit, is his Aunt Mary. There was no-one else; Alice's witness had been borrowed from another wedding party, and had not wanted to be photographed with theirs.

Mary is Harry's only living relative. She and Alice have met rarely, the last time being at Jesse's christening thirteen years ago. Mary had stayed only long enough for a single glass of champagne, a single snap holding the baby as if he was an armful of firewood. But where else would Harry go?

If he's left Alice. She knows there could be any number of answers to that question, but she has to start somewhere; every ending calls forth another beginning.

She picks up the phone warily, half afraid she will still be able to hear Basil and Isabella bickering, and dials Mary's number. It's after ten, she realises, as she listens to the ringtone; Mary's probably in bed, but she sounds sharp and wide awake when she picks up the phone and says,

'Brenkley 451,' as if she is Margaret Rutherford in a Sunday afternoon movie.

'Mary, it's Alice...Alice Theobald.'

'Alice, dear. Yes, I did recognise your voice.'

'Sorry. I wasn't sure...'

'What can I do for you?' Brisk, to the point, a squat, square figure, unsmiling in the wedding picture, giving nothing away now.

'I just wondered...'

'Yes?'

'Has Harry been in touch?'

'Not since my birthday. Why?' The question is put hard, it has purpose behind it.

Alice welcomes this because it means she doesn't have to put up a smokescreen of small talk. 'He went away for the weekend,' she says. 'He hasn't come back. I thought maybe...that is, I couldn't think of anyone else who might know where he is.'

'It's only Sunday.'

'He was due back this afternoon. He promised. There was something he didn't want to miss. His phone's switched off, or out of battery, or...'

'Have you called the police?'

'The police? No, it hadn't occurred to me. Oh god, d'you think..?'

'Good. Don't want to get them involved just yet.'

Just yet? As if Mary is certain a time will come when the police have to be called.

'I'll come over,' Mary continues. 'I'll look up tomorrow's trains and call you back.'

'There's no need, really.' Suddenly Alice does not want Mary at Wildwood, contaminating her home with thoughts that lead to that terrible phrase, *just yet.*

'It's no trouble. I'll call you back as soon as I've looked up the trains.' Mary puts down the phone without saying goodbye, without any softening of attitude that might blunt the edge of *just yet.*

When she calls back to tell Alice she can catch a train into London just after eight next morning, and will reach Norwich around midday, Alice listens as though every word means something else. She jots down the train times as if they are a code she has to crack and leaves them on the kitchen table. Later, when she has taken the dog out and locked up the house, and lain for a while in her bath, weighed down by the still, empty air and the silence after the storm, she goes to bed and dreams she is stripping away old varnish from her kitchen table, stripping and stripping till there's nothing left.

Something wakes her. Something harsh and sudden. A fox barking? A rabbit as the shriek owl sinks in her talons? She lies, stiff and still in the middle of the big bed, feeling her sweat cool, waiting for the sound to identify itself. There it comes again, more muffled than sharp, but eerie, a moan that seems to carry an echo with it. It's Jesse having one of his nightmares. She gets up and goes to him, padding urgently along the gallery that links her and Harry's landing to the children's, in and out of the bars of rinsed moonlight that pours, now, through the unshuttered windows and spills from the gallery into the staircase hall below. A thin strip of bluish light showing beneath Polly's door seems to underscore, tonight, some awful shortcoming in Alice's capacity for motherhood. Even Polly, at fifteen, cannot sleep without a nightlight.

Jesse cries out again, then settles to a semi-articulate muttering, his words just out of reach. Alice enters his room cautiously, never sure whether it's best to wake him from these dreams or let them run their course. His window, curtained in dark blue, faces away from the moon and the room is in almost impermeable darkness, his body a shadowy mound beneath his duvet. She sits on the edge of the bed and lets her hand hover over Jesse's forehead, and gradually, he falls still and quiet, his breathing steadies, his eyes stop flicking beneath their thin, pale lids. Somehow, she is sure he knows she's there. She sits for a while longer, wondering what these dreams are that he never seems to remember or be touched by. She hopes his insouciance is true, that his dreams will never gnash their teeth in quiet corners the way hers do.

When she's sure he is settled, she returns to her room, finds her pack of Camels in her handbag, and leans out of the window to smoke one. The wind has died away now and the garden in moonlight is a tangle of fantastical silhouettes. As she draws the fragrant smoke deep into her lungs, a sudden dizziness animates her view, as though the garden too has taken a breath and is holding it. In the stillness following the storm she can hear the sounds of the house at her back, the creaking of floorboards and ticking of pipes, but the comfort this usually brings her seems to have become perverted. These are no longer, she feels, the sounds of the house settling to sleep but of something awakening.

DAY TWO

'Well, dear, I can't pretend you're looking your best.'
Alice leans forward to kiss Mary's cheek, but Mary
thrusts out her hand. Alice fumbles the shake. Both women
reach in unison for Mary's case and the backs of their knuckles clash. Alice bursts into tears. Mary picks up the case and
hooks her free hand beneath Alice's elbow, guiding her to a
bench beneath the arrivals board.

'I'm in the short term car park,' Alice protests, sniffing.

'Sit down,' says Mary. 'You've got more to think about
than a parking ticket.' Again, that sense that she and Mary
are reading from different scripts.

She drops down on to the bench, suddenly unable to
trust her legs. The London arrivals have dispersed and the
station is temporarily deserted. A long-limbed man, pliant as
willow, pushes a cleaning trolley across the forecourt as if in
slow motion. A girl with purple hair is slumped at one of the
tables outside the cafe. Mary fishes in a voluminous handbag
and produces a tiny, lace edged handkerchief. Alice spreads
it in her lap, smoothing it and smoothing it over one thigh.

'Something happened on the way here,' she begins,
once she feels able to speak without crying. She takes out
her Camels, lights up and sucks smoke deep into her lungs.
The cleaner wags a finger at her, but there's sympathy in his
sad eyes. She wonders if she should offer him one.

'What?' asks Mary. 'Some news? Something to do with Harry?'

Alice gives a negative shake of her head, then corrects herself. 'Well, I don't know, maybe. I stopped to fill the car up. Then I couldn't pay. None of my cards worked. I had to leave them my watch.' She takes another long drag on her cigarette to fight the tears which are threatening to well up once more. 'Harry gave it to me.'

'Never mind. We'll go back that way and I'll pay.'

'No...I mean I couldn't possibly. That's not...'

'This is hardly the occasion for polite protestations, Alice. I'll pay for the petrol, you'll get your watch back and then we can think about what to do next. Come on.' She pats Alice's shoulder and rises from the bench. A tired-looking railway official is coming towards them.

'I'm sorry, madam,' he begins but Mary waves him away.

'Yes, yes, alright, we're going.'

'You can't smoke in the car park either,' he shouts after them. Mary turns and gives him a withering look.

'Bloody little Hitler,' she mutters, with a venomous spirit which gives Alice hope.

The two women sit facing one another across the kitchen table, a half empty bottle of Manzanilla between them. Alice never drinks sherry and now her mouth tastes as though it's lined with a thin sheet of rusting metal. She knows, however, that the Manzanilla is of the highest quality, selected by Harry's wine merchant, and they are drinking it from rare Bristol green glasses, which lend the pale sherry the colour of spring barley. Before the incident at the garage, she realises, she would have given neither of these details a second thought.

'I'll have to phone the bank,' she tells Mary, her voice constricted with worry.

'Could have been the garage's machine.'

'It took your card OK.' Their eyes meet, and Alice perceives the emptiness of Mary's remark. She refills their glasses. 'Mary, are you sure you haven't heard from Harry? Not in the past few days necessarily. I just wondered...' she takes a swig of sherry, '...if he'd said anything...out of the ordinary.' She is seeing slightly double, as though she is in the process of splitting apart from herself. Her voice sounds squeaky and unnatural, but Mary doesn't appear to notice. Mary looks flushed and her eyes are watering, and Alice knows she should offer her lunch, but her mind is so focused on what Mary might say in response to her question she cannot think about anything else.

'No, dear, nothing. Why? What do you think he might have said?'

She peers at Mary, trying to assess whether or not she's lying. Mary peers back, her gaze sharp in spite of the sherry on an empty stomach. Alice shrugs, affects carelessness. 'I don't know. I just thought, well, you know, men of his age, mid-life crises and all that.'

'Has he been behaving oddly?' Mary laughs as she puts the question, but her eyes remain cool, assessing. 'Recently,' she adds, as though there was perhaps a time when Harry was in the habit of behaving oddly.

Alice tries to picture Harry with childhood fetishes or teenage eccentricities but fails, and wonders if he has ever tried to do the same with her. If, somewhere, he is trying now. 'No,' she says, 'you know Harry, he's always the same. He's the most equable man I know.' Her eyes search Mary's for evidence of demurral.

'Nothing to worry about then, eh?' Mary leans towards Alice and pats her hand.

'All the same, I think I'll give the bank a quick call before lunch.'

She goes into Harry's study to make the call. If she is going to hear shocking or embarrassing news she will do so in private. The air in the study is still, a little stale, as though the room hasn't been used for a long time. It holds a residual smell of Harry mingled with furniture polish and old books. Alice feels like a trespasser; she can't remember ever entering Harry's study before except in his company. His facsimile of the 1597 Gerard, a couple of Wildwood's Repton red books and the first edition Robinson he'd bid silly money for at auction last year are stacked beside his laptop, giving her the sense that at any moment he'll appear in the doorway behind her and ask her what she's doing.

The files of bank statements are ranked in a glass-fronted cupboard which once held china, when the study had been the housekeeper's parlour, before the house became a sana-torium for burned airmen in 1940. Alice carries them to the desk and puts them down on top of the books. The corner of one catches the Airfix Apollo, which is already precari-ously balanced because one of its rocket boosters is snapped off. God knows why Harry keeps the old toy, but when Alice broached the subject of throwing it out, Harry came as near to being angry as she has ever seen him. Had she got some problem with his past, he'd demanded. What past, she'd retorted, then they had both pulled back from the brink.

'What's happened, Harry?' she whispers as she puts out a hand to steady the rocket. 'Where are you?' She opens the first file, both hoping and fearing it will contain answers to her questions. She calls the banks, one after the other. One after the other, she assimilates their replies, the bal-ances given by misfitting automated voices, like auditory identikits, the apologetic sounding Indians with improbable names like Dean or Marjorie. Small credits, unauthorised overdrafts, direct debits returned unpaid, people who won't talk to her because she doesn't have Harry's passwords, but she can tell by their tones they guard dark and weighty secrets about Harry's finances. Apart from her own limited earnings from her interior design and restoration business, it seems they're broke.

She remains at Harry's desk, staring at the last opened file, statements from some bank she has never heard of with an address in the Cayman Islands. She and Harry went there once, she remembers; Harry was collecting banana orchids, she spent her time by a swimming pool with Polly and Jesse and ranks of bony, rhino-skinned American women on sun loungers. She wonders if the orchids survived; she rarely goes into the orchid house because the plants, obscene in their voluptuousness, unnerve her. Finding her eye drawn to the bulging, vegetal curves of a Palissy ware jug on top of Harry's Ashbee bookcase, she ponders Harry's taste and wonders how he ever came to choose her. Alice likes bee orchids, hidden and secretive, camouflaged by modesty rather than flamboyance.

She'll sell the jug; through Harry, she knows other collectors with whom she can deal directly and discreetly. She'll sell everything she doesn't like, because what matters to her is the house itself, its function and honesty, which make it beautiful in her eyes. Guilt jolts her out of this line of thought. She's already behaving as though Harry isn't coming back.

She looks again at the Cayman Island statements, her eye drawn by a repeating pattern of print on the page. On the 21st of each month, a payment in, from another of Harry's accounts. On the 22nd, a payment out of exactly the same amount: £2,846.82 to Elysium plc. The last payment had been made in May. Today was June 24th. What was Elysium plc? And why route the money through a separate account? Why not make the payments from their main current account along with all their other direct debits? What might Elysium plc do when it discovered its June payment had not been made? She scans the statement for a phone number. She thinks about looking up the company on the internet, but she can't bring herself to open Harry's laptop; it would seem like a betrayal, an admission of some kind. Even when she finds the number, she hesitates to pick up the phone. Harry has his own line into the study, and she is haunted by the sense that he is there somewhere, strung out along the wires, listening. Perhaps she should wait. For something in the post. There could be something today; she hasn't been down to the gatehouse yet, to collect the mail from the security guards. But no; they phone these days, don't they, when bills are overdue? She tries to remember if she has heard Harry's phone ringing recently, but can't. There's nothing for it, she concludes, but to call the bank herself.

'Alice, dear?' Alice starts out of Harry's chair, but it's only Mary, her face around the door less flushed now, and tired-looking. 'Shall I start some lunch?'

'Oh...if you like. There's some soup in the fridge. Mary, have you ever heard of a company called Elysium?'

Mary advances into the room. 'They run old people's homes,' she says, with a decisiveness which surprises Alice. Immediately suspicious, she snaps,

'How do you know?'

'Well it's not a crime, dear. I have a friend who lives in one, and a few shares, you know, if need be. They're very nice places, but expensive. Shareholders get a discount.'

' Does Harry know your friend?'

47

'Oh no. She was a member of the bridge club. Alice, what is all this? I'm very hungry and a little tipsy and in no mood for the third degree.'

Alice knows she should apologise, and she will, as soon as she's found out why Harry is, or was, paying out nearly three thousand pounds a month to an old people's home when Mary, who has a bungalow in a village in Wiltshire, is his only living relative. She finds she resents Mary for this. 'Look,' she says, beckoning Mary forward and wheeling her chair aside so Mary can look over her shoulder at the bank statement. She points at the direct debit. 'What do you suppose that is?'

Mary appears to have no answer. She remains staring at the page over Alice's shoulder; Alice can smell the sherry on her breath.

'Well?' she demands.

'I had no idea just how high their fees are,' says Mary.

'You know something, don't you?' Alice leaps up from the chair. It's all she can do to restrain herself from grabbing Mary by the collar of her seersucker dress and shaking her. 'You've been lying to me. You know where he is, don't you?'

'Alice, Alice. I haven't lied to you. I haven't spoken to Harry since my birthday, as I said. I have no idea where he is. Look, half a bottle of sherry on an empty stomach isn't good for anyone's peace of mind. Let's have some lunch and then we'll be able to make a more sensible decision about what to do next.'

'I can't eat. I'm going to phone Elysium.'

'They won't talk to you. The account's in Harry's name.'

'I'll manage.'

'Look, I really...'

'I said, I'll manage.'

Mary looks as though she is about to say more, but Alice, making her face a mask of determination, continues to stare at her until Mary retreats to the kitchen. Alice sits back down and picks up the phone, her hand around the receiver slippery with sweat. She gets the number for Elysium's head office from directory enquiries.

'Elysium. How may I help you?' The voice is American, female, with the bland, singsong tone of a cocktail waitress in Orlando.

'Could you put me through to your accounts department, please?' Alice struggles to keep the shake of fury and alarm out of her voice, but the girl on the other end appears to hear nothing out of the ordinary.

'Putting you through,' she chants, followed by a snatch of muzak, then a male voice says,

'Finance.'

Alice hasn't thought about how she's going to do this, but as soon as she begins to speak, the lies come. 'I'm calling from Cayman Caribbean,' she says. 'I'm running a security spot check on account number 65730909. A regular transaction with yourselves.'

'Can you hang on a minute?' The voice on the other end sounds young, unsure of itself.

'Very well,' she concedes, with a sigh of authoritative impatience. She waits, hearing various electronic clicks and snatches of muffled, tinny speech from down the line. She wishes she had a cigarette, and immediately sees Harry's face wearing a mildly reproachful expression. The face floats, disembodied, before her eyes. It is transparent; she can see everything through it, the window framing a patch of white cloud, the clematis Dr. Ruppel pressing its flat blooms against the glass.

'Just had to get the right screen up,' explains the boy on the other end of the line. 'Sorry to keep you waiting.'

'That's alright,' she says, in a tone that makes it clear it isn't.

'So, what do you need to know?'

What indeed? 'I'm looking at a regular monthly payment of £2,846.82. I need to know when you last received it and where it's allocated.'

'Looks like a resident's fee.'

'I'd assumed that much. As I said, I need to know when it was last paid and where it goes. The name of the home,' she draws a sharp breath, 'and the resident.'

'I'm not sure...'

Bugger.

'I mean, residents' details are confidential...'

'My bank built its reputation on discretion. If you can't give me the information I need, then you'd better hand me over to someone who can.'

'Well, I suppose...Cayman Caribbean, you said? Just a sec...'

She hears the soft chuckle of computer keys, and a sudden laugh from elsewhere in the Elysium office, which makes her cheeks hot, as if someone is jeering at the ineptness of her subterfuge. When, she wonders, did she become so deep-in-the-bone honest?

'Yes, here we are,' says the boy. 'The payments go to Autumn Glade, in Wortley. That's in Yorkshire.'

'I know where it is,' she snaps, forgetting, for a moment, who she is supposed to be. 'And the name?' she continues, when she remembers.

'They're for the care of an...Abigail Jones.'

'Thank you,' she says, and hangs up. Wortley. What connection does Harry have with Wortley? She supposes there might be a GardenMart there, but that does nothing to explain why Harry is paying for the care of one of the village's elderly residents.

The smell of warm bread greets her as she returns to the kitchen. Mary is setting out bowls and spoons on the table. Alice approaches the Aga and lifts the lid on the soup pan. Courgette and rosemary, made a few days earlier, when her most pressing concern was a glut of early courgettes. Rosemary, she remembers, from one of Harry's historic herbals, was once believed to ward off madness. She hangs her nose over the pan and breathes in deeply, feeling the astringent perfume cut through the fog in her brain.

'Well?' asks Mary.

'Abigail Jones. A resident of Autumn Glade in Wortley. Honestly, Mary, I feel like Jane Eyre.'

'I doubt Harry has a wife hidden away in an Elysium home, dear. Average age of eighty something. She'd be a bit old for him.' She hasn't asked where Wortley is, yet Wortley is tiny, one of a cluster of former mining villages in South Yorkshire, bypassed by history, not the sort of place anyone knows unless they have good reason to.

'You know who she is, don't you?' demands Alice.

'No, I don't. Now, I found some of those half-baked bread buns in the fridge. I'm guessing they should be done by now, though I'm no expert on Agas.'

'But you know who she is.'

'Mmm, they certainly smell done. Don't let them burn, dear.'

Alice takes an oven glove from the Aga's front rail and opens the oven door. Mary holds out a plate while Alice piles on the rolls. 'I'm going up there,' she tells Mary. 'I'll go in the morning.'

Mary puts the bread on the table and hands Alice the soup bowls. 'I don't think you should,' she says. 'And what about the children?'

Alice ladles soup into the bowls, noting how steady her hands are now she has a plan. 'What about them? I'll only be gone for the day, and you'll still be here, won't you?'

'I'm not sure, I probably need to get back. I've left my neighbour with the dog and she's ever so old. Scared to death of thunder, you know.' The dog or the neighbour, Alice wonders, without asking. Mary sits down. She crumbles a bread roll on to her plate but doesn't eat any of it, pouring herself more sherry instead and draining it. 'I think it's time to call the police,' she announces. Daisy shuffles about under the table, manoeuvring for crumbs.

'The police?' Alice sets the soup bowls on the table with exaggerated care. 'But you said...' Suddenly she feels as though she has piano wire knotted around her stomach.

'That was before I knew about the money. Or this Abigail Jones. Things seem a bit different now, wouldn't you agree?'

Alice doesn't know what to think; she doesn't know what 'things' Mary is referring to or how they might have changed. What she is certain of, however, is that she doesn't want the police poking into her life, trampling over Wildwood, asking intrusive questions about her marriage, leafing through the bank statements with their inexplicable rows of zeroes and minus signs. She scoops up a spoonful of pale green soup and lets it fall back into the bowl with a series of mildly scatological plops. She turns her gaze full on Mary, feeling her face naked with pleading. 'Let me do this my way,' she says, 'at least until I've been to Wortley. Then, well, if nothing comes of it, I'll go to the police, I promise.'

Mary's shoulders slump. 'What about the children?' she repeats.

'Couldn't you stay, please, go back Wednesday if you must?'

'What will they think if you go haring off tomorrow, leaving them with me? They hardly know me. And they must be unsettled enough as it is.'

'They know you're Harry's aunt. You're family. It's not like I'm leaving them with a stranger.'

'And if you and Harry were going away? In the normal run of things they'd stay with friends, wouldn't they?'

'Mary, why don't you want me to go and see this woman?'

Mary sucks up a mouthful of soup, pursing her lips around the edge of her spoon. She says, 'I just think you should pay more attention to your children, that's all. This must be very upsetting for them.'

'How dare you!' shouts Alice, banging her spoon down into her bowl so soup splashes everywhere. Fury wracks her, blots her vision, convulses her hand so the spoon continues to rattle against the edge of the bowl. Daisy, still beneath the table, leaps to her feet and thrusts her snout into Alice's lap. Alice can feel her trembling. 'How dare you tell me how to look after my children. What gives you the authority? Do you have any children? No. Have you ever taken the slightest interest in mine? No. The best thing for them would be to find out as quickly as possible what's happened to their dad. And get him back here or...or...be able to move on. And that's what I'm trying to do, however hard you try and stop me.' She comes to an abrupt halt, shocked by her own vehemence, her anger drained as suddenly as it had arrived. Unable to look at Mary, she stares at the viscous splatter of soup on the table; it looks like sick. 'I'm sorry,' she says, deflated, 'I should never have involved you in all this. If you want to go home, I'll take you back to the station.'

'No, you were right to call me, and now I'm here you should take my advice. I can be more objective than you, he's not my husband.'

'You know how private he is. The police are the last thing he'd want. Then there'd be press and...'

'Not necessarily. They can keep the press quiet if they think it's in their interests.'

'It's Harry's interests I'm concerned about.'

'Don't split hairs. You know what I mean. Kidnap, for example.'

Feeling Mary's eyes upon her, Alice forces herself to look up and meet the other woman's gaze. Mary's expression is insistent; she seems to be urging Alice to understand something which remains unuttered. 'There'd have been a ransom demand. There's been no ransom demand. You don't think...I mean, I'd have gone straight to the police if... Of course I would.'

Mary makes no reply, but Alice cannot interpret her silence. 'I'm going to Wortley,' she says again, 'first thing tomorrow morning. You do as you please.' She pushes her chair back from the table and stalks out of the kitchen, slamming the door behind her. She knows she's being childish but she can't help herself. She's cornered; she has to avoid involving the police for as long as she can, at all, if possible, but she can't explain that to Mary so it seems her best recourse is to avoid talking to Mary until the subject can be changed.

Somehow, Mary's presence seems to fill the public rooms of the house, even though she remains in the kitchen. Alice feels she will have no privacy anywhere except in her bedroom. She could go into the garden, but she won't. The garden is Harry's; if she goes out there, George will seek her out, and she can't bear the mute enquiry she knows she will see in his eyes. She longs for peace, for a refuge which will protect her from fractured conversations and silences with jagged edges. Yet, even as she climbs the stairs, moving among fittings and furniture and ornaments she knows with the tender intimacy of a lover, she becomes aware she won't find it. Every object she notices, every angle of light glowing through the leaded panes and on to warm oak beams and floors is threatened now by the empty bank accounts.

She had expected to live out the rest of her life here; from the moment she had first seen the house, on a dank December afternoon with snow just beginning to fall, her heart had relaxed and expanded to fill its space. She had known she could live and, more importantly, die here in contentment, in the fullness of small things achieved. She had envisaged herself and Harry, sitting on the broad terrace overlooking the sunken garden, watching their grandchildren in companionable silence, illuminated by late summer sunshine.

Entering her bedroom, she throws open the windows so she can smoke without setting off the alarm. It is a perfect midsummer afternoon, the sky cloudless and gulls glinting like tinsel as they ride the air currents, almost impossible to believe the previous night's storm had ever taken place. George is mowing the strip of terraced lawn on the far side of the sunken garden which Jesse uses for cricket practice; head down and immersed in the roar of the mower, he will not notice her at the window. Then suddenly the roar is curtailed as one of the security guards, she can't identify which, Doberman at his heel, approaches George. Alice withdraws behind a curtain and watches them. The dog sits and the two men chat for a moment. She hears male laughter drifting across the garden and is shocked by how unfamiliar it already sounds.

Despite the laughter, and the relaxed demeanour of the two men, the guard's presence seems to have introduced a darkness into her view, as though the black of his uniform has leeched into the air. Her dream of the future, she thinks, had never included security men with dogs patrolling

Wildwood's perimeters. Has something else been going on here all along, something to which her contentment has made her oblivious?

For the first time in many years, she finds thoughts of her parents imposing themselves on her mind, of her father in particular and the reticence that enfolded him, intangible and impenetrable as thick cloud. She remembers how, when he had what her mother termed his 'moods', they had to tiptoe around him as if he were a mine they were in danger of stepping on. His moods were rare, which made them all the more frightening, and unpredictable, so she and her mother lived in a state of perpetual threat. She thinks, now, that he probably used to hit her mother, and that she always knew it, in some half-buried region of her psyche, but when she tries to focus her memories, they elude her. She is so changed from the girl she was then that she cannot cast her feelings in the same mould as theirs, and she is a wife now, not a daughter, and comparisons between the two states work only superficially. Her trepidation is not something gone cold over time, it's here and now, knotting her stomach and vising her temples and making her hands shake on the window ledge. She has to see Abigail Jones and find out what she knows, and she has to do it alone, without the police, keeping her intent focused and strong.

She flushes her cigarette down the lavatory in the en-suite bathroom and goes back downstairs, briskly this time, not pausing to savour the things she loves for fear pieces of her heart might splinter off and stick to them like iron filings of emotion. She must direct all her power of attraction to finding Harry before it's too late. At the turn of the stair she hears Mary's voice and freezes, listening. Alice can't see her, but Mary's words fall clearly on her ears.

'No,' she says, 'I'm sure not, and I imagine you'd agree it would be best to keep it that way for now.' Her voice sounds younger, stronger, as though their argument has invigorated her. Alice wonders if Mary is one of those people who thrive on a crisis. A listening silence ensues. Alice realises Mary is on the phone.

'You don't want to do that yet, do you? I think we'll have to risk it...another day or two...I know I shouldn't, but it's a good job I did, isn't it? He's clearly fallen off everybody else's radar...Yes, well, that was a bloody silly condition. What did anyone expect?...Not that I'm aware of...Yes, he might have a motive but I don't know. Presumably someone does, unless he's disappeared off the system too...For the time being, yes. I want to keep a close eye on things... With respect, you can't tell me what to do any more...No, can't be doing with them. You'll have to wait for me to call you...Yes, well, let's hope so. For your sake. Could be very embarrassing.'

Daisy, at Alice's heels and impatient with her immobility, darts off down the stairs. Alice follows, just as Mary walks in from the terrace. She seems unaware of having been overheard. No doubt she thought the terrace would afford her a degree of privacy; she doesn't know about what Harry calls the space heater, Arts and Crafts style. There is a cavity in the wall abutting the terrace, in which sits a large and ornate central heating radiator designed to distribute heat outside as well as in, to create a sense that the terrace is an extension of the house, the boundary permeable between nature and artifice. The children had discovered early on that sound carries with freakish clarity through the radiator's fins, and used to relish using their arcane knowledge to stage hauntings of unsuspecting school friends.

The game, Alice feels, has suddenly turned serious.

Day Three

Ian's never been to Norfolk before; since childhood, he has moved steadily west, towards the setting sun, from the bleak cockle sands of Lancashire to the tragedy of Ulster that corroded his heart to its own shape and became his tragedy too. Even hunkered down in the roomy back seat of a Vauxhall Vectra, among boxes of groceries and a large duvet, he feels exposed. The air seems thin, it lets in too much light, and there is no cover, just vast stretches of flat, open fields bordered by scrappy hedgerows and squat farm buildings. Occasionally, he sees a church tower standing like an exclamation mark, a warning note from God.

They could take him all the way to Aylsburgh, his lift said, a dumpy couple called Bunty and Annabel who had a caravan there.

'Got up this morning and thought we'd go over for a few days while the weather's fine, didn't we, old girl?' said Bunty, enjoining Ian to 'hop in'. 'That's the beauty of being retired. No-one's beck and call but your own.'

Ian had been surprised a couple like Bunty and Annabel would pick up a hitcher, but he didn't demur; a lift right into Harry Theobald's village was far better luck than he'd bargained for. They had picked him up on the edge of Wroxham, and their conversation since had kept reprising what a remarkable, happy coincidence it was that he should be heading for Aylsburgh too as if it were the refrain to an uplifting hymn.

When they asked him why he was going there, he told them he was meeting an ex-Army pal who worked in a pub there.

'The Dog's Head?' asked Bunty.

The Dog's Head. 'That's right.'

'What's his name? We might have met him.' That was when they told him about the caravan. *Fuck.*

'Tom,' he said. It was a common enough name. Bunty and Annabel exchanged puzzled looks and shook their heads.

'Don't think so,' said Bunty. 'There's a lad in the kitchen but his name's...'

'Sean,' interrupted Annabel, 'or is it Sam maybe? Anyway, it's not Tom.'

'We've only ever seen Bernard behind the bar, haven't we dear?'

'He the landlord, is he?'

'That's right. Been there about a year. Used to do something in London before, I think. Not a bad chap.' Bunty smiled at him in the rear view mirror. Ian felt transparent as glass, and as fragile. He was exhausted and footsore and wanted nothing more than to lay down his head somewhere dry and quiet, away from the bruising cheerfulness of his hosts. He closed his eyes, listened to the Vauxhall's tyres whispering along the road, inhaled the scent of apples and bananas among the groceries and was a child again, sitting at the kitchen table, hair freshly washed and still smelling of his mother's apple shampoo, slippered feet swinging inches above the floor, Horlicks coating his mouth with pale, sticky-sweet maltiness. This scene has no ending or beginning, it is the whole of his unchanging life, the evening sunlight on red Formica, the swell of his mother's belly that will never mutate into his baby brother, his father sucking his tea through his teeth as he reads the *Star*. This is forever.

And then it stops.

'Ian..? We're here, Ian.'

His mother's kitchen streams away from him, until it is a pinprick of reddish light under his eyelids, then nothing. He opens his eyes and sits up. 'Sorry,' he says to Annabel's creased, kindly face, swivelled like an owl's to face him in the back seat, 'must have dropped off.'

He helps them unload the car and carry their provisions into an immaculate caravan with pristine lace curtains.

'I suppose I let her put too much into it,' says Bunty, seeing him looking around. 'After all, whole park'll be in the sea in ten years. Most of the vans are empty already, especially the ones near the cliff edge, but the way I see it, that won't be our problem. We won't be here in ten years. That'll be one for our Alison.' He nods towards a framed photograph on a coffee table in the saloon, a family of four, mother, father and two boys. The mother has Annabel's owlish face though smoother, less formed, and she is wearing glasses.

I want a big family, Ian, I warn you. I like the craic. He is suffocating, his eyes smart and his throat contracts in a smog of air freshener complacency. He puts down the box he is carrying with exaggerated care and walks out of the caravan.

'Well, I...'

He hears the hurt indignation in Bunty's voice and he's sorry, but he's also in the grip of a vicious fantasy of setting fire to the caravan, of watching the paint blister and the steel body buckle and twist and the lace curtains turn to a confetti of ash and drift out to sea. He sees Bunty and Annabel dancing in death's embrace as they try to damp down one another's burning clothes, hears the spit and crackle of their fat evaporating until they are as sere and emaciated as he is, until their hearts are ash.

Alice makes bets on raindrops racing down her car windscreen. If the one on the left reaches the folded wiper first, Harry will arrive home while she is away. If the one on the right, Abigail Jones will hold the key to his disappearance. It's a forlorn game, from before, from childhood, but she just needs something, anything, to take her mind off the shock of seeing a GardenMart van at the petrol pumps.

What's wrong with her? How many thousands of GardenMart vans must there be all over the country? There's nothing surprising about seeing one at a petrol station. Yet she can't escape the sense of being stalked, spied upon, and wonders what she's doing here, in a service station on the M1, in the rain, heading towards a place she thought she'd never see again and knows she'd be wiser staying away from. What if Harry was even now on his way home? What if he arrived there to find her gone and the children in Mary's charge? What would he think of her? He wouldn't be angry, Harry is never angry, but sometimes Alice feels anger swelling in him like a storm that doesn't break. Sometimes he will take himself off into the garden and lose himself in hard, physical work, but sometimes he will shut himself in his study for hours, and she imagines some kind of Jekyll and Hyde struggle taking place behind the panelled door.

She learned early in her marriage that the best deliverance from these moods of his was sex, and that the sex that erupted from them was the kind she enjoyed. She remembers now, with a fierce, lonely stab of desire, that Harry had been engaged in a long telephone wrangle about the purchase of some land. She had gone into the sitting room of the house they lived in then, in Lincolnshire, in the midst of Harry's bulb fields, to tell him supper was ready. As he ended his call and rose from the settee, she read both rage and arousal in his body, and came close and slid her arms around him, to soothe him. Tensing her hands on the steering wheel, she feels again now the vibrato of his heart beat, the jut of his hipbones against her forearms and his erection pressed into the base of her belly. He had fucked her there and then, on the settee she had upholstered for her final college project, with an inwardness that negated her self consciousness and freed her to discover the kernel of passion in her own wary nature. She has always fancied that was the day they made Polly, a nugget of new joy formed and nurtured and entered into the world as her daughter. She has kept the old settee, in her studio now, for that very reason. Sometimes, when she is tired, or needs to gather her thoughts for the next stage in a piece of work, she will sit there, leafing through her scrapbook, listening to the hollow song of broken springs shifting beneath her weight.

The rain running down her windscreen begins to veer out of its tracks to form the shape of Harry's face, ghostly and translucent, and as she reaches out to it, it dissolves. She will go home. She will call Mary now and tell her. But as her finger hovers over the keys of her phone, she hears Harry's voice, Harry nowhere yet everywhere. When you've made a plan, stick to it, he's telling her; even if it's the wrong plan, indecision is worse. She goes into the service station to buy water and a Snickers, then pulls back on to the motorway to continue her journey.

Autumn Glade is more like a country club than a care home for the elderly, the sort of place, thinks Alice, feeling as if she is trapped on some nightmare fairground ride, where

Isabella might take her if Harry was having an affair. The foyer, behind a lugubrious neo-Gothic facade, is an expanse of blond wood with a corner reception desk set in the sweeping embrace of a grand staircase. It smells, not of cabbage and urine as she had expected, but of air freshener: synthetic rose and lavender with a sharp, antiseptic note. Her voice, as she asks the plump, well-scrubbed girl behind the desk if she can see Mrs. Jones, falls on a carpeted hush rather than having to compete with the blare of daytime TV.

'Are you from St. Mark's lunch club?' asks the receptionist.

'No, I'm...' But what is she? What can she say?

'Oh, sorry, it's just that they usually send someone to see Hilda on a Monday.'

'Hilda? No, it's Abigail Jones I've come to see.'

'Abigail?' The receptionist looks puzzled.

'Is there a problem?' Alice feels a thin, clammy sweat spring from all her pores. She clutches her bag with both hands to stop them shaking. Harry has found out she was coming and told them not to let her see Abigail. He has removed her to some other, more secluded place. She has died and taken whatever linked her to Harry beyond reach. Alice waits, tensed against the inevitable advance of some discreet security officer who will place a polite hand on her shoulder and ask her to leave.

'No,' says the receptionist, and Alice breathes again, 'it's just a coincidence, I suppose, but I can't remember anyone coming to see Abigail in all the time I've been here and then, suddenly, this morning someone phones and asks to speak to her, and now here you are. It wasn't you that phoned, was it? I thought it sounded like an older lady.'

Mary. 'I hope it won't be too much for her, a phone call and a visitor.'

'Oh, she didn't speak on the phone. She was with the physio and the lady never called back. She wanted to leave a message but I told her there wasn't much point with Abigail. She's got dementia, but I suppose you know that. If you're visiting.'

Alice smiles non-committally. So, if it was Mary who called, that was why she hadn't bothered to call again; she had supposed that, whatever Abigail Jones' connection with Harry was, it could no longer be retrieved from her memory.

'Hang on, will you, while I call Abigail's carer?'

Alice will hang on, she will hope. What else can she do? The receptionist picks up a walkie talkie, mutters into it then listens to the crackled response. Then, smiling at Alice, she says, 'Stefanya will be here in five minutes if you'd like to take a seat.'

Stefanya has a small, sinewy body and dyed blond hair scraped back in a ponytail, so her face, acne-pitted beneath a layer of chalky foundation, is framed by dark roots. Her pale gaze is more defensive than welcoming. 'You come to see Abigail?'

'Yes.'

'Why? Who are you?' She has the accent of a torturer in a Cold War spy movie.

'I'm...an old friend of the family.'

Stefanya looks justifiably sceptical. Alice takes a step towards her, where she stands with her back to a corridor which, Alice assumes, leads to the residents' quarters, but Stefanya holds her ground. 'Abigail frighten easily,' she says. 'Her memory is not good. If she has not met before, well...perhaps is best not see her.'

'OK,' says Alice, now close enough to Stefanya to speak without being overheard, 'the fact is, I have to see her. I've just found out my husband pays for her to live here and I have no idea why.'

'You can't ask him?'

'No.'

Stefanya waits. Alice says nothing more. Stefanya shrugs, turns and leads Alice along the corridor, which has a row of tall windows giving on to the car park. As they pass a series of alcoves where residents sit grouped around low tables, reading, knitting, or just staring at their memories, Stefanya talks to Alice over her shoulder. Harry's money, it seems, has bought her trust. She tells Alice she has been Abigail's keyworker for seven years, ever since Abigail came to live at Autumn Glade, already suffering from dementia. Though her physical health is good, her mental state is now very frail and Alice must not expect much. They cross a high-ceilinged drawing room where Fred Astaire is singing, accompanied by an old man wearing a yellow cardigan who sways and twirls as he quavers out the words.

'*There may be trouble ahead*

But while there's moonlight and music and love and romance...'

'Turn off music,' says Stefanya, 'he cannot stand without frame. Always this song.'

'Sad,' says Alice.

'Not sad. He is happy. Replays over and over a happy time. Worse ways of living, I think.' Stefanya pauses outside a door marked SYCAMORE, between CHESTNUT and ALDER. 'A curious thing,' she says, turning to Alice, 'a thing perhaps will help you. Abigail has a tin...'

'This is Abigail's room? She's in here?'

'Yes, yes. In here. A tin for biscuits. Old. For wedding of Prince Charles and Lady Di. There are...what's the word?' She makes a scissoring gesture with the first two fingers of her right hand.

'Cuttings? Newspaper cuttings?' Alice's heart begins to thud urgently. She feels breathless with an impatience oddly like that of waiting for a lover to call. She keeps newspaper cuttings too; she pastes them into a scrapbook and scans names and faces, dates and numbers for clues. 'What are they about?'

Stefanya shrugs. 'Don't know. I just see her sometimes with tin open in her lap. If I ask what is, or try to see, she very distressed. Tries to hide tin. So now I not ask.'

Elation yaws towards despair. 'So you don't think I could ask either?'

'Perhaps.' Stefanya shrugs. 'Perhaps not. We see how she is with you, eh?' She flashes Alice a brief smile; she has a silver tongue stud.

'Can I talk to her alone?'

'I think no, this time. Perhaps another time.'

Alice glances at her redeemed watch. It is approaching two o'clock. Harry has been gone for six days. She has no time, it is now or never. She nods her acquiescence; she cannot afford to lose Stefanya's good will. Stefanya knocks softly on Abigail's door, then puts her head around it. 'Hello, Abby.' Her voice loses its staccato quality and takes on a singsong tone, as if she is talking to a small child. 'I got a visitor for you. A nice lady.'

The room is comfortable, with a bay window overlooking a garden and the kind of furnishings you would find in a decent chain hotel room, robust, functional, impersonal. There are no photographs, no ornaments other than a vase of silk tulips on the windowsill, nothing to offer any clue as to the identity of Abigail Jones. Her high-backed chair is turned towards the window, so all Alice can see of her as she enters the room is the backs of her legs, bird-thin and clad in thick, flesh-grey tights. Her shoes gape around her heels as though her feet have shrunk since they were bought. They are made of cheap imitation leather and are badly worn. Alice is seized by a sudden anger that Harry, with all his wealth, should let Abigail wear cheap, ill-fitting and worn out shoes. What does it mean, to care enough to pay her fees for this expensive place, yet so little that she has to wear those shoes? Alice wants to say something to Stefanya, to empty her purse on to the narrow bed and say, there, take that, buy her some decent shoes. She is a prisoner in those. But Stefanya is busy turning Abigail's chair to face her visitor and all Alice can do is blink, to clear the anger from her eyes, and smile.

Abigail would have been pretty once. The fine bones of cheek and jaw are still there, folded in a tissue of desiccated skin. Though her clothes, like her shoes, are cheap, ill-fitting and anonymous, there is a certain flare in the way her blouse is fastened at the throat with a bar brooch studded with marcasites, the kind of piece a Victorian clerk might have given to the girl of his dreams. Perhaps it is her only jewellery; she wears no wedding ring and no watch on her knobby wrist. Did Harry give it to her, Alice wonders? Yet, like the shoes, it would seem to be a gift of the kind of calculated meanness of which she would have believed Harry incapable.

'This is Alice,' says Stefanya. 'She come to see you. Nice, yes?'

Alice steps forward, holding out her hand to Abigail. 'Hello...Mrs. Jones?' Mrs? Miss? Abigail? Etiquette depends on each of them knowing who she is and what they are to each other. They shake, Abigail's hand in Alice's feeling like a pouch of knuckles and bones for casting.

'Hello,' says Abigail. 'How kind of you to call.' Her vowels have been tortured into refinement, but the accent they conceal is still disturbingly familiar to Alice. 'I'll make some tea in a minute, when the electric's back on.'

'That would be very nice, thank you.'

'Two doors down, they're on the same grid as the hospital and they never get the cuts. I shan't be voting for Mr. Heath again, I can tell you.'

Alice nods and smiles.

'Please sit down,' says Abigail, with a gracious wave of her hand.

As the only chair in the room is the one in which Abigail is seated, Alice perches on the bed. A single chair, shoes in which merely shuffling to the bathroom must be fraught with risk. Abigail is the victim of a subtle incarceration.

'Have you come far?' Abigail resumes. 'My son came yesterday.' *My son.* The phrase scores itself emphatically in Alice's mind. 'Yes. The yesterday before today.' Stefanya, leaning against a chest of drawers made of white MDF, gives a discreet shake of her head.

'That's lovely. I expect you enjoy seeing him. What does your son do?' asks Alice.

'Do?' Abigail looks nonplussed. 'What a funny question. He's only sixteen months. His dad wants him to be a footballer. Wednesday, mind, not United.'

Alice glances at Stefanya, whose expression says this is a story she has heard many times before.

'Would you like some tea? We'll have some tea when he gets here.'

'Does he have far to come?'

'He comes from the other side, love. I never know when he's going to turn up. I always keep a cake in. He likes chocolate cake.'

'My son likes chocolate cake too.'

Suddenly Abigail begins to whimper, cowering back in her chair as though Alice's words carry some physical threat.

'It's alright,' says Alice, reaching out a hand to her, trying to emulate Stefanya's soothing, singsong tone. She

68

mustn't lose Abigail now, just as she appears to have said something which has broken through the veneer of Mad Hatter courtesy. Stefanya squats beside Abigail's chair and strokes her hand, clawed now around the chair arm. Abigail brushes her free hand again and again across her forehead, as though trying to sweep aside a stubborn stray hair. Is she trying to erase a memory or capture one, Alice wonders.

'You leave now, I think,' says Stefanya.

'No, please, just a few more minutes. Let me try again. I have to find out...'

Stefanya shakes her head. Alice rises, but feels more as though she is a plunging sky-diver with nothing between her bones and the uprushing ground but the air streaming through her fingers. 'Look,' she says, 'you have to let me stay. The thing is, my husband's disappeared. This money he pays for Abigail, it's my only clue.'

Abigail is watching them, her eyes flicking from one to the other as if she is watching a tennis match. Her expression is one of vacant cunning, of a mind that follows a Mobius strip of reasoning. Alice is almost in despair, but Abigail's memory is all she has; she has no option but to keep trying. 'Please,' she says.

Stefanya straightens up, though she keeps hold of Abigail's hand. With her head cocked to one side, she considers Alice, her eyes hard, bright and unreadable as a bird's. 'I am from Silesia,' she says, and for a moment, Alice wonders if the Mad Hatter's tea party has resumed. Though she feels like wrecking the room in her impatience, she makes a murmur of polite interest and waits.

'My grandfather was conscript in German army in World War Two,' Stefanya continues. 'After war, when we were liberated by the Russians my grandfather was taken away by Russian soldiers. We still not know what happen to him. The worst thing, not to know. No grave, no papers. You have a picture of him, maybe, of your husband?'

'No, I'm afraid not.' Alice feels as though she has let Stefanya down. 'I have one of my son, though. They look quite alike. D'you think I should show her that?'

'OK, says Stefanya, tightening her grip on Abigail's hand. Abigail gives her a trusting smile, whatever so upset her now wiped from the whiteboard of her mind. Alice fishes in her purse for the photo, just last year's school portrait, Polly an image of studied cool, as though her face and uniformed torso come from two different cards in a game of Tops and Tails, Jesse grinning to camera with his tie crooked. Jesse's eyes the blue of cornflowers, like Harry's. She hands the photo to Stefanya, who places it in Abigail's lap. Alice senses a stillness, a kind of cosmic hush, as Abigail's gaze rests on the images of her children.

Then, before either Alice or Stefanya realises what is happening, Abigail is ripping the photo to shreds, arms and hands working with a force of which Alice would not have thought her capable. 'Little bastard!' she shrieks. 'That little feckin' bastard. Him and the other one.' Her accent is now pure, guttural South Yorkshire.

'Abigail.' Stefanya, too, has raised her voice in an effort to regain control of the situation. 'Ab-i-gail,' she says again, with equal emphasis on each syllable, her voice the percussion holding the performance together.

'What happened, Abigail?' demands Alice, desperate for an answer before whatever gateway to Abigail's past has opened up closes again. 'What other one?'

'Feckin' little coward. My poor little Jimmy.' Abigail begins to cry with loud abandon, hugging herself and rocking back and forth in her chair, the confetti of Alice's photo scattered in her lap.

'OK, Abby, it's OK.' Stefanya reverts to her singsong, baby-coddling voice and tries to put her arms around Abigail, but Abigail struggles free. Her hands claw the air as if she is scrabbling to the surface of something.

'Tin soldier!' she yells. 'Fuckin' tin soldier. Stood there and said he were fuckin' tin soldier.'

An image is forming in Alice's mind, of the bookshelves in Harry's study, of one book in particular; an old, cloth bound copy of Hans Andersen's *Fairytales,* its corners battered and threadbare, much of its gilded lettering rubbed away and the scarlet cloth of the spine sun-faded to the colour of a tea stain. It has always been there, among his gardening books and business magazines. The children had had their own books of fairytales, with laminated boards and gaudy illustrations, and the old, battered book had become no more than a mild curiosity, a question she did not ask because there were so many questions she did not want to have to answer.

But now she has to ask; her marriage, Harry's life may depend on it. And the image in her head is becoming clearer. There is an inscription in the frontispiece of the book, a girl's name, on an *ex libris* label which has partly peeled away, leaving a brown rectangle of dried glue. She can't remember the name; she tries to visualise the letters but it's impossible with the racket going on around her and the jangling urgency in her heart. 'Was it *The Steadfast Tin Soldier,* Abigail?' she asks.

'Where's me tin?' demands Abigail, struggling to rise from her chair. 'Me tin, I want me tin.'

'Alright, alright, I get for you.' Abigail subsides with a shallow sigh. 'Sorry,' Stefanya says to Alice, 'so sorry, but is enough. You have to go now. Try again another time, yes?'

'But I can't...I mean, I live in East Anglia. And my husband's missing now. Now, not another time.'

'You get my tin! Wretched girl.' Abigail fetches Stefanya a feeble clout to her side. A shadow passes over Stefanya's face but all she says is,

'Please. This was big mistake. If I have to get nurse, I will have trouble. You go.'

'She's stolen it, hasn't she?' shouts Abigail, pointing at Alice. 'She's with him. Little cunt. Him and that other one. I said no good would come of it, I said, to that man from the papers. Should have thrown away the fuckin' key.'

'Please,' implores Stefanya, struggling to hold Abigail in her chair. It is a real struggle; Abigail's ancient limbs shove and twist with a force that seems impossible. The torn scraps of the photo are scattered, now, all over the green carpet.

'Took everything!' screams Abigail. 'Everything!'

Stefanya glances anxiously towards the door. Alice, too, is certain the commotion will be overheard and bring someone running. She feels guilty about Stefanya, but she can't leave, not like this, with nothing but a jumble of disconnected clues, a trail as meaningless as the pattern of torn paper on the floor. She wonders if, perhaps, she can reassemble the pieces of the photo sufficiently to show it to Abigail again; after all, given the condition of Abigail's mind, there is no reason why her responses should be consistent, no reason why, a second time, she might not be better able to articulate what the faces of Alice's children mean to her. Alice slips off the bed, on to her knees and begins to crawl around the floor, picking up the scraps of card.

'What you doing?' demands Stefanya. She is breathless and a few lank strands of hair have escaped from her ponytail to hang in her eyes.

'I'm going to show her the photo again.'

'You're mad. I call security. You want lose me my job?'

'I want to find out what's happened to my husband.'

'She know nothing, Alice. She just poor old demented woman, know nothing.'

'She knows something, I'm sure of it. What about the tin? The newspaper cuttings?' Alice's scrapbook contains all the keys to her life. You just have to know how to look. 'Where does she keep the tin? I'm going to get it out. Imagine if you thought it contained something about your grandfather. How would you feel then?'

Stefanya hesitates. Alice makes a lunge for Abigail's wardrobe, hooking her fingertips around the edge of one door and pulling it open. The wardrobe totters with the force of her action. At the same time, Abigail frees herself from Stefanya's grasp, pushes herself up out of her chair and stands, her uncertain sway mirroring that of the wardrobe. Stefanya is between them like a referee in a boxing match, feet splayed, arms outstretched. But she cannot keep them both from falling. Suddenly shocked at her own recklessness, Alice manoeuvres herself until she can throw her weight against the wardrobe to steady it.

That must have been the moment, she realises later, as she was getting sheepishly to her feet while Stefanya pushed the wardrobe back more firmly against the wall, when Abigail pulled the alarm cord. Was it a second's rationality to counter Alice's loss of control, or merely a childlike attraction to the bright red bell-pull? Either way, within seconds, three or four more people had crowded into the room, a syringe was produced from somewhere and a bulky man, replete with the ironic courtesy of the nightclub bouncer, had taken Alice by the elbow and was escorting her back through the drawing room, where the old man in the yellow cardigan still blithely faced his music and danced, towards the front door.

She sits in her car for a long time, smoking. The rain has cleared while she has been with Abigail and Stefanya, and the shadow of an ancient cedar, blurred by weak sunlight, crawls across the car park as she loses track of the number of cigarettes she has consumed. She cannot stop until the trembling ceases, the aftermath of vehemence like a recuperation from a powerful illness. She has to smoke until she can breathe evenly again, and her heart stops racketing around in her chest, until she can think clearly. What now? The question plays through her mind in a loop. She hopes Stefanya won't lose her job, but whatever happens, she can't make another visit to Abigail; she would never be allowed near her. Her trip has been a complete waste of time, and petrol she can ill afford now, and she has nothing to show for it but a torn photograph.

Yet there has to be a connection, she's sure of it. If she can only stop her brain from racing and think calmly she will be able to grasp it. She knows it's only just out of reach, around the next corner, waiting for her when the fog of anger and worry lifts. Mary must know; she is the same generation as Abigail; if Abigail had some role in Harry's childhood, then Mary must know about it. She has tried to speak to Abigail, no doubt to warn her of Alice's visit, and who was she on the phone to yesterday, when Alice overheard her? Mary is the key, she's sure of it. She glances at the clock on her dashboard. Four seventeen. If she leaves now she should be home in about four hours, plenty of time to get the children to bed, or at least up to their rooms, and have a serious talk with Mary.

Ian's back prickles with a sense of exposure as he walks towards the village, as though the sea and the sky and the empty caravan windows are all made of eyes, watching him, pelting his skin with eyeball bearings. The Dog's Head is ahead of him, a tall, narrow building with a yard abutting the caravan site. The yard is in heavy shade, evidence that somewhere inland, the sun has begun its decline. The trestle tables are empty except for one on which a gull struts up and down, stabbing its beak from time to time at invisible crumbs. A roost of sparrows chatters at the gull from the branches of a tree overhanging the yard, but the gull ignores them. Ian, however, drawn by the cacophony, notices among the leaves a shape which is not that of nature, flat-sided and sharp-cornered. A surveillance camera. The tree is behind a discreet fence of living willow, entwined with climbers and creepers of various kinds, but Ian's trained eye picks out the razor wire they do not quite disguise, running along the top of the fence which, he now observes, borders the length of the caravan park down to the sea.

Even before he has seen the fancy chimneys protruding above the vegetation, he knows he is looking at Harry Theobald's house, and he thinks the boy who became Harry Theobald is probably the only person he knows cold enough to fall in love with a pile of bricks and mortar. He flexes his hands, whose joints are still stiff, and wonders what he's going to find inside The Dog's Head. It crosses his mind briefly that he might find Harry himself in there, wearing a rollneck or a scarf, like some ponce, to hid the bruises on his neck, but then common sense, and everything he knows about killing and dying, prevails.

The man behind the empty bar has a florid complexion and a shock of white hair, tobacco stained at the front. 'What can I get you?' he asks, bearing his horse teeth in a practised smile as Ian approaches the bar. He surveys the beer pumps ranged along the counter.

'Which do you drink?' he asks.

'I don't.'

'I suppose you see too much of the damage it can do in this job.'

The landlord purses his lips; his gaze flicks critically over Ian, as if to suggest he has a fine example in front of him of a man undone by drink. Ian rakes his fingers through his hair in a vain attempt to tidy it, and wishes it were that simple.

'I'll have a pint of...Wherry, then.'

The landlord nods, takes a glass from beneath the bar and begins to pull the pint. Ian watches the beer swirl into the glass. 'Can I get anything to eat?'

'Crisps, nuts. Kitchen's not open till seven.'

Ian glances at his watch. Just before four. 'I'll have a bag of peanuts, then. Plain salted.'

The landlord places his pint and packet of nuts before him. Ian holds out a note, half expecting the landlord to notice it isn't his but Harry Theobald's, but he merely takes the note and busies himself at the till, leaving Ian free to look around the bar. It is well kept, the brass and woodwork gleaming, the tiled floor spotless and the beer, when he takes a draught, clean-tasting. The landlord, reading his satisfaction, smiles, a smile whose grim warmth reminds him suddenly, shockingly, of fat Janet at Appsley House. He hasn't thought about her in years. He drains his beer and orders a second.

'Not seen you round here before, have I?' asks the landlord, setting the second pint on the bar.

'No.'

'So what brings you here?' The man's eyes, beneath heavy, pleated lids, are keen and curious.

'Maybe the fact I've never been here before?' He flashes his most dazzling smile, the one that makes men trust him and women think he's dangerous.

'Staying long?'

'Depends. Is there work to be had?'

'You could try the site.' He juts his chin in the direction of the caravan site. 'They'll be getting ready for the summer now, might need some odd jobs done.'

'What about that big place I passed on the way here? Fancy chimneys.'

'You mean Wildwood? Harry Theobald's place?' The landlord says his name with studied nonchalance. 'I don't think you'd get anything there.'

'Why not?'

'He's very security conscious. Has to be, I suppose, in his position.'

Ian continues to smile, wondering if the landlord has any idea what Harry Theobald's current position is.

'I don't think he'd take on just anybody. Don't get me wrong, he's a decent sort, no airs and graces, just...private, if you know what I mean.'

Ian nods. He knows. 'I'll try the site, then.' He drains his glass. 'See you later. I'm Ian, by the way.' He holds out his hand. The landlord takes it.

'Bernard,' he says. His grip is weak, provisional.

Traffic on the Tinsley viaduct is stationary. Persistent rain has brought with it an early twilight, a slush of grey filling Alice's windscreen, streaked with red and yellow smears of headlamps and rear view lights. She is maddened by the slap and swish of the wipers, marginally off-rhythm, and the parched roar of the de-mister in which something is rattling like the lungs of a tubercular mouse. Desperate to be away from here now, she slams her palms against the steering wheel and shouts, 'Get a fucking move on!' at the top of her voice.

The final few miles of the journey to Autumn Glade, once she had left the motorway, hadn't been as bad as she had expected. She had spent most of the time staring at her satnav rather than her actual surroundings, seeing not the steep, narrow streets with their stepped borders of terraced cottages but a grid of coloured lines that transformed her journey into a kind of computer game. Only on the return did she begin to notice familiar landmarks and how they had been changed by time and circumstance. The corner shop on Hermit Hill was a community centre now and the church in Pilley had been cleaned, giving the stone a raw, unsettled look as though it had been recently quarried. Passing the entrance to Wortley Golf Club she was assailed by a memory that still clings to the inside of her skull as she sits on the viaduct, staring into the grey space that used to be filled by the sweeping flanks of the cooling towers.

She's on her chopper, cycling up the long drive towards the clubhouse, thin legs pumping furiously to keep up with the other kids who have proper bikes with full-size wheels. The slope is shallow, but for her, peddling twice as fast as everyone else, exhausting, and she begins to fall behind, her legs turning to lead, her heart to dreams, until she's in another place where she is mistress of a house like the clubhouse, sweeping from room to room in a crimson satin dress, touching silk-gloved fingertips to the furniture as she passes. Music is playing beyond a gilded double doorway, opened as she passes by footmen who are invisible, though she knows they are wearing powdered wigs and silver-buckled shoes. There's a perfume like the *Rive Gauche* that her mum wears on the rare occasions her dad takes her out, and something else, sharp and feral, that makes her skin tingle. She knows it comes from the figure at her side, whose shoulder and hip she can feel in rhythm

with her own, but when she turns to look at him, he isn't
there. Not yet.

Of course she's late, and earns fewer pennies for retriev-
ing lost balls than the others, but Nathan gives her half his
so she ends up with the most. By the time they arrive at the
newsagents, just before closing, she's already forgotten she
didn't earn them all herself. She buys a quarter of rhubarb
and custard and three flying saucers, then she's five pence
short for *Princess* so Nathan buys her that as well.

Nathan. She hasn't thought of him in years.

The two girls in the site office are pathetically grateful for
Ian's offer. They haven't had an on-site handyman before,
they tend to use labour from the village, which is expensive,
and the rents are going down all the time as the sea eats into
the cliff. He agrees to work for a low wage, in exchange for
one of the empty vans to live in. They tell him he can buy
supplies at the Co-op in the village, and that they're sorry
there's no electricity or mains water, but he's welcome to
use the shower block, and give him the key to a van right on
the cliff edge, nothing between it and the beach but a narrow footpath and a rickety post and wire fence. It's high tide
when he goes down there, and looking out of the bay window that takes up most of the van's end panel is like looking
down from the bridge of a ship, straight on to the sea, a
flat, brassy expanse in the late afternoon sun that looks as
though it couldn't even roll a pebble, let alone pulverise the
shore.

The journey and his mid-afternoon beers have taken
it out of him, and he's tempted just to lie on the balding
velour window seat and watch the sea until he falls asleep,
but he forces himself to walk into the village. It will give
him a chance to look at the evening papers. If either Harry

Theobald or his car has been found, it's certain to have made the front pages.

The Co-op is under siege from a hoard of school children in grey and maroon uniforms. It's hard to believe such a small village could have spawned so many of them. The cacophony of ringtones and chatter does little to assuage his burgeoning headache as he flicks through the titles on the newsstand. The *Aylsburgh Gazette* headlines with the plight of a duck shot with a crossbow, the *Eastern Daily Press* with plans to introduce wind power to Norwich City Hall. There is no mention of Harry Theobald. Ian is shaken by a sudden, fierce terror of loneliness; for the first time, his mind is consciously processing the prospect of a world in which Craig Barnes no longer exists. His hands shake. He thrusts them in his pockets, glancing around him to see if anyone has noticed.

The whispers, the pointing as he enters the dining hall. He'll keep his hands in his pockets, he tells himself, and that James Dean scowl on his face, and he won't care. 'I don't have to explain anything to anybody,' Jimmy's mumbling, right in his ear, straight out of Rebel Without A Cause. *Then one of them says it, not to his face but behind his back as he slouches to his place, a whisper loud enough to reach the ear of God. 'Cry-baby,' she says, and his hands are out of his pockets in an instant, balled into fists, smashing into her teeth whose braces leave cuts on his knuckles. And he's back in the house mother's study again, bent over her desk and listening to the whistle of the cane, the way it stops just before it hits him, like one of Hitler's doodlebugs.*

The memory fades as he becomes aware of a girl standing next to him, flipping through some garish teen magazine, so close he can smell her, shampoo, ironed cotton, an echo of chlorine that tells him she's been swimming this afternoon, and taken a shower afterwards. Without turning his head, he looks at her, and it's like opening his eyes under cool, clear water.

Like most of the others in the shop, she's in school uniform. White shirt, grey skirt, maroon tie with diagonal stripes. Her hem rides several inches above the knee and her legs are bare, tanned, swimming-pool-scuffed. She is wearing white ankle socks with her kicked-heel school shoes, but she's not a child. The outline of her bra beneath the thin cotton shirt draws his attention to the swell of her breasts and makes his mouth dry. He forces his gaze back to the headlines on the newsstand, but the letters jumble in front of him and his eyes slide away, over her throat, exposed by her undone top button and loosened tie, her hair which has the gleam of wet sand, a fine wrist that glitters with beads and plaited friendship bracelets as she runs a finger along the magazines, looking for the one she wants. How old is she, he wonders. Old enough, whines the voice of longing inside him, that is still, itself, the voice of a child, needy and jealous, always peering through from the wrong side of the fence. The girl, sensing his attention, casts him a smile so brief it's little more than a second of light on water, and her cheeks turn shell pink. She is, quite literally, breathtaking, not beautiful but cool and clean and new-looking with, he thinks, not the faintest idea of the effect she is having. The ache of longing, which is always there, intensifies, seems to tighten like a band around his chest. A heart attack, he thinks, an attack on the heart.

By the time he has taken his basket to the checkout and paid, the children have drained away from the store and are gathered in chattering knots outside. Instinctively, his eyes seek her out and, though he looks at her for barely a second, he knows, from the intentness of her concentration on the conversation in which she is engaged, that she is aware of it.

With Daisy capering around her feet, Alice follows the sound of machine gun fire into the snug. Jesse is lying at full stretch on his front, absorbed in a computer game. Alice is too glad to see him even to worry about the violence of the game, or be irritated by the fact that she has to say his name twice before he hears her.

'Hi, mum,' he says eventually, still staring at the screen, thumbs working the controls with convulsive rapidity. She is content she merits only a minute fraction of his attention because this is normal, the way life was before Harry went away.

'Hi yourself,' she replies, smiling at the nape of his neck, his dark curls so like Harry's. 'Where is everyone?'

'I'm here. Polly's upstairs. Don't know where Aunt Mary is. She didn't like me playing *Assassin's Creed* but I said I was allowed so she went off somewhere. Bugger off, Daisy,' he adds as the dog inserts herself between him and the screen.

'Language.'

'Mu-um.'

Alice laughs. She stoops to ruffle his hair, feeling the stretch in the muscles of her back and legs like a blessing after the long hours hunched over the steering wheel. Leaving Jesse to his game she goes in search of Mary. As she walks towards the drawing room, she replays Mary's behaviour since she told her about the payments to Elysium plc, her antipathy towards Alice going to see Abigail Jones, her sudden volte face over the police, the overheard telephone conversation. It all adds up; she is more certain than ever that Mary knows something that connects Abigail Jones with Harry.

She finds Mary seated beneath the Benson lampstand, absorbed in a book, apparently unaware of her as she pauses in the drawing room doorway to gather herself. She watches the methodical way Mary turns a page, smoothes it with the flat of her hand and clips it in place with one of those book-marks that looks like an ornate hairpin. Her face, toplit by the circle of yellow light from the lamp, frowns in concentration. She is as lost in her reading as Jesse in his game. Alice has an image of the four of them, herself and Mary and the children, each moving around inside the empty vastness of Wildwood in his or her own circle of light, bumping into one another, overlapping sometimes, like Venn diagrams, but the circles remaining intact, inviolable. Was it Leonardo da Vinci who said the circular fortress was impregnable? She seems to remember something like that from the architecture unit of her interior design course. Well, even Leonardo could be wrong about some things.

'Hello, Mary,' she says.

Mary looks up, the light glinting in her spectacle lenses so Alice cannot see her eyes. 'You're back, then,' she says, closing the book and beginning to fiddle with her page marker. A statement of sufficient banality, thinks Alice, not to merit a reply. Mary removes her glasses; the skin around her eyes looks crumpled and fragile, like very old paper suddenly exposed to the air. 'Earlier than I expected,' she adds.

'Not enough time to bury the bodies?' asks Alice, advancing into the room. To her credit, Mary doesn't feign ignorance but casts Alice a rueful look which seems to admit complicity. But in what?

'Jesse has done his homework,' she says. 'Maths and geography. His understanding of crop cycles in Bengal seems serviceable but I can't vouch for his quadratic equations. Not my strong suit, I'm afraid.'

'Abigail Jones got very excited over a photo of Jesse. I have no idea why because she's quite off her head. But of course, you knew that, didn't you? They told you when you phoned.'

Mary nods.

'So what else do you know about her?'

'Very little.'

'Little doesn't necessarily mean unimportant.'

'It means what it says, Alice. I know of Abigail Jones, but I know very little about her.'

'Then tell me what you do know. *How* you know. If Harry's been paying her care home fees, I've got a right to that, surely.'

Mary pinches the bridge of her nose between thumb and forefinger, massaging the patches of skin reddened by her glasses. 'No, dear, I'm afraid you haven't. While Harry's alive...' She pauses and glances up at Alice to gauge the effect of her words; Alice glares back; of course Harry's alive; she'd know if he was dead, the way animals know when the pressure of the air changes. '...you have no right to know anything about him he chooses not to tell you. The fact that he's kept those payments away from your joint bank accounts makes it clear he didn't want you to know about them.'

'I'm his wife, Mary. Why should he keep secrets from me? You're not married, you don't understand.'

Mary heaves a deep sigh. 'I knew something like this would happen,' she says, as if to herself.

'Like what? What *has* happened? I'm sick of this, being treated like some child being kept in the dark for her own good. I'm not a child,' she insists, though her tone seems to her to be exactly that of a peevish little girl, 'I've made up my mind. I'm going to call the police. That's what you want, isn't it?'

She turns away from Mary, preparing to walk back out of the drawing room, into the staircase hall where there is a phone extension. When Mary says, 'I've already spoken to them,' she doesn't know whether to be angry or relieved.

'Sit down, Alice,' says Mary. Alice compromises by perching on the arm of the chesterfield before the fireplace, keeping an expanse of polished parquet and a Voysey rug between her and Mary; the rug, she notes with a sharp clutch of despair, is slightly damaged at one corner; by how much, she wonders, will that reduce its value, if she has to sell it?

'The call you made yesterday?'

Surprise flickers across Mary's face before she nods her affirmation. Remembering how different she sounded on the phone from the Mary she knows, Alice finds herself somehow more disturbed than reassured.

'Whatever Harry's done,' says Mary, 'he's done because he loves you. You and the children mean everything to him. You know that, don't you?'

She used to think she did. 'Well he's got a funny way of showing it. Keeping secrets to the tune of nearly three thousand pounds a month, telling me he's gone fishing and then...vanishing.' Alice clicks her fingers. Daisy jumps up, stern wagging. 'And leaving us penniless, it seems,' adds Alice, staring at the frayed corner of the rug. 'What did the police say? I suppose they'll want to talk to me. When they do, I shall tell them about Abigail, even if you won't. I mean, she could be the whole key...'

'The police have all they need for now.'

'What do you mean? Of course they'll want to talk to me.'

'I've impressed on them the need for discretion because of Harry's position. They won't come to the house unless... they have to.' The pause lasts a fraction of a second, but it's like playing a damaged CD, when the laser suddenly jumps to a different track.

'You think he's dead, don't you?' Alice jumps up from the arm of the chesterfield. 'That's what you and the police were talking about, him being dead,' her voice rising, spiralling up into a shriek, 'and you thought...you thought if I went haring off to Yorkshire it'd take my mind off it, get me out of the way while you...oh fuck knows.' She turns away from Mary and presses her head against the edge of the mantelpiece, calmed by the manageable pain of it digging into her brow.

'I think it's a possibility we have to consider.'

'We?' yells Alice, whirling away from the mantelpiece. '*We?* You can consider it if you want to but not me. He's not dead. I'd know. Why would he be dead? If there'd been an accident or something, I'd have been told by now.'

'If he'd been found,' says Mary quietly. 'Until I spoke to the police, no-one had any reason to go looking for him.'

Horrible images assail Alice, of Harry drowned, his water-logged body caught on the edge of a remote burn; of Harry at the bottom of some unforgiving Highland valley, his dead fingers still clawed around the jammed door of the crashed Range Rover; of Harry riddled with bullet wounds after a kidnap that has gone wrong. She tries to push them away, wishing she didn't have such a well-nourished imagination for disaster. She forces her mind back to Abigail Jones.

'She's his mother, isn't she?' Alice is unaware that this is what she's thinking until she says it, so repeats her conclusion, as if to test its viability. 'Abigail Jones is Harry's mother. He changed his name for some reason.' People do.

Mary's mouth sags open as if the muscles of her jaw have been suddenly severed and, to Alice's astonishment, she begins to laugh. There are tears of mirth in her eyes by the time she recovers herself sufficiently to say, 'Abigail Jones isn't Harry's mother, Alice, I can promise you that.'

Then..?' Alice feels foolish. Whatever the joke is, she's failed to understand it.

'Alice, I really can't say any more about her except that she isn't the solution to your problem. She won't lead you to Harry.'

Suddenly Alice can't bear to look at Mary any longer, can't stay in the room whose twilit air seems thick with lies. 'I'm going to check on Polly,' she snaps, and flees, thinking she wouldn't care if the drawing room, with its artfully placed furniture and the frayed rug, and Mary in it, simply went up in flames.

'Can I come in?' she calls, tapping on Polly's door.

'Hi, mum. Sure.'

She hears the metallic smack of a laptop being closed as she enters. Polly is sitting on her bed, computer balanced on her knees, mobile beside her. She is wearing a skinny vest and pyjama bottoms patterned with Scottie dogs with red bows around their necks. The phone trills and buzzes into life. Polly looks at it, smiles, and sets it aside.

'Text from Mads,' she says. 'Wants to know if she can borrow my orange skirt for Saturday.'

'What? The satin one? Bit dressy for a beach party, isn't it?'

Polly gives her mother a sharp look. 'Oh, so I can definitely go, then?'

'Yes, I suppose so.' Why argue with her precious daughter about something as insignificant as a summer party?

'Cool.' Polly doesn't say thank you, doesn't leap off the bed to hug her mother, but the smile in her eyes is fulsome and genuine. Alice can feel Polly's gratitude wash over her like a warm tide and she's suddenly so tired she wants to sink down into it, into the love of her family that holds Wildwood together as surely as the mortar in its walls.

'Oh, someone came,' says Polly. She's texting now, looking not at Alice but at her phone as her fingers dance over the keys.

'Who?'

Polly shrugs. 'Bernard, from the pub. He was just leaving when I got home.' She giggles. 'I think he and Aunt Mary might have been on the gin. Bernard was a lot less... you know...than usual.'

How long had Bernard been there, she wonders. What had he and Mary talked about? The thought of them together makes her feel somehow violated. 'Did you come straight home?' she snaps. 'Have you done your homework?' The guilt and apprehension lasts only a second, but Alice spots it. 'You haven't, have you? I suppose you've been messing about on Facebook all evening or something.'

'Chill, Mum, I've done most of it. I can do the rest on the bus in the morning.'

'Of course you can't. And don't you talk to me as if you were some kind of street kid, Apollonia.'

'What? What's with the Apollonia all of a sudden? You know I think it's gross.'

If you want to go to that party on Saturday, you'd better finish your work and smarten up your attitude, young lady.'

Polly flings the phone away from her and turns over on to her side, facing away from Alice and towards a wall decorated with a giant poster of a bare chested Robert Pattinson. 'I wish Dad was here. You don't go on at me like this when he's here.'

'Well maybe I should, and then maybe you wouldn't be so rude and disobedient. You think your dad would like to hear you talking to me like this? He'd be furious.' No reply. Alice stares at the nape of her daughter's neck, wondering how the conversation took this turn. 'Lying is very serious, Polly. When dad does get home, I shall have to tell him.'

Polly turns over. Lying facing Alice, with her knees drawn up to her chest, she twists a hank of hair round and round her finger the way she used to when she was a toddler, and tired, and fixes her gaze on her mother. Her eyes have a dull, hollow look. 'He's not coming, though, is he? I'm not stupid, mum. He's gone off with someone, hasn't he, like Lee Abbot's dad and Mrs. Stark from the art department?'

The idea that Harry is comparable in any way to Charlie Abbott, with his Norwich City shirt stretched tight across his gut and the battered white van in the back of which, it was rumoured, he had exerted his peculiar charm over Mrs. Stark, is laughable. But it also makes Alice feel sick to think that she and Harry might be the subject of the same kind of schoolyard gossip as Charlie Abbott and Mrs. Stark. She doesn't know Lee, but she remembers how unfair and unfeeling she had thought it when the school suspended him for hitting another boy who had teased him about his father and the art mistress.

She reaches out a hand to Polly, but Polly just tucks herself into a tighter ball.

'Are people at school talking?' Alice asks.

To her surprise, Polly laughs. 'God no. Why would they? It's not like there's any teachers involved. And anyway, no-one knows. I mean, no-one even knows what goes on inside here, do they? We're like, sealed away in here. Once I get home I might as well be in outer space for all anyone knows. Or cares.'

'Oh Polly, don't be like that. You've got lots of friends.'

Polly sits up, swings her legs over the side of the bed so she is facing her mother full on. 'No, Mum, I don't. The people who come here from school are no different from the ones that come to look at Dad's plants. We're freaks, me and Jesse. It's like we have two heads, or a relative who was murdered or something. I wish you'd sent us to some posh school where being rich was normal instead of putting us in that zoo.' She pauses, dashes tears from her eyes. Alice stares at her face, blotchy with emotion. She wants to tell Polly she understands, but she can't. The part of her that understands has nothing to do with being Polly's mother. Polly's mother, it seems, is the one who, ostrich-like, believed that if she pretended her family was ordinary, no-one would be able to see otherwise. So she says nothing, merely reaches out to touch Polly's knee, hoping, somehow, that her touch can synthesise the different parts of herself and communicate her sympathy. Polly stays still, but she is tense, wary, as though a wasp has landed on her and she's afraid that, if she moves, it will sting her.

Alice thinks about the police, about what will happen if they do come to the house. Will they arrive in unmarked cars, or in full livery, complete with flashing blue lights? Will they ring first, or just turn up? Then people will start talking, and if Polly thinks school is a zoo now, she'll know it's a jungle once the gutter press are at the gates. 'OK, you're upset. I'm upset. We shouldn't make it worse by falling out. You can go to the party,' Polly clenches her fist and gives the air a tiny punch, 'but you have to promise me something in return.' Alice pauses.

'Cool.'

'You come straight home after school every afternoon, and I mean *every* afternoon, unless I know in advance where you're going. And you *don't* try to do homework on the bus. You're a bright girl, Polly, don't waste it.'

Polly mumbles something. Alice concludes it's probably best that she fails to hear what it is.

'Good. We've got a deal, then.'

'Deal. I know why Bernard was here, by the way.'

'..?'

'He brought the ACDC minutes. For Dad.'

The site office is locked by the time Ian walks past it on his way to The Dog's Head, and most of the vans are in darkness, just a few rectangles of curtained light here and there like sticking plasters on the face of the summer's night. He might have wondered which one was Bunty and Annabel's, but he doesn't, because his attention is focused entirely on Bernard.

Bernard's hand is already curled around the Wherry pump as he approaches. He orders a whisky chaser as well, and takes a menu from a stack on the end of the bar.

'What do you recommend, then?' he asks, though he isn't hungry. He just wants a means of getting into conversation with the landlord.

'Fish is always good,' says Bernard. I bet you say that to all the girls, thinks Ian, and is about to make some remark about eating fish at the seaside when Bernard's attention is distracted by a new arrival. He's a squat figure wearing a worn tweed jacket and a greasy flat cap, his bow legs encased in gaiters as though he's stepped off the set of an Edwardian country house drama. He is clutching a bundle wrapped in newspaper and secured with string, which he places on the bar as he accepts a half pint glass from Bernard. 'Be rain later,' he says.

'Evening, George,' says Bernard.

'Runner beans,' says George. 'Picked um this evenin'.'

'Thanks, George. Much appreciated. I'll just call your supper through to the kitchen. Usual, is it?' Bernard picks up the bundle.

'Do well, mister.'

'Back in a minute.'

The old man gives Ian a nod and goes to sit at a corner table with the air of a man who owns it. Ian fancies he can almost see the groove in the floor worn by George's feet as he trudges from bar to table, table to bar, year in, year out, drinking his pint, eating his usual. He imagines every village has its George, whose burden of habit counterweighs the drift of people like himself who wash in and out on the tide.

'Harry Theobald's head gardener,' says Bernard, in a confidential tone, as he re-emerges through a door behind the bar. 'He comes in for his supper most nights since his wife died.' It's a banal enough remark, yet to Ian it seems pointed, as though Bernard knows he has a particular interest in Harry Theobald. The low babble of background chatter in the pub seems to form itself into the words Craig uttered in the Head of Etive car park. *...he got my hackles up... used to be a private dick...something stinks, Arthur, something definitely stinks.* He fights the urge to run; if this man knows the truth about him then he has to find out, and deal with it. Quickly, before anyone notices Theobald's Range Rover abandoned in the service station car park.

'That's a bit of a coup for you,' he says, draining his whisky and pushing the glass towards Bernard, 'having the big man's head gardener as a regular.'

Bernard bridles. 'Harry and Alice come in here a lot,' he says. You pull the trigger, the gun fires, thinks Ian, handing one of Harry Theobald's crisp twenties across the bar and telling Bernard to get one for himself out of it too.

'You know him quite well then?'

'A landlord's business to be hospitable, isn't it?' Bernard's defensiveness comes as a relief to Ian; it tells him

Bernard isn't as familiar with 'Harry and Alice' as his casual use of their first names would suggest.

'Mate, I'm just making conversation, yeah? You have a name as big as Harry Theobald coming in your pub, people are bound to be curious.'

They fall into an uneasy silence as George approaches the bar with his empty pint pot.

'Turn up seeing Alice in here for the ACDC meeting Sunday,' Bernard remarks as he pulls George a fresh pint.

'Ar,' George agrees. 'She unt never seen the point of it. Can't stop nature, she says.'

'Odd view for the wife of a garden designer.'

George says nothing; if he has an opinion, he isn't going to share it.

'Harry still away then is he?' Bernard asks, and Ian's hearing seems to sharpen.

'Fishing,' says George, with an air of muted puzzlement that seems to hang in the air like a question mark. Ian's scalp crawls; as the pub door opens, he shivers, even though the evening is mild.

'Someone walked over my grave,' he remarks, with a smile that feels like a muscle spasm.

'Oh, hello. Did you find your friend yet?' *Shit. Bunty.*

'Not yet.' He forces himself to apologise to Bunty and Annabel for his earlier abrupt departure and offer to buy them a drink. Good manners will make him unremarkable to a couple like Bunty and Annabel, and he doesn't want them to remember him. 'You, George?' he adds, casually inclusive. It's Harry Theobald's money he's spending after all; he pulls another note out of his back pocket, the texture of it acute, distinct between his fingers, this paper that also carries the imprint of Craig's hands. Suddenly he sees them as they were that day, knuckles skinned and thumbnails gnawed to the quick, curled around the neck of the bottle of gin and orange as he tipped it to his lips. He blinks the image away as Bunty says,

'We gave him a lift.' He orders a half of bitter and a lemon and lime. 'From Wroxham. Said he was meeting a chap who works here. What was his name..? Tom, was it? Can't say I remember him but then, I suppose you get a lot of casuals in the summer, eh?'

Bernard murmurs non-committally, but his eyes flick briefly in Ian's direction and his brows, one white, one pipe smoke yellow, rise a fraction. The whites of his eyes are opaque as the whites of hard boiled eggs. Ian sets down his drink and heads for the gents; he needs time to spin himself a cover, just something vague and simple about miscommunication, but plausible, something Bernard can't question.

Bernard cuts him off just outside the door; they have to shuffle to one side in the narrow corridor to allow a girl in shorts and hiking boots access to the neighbouring ladies' room. They both look at her legs.

'What are you doing here?' demands Bernard. 'Asking questions about Harry Theobald and my pub. Eavesdropping.'

'Eavesdropping?' Ian is genuinely astonished. He wonders what conversation he has overheard that he shouldn't have, then remembers George's odd lack of confidence as he pronounced the word, fishing, as if he suspected his boss had gone fishing for more than salmon.

'Well you're not here to meet this Tom character, that's for sure. I never employ anyone here except the lad in the kitchen and some local school kids to wait tables. There's no call for anyone else behind the bar. Just the regulars and a handful of caravaners who haven't been driven off by the erosion. Are you police? Scotland Yard went through everything like a dose of salts. Notebooks, computer, bank account. And they couldn't find a thing,' he concludes with an air that suggests there had been plenty to find but Ian, though mildly curious, isn't concerned about what Bernard had to hide from Scotland Yard. What matters is that, unless Bernard is playing a game of improbable subtlety, Craig's fears would seem to be unfounded. Whatever Bernard knows about him, he has made no connection with Ian.

'I'm not police, mate, and I'm not interested in your bank account unless you've just won the lottery. Alright? I was just looking to hook up with someone, but I guess I got the wrong place.'

Bernard gives a sceptical grunt, but he doesn't pursue the conversation and Ian, with a small thrill of power, knows the landlord believes he's said too much. He will tread carefully around Ian from now on, but Ian has what he came for, and there is no longer anything to keep him here, on this strip of crumbling coast. He will sleep the night here and leave in the morning.

The clock on Alice's desk reads eight minutes to midnight. She knows she should go back to the house; her stomach growls with hunger and her limbs are stiff and cold. She has no idea if the children have gone to bed. But she cannot move from her place curled up in the corner of the old sofa, the sofa where Polly was made, her scrapbook open on the cushion beside her. She reaches out stiff fingers and turns a page, the crackle of desiccated newsprint the only sound in the studio. *The noise was horrendous from start to finish,* she reads, - *a terrible, unbelievable metallic grinding noise. Bottles of perfume and whisky were flying around,* she reads. Yet doesn't read, because the studio is in almost total darkness, the unexpected geometry of half-restored furniture drawn in by the circle of light from the desk lamp like strange creatures attracted by firelight. Her fingers move over the pasted pages whose words she knows by heart.

He's called Simon Osborne, the man who wrote this account of the sinking of the *Herald of Free Enterprise* on the sixth of March 1987. He's a journalist now, but two of the friends he was travelling with died. She turns another page. The wounded furniture seems to draw closer. *Charlotte and Marcus were fourteen and on holiday when the tsunami struck,* her moving fingers tell her. *They never saw their mother and father again.* Her scrapbook is full of them, the suddenly dead, the disappeared, the people she looks for in crowds.

DAY FOUR

Afterwards, even then, Ian would always be clear in his mind that he had gone to bed, such as it was, intending to leave Aylsburgh next morning. He had rolled himself in the sleeping bag borrowed from the site's lost property store with the sense of tarmac beneath his feet and places to go to where there were hills, high buildings, shadows in which to lose himself. But his sleep was infected by the dead, stifling air in the unused caravan, and he dreamed.

He dreamed of twisted chimneys that transformed into the fingers of an arthritic witch, tangled in his hair, yanking him backwards. As he struggled the witch grew and grew, until she was pulling him into her mouth, which was really the door to a gingerbread house, and he knew he mustn't cross the threshold, but it was sweet, so sweet, and he was hungry...He awoke briefly, with a stiff neck and growling belly, before falling into a second dream, in which he was pursuing someone he couldn't see along dark, knotted passages that were hot, and stank, and pulsed...and were the intestines of the little sapper he'd watched die in a doorway in Derry. *Don't call it Londonderry, Ian, me da would kill youse.* He woke again, sweating and shaking, and the boy's voice was in his head, begging for water. Yet, when he got up, and went into the saloon in search of a water bottle, the image that lingered behind his eyes was of the bare calves and white socks of the girl in the Co-op.

'I made muffins,' says Alice, ice-bright and brittle. She had lain in bed as long as she could bear, listening to the wisteria scratch at the bedroom window in a rising wind, and then the rain that followed it, gurgling in the downpipes, and further away, the restless bass note of the sea. Creeping back into the house in the early hours, she had gone into Harry's study and taken the old copy of Andersen's *Fairy Tales* from the bookcase, hoping it would have something to tell her. She had carried it upstairs and lain it on Harry's side of the bed, and forced herself not to open it until she had completed her customary preparations for sleep, going through each ritual with the rigorous conscientiousness of a priest who does not quite believe in what he is doing.

Then she had fallen asleep reading *The Steadfast Tin Soldier* and into a dream of Harry swirling away from her in a fast flowing stream, his face in the eddies of water like the face of Munch's *Scream of Nature*. She was running, slipping on the riverbank, stumbling over tree roots, the leaves of the trees glittering, falling, studding her skin with marcasite, tinkling like tiny bells... Birdsong.

She woke to the cacophony of the dawn chorus that seemed to resolve itself into words as she thrashed reluctantly back to consciousness:

Flee, warrior, flee!
Death is after you!

As soon as her heart rediscovered its natural rhythm and the dream cleared from her head, she got up and went down to the kitchen in slippers and dressing gown, dry mouthed and gritty eyed, all the unanswered questions still burning inside her. She baked to console herself, measuring and stirring, measuring and stirring in the cool grey light, letting her mind empty along with bowls of flour and jugs of milk.

'Almond and blueberry,' she announces, setting the plate down before the children. Polly pushes the plate away and selects a nectarine from a bowl on the table. Jesse helps himself to two muffins, which he then proceeds to dissect in order to remove all the fruit. Daisy licks up crumbs from around his chair, leaving a slick of saliva on the terracotta tiles. Alice turns to the Aga and busies herself making coffee. She clangs down the kettle on the hob, clatters a spoon against the lip of the cafetiere. Anything to counter the sullen silence of the children which seems to hang like a storm cloud at her back.

After breakfast, Ian decides to walk up to the village. Just to clear his head, he tells himself. The morning is bright and blustery, the sea sparkling, a scarlet fishing boat bobbing across the view from his saloon window like a toy, a smoke of gulls streaming out behind it. The breeze, he tells himself, will blow away his dream. The school bus, he tells himself, will have picked up the children and driven them away by now. Or perhaps it will be late and he will see her, hanging out with her friends, whispering and giggling and picking at her nail varnish, the breeze teasing wisps of hair out of her ponytail and sticking it to her lips so she has to keep brushing it away. Her lips, pale pink and slightly cracked.

He's walking in a daze, his dream, and thoughts of the girl, part remembered, part imagined, still clinging to him the way fog lingers around the bases of trees. But as he emerges from the caravan park into the lane which runs between the pub and the church into the village, something makes him look up and bring his surroundings into focus. Suddenly, finally, he's fully awake, the echoes of the night silenced, and staring at the back of a stout woman, in a raincoat and sensible shoes, walking a Dalmatian dog on a lead.

There is something familiar about her. His heart begins to beat faster and he feels sweat spring on his upper lip then cool in the stiff breeze. He doesn't know who she is, but the sight of her evokes the memory of distressing emotions, of fear and revulsion, and a sense of malignancy so strong it feels like a weight at his back, pushing him forward, down...

The fire escape outside the dormitory window. Like the skeleton of a giraffe, says Craig. How do you know, demands Arthur, bet you in't never seen one. Because he doesn't like Craig's flights of fancy; they make him feel oddly inadequate...

The woman stops, turns her profile to him as she watches the dog take a piss on the grass verge, and his remembered feelings coalesce around the figure of WPC Mary Canter. It's Mary fucking Canter. The realisation seems to paralyse his brain. For a second it's as though he no longer knows how to use his legs, and even when sensation returns, he doesn't know whether to run, or call her name, or simply walk past her and hope she fails to recognise him. After all, he must have changed even more than she has in the years since they last met. She must have been in her early twenties, not much more than ten years older than he was, though she was in uniform, in charge, and he was just a scared kid.

But what is she doing here? What does her being here mean? As he hesitates, wondering, Bernard comes into view, walking towards him, carrying a couple of shopping bags. Not wanting to be seen, Ian ducks into the churchyard, from where he sees Bernard stop to talk to Mary; they chat and laugh as though they're well acquainted, as though this is not the first time Mary has been to Aylsburgh. He strains to hear what they're saying, but he can't get close enough without drawing attention to himself, and after a few minutes, they go their separate ways, Mary with the dog, Bernard with his shopping.

He roams around the graveyard in a fury of curiosity. Remembering Mary and Bernard chatting, he feels excluded, shut out of some magic circle whose initiates have knowledge he covets, needs. He kicks out randomly at the headstones, dislodging flakes of pus-yellow lichen; it reminds him of his room-mate at his first place, a kid called Sammy who was always picking at his acne. Memories gnaw at him like there's a rat in his brain. His head thuds. Climbing away from the lane, towards the church which stands atop a slope whose steepness surprises him, he spots a bench in the lee of the church wall, facing out to sea. He flings himself down and lets the wind lift his hair, cool his forehead and temples, rake away the dead, rotting leaves of his past.

He should leave this place. He should never have come here. What does it mean, almost bumping into Mary Canter like that? She didn't look like a woman who had just been told of a disappearance, a death... Yet why else would she be here, unless drawn to Aylsburgh for the same reasons as him? If he turns to his left, the barley twist chimneys of Wildwood snag at the tail of his eye, poking up from among the trees in the grounds, and he wonders what is going on under that ornate roof, behind the cameras, the concealed razor wire, the teasing discretion of Bernard who is so full of pride in his acquaintance with Harry Theobald Ian thinks he could be lanced like a boil.

But the pub won't be open yet and besides, he has no wish to provoke Bernard into asking him any more questions, so he'll go to the Co-op and look through the newspapers. He glances at his watch. Nine twenty seven. The school bus couldn't be that late, he tells himself, but his heart is stubborn; it hopes; it won't sink.

'You going to buy any of those?' demands the girl behind the counter, popping her bubblegum. Ian smiles, shrugs, and walks out of the store. He hasn't the money left for buying newspapers with nothing in them. Nothing of interest to him, anyhow. The headlines are all the usual stuff – Afghanistan and the credit crunch, dead soldiers whose faces he recognises, fat bankers whose complacency he both hates and envies. The sort of people Harry Theobald's wife entertains to dinner. He can just see it, the men with their snouts in the trough, the women flashing their diamonds and neighing about holidays on yachts, or how well their toffee-nosed brats are doing at Eton.

As the shop door swings shut behind him, he remembers he meant to buy food for breakfast. His stomach growls at him reproachfully. Glancing around the square, with the war memorial standing on a patch of withered grass at its centre, he sees, between a thatched cottage and a more modern house whose roof gleams with solar panels, a wooden sign with the word CAFE painted on it in Day-Glo orange, and an arrow. To Ian, a cafe means a fry-up and a pint mug of strong tea and his hunger dislodges, for now, the ache of his curiosity.

His pursuit of a fried breakfast leads him along a lane which runs from the square, past a row of derelict-looking terraced cottages, towards the sea. Just beyond the last of the cottages, he finds himself forced on to the verge by a speeding van which then sways to a halt about a hundred yards ahead of him. Before he can step back out on to the road, a second van passes him and stops just behind the first. Which is not, he now realises, the first at all.

Occupied by looking for signs of a cafe, he had failed to notice that the lane ahead was blocked by TV satellite trucks. No longer in the least hungry, he wills himself forward, his mind whirling. He is aware, now, that the lane is bordered to his left by the same razor wire concealed in thick hedging, the same cameras lurking like hedgerow robots among the blackthorn and copper beech. As he draws closer to the knot of satellite trucks, he sees most of them are pulled into the broad mouth of a driveway cut off by ornate security gates and overlooked by a pretty lodge which threatens to drag him back into his dream of the witch and the gingerbread house. He crosses the road and saunters slowly past, hands in pockets, taking in the scene at Wildwood's gates out of the corner of his eye.

Camera operators pace slowly back and forth while reporters brandishing microphones make scurrying sorties on the lodge, whose entrance is blocked by a large, stolid man in uniform, a Rottweiler at his heel on what looks to Ian like a distinctly inadequate leash. He feels sick, exposed. He has to ask what's going on, what's happened, yet he feels that the moment he crosses back to Wildwood's side of the lane, he will be recognised, and accused, and perhaps this time they'll be right, perhaps this time Craig Barnes has turned him into a murderer. Pulling in a deep breath to steady himself, he walks towards Wildwood's gates.

The trill of Alice's mobile distracts her from her plans for the redesign of Isabella Keats' drawing room, though the distraction was there already, running like an underground stream beneath the thin crust of habit, eroding what is left of her daily life. As she picks it up from her desk to answer it, she notices the time is eleven minutes past nine. She also notices the caller has withheld their number, but she answers anyway, her heart torn between hope and fear. 'Alice Theobald.'

'Mrs. Theobald, Ralph Bellamy from *The Sun.* Just wondered if you'd got any comment for us on your husband's disappearance?'

She dashes the phone from her ear as if it's burned her. It takes several attempts, her fingers palsied with shock, to switch the thing off. What..? How..? The police, she decides, some underpaid officer looking to augment his pension with a backhander from a journalist. Whatever assurances Mary gave her, it must have been the police who gave the newspaper the tip-off. Who else could it have been? Isabella? Surely not. Isabella is her neighbour, her friend. She wouldn't even have thought of Isabella if she hadn't been at work on the designs for her drawing room. Would she? She picks up the landline on her desk, intending to call Isabella, then puts it down again. If the press have got her mobile number, what's to say they don't have that one too? And the number for the house. They could be listening in; there had been some furore about phone hacking, she recalled; Harry had become nervous about it and she had teased him, joking that anyone who was listening to their calls was more likely to fall asleep from boredom than hit on a juicy scandal.

Or Bernard? Hadn't he been a journalist himself at one time? And he had been, she thinks now, looking back, unusually interested in her taking Harry's place at the ACDC meeting. Then again, perhaps it was no more than his usual friendliness which, she points out to herself, she has always found oddly intrusive, even though Harry told her she was being paranoid. And she trusts Harry's judgement on these matters; though it is something they have never much discussed, they have always been on one another's wavelength over the need to keep their private life private. Most girls he went out with wanted to flaunt him, he told her, when she plucked up the courage to ask him why he was still unmarried in his mid thirties, and she had smiled, said nothing, stored up his use of the word 'most' in her heart as a kind of memento mori. She had been very afraid of falling in love, a process which seemed to her, as she watched others go through it, a terrible descent into chaos.

She must find Mary. Mary will know what to do. She can call the police again and they will sort it out. Picking up her mobile between thumb and forefinger, as though it's contaminated, she returns to the house, calling Mary's name as she enters the kitchen. No response. She can tell immediately that the house is empty. Mary must have taken Daisy for a walk. She runs through to the staircase hall and out of the French window on to the terrace, hoping to see Mary returning through the garden, but there is no sign of anyone, not even George. Small clouds scud across the empty blue sky, staining the lawns indigo with their passing shadows. Leaves glitter and flowers nod in the breeze, the garden as it should be, but empty, a barrow in one of the paths through the sunken garden, with a rake leaning against it, like an echo, as of someone just gone. She shivers and returns indoors.

As she hovers in the staircase hall, wondering what to do next, the house phone rings, loud in the emptiness. Her first instinct is to ignore it, but its persistence infuriates her; she'll answer it if only to shut it up. Striding across the hall with the dog skittering at her heels she yanks the receiver from its cradle and clamps it to her ear. 'Yes?' she snaps.

'Mrs. Theobald? *Lynn News*. We just wondered if you had any comment...'

'Where did you get this information?' A short silence. 'And don't tell me you have to protect your sources. My husband's solicitors...'

'Do you have any comment, Mrs. Theobald?'

Alice closes her eyes. She holds the receiver away from her, until the voice of the woman on the other end is nothing but a tinny buzz. Once it stops, she lays the handset down beside its cradle. Then replaces it. What if Harry calls? Or the police? Or school? The press might contact the children's school. She groans, listens with detached embarrassment as her groan crescendos to a howl of frustration. How is she is going to defend her family? She must change all the phone numbers, but if she does that, how will Harry contact her if – *when* – he's ready? She wonders if the press have got hold of his number, if maybe that's why his phone now seems to be switched off. Briefly, she is relieved. She will call the solicitors; there must be something they can do, but how can she pay them? Letters have already arrived from the electricity company and the council. There are others, but she's stopped opening them, she leaves them piled up on Harry's desk.

Calmer now, though with a raw throat and a throbbing behind her eyes as though she is coming down with flu, she takes the phone off the hook once more, thinking she'll put it back once she has given herself a little space to think. She goes into Harry's study, her eyes flinching from the unopened bills, and unplugs the phone there also, then upstairs to their bedroom to disconnect the extension beside their bed. As she is rummaging behind the bed for the plug, the phone rings. She picks up the receiver, intending to put it straight back down again and cut the caller off, but something makes her hesitate. Holding it an inch or so from her ear, she listens to the hum of white noise, into which a word drops, like a stone into a pond.

'Mo?'

She slams the receiver down and yanks out the plug with shaking, sweating fingers.

'What's this about, then?' asks Ian, hoping his casual joviality doesn't sound as false to the girl with the clipboard as it does to him. Removing a pen from her mouth, she says,

'There's a load of internet chatter says Harry Theobald's disappeared. We're trying to stand it up. Do you know him?'

'Me? No. No way. Just...being nosy, I guess. I mean, you're not exactly discreet, are you?'

The girl tosses her hair contemptuously and struts away, BlackBerry stuck to her ear. As he walks on in the direction of the sea, Ian wonders how he can gain access to a computer. What he needs is an internet cafe, somewhere busy and anonymous, and for that he needs the city, and money. By the time he's bought breakfast, he will have very little left of the two hundred he lifted from Harry Theobald's wallet. He'll have to ask the girls on the site for an advance; he reckons it won't be hard to charm them into it, especially the tall, skinny one whose cow eyes follow him every time he walks past the office window. Though he'd rather fuck the other one; he likes his women with a bit of meat on them.

His thoughts have wandered to Tara's breasts when he stumbles across the cafe almost by accident. It's a brick built bungalow, just a private house with a conservatory stuck to one side, distinguishable as a cafe only by a board leaning against the gate on which the word is written in the same Day-Glo orange paint as the sign in the village. What would have originally been the front hall now contains a counter, behind which a faded woman in a faded floral overall waits, pencil poised, to take his order. The expression on her face, wary, distasteful, tells him how he looks. He needs a shave, a haircut, a change of clothes.

He asks for a bacon sandwich and a large tea, and a buttered teacake because it might assuage the ache left by remembering Tara's tits, and goes to sit at a table in the conservatory. A couple of walkers, the cafe's only other occupants, glance up as he enters then return to their morning papers, shuffling their chairs together as though seeking mutual protection. They'll have something to read tomorrow, he thinks.

'Bit of a to do up at the Theobalds,' remarks the faded woman when she brings him his tea and sandwich. His table affords him a clear view of the cluster of satellite trucks at Wildwood's gates. 'Still, it's a wonder it doesn't happen more often, him being so well known. I'll bring your teacake a bit later, shall I?' The sort who chatters to cover her nerves.

'Thank you.'

The sandwich is anaemic, the bacon undercooked and the white sliced bread slathered with too much margarine, but the tea is hot and strong and suffuses him with a sense of wellbeing. He will sit here awhile, he decides, and see what happens. The walkers leave in a rustle of maps and waterproofs. The morning sun warms his back, making him drowsy. His eyelids are growing heavy when the faded woman returns with his teacake, setting the plate down sharply so his eyes snap back open and he sits up straighter in his chair. The woman hovers at his table. He casts an eye over the teacake, wondering if she's expecting thanks for it, if there's something special about it that he hasn't noticed, then realises she isn't paying attention to him but is looking through the window in the direction of Wildwood. He follows her gaze.

A small crowd of people has billowed out from among the trucks and is blocking the lane. Mary Canter is walking towards them with the Dalmatian.

'That's the Theobalds' dog,' says the faded woman, 'but don't ask me who that is walking it.'

Don't ask me either. 'Well she doesn't look like a stray from *Celebrity Big Brother.*'

'Get away with you,' the woman says, and smiles, a smile that seems to bring colour even to her washed out overall. 'Shall I bring you a fresh brew?'

'That'd be nice, thank you.'

She returns to her kitchen, and Ian watches as Mary and the dog are engulfed by the mob of reporters. He feels oddly cut off from his own life as he sits behind the conservatory glass watching Mary deal with the consequences of his action. He wonders if, as she casts about for answers to the reporters' questions, the name Arthur Ingliss comes into her mind. Perhaps it's just the steam from his tea condensing on the glass, but as he looks, the figure of Arthur as he was then, skinny, pasty, thick hair stuck up at all angles, fists clenched in pockets, seems to materialise on the edge of the jostle of reporters. Laughing. Dislocated. Sidling, unnoticed, towards the high gates. In his head, a voice. *I can give you money, help you get away.*

Well, why shouldn't he take his cut of Harry Theobald's fortune? God knows, he deserves it. With the beginnings of a plan in his head, he dashes out of the cafe, the faded woman's indignant, 'Hey!' ringing in his ears as he slams the door. He keeps running until he arrives at Wildwood's gates, and lets his momentum carry him, fists and elbows flailing, through the mob of reporters to Mary at its centre.

'You alright, love?' he asks, winding a firm, protective arm around her shoulders. Her hair has come loose from its bun and grey tendrils hang across her eyes. He can feel her body shaking in his grasp, but her muttered, 'Yes, yes, I'm perfectly fine, thank you,' has all the no-nonsense firmness he remembers. The dog seems to have taken its cue from him and is now barking wildly at the reporters, keeping the thicket of microphones at bay.

'As soon as they get the gates open...' she adds, and he notices, behind the yapping, and the disconcerted babble of the reporters, the expensive sigh of the electronic gates as they swing open. His grip on her shoulders tightens. Doubt flickers over her face. She hasn't recognised him; she'd look more than bloody doubtful if she had.

'I wouldn't,' he says, 'not just yet,' and nods in the direction of the gaggle of reporters, now rushing the gate, now milling about in consternation as the burly security guard steps in front of them, the growling Rottweiler barely restrained by its lead. He propels her down the lane towards the cafe, the Dalmatian skittering in their wake.

'Tea, love,' he tells the faded woman, 'big, hot and sweet,' and winks, bringing a faint flush to her cheeks. 'And put the dog somewhere, eh?' It's the Theobalds' dog; she'll be able to dine out for weeks on having had responsibility for it, even for five minutes, though Ian expects his plan to take a little longer than that to put into action.

Too shaken to concentrate on her work, Alice digs out her scrapbook from the bottom of a drawer full of colour charts. Closing the drawer, she sits with her back to it, hunched between the desk and the chair legs, balances the book against her bent knees and carefully opens it.

In total, she reads, *25 victims had their hands removed. Their families were told they could not see the bodies because their deterioration would be too upsetting.*

Judy Wellington, she reads, *whose son, Simon, had his hands removed, said the family was initially given the body of a white man although Simon was of Caribbean origin.*

'I lost someone in the *Marchioness* disaster,' Harry told her. He had taken her to lunch at the River Cafe, not a date exactly, but he had allowed his hand to brush the small of her back as he ushered her through the door to the restaurant, and the sensation remained, like the echo of half-heard music to which the nerves in her skin were still dancing. She sat straight in her chair, as if leaning against its back might crush something fragile and precious. It was the third time he had taken her out to lunch, but the first he had touched her.

The conversation had begun, after a short silence which made Alice nervous, with her telling him how she loved listening to the late night shipping forecast. She had meant to say that the reflection of Canary Wharf in the river, its aircraft warning light winking like a secret signal from the deep, put her in mind of the drowned city of Is, but she was afraid he wouldn't know what she was talking about. Or that he would, and that would be worse.

'Why?' he had asked, staring at her with the expression that still makes her heart flap like a loose sail, that expects something of her, that says, you're there, *there* you are, and here I am, and isn't it both a miracle and a tragedy that each of us is trapped inside a separate skin?

'Because...' She hesitated, searching for the right words, that would be both true and safe to utter, '...you know the bit where they give the twenty four hour report for inshore waters?'

He shook his head. He wore an amused and indulgent expression, not quite a smile.

'Well at the end, the last bit they do is go round the coast, clockwise, Cape Wrath to Rattray Head, Gibraltar Point to North Foreland...such lovely names. And it gives me a sense of being held in place. I don't know. "This sceptr'd isle, set in a silver sea". That sort of thing.'

'*The Ancient Mariner*,' he said.

'*Richard II*,' she countered, surprised; she had assumed a man like Harry would have had an expensive education.

Harry looked mortified; as he fiddled with the napkin in his lap, she could almost imagine he was blushing, though his faintly golden skin did not change colour.

'Sorry.' She reached a hand across the table. 'I was always good at English.'

He looked up. He did smile this time, but the expression was mechanical and his vivid blue eyes were darkened by something she thought then was hurt pride, that drove him to tell her, 'I lost someone in the *Marchioness* disaster.'

'Lost?' she queries. 'You mean died?' When all is chaos, you must use words precisely, with care. When there is no meaning, words are what you have. He nodded, and behind his exactly broad enough shoulders in the artfully crumpled Margaret Howell shirt, she saw them, the handless ghosts, gathered as if they had just risen up from the river's deep, waving their stumps, all neatly sewn like small bolsters.

Now, as she strokes the brittle newsprint with her fingertips, she asks herself if the darkness in Harry's eyes could have been something else.

Ian watches Mary as she tries to push the stray hairs back into her bun, remembers she used to wear her hair back combed, with kiss flicks, like Dusty Springfield.

'You're very kind...,' she begins, but he cuts her off.

'You don't remember me, do you?'

She hesitates, hands poised in the air. Her forehead puckers into a frown. Beneath a layer of face powder her skin is grey and tired, and weathered with fine veins. She's an old woman now. She'd been in her first job when they met, a WPC fresh out of training; she used to look at him sometimes and complain she hadn't joined the force to be a babysitter, though her expression would soften when she looked at Craig.

'Do you?' he repeats, as the faded woman places a cup and saucer before Mary and tells her she's given the dog a bowl of water in the back garden. Ian glares at her, just so she knows her obsequious hovering isn't appreciated. She disappears, and Ian and Mary have the conservatory to themselves.

'I...'

Ian runs a hand through his hair in exasperation. At her for not knowing him. At himself for being upset about it. As he does so, he sees her frown smooth and a light of dubious recognition comes into her eyes.

'Arthur..?' she says, her voice querulous, wondering, but not in a good way.

'Not pleased to see me then? Not just a little bit grateful I got you away from that lot?'

'Yes...yes, of course I am...pleased, I mean, grateful...'

'It's alright, Mary.' He pats her hand; she flinches. 'No need to put it on with me. To be honest, I wasn't that fucking chuffed to see you either, but then I thought....'

'What are you doing here, Arthur?'

'Ian. My name's Ian now, right?'

'Ian,' she repeats, as though learning a foreign language.

'Like I was saying, then I thought, maybe it's a stroke of luck after all. I'm not asking why you're out walking "Harry Theobald's" dog like you owned the thing, you get me? But I have got something I'd like to tell his wife.' *I love my wife very much, Arthur, and she loves me, but she's a tender-hearted woman, a good mum...You know what I'm saying?*

'What have you done, Arthur? Where's Harry?'

'*Ian.*' A savage whisper, forced between bared teeth. She looks chastened, frightened even. Good. He sits back in his chair, stirs his tea, which is stone cold now and surfaced with a greasy scum. He smiles. 'Like I said, I'm not asking you any questions, so you just shut up and listen to me. Right?'

She nods.

'You tell Mrs. Theobald I might know where she could start looking for her husband. For the right price.'

'Alright...Ian, that's enough. I'm calling the police.'

'No you're not. For one thing, I bet you don't take a phone out dog walking with you, do you?' She blushes. There's an uncertain flicker in her eyes, beneath her pleated lids. 'And for another, you phone the police and they'll be as interested in you being here as me. The two of us turning up here, in a place this size. That's got to be more than a coincidence, wouldn't you say?'

'The locals already know I'm here.' Her doubt disappears. Her face seems to harden, as though the powder's setting, a scrim of pale pink concrete. 'That surprised you, didn't it?'

'And that lot?' He nods in the direction of the gaggle of press blocking the lane. 'Do they know who you are? Who Harry Theobald is?'

'You're the last person who's likely to tell them, though, let's face it.'

'I remember what you said to me, Mary. You said what a brave boy Craig was, not giving me away, and how he'd suffer for his loyalty. You said he'd made it easy for me.' His mouth feels suddenly dry; he's about to say something no-one but Craig has ever known, till now; he takes a sip of the cold, scummy tea which films the inside of his mouth like a fine layer of wax. 'But what if I told you it was the other way round? That the song I sung then was a lie, a lie I've gone on singing for forty years.' He leans towards her, elbows on the table. To her credit she holds her ground, and he's so close to her now he can smell her sour old woman smell, coal tar soap and over-washed underwear. Beneath her face powder, the broken veins in her cheeks are purple. 'That lie,' he says, his voice almost a whisper, 'that's why Craig came looking for me.'

'He..?'

'Shut up and let me finish, right? He came to tell me he thought he'd been rumbled, by the bloke that runs the pub. I saw you talking to him earlier. Very chummy, you looked. I might think you were in it too if I didn't know what an upright citizen you are. Sworn copper an' all that. He said if the shit hit the fan, it'd stick to me too, and he was worried I might decide to tell the truth. Said he was willing to pay handsomely to stop me, to save his marriage, he said.'

'I don't know what you're talking about. My guess is you've seen a photo of Harry somewhere, recognised him and come here to blackmail him. Only, as you see, he's not here. So I suggest you move on, or I will call the locals and tell them you're in breach of your licence. You'll find yourself back inside before your feet can touch the floor.'

'I'll tell you what I'm talking about,' he says, but hesitates. These are words he has never spoken and he isn't certain of the feel of them in his mouth. 'I'll tell you what I'm talking about,' he repeats, and this time the words tumble out of him, fully formed, as if they've been there forever, lined up in his throat, waiting. 'I never killed that kid, Mary. It was Craig all along.' She looks as though she wants to interrupt him but he holds up a hand to prevent her; if he loses his momentum he may never get it back. '*...he was just about to weep tears of tin, but that wouldn't be proper. He looked at her and she looked at him, but neither said a word.' – Craig closes the book and looks up. – There, see, he's fast asleep now.* 'I don't know what happened. I went outside,' *the smell of wet wood and diesel; dusk falling over everything like a thin blanket,* 'and when I came back in, the kid's head was lolling sideways and his eyes...his eyes were like doll's eyes. Staring.' The memory crawls over his skin, as vivid as if it was yesterday, yet it's something he's never even dreamed of in all the years since. He doesn't know why. He dreams of Orla often.

'Are you telling the truth?' asks Mary, peering up at him from beneath concentrated brows. 'You are, aren't you? Why? I mean, why now? Why not then?'

'Because no-one would have believed me.' It had been there, in the eyes of the jurors; the three women even smiled at Craig once or twice, but never at him. They hated him, all of them. He scared them. He never stood a chance. That was why he'd changed his plea, and relied on Craig to remember the promise he'd made when they cut their thumbs and mingled their blood, just after he'd pushed the pram down the embankment. It'll look like an accident, he'd said. Keep your mouth shut and let me do the talking, he'd said. And Craig had. 'I thought, if I confessed, I'd get a shorter sentence and Craig'd get off.'

'You always were a sly, clever thing, weren't you? You didn't give a damn what happened to Craig as long as you saved your own skin, did you? You had that boy in your pocket from the outset.' She shakes her head, her lips compressed in a disapproving line. 'I remember how he never took his eyes off you in the dock. As if you were the only other person in the universe as far as he was concerned. You saw which way it was going and decided to chuck him overboard. Do you know what happened to him?'

'Much the same as happened to me, I guess.' Ian gives a short, bitter laugh. 'He obviously learnt gardening. I learnt gardening too.'

Mary fixes him with a cold glare. 'He was sent to St. Helier Place.'

'You say that as if I ought to know what it means.'

'I thought you might have heard of it. It was notorious. When it was closed down the papers called it a juvenile Broadmoor. I'd say Broadmoor was pretty enlightened by comparison.'

'Well it doesn't seem to have done him any harm.' He thinks of the man in the car park at the Head of Etive, solid, confident, still so handsome you couldn't quite believe he was real. A blest man. And blessings should be shared. 'How do you know all this anyway?' he demands of Mary. 'What business is it of yours? How come you're out walking the dog like you're an old family friend?'

To his astonishment, Mary blushes. He's never thought of old women blushing before, somehow imagined they'd grow out if it, if he thought of it at all. His mind is generally more occupied with young women. The blush makes her look younger, more like she used to when he first knew her. He can hear her suddenly, as clearly as if she was saying the words now, except that she had a Yorkshire accent then, which she seems to have mislaid somewhere in the intervening years. *You should be more like that Craig,* she's saying, *he could make a success of himself if he'd been brought up right, kept away from tykes like you.* He starts to laugh, because what he's thinking is ridiculous, and it hurts, and he doesn't want her to know that. 'You're not..? You're not pretending to be his mother, are you?'

Her blush deepens. 'Aunt,' she confesses, the blood accumulating in furious blotches on her cheeks and neck.

'Well it's certainly a day for revelations.' Ian grins, swings back on the hind legs of his chair with his hands clasped behind his head, then forward, the chair's front legs hitting the tiled floor with a crack like gunshot. Mary flinches. 'But we don't want any more, do we? We don't want that lot,' he jerks his head in the direction of Wildwood, 'finding out you're not Harry's auntie, and he's not Harry, and I don't know what else. Do we? And you can see how easily it might happen. Plod knows you're here. Plod chats to hack over a pint. Maybe Bernard pulls the pint, and Bernard used to be a sniffer dog for the red tops, Harry reckons.' He gives a theatrical sigh. 'What a bloody mess, eh? What a tangled web.'

'What do you suggest?'

'You persuade Mrs. T to do what her husband promised me, then I might be prepared to tell you what I know.'

'What did he promise you?'

'Two hundred and fifty k and a passport.'

Mary looks aghast; for a few seconds her features are all over the place, mouth agape, eyes blinking as if the circuitry behind them has sprung a fault. But he admires the speed with which she collects herself. 'I don't believe you,' she says, 'you're trying it on.'

He shrugs, spreads his hands. 'Take it or leave it.'

'If you know where he is, why can't you just ask him? Why this pantomime?'

'You'll have to ask him that when you find him. If you find him.'

'Bullshit,' she responds, improbably.

He withdraws Theobald's signet ring from the ticket pocket in his jeans where it has been since he took it, and holds it out on the flat of his palm. Mary snatches at it. He closes his fist over it, squeezing till his knuckles whiten. 'Oh no you don't. You go and tell Mrs. T what I asked you to tell her. You make sure she knows I'm a good authority. You tell her, if she wants to find her old man, she can meet me...' he glances around the empty cafe, '...here's as good as anywhere, day after tomorrow, with a quarter of a mill in cash. Used notes, all that shit. Yeah?'

'How did you get that?'

'Let's say he gave it to me. Like one of them old fashioned kings. So everyone'd know I was his authorised mes-
senger. Let's say I'm Mrs. T's knight in shining fucking
armour.' He waits, watches Mary weighing his words. Time
feels like a falling drop of water, about to burst.

'Alright,' she says finally, 'I'll tell Alice what you've said.
How can I contact you? Do you have a phone number?'

'Alice eh? Very cosy. You can leave word at the caravan
site office.'

'Very well.' She stands, smoothes her hair, her sensible
skirt. 'But I'm not making any promises.'

He shrugs. 'Craig seemed to think he was happily married. If he's right, she'll pay up, won't she? And you'd better
persuade her, or she might be finding out you're no more
Harry's auntie than I am,'

'You wouldn't dare.'

'Try me.' He holds her with his gaze. Behind his eyes
the cinema is exploding, and the eyes of God weep cellu-
loid from a molten billboard. Behind his eyes is the pink
mist that human beings are turned into by the alchemy of
Semtex.

Mary flees. As he watches her pass through the conservatory he tosses the ring up in the air and catches it several
times. Not bad, he tells himself, not half bad. With any luck,
by this time next week he'll be somewhere new, somewhere
with sunshine and siestas, and willing girls to share them.
Leaving the table to go and pay his bill, he finds he's slipped
the ring on to his own finger almost without being aware of
it. He fiddles it around with his thumb as he waits for his
change from Harry Theobald's last twenty, settling it, making it comfortable. By the time he's reached the end of the
lane, where the tarmac breaks off like a torn liquorice stick,
he hardly knows it's there. He clambers down the cliff, over

a scree of loose bricks and chunks of mortar ripped away from the side of a house by the wind and the sea. Glancing up, he sees a wall covered with faded wallpaper, bent joists and ragged floorboards, a woodburner capsized in a crazily-angled hearth. It reminds him of Belfast.

Walking along the beach towards the caravan site, he's aware of Wildwood, the twisted chimneys behind a green-gold wall of copper beech atop the cliff edge. The house feels like a weight on his left shoulder; the roots of the hedge, some already bare where the cliff is crumbling around them, pluck at the edges of his mind. He flexes his back, as though shrugging it off, and scrambles over the tumbled sea wall to walk between it and the sea. He can do this, he tells himself, he's nearly done it. A couple more days, that's all...

Hearing footsteps in the drive, Alice pushes the scrapbook back into the drawer beneath the paint chart and hurries outside. Mary is crossing the carriage yard to the back door, Daisy at her heel.

'Mary! God, where have you been? You wouldn't believe...' Her voice tails off as she approaches Mary and takes in her dishevelled state. Her usually severe chignon has largely unravelled, her blouse has been pulled askew at the neck as though someone has tried to grasp her by the collar, and there is a gash in her shin. Daisy's hackles are raised and she is skittish with nerves. Full of guilty solicitude, Alice wraps an arm around Mary's shoulders and draws her into the house.

'Did you fall?' she asks, once she has sat Mary down in the kitchen and is dabbing at her cut shin with cotton wool and Savlon. 'Daisy's dreadful on her lead. She can tug so hard sometimes. I shouldn't have...'

'I didn't fall, Alice. I'm not that old and feeble yet. Haven't you noticed what's going on at the gate?'

'No, I...' She feels suddenly foolish and inadequate, emerging from the cocoon of her memories like some ungainly and impractical insect. Is she, she wonders, any longer capable of existence outside Wildwood?

'Well there's an ugly crowd of television people outside, saying they've heard that Harry Theobald has disappeared. They asked me what I knew...rather forcibly, as you see. But happily I was able, equally forcibly, to tell them nothing. Your security men were most helpful.'

'You should set the police on them.' Alice dabs angrily at Mary's shin. 'This is quite deep. It probably ought to have stitches.'

'It would be a lot better if you stopped prodding it, dear.'

'Sorry, sorry. I'll just...' She peels the back of a sticking plaster and smoothes it over the cut, tearing away the laddered edges of Mary's tights. 'I've had calls,' she says, sitting back on her heels to assess her handiwork, 'from *The Sun* and the *Lynn News*. They said they'd seen something on the internet. I unplugged the phones.

'The internet. So that's it.'

'What?'

'How they found out.'

'Yes, but who put it on the internet?'

'I'm really feeling a bit wrung out now, Alice. I think I'll go and lie down for a while if you don't mind.'

Both women rise. 'Yes, yes of course.'

Alice accompanies Mary to the staircase hall, her arm curved behind Mary's shoulders though not touching her. As they reach the hall, Mary shakes her off, making her feel that it is somehow she who has been cared for, protected, humoured. She watches Mary cross the hall and stump up the stairs. Though her head is bowed, her tread is firm. Alice feels helpless, irrelevant.

By the time Mary comes back down, an hour or so later, Alice has a rosemary loaf cake in the oven and is cooking rice to make a salad for the evening meal. With all the phones disconnected, the house feels serene, as though it has breathed a sigh of relief and settled around her, calming her in its embrace. She stirs and ladles, ladles and stirs as she adds stock to the risotto pan, listening to the timeless sounds of the house, its creaks and sighs, the rustle of the daphne growing under the kitchen window as the breeze blows through it. Her limbs feel indolent and heavy, as if she has come to rest after great physical exertion, her mind empty of everything but the slow rhythms of cooking.

Yet Mary's step in the passage leading to the kitchen runs through her muscles like an electric shock, hunching her shoulders, tensing her jaw. She turns away from the Aga, the smile on her face stretched, as though her mouth has somehow shrunk since the last time it smiled.

'Are you feeling better? Let me make you a coffee. Or maybe we could have an early lunch.'

'Sit down, Alice,' says Mary, seating herself at the table. 'There's something I need to tell you.' Her words fall on Alice's skin like cold stones. She sits, as if hypnotised, as if suddenly thrust into a looking-glass world in which the avoidable has become inevitable.

Mary clears her throat. 'I said there were things you didn't know about Harry, things I couldn't tell you. I was wrong. In the circumstances...' She is cut short by the pulsing shriek of the smoke alarm.

'Oh fuck!' Alice leaps up from her chair, snatches the smoking risotto pan off the hob and hurls it at the twin butler sinks; it lands with a tinkle of smashing crockery and a deeper, more ominous crack. 'I'd completely forgotten the bloody thing.' She turns on the cold tap, drags a chair to stand beneath the alarm, then climbs on to it to extract the battery. The sound of it is like a knife being stabbed repeatedly into her brain.

'Sink's cracked,' says Mary, once the alarm has been silenced. There is something almost smug about her tone that makes Alice want to hit her. Of course Mary would never burn rice or crack sinks; of course Mary would never lose her husband because she's never been stupid enough to acquire one to lose.

'Never mind,' says Alice, but she does mind. She has inflicted violence on her house, her beloved Wildwood. She wishes she could stick a plaster on it, as she did on Mary's leg. Cracks terrify her, hoarsely whispering of precariousness and impermanence. She wants to cry, she wants Harry. As she stares at the jagged fault in the enamel she remembers the small scar on the tip of his left thumb, the result, he told her, of an accident with a penknife when he was a boy. When he makes love to her, he strokes her with that thumb, knowing the fine ridge of scar tissue brings her a sharper pleasure. The memory of it now shakes her with a perverse orgasm of grief.

'What we were talking about,' begins Mary, turning off the tap and sitting back down at the table. Alice grips the back of the chair she had been standing on, more for support than to return it to its place. The bones in her legs feel like plasticine.

'D'you mind if we don't? I mean, I can't... Mary, I think you should go home.'

'But..'

'Please, Mary. It was good of you to come...'

'I came because you asked me.'

That isn't how Alice remembers it but she's too tired now to argue. 'But I can cope. The children and I, we'll be alright...better on our own. It just makes things simpler.'

'I suppose it does. Yes, I suppose it does.' Mary repeats the phrase as though it is something recently learned and imperfectly understood, as though she is pushing it out into the light so she can examine it more closely. 'Very well, dear, if that's what you want. Shall I get a taxi? To save you running the gauntlet of that lot at the gate?'

'I shall have to go out to collect the children. I don't want them exposed to those hyenas. I'll take you into Norwich first.'

'I'll go and pack, then.'

Mary goes to her room. Alice returns to her studio in search of her mobile phone, intending to turn it on for just long enough to call the school and let them know she will be collecting the children in person and not to let them catch the bus. The roar of the lawnmower greets her as she steps out of the back door, but in the intermittent silences, when George turns it off to empty the grass box, she can hear the voices at the gate, the general hubbub punctuated by occasional shouts from Stan or Ollie. At least, she thinks they're the team currently on duty; she never remembers; security is Harry's responsibility.

DAY SEVEN

'Mum? Have we got any hair straighteners?' Polly, wearing her dressing gown and flipflops, her freshly varnished toenails separated by wedges of tissue, throws open Alice's studio door, then hovers on the threshold in a slice of golden evening sunlight hazed with dust motes. Alice sits back on her heels and wipes her hands down the thighs of her overalls.

'Not unless Jesse's got some hidden away somewhere.' Jesse has his father's tight, dark curls, Alice and Polly the same dead straight, sandy blond hair.

'Mum.' Polly stamps one foot then gasps, peering closely at her toes as dust rises from the floor and swirls in the thermals. 'It's not funny. Maddie's forgotten hers and she's going totally postal.'

'Maddie's got lovely hair. What does she want to straighten it for?'

'Yeah, I know, I told her but...' Polly shrugs. 'Can you come and help?' She hugs her dressing gown around herself and fixes wide eyes on her mother, a child still, manipulative in her fragility.

'OK, give me a minute.'

'Thanks, Mum.' Polly races away, banging the studio door behind her. Alice lays aside her tools, strips off her overalls and goes to wash her hands. Outside in the carriage yard the sun is still bright enough to make her blink as her eyes adjust and her heart resumes the rhythm of the world beyond the studio. It will be a clear night; she must tell the girls to take sweaters, in case it grows cold down by the sea.

Heading for whatever drama is about to confront her in Polly's room, where she and Maddie Manning are dressing for the beach party, she passes the phone on the kitchen dresser, the phone behind the closed door of Harry's study. Her shoulders tense, even though she knows they are all disconnected. The only communications have been a flurry of urgent texts between Maddie and Polly culminating in Maddie's arrival earlier that afternoon with a suitcase big enough to hold everything she might need for a fortnight's holiday. The plan is for the girls to get ready at Wildwood then return to the Mannings' overnight. One other call has come, to Alice's mobile from Isabella Keats, inviting her to join her and Basil for supper at The Dog's Head. As Jesse has gone into Norwich to the cinema and will be delivered home later by a friend's father, Alice can think of no reason to refuse, but she has not yet committed herself because she knows all Isabella will want to talk about will be the press at the gates and what implications their arrival has for the whereabouts of Harry. On the other hand, Basil's wry imperturbability might be just what she needs, along with a couple of large gins and a plate of Bernard's surprisingly good Thai curry. She wonders, sometimes, if he has a Thai bride hidden away in his landlord's flat. She often finds herself thinking about people who have been uprooted and transplanted into new lives, wondering if they carry the secret marks of their transformation the way adapted furniture does, or grafted plants. The moment of hearing Nathan's voice on the phone returns to her, the single word question – 'Mo?' – like a full stop, or perhaps the closing of a bracket that contains her life with Harry.

Outside Polly's door she pauses long enough to compose her expression into that of smiling, competent mother then knocks. The voices in the room, Maddie's a little hysterical, Polly's placatory with a hint of exasperation probably only Alice notices, cease abruptly.

'*Entrez*,' says Polly.

'Mercy bucket,' replies Alice, smiling. 'Now then, what's the problem?'

'It's a disaster,' says Maddie, turning away from the dressing table mirror. Her round face is framed by a cloud of fine auburn curls. 'I've brushed it and brushed it and now it's gone all static.'

'It looks great,' says Polly, with the air of having said this several times already.

Alice is back in her studio, she is considering Maddie as if she were an intransigent room.

'Mum,' prompts Polly, 'don't stare. You're making Maddie blush.'

'Sorry. Sorry, Maddie, I was just thinking...hold on a minute. Back in a tick.'

She crosses the galleried landing to her own room and rummages in a drawer full of scarves. Maddie is wearing Polly's orange satin skirt and a white top. Alice selects three scarves in colours which will complement the orange and is about to return with them to Polly's room when her phone springs to life with a voicemail alert. She hesitates, watching the phone on her bedside table as the screen light fades. It will be Isabella, she decides, badgering her about the invitation to the pub. Still uncertain whether or not to accept, she leaves it and carries the scarves back to Polly's room.

Maddie sits quietly, though she wears a bit of a scowl, as Alice tries various ways of dressing her hair with the scarves. Polly, toenails now dry, delves into the bottom of her wardrobe and throws out several pairs of shoes which she begins to try on.

'Oh I like that one,' says Maddie, her scowl relaxing into a smile as Alice ties a peacock green scarf decorated with sequins into a bandeau around Maddie's forehead. Polly, standing on one leg, glances up and overbalances, toppling into her desk, which jars her open laptop into life.

Her Facebook profile shines out into the room, catching the corner of Alice's eye as she concentrates on making minute adjustments to the scarf around Maddie's head.

Except that it's not Polly's profile.

Please Find Polly's Dad

reads Alice at the head of the page, and next to it is a photo, a photo Alice has forgotten about, or perhaps never knew existed, of Polly and Harry at Harry's fiftieth birthday party. Polly in her first evening dress, shadows pooled in the hollows behind her collarbones, wisps of hair escaped from the knot at her neck floating around her face, lit up by the camera's flash like a halo. Harry with his bow tie undone and his hair ruffled, grinning into the camera, his arm around his daughter's waist. Perfect dad. Romantic hero. Who had taken the picture, she wonders? Not her; she and Harry never take one another's photo.

Whirling away from Maddie at the dressing table, she pushes Polly out of the way and stares, horrified, at the computer screen.

my dad went missing in glencoe thats scotland on june 14. noones doing anything about it. my mum doesn't care. my brother just thinks its cool and thinks hes living in a movie. its like my dad matters less than our house or something but like we wouldn't have all that stuff our lives and everything without him. so if anyone out theres seen him or even thinks they have tell me coz i want him back.

'You set this up?' Alice demands. Her voice shakes with rage.

'Yeah, well, nobody else was doing anything.'

'You realise what you've done?' Alice scrolls down the page. There was a long list of comments, mostly platitudes, some religious, some weird:

My dachshund is psychic. I'll show him the photos and get right back to you. Meryl.

Meryl was in Texas. Iolanthe, on the other hand, was in Glastonbury and urged Polly to buy a crystal from her website (all major credit cards accepted). When suspended from a cotton thread (no manmade fibres) the crystal would point towards her 'absent significant other' and sing a siren song to lure him home.

Meryl likes this was followed by a little thumbs-up sign.

How dare they, these wackos and charlatans? How dare they prey on a desperate and lonely young girl this way? She doesn't know who she's angrier with, them, or Polly for being so stupid. She turns to glare at Polly, who is now sitting on the floor, fastening a pair of glittery jellies with a valiant air of unconcern. Maddie remains at the dressing table, shoulders hunched, eyes fixed on her reflection, cheeks blotched with embarrassment.

'That's why we've got those wretched reporters hanging about,' yells Alice. 'You stupid, STUPID girl!'

'Well what's *wrong* with people knowing?' Polly shouts back. 'Maybe if Dad saw something in the papers he'd realise what he'd done and come home.' Polly is fighting back tears; she stares at Alice without blinking, the tears threatening to brim over and dissolve her mascara. Alice tries to put her arms around her.

'It's not that simple,' she says.

Polly struggles free, fists pushing against her mother's chest, all sharp angles, unyielding, untrusting. 'WHY isn't it that simple? I'm not a kid, you know, you can tell me what's going on. It's a whole week now and you haven't even called the cops. Don't you want Dad back? Is that it?'

Alice casts a glance at Maddie, whose reflection in the dressing table mirror looks mortified. 'We'll talk about this later, Polly. It's not very nice for Maddie to have us arguing in front of her.'

'Maddie's cool. Aren't you, Mads? She's always fighting with her mum when I'm there.'

Maddie gives a meek nod but says nothing.

'We're not fighting,' says Alice.

'You think? What's this, then? Like, some kind of love-in?'

'I haven't spoken to the police, but Mary has.'

'Aunt Mary? Why? Why not you?'

It's a good question. 'She has. That's all you need to know for now. Everything's under control. Now, go to your party and enjoy yourself...yourselves,' she adds, smiling at Maddie's reflection. 'You really do look lovely in that scarf, you know.'

'Thanks.' Maddie's voice is small, as though she wishes she could make herself disappear.

To Polly, Alice says nothing, because Polly, in a float-ing, floral dress over skinny jeans, is perfect. In response to

Alice's urging to take something warm, she adds a denim jacket and one of the scarves discarded by Maddie.

'Stay together,' she admonishes as she follows the girls downstairs, 'and no drinking,' she calls after them as they set off along the drive. She has arranged for one the Jedwards to meet them at the gate and escort them to the party, which goes some way towards palliating her nagging unease.

'D'you think we'll be photographed?' she hears Maddie ask, wary, yet hopeful, as they walk away from her, shoulders touching. She doesn't hear Polly's reply, just a burst of laughter. They are careless, she thinks, careless children who set up Facebook pages and have no fear of being photographed.

Going back inside, she is assailed by the awful silence of the house, and decides she cannot bear to spend the evening there alone. She runs upstairs, drumming her feet loudly on the wooden treads, to collect her phone and ring Isabella back.

But when she looks at the voicemail alert, she sees the call has come from Harry's number.

She sits down on the bed as if pushed, feeling the chill of its emptiness at her back. With the phone in her lap she fumbles the keys, pulling up first of all her text messages, from the children about things they'd forgotten to take to school, from a supplier to tell her a paint she had ordered to be specially mixed is ready. She catches herself scrolling through them, as if their banality will somehow communicate itself to whatever message Harry has left on her voicemail. The final text from him. *Love you. Miss you. Sweet dreams. Big hugs. Hxxxxx*

As she dials her voicemail, she holds the phone an inch or so from her ear, as if she expects it to burn her. Following the recorded instructions, at first she thinks she has hit the wrong key again and deleted the message. But then the electronic voice tells her it is still there, and that it was sent at five seventeen pm. It begins with a rustling, a sound she recognises from the many times Jesse has left his phone unlocked in his pocket and it has inadvertently dialled home. The threat of tears makes her nose prickle. He had never meant to call her; the phone is stolen; it's all a horrible, pointless mistake. Then, as she listens, a whispered voice emerges from the background.

'Alish...,' it says, and again, 'Alish...' He's drunk. Harry never gets drunk. Merry, perhaps, but never so drunk he slurs his words. She's angry now, then panicked as it occurs to her he might be hurt. She listens on, straining her ears for clues. More rustling, or perhaps hoarse breathing, then, '...tell you...Jimmy.' Jimmy? Alice searches her memory for anyone they know called Jimmy. She can come up with no-one other than James Guy, a ceramics specialist at the V and A whom Harry once called in to authenticate a piece of De Morgan lustreware he had bought in a private house sale. And Jesse, of course, but Harry never calls Jesse by his given name. How odd, she thinks, to know so few people with such a common name. The phone is pressed to her ear now, to pick up the slightest whisper, anything to tell her what he is talking about, where he is. How he is. But he says no more, and, after a few seconds, the recording ends. Alice dials his number immediately, but it goes straight to voicemail. She listens to his message, to the joke about curiosity and the cat which seems to have lost its endearing corniness and taken on a ghostly quality, as though his disembodied slurring of her name now shadows it. As soon as the line clears, she calls Isabella.

'Can I come round to you before the pub?' she asks.

'We were just about to leave. Basil booked for seven thirty, but I suppose...'

'Please. It's important.'

'What is it, Alice? What's happened?'

'I can't say. I think...there are people listening in.'

'Oh God, I've seen the vans outside the gate. I suppose it's Polly's Facebook wall. I'd seen it of course but...'

Isabella's improbable enthusiasm for social media normally amuses Alice. Now the thought that she has seen what Polly had done and not bothered to mention it makes her want to seize Isabella by her scrawny shoulders and bang her head repeatedly against a real wall.

'It's being dealt with,' she cuts in, feeling sick and cold at the thought of the thousands, maybe hundreds of thousands, of people who must have seen Polly's appeal.

'Just as well,' says Isabella, 'it's attracted a few trolls.'

'What?' In Alice's mind is an image of the shoebox full of plastic trolls she had collected as a child, both freakish and endearing with their stunted, sexless bodies, their bushes of bright hair and puggish faces. She had made them beds of paper tissues and cried whenever she lost one in cutthroat playground trading.

'You really must get with it, darling. Trolls. People who post off-topic messages.'

'Isabella, please, can I come over? It's urgent.'

'God, sorry, I do ramble on, don't I? It's just that...'

'*Please.*'

'Of course. I'll get Basil to phone Bernard and postpone for half an hour. See you in...what?'

'Five minutes.' She would walk, normally, but tonight she will take the car. Without pausing to so much as comb her hair or scrub the dirt of the studio from under her nails, she grabs her bag and leaves the house.

It's a beautiful evening beyond the smeary bay window of the caravan saloon, the sky luminous, with a bright coin of a moon set among the stars. Ian tells himself he should appreciate it, but he can't. His seeing is as clouded as the window, with the tyranny of waiting, with trying to seem unconcerned when he goes up to the site office and all they have for him is chores, never a message from Mary. He's started biting his nails again; he hasn't done that since he was seventeen, and someone else; Ian Slight doesn't bite his nails, only Arthur does...*did* that. He looks at his watch; five minutes since he last looked at it; he'll go up to the pub, have a meal, make a casual enquiry of Bernard. If he hasn't heard from her by tomorrow lunchtime, he'll cut his losses and leave. Maybe Alice Theobald doesn't want her husband back.

When he steps outside, the sough of the sea is overlaid by a hubbub of voices and a dubstep beat. It sounds as though there's some kind of party taking place on the beach. Maybe he'll take a look. Sure enough, as he approaches the cliff top path, the conversation grows louder and the music more distinct, and he sees the bloom of a bonfire, its light setting the red cliff wall aglow and staining the surf at the tide's edge a frothy pink. Like the blood of a man shot in his lungs.

He walks past the scaffolding tower that supports a flight of aluminium steps leading from the caravan site to the beach, thinking he will find another way down the cliff, away from the partygoers whose shadows flit like giant moths around the fire. He could score down there, he tells himself, but he isn't in the mood. As he passes the wartime gun emplacements that look like giant concrete bus shelters, a single word graffitied in thick, round letters five foot high glares at him in the moonlight. TWAT, it says. You're right, he thinks, breathing in a whiff of stale urine, you're so fuck-ing right. Mary isn't coming. There will be no bag of used notes, no tropical paradise full of bare breasted girls with flowers behind their ears, not even a B and B in an English seaside town with Sandra turning out fried breakfasts and pie and peas. What made him think his luck might change, now, after all these years? And *what* made him believe any good could come of his reunion with Craig Barnes? Furious with himself, he kicks out at the base of one of the concrete walls.

And hears screaming.

For one mad second he stares at his stubbed toe, won-dering if that is where the screams are coming from, then he thinks it's just the partygoers, just cheap drink, a few tabs and high spirits. But then it comes again, closer this time, the terror unmistakable. He could just ignore it, that would be for the best; things always go wrong when he gets involved. But he's already at the cliff edge, looking for a way down.

Spotting a break in the fence, he steps through it, slides and scrambles down loose scree to the beach. At the base of the cliff, he pauses, listens, trying to determine which direction the screams are coming from. There are words now. A high, thin, 'Noooo!' like the cry of a nocturnal gull. A man's voice, deeper, indistinct, but the tone of angry frustration unmistakable. Ian looks both ways along the beach but sees nothing.

In front of him, a barrier of broken storm defences, tumbled concrete blocks with rusting reinforcement bars poking out of them like dead plants, lies between him and the sea. He stumbles over the concrete slabs, slippery with weed, then stops, straining to hear something other than the sounds of the party and the rush of his own blood in his ears. He curses the years of working in bars, the alcohol, the cigarettes, the stupid hours and lack of exercise. When he was in the army...but he isn't going there now.

The man's voice comes again, slurred and domineering. 'Stuck up little bitch,' he says, 'Cop a feel of that. That'll make a tame little mare of you.'

'Screw you,' yells the girl. She sounds young. She's putting up a struggle, though. Scuffling now, skin scraping against concrete, glass breaking, a sudden 'ooff!' from the man. One where it hurts, thinks Ian, now's his chance, move in fast before the bastard has time to recover. He bursts over the angled ridge of one of the broken blocks and hangs there, his arm hooked around a reinforcement wire, his feet slipping on seaweed.

They're below him, in the sand, the girl's bare legs kicking and twisting, the man's jeans and underwear pulled down to reveal pale buttocks and thighs scattered with dark hairs. The moon is merciless. Ian lets go the wire and leaps clear of the slippery concrete, on to the sand, which swallows the sound of his feet. He lunges for the man, grabs him by the collar and hauls him off the girl, who rolls away, howling, into the shadow of the broken storm wall.

The man tries to twist out of Ian's grasp but he hangs on, ignoring the sudden stab of an elbow in his ribs. He hooks his free arm around the man's neck and yanks backwards, not hard enough to break the little shit's neck but hard enough to make it clear he could, if he wanted to. But the little shit has hidden talents, it seems. The next thing Ian knows, he's cartwheeling through the air like a kicked dog and then he's on his back in the wet sand, winded, and the little shit is lunging for him, his contorted face blue in the moonlight, his naked dick shrivelled, the glint of a broken bottle in his hand. But he's forgotten the jeans and boxers tangled around his knees. He trips, stumbles. Ian rolls out of his reach. The little shit falls, thuds down beside him. There's a sickening crack, a small sound but the sort you'd hear above any level of background noise, and the little shit isn't moving.

Ian gets to his feet, slower than he'd like, his spine, ribs, knees all reminding him this is his second fight inside a week. Somewhere, he can hear the girl whimpering. He prods her attacker with the toe of his boot; he rolls over far enough for Ian to see his half closed eyes, slack mouth and a smear of blood, dark on his forehead. He isn't waking up any time soon. Ian lets him fall back and goes in search of the girl, feeling every step judder through his bones. He finds her crouched among the concrete blocks, just where the light of the bonfire begins to lick their outlines, but she is in darkness, a huddle of torn clothing and clenched limbs, her head bowed, face obscured by fair hair. He squats at a little distance from her, to make it clear he presents no threat. His knees crack. Fishing his cigarettes out of his pocket, he holds the pack out to her. She shakes her head and seems to shrink back against the concrete.

'It's alright, love,' he says. 'I won't hurt you and he's...' He glances over his shoulder to where the little shit is still lying face down in the sand, one arm trapped beneath him and his head rammed up against the edge of one of the blocks. He can't think about him now. 'You're safe.'

The girl looks up, pushes her hair off her face with shaking hands, and Ian's heart gives a lurch. He is staring into the tear-filled, bush baby eyes of the girl from the Co-op. For a moment he feels as if he has been struck to stone. Though he takes in her grazed cheek and bruised mouth, the blood trickling down her shin from a cut in her knee, he cannot move to comfort her. One breast is exposed, so perfect in its delicate contour, the pinkness of the wind-teased nipple and the pale flesh around it, that his mouth goes dry. As if he is watching the scene from somewhere outside himself, he sees the panic in her eyes as she reads his expression and pulls her torn clothing over her breast. He reaches out a hand as if to stop her, and the spell is broken. He blinks, shakes his head, and the vision of the sea siren is gone, replaced by a child, shivering with cold and shock.

'Come on,' he says, 'we need to get you home.' He pulls off his hooded top and holds it out to her. She stands up, awkwardly, patting and pulling at her flimsy dress to keep herself covered. There is a moment of confusion while she tries to work out which hand she can safely free up to take the top from him. He wants to go towards her, close enough to wrap the soft cotton fabric around her and hold her, to feel the slenderness of her limbs and the animal race of her heart, and inhale that shampoo scent he remembers from the Co-op. But the watcher outside himself knows better. He turns away from her, reaching the top out behind him. There is a light tug as she snatches it out of his hand, followed by some rustling and a softly-uttered, 'Shit,' before she says, in a small, childish voice, 'You can turn round now.'

The top falls almost to her knees, and her hands, one of which she raises to hitch up the loose neck, are entirely covered by the sleeves. Inside him, everything settles. She is just a child, a little girl who's fallen in the sea, maybe, wrapped up in her father's sweater. 'It smells of cigarettes,' she says, wrinkling her nose.

'Sorry.'

'That's OK, my mum smokes.' She gives a wan smile.

'Come on, then.' He sets off back towards the steps up to the caravan site, but quickly becomes aware that she isn't following him. He stops and turns to look at her; she has taken a couple of steps away from the tumbled sea defences, he can see her footprints, dark in the moonlit sand, but now she hesitates, shifting nervously from foot to foot like a race-horse at the starting line.

'I can't,' she says.

'What do you mean?'

'Go that way. Walk past...him.'

'OK,' he says, and they begin to walk towards the bon-fire and the partygoers, who are quieter now; someone has produced a guitar and is strumming old Dylan numbers, accompanied by sporadic bursts of familiar choruses that tug him into his legacy years. He can no longer remember what music he was supposed to like, a realisation which makes him feel empty inside, and sullenly angry, even though he knows it doesn't matter now; the lie has become truth as so many real stories have been layered over it.

He and the girl walk shoulder to shoulder, but not touching, and he matches his pace to hers as she swerves away from the fire, moving faster now, despite the wet sand, legs pumping, shoulders set square as she follows the path of the moon towards the sea. But he is so deep in the thoughts triggered by the music, he is surprised to find he has wet feet, and the girl is wading away from him, the water already above her knees, the hem of his sweatshirt floating around her. Almost before he realises what she is doing, he is crash-ing through the shallows after her, small waves tugging at his ankles.

'Hey!' he shouts, but the sea's low roar swallows his voice. 'Where are you going?' he tries again, blundering on, his shoes full of sand and water, his sodden jeans feeling like lead casings around his calves and ankles. Compared to him, the girl seems to glide along the moon-path, moving effort-lessly through the water, the gap between them widening.

Wavelets lap her waist and she pats them down with sharp, nervous jerks of her hands. She'll start swimming in a minute, he tells himself, but she doesn't. He plunges forward, into a clumsy front crawl, remembers doing life-saving at the place with the pool, that's closed down now; you swam in pyjamas and bare feet then, though, not jeans and work boots, not driven by a heart that has been too long in the world. Would she save him, he wonders, his mouth full of salt water, and then, somehow, he has hold of the sweatshirt, the fabric knotting as she twists and turns, her voice an effortful grunt as she says, 'Get away from me. Let me go. Got to get clean.'

Alice replaces the handset on its stand and goes into Basil and Isabella's drawing room. Despite the agitation of the moment, a part of her mind registers, out of habit, the plate glass windows whose angles she has been charged with softening, the stone-clad fireplace to be ripped out, the avocado hessian wallpaper whose glue, she knows, will be as tenacious as skin.

'The police will be here in half an hour,' she says, as Basil advances across acres of oatmeal carpet, brandishing a gin and tonic. 'I'm so sorry about dinner. I could always arrange to meet them at home...'

'Out of the question, old girl. We don't want the gentlemen of the press catching sight of them.'

'It's odd, though,' Alice sits beside Isabella on the gold Dralon settee and puts her drink on the glass-topped coffee table in front of it, 'they said they already knew about the call, because they have a trace on Harry's phone. They said they'd tried to contact me but couldn't get a reply. D'you mind?' She fishes her cigarettes out of her bag and holds up the pack.

'Like fresh air after Basil's cigars, darling,' says Isabella, pushing the onyx table lighter towards her. In its way, she thinks, the Keats' bungalow is as much a period piece as Wildwood, and wonders if what she has planned for this room is really vandalism.

'Well you've switched off the phones, haven't you?' asks Basil.

'They have my mobile number. There were no missed calls. Only the message from Harry. Then they said they'd spoken to Mary, as if that explained everything. Don't you think that's odd?'

'Don't suppose they're all like the detectives in those TV shows Izzie's always watching. Don't suppose they have the resources to send Inspector Morse after every clue.'

'Don't be ridiculous, Basil. This is Harry Theobald we're talking about. Of course they should be doing everything possible.'

Of course they should, *of course* they should. Alice's heart feels ready to burst with emphasis, yet at the same time, she knows Harry's disappearance is no more or less important than the catastrophic vanishings that happen every day, some sudden, an eye blinked, a corner turned, an empty space where the beloved once stood; some gradual, Cheshire Cat fades. 'They're coming now, anyway,' she says, emollient, and Basil and Isabella stare at her, shame-faced.

'I'd better cancel the pub,' says Basil, pausing to replenish his whisky as he heads for the phone in the hall.

'I'll see what I can rustle up here.' There is a deflated set to Isabella's mouth. She was not, thinks Alice, cut out to deal with the mundane fall-out from dramatic events. They drink in silence for a moment, hearing only Basil's side of his conversation with Bernard. He is telling Bernard Isabella has been taken ill. Then Isabella asks,

'What was in the message, then?'

'Nothing really. He sounded drunk...'

'Drunk? Harry? Are you sure it was him? I mean, the phone could have been stolen.'

She hadn't thought of that. 'He said my name.'

'He could have got that off Harry's contacts. Probably just some little criminal having what he thought was a good laugh.' Isabella goes on in the same vein, but Alice lets the words pass her by. Was it Harry? Had she just assumed it was him and so not listened carefully enough to the voice? If it wasn't him, that would explain the mysterious reference to Jimmy. She delves in her bag, searching for her phone. She must listen to the message again, perhaps get Basil and Isabella to listen to it as well. But where is the phone?

Suddenly she can see it, as clearly as if she were standing in her own bedroom, lying on the bedside table. Damn. What if Harry has tried to ring her again? Or Polly? Or Jesse. She rises, abruptly, barking her shins on the sharp brass edge of the coffee table. 'I must...' Then the doorbell rings.

'I sent my sergeant to the beach,' says the boxy woman in the ill-cut trouser suit. 'He needs a bit of a holiday.' She pauses, like a bad comic in a working men's club, waiting for the laugh that doesn't come. 'To investigate the row,' she adds, now stony and efficient.

'There's a midsummer party,' says Alice.

'Would you like a cup of tea, miss...er..?' Isabella steps out from behind the coffee table, wobbling slightly on her kitten heels.

'Roberts. Detective Inspector. No thank you.'

'Mrs. Theobald?' Alice nods. Without waiting for an invitation, Detective Inspector Roberts sits beside her on the settee, in the place vacated by Isabella. In her black polyester suit and square-toed vinyl shoes she looks thoroughly at home on Dralon. 'So, what can you tell us about this phone message?'

They go through what Alice has already told them on the phone. ('Not me, Mrs. Theobald, the duty officer, so if you wouldn't mind going over it again.') By the time they have done this, Roberts' sergeant has reappeared. He is as tall, slender and courteous as she is dumpy and blunt, and dressed, Alice is certain, in a bespoke suit, a pale grey Prince of Wales check with a blue silk lining. Sand clings to the polished toes of his black brogues.

'Sound and fury signifying nothing,' he reports cheerfully to his inspector, who gives him a blank look.

'Oh dear,' mutters Alice, and Isabella giggles.

'Mrs. Theobald's daughter is there,' she says, more to the dashing sergeant than Inspector Roberts.

The sergeant gives Alice a well bred, reassuring smile. 'Well I'm sure she's enjoying herself,' he says.

'How old is your daughter, Mrs. Theobald?' demands Roberts.

'Fifteen,' she replies, and the word has scarcely left her mouth before she is kicking herself for not lying. Her face blazes with embarrassment and worry. Polly is too young; she shouldn't have let her go, even with Maddie and the Jedward. Without Harry, she can't make proper decisions. Bloody Harry. Where is he? How could he leave her like this, stranded between gossipy Isabella and this po-faced policewoman like Scylla and bloody Charybdis? She'll kill him when, if…God, what is she thinking?

The inspector looks at her as if she knows, as Alice adds, lamely, 'She doesn't drink. She's with a friend.'

'You have to let the young go, don't you, inspector?'
Alice knows Isabella is trying to make amends but wishes
she would just shut up. Roberts glares at Isabella, and the
expression on her face reminds Alice suddenly of her father.
His eyes, that she still dreams about sometimes, following
her, around rooms, up and down stairs, along the street to
school and back again. Following her by proxy, through the
eyes of teachers, and her friends' parents, and neighbours.
Isabella's right, because it makes no difference; children
always leave, one way or another.

'I imagine you'll be wanting to get home before she
does,' says Roberts, with all the warmth and flexibility of an
iceberg, 'so let me update you on where we are now. As you
know, we were alerted to the call, and we did try to contact
you. When we eventually got through to Miss Canter, she
said she'd speak to you but clearly she hasn't been able to
get hold of you either. As far as you know,' she pauses for
emphasis, 'your husband hasn't tried to contact you again?'

'He hasn't. In fact, I do wonder now if it was him at all.
The phone could have been stolen.'

'That's obviously a possibility, but it's the only lead we
have at present. Our technoheads didn't manage to triangu-
late the call, it wasn't long enough, but they did pin it down
to somewhere around Carlisle. Do you have any idea what
your husband might be doing in Carlisle?'

'No. Driving home? He's been in Scotland, as you know.'

'We've asked the local force to look out for his vehicle.
Nothing so far. Mrs. Theobald..? Had he got any reason to
disappear deliberately? You see, that might explain why we
haven't been able to trace him. If he'd planned it. With his
money...'

'No, inspector, no reason.' And no money. Unless...Had
he cleaned out the bank accounts on purpose? Should she

tell the police? About the rows of zeroes, the unpaid bills, Abigail Jones with her cheap shoes and her tawdry brooch? She glances around the Keats' hard-edged drawing room, everything now stained a greyish-yellow as lamplight begins to take over from the remains of the day. At kindly Basil, and Isabella, who means no more harm than the bull in the proverbial china shop, at the dashing sergeant standing beside the ghastly fireplace as though about to ask Basil for his daughter's hand in marriage (not that Basil has a daughter), at Roberts who looks as if she wouldn't blame Harry if he had deserted his family on purpose. 'We were happy,' says Alice firmly. 'Unfashionably so, perhaps, but there it is. Harry hasn't left us. Not in that way.'

'In what way might he have left you then?' Roberts perseveres.

'I don't know, inspector. I rather think it's your job to find out.'

Ian's teeth chatter convulsively and, despite the mildness of the night, he feels cold to his bones, his wet clothes clinging to him like a dead skin, but the girl worries him more. She is withdrawn and sluggish, feet dragging in the sand, weight slewed against him as if she no longer has the will to hold herself upright. She hasn't said a word since he dragged her from the sea and lay with her for a moment, side by side on the shore, the pair of them gasping and moaning like lovers in the aftermath of a violent coupling. As soon as he had caught his breath, he had felt the evening breeze knife through him and knew he must get them both to shelter as quickly as possible.

He's afraid the girl is already hypothermic. He'd call an ambulance, he tells himself, if his phone wasn't waterlogged.

Just call an ambulance, tell them about the girl and the little shit with his head cracked, and leave. Decent thing done.

As they skirt the bonfire, unnoticed by the other party-goers grouped around it, his eye is caught by a jacket, discarded on the sand. Pulling the girl with him, he swoops in and grabs it, then bundles it around her shoulders, chafing her upper arms as he does so. For some reason, this makes her giggle, and her gaze comes back into focus.

'Hello,' he says, and tries to smile through his chattering teeth. She presses herself suddenly against him, her cheek to his chest, her small, freezing hands coming up to cover his where he is still holding her upper arms. He lets them stay that way for a few seconds, before he pushes her away, their bodies pressed together, generating a thin warmth as the rising breeze whips at their backs. 'Come on,' he says, more roughly than he intends, 'let's get you out of the cold. Can you show me where you live?'

She nods and leads him, briskly now, over hard-packed sand, until, a hundred yards or so past the campfire, she turns towards the cliff and begins to climb. Following, he realises they are on a steep, crumbling path, narrow, a sheep track probably. He scrambles up behind her, uncomfortably aware of the flex of muscle in her buttocks and thighs beneath the ragged wisps of her dress. Whatever underwear she had been wearing, she isn't any more. She seems so blithely, dangerously unaware of herself. He's not out of sympathy, he reflects, with the intentions of the little shit he's left for dead on the beach, just with his methods. Where's the challenge in mounting a direct offensive on such a weak target? What kind of mother, he asks himself, to sabotage his previous train of thought before it takes him over, lets her teenage daughter out dressed – or undressed – like that?

At the top of the path, she turns and stretches out her hand as if to help him up the final few feet.

'I'm OK,' he says, somewhat hurt she should think he needs help yet at the same time shocked at how out of breath he sounds.

'Now we go through here,' she announces, and disappears into a hedge. A high beech hedge, its pale leaves glittering in wind and moonlight. His heart races with more than exertion as he follows her through what turns out to be a tunnel-shaped gap in the hedge. She is leading him into the grounds of Wildwood House. She must be one of Craig's kids. He wants to laugh out loud, he wants to plant a great, smacking kiss on her sweet little mouth and whirl her into a dance in this clearing into which they have merged, as if they were fairy folk. One door closes, another opens.

They move away from the hedge, into a woodland walk, the house visible then invisible ahead of them as the path snakes through stands of trees and shrubs. Pale-barked eucalypti glimmer like bones in the broken moonlight. His stockinged feet crunch on dry leaves and beech mast. His boots, he supposes, are somewhere at the bottom of the North Sea. He strains to see the house properly but can gain nothing but impressions, the barley-twist chimneys, a jumble of ornamented gables, facades mosaiced with tiny windows winking in the security lights. The glimpses set up an echo in his memory, something real but not concrete, vivid yet elusive. Then he grasps it. The gingerbread house of his dream, the dream that had entangled him somehow and kept him in Aylsburgh. It's all falling into place. His luck is changing.

The woodland path debouches onto a raised grass walk bordering a sunken garden. The house now blazes ahead of them in all its quirky magnificence, a broad terrace scattered with chairs and tables, and a boy's bike, stretched between two wide angled wings. Remembering the guards on the main gate, and the press outside it, Ian feels nervous, exposed, as Craig's daughter leads him into the aureole of the security lights.

'Look,' he says, 'you'll be OK now, won't you? I'll be off.'

She turns to him, grabs bunches of his sodden teeshirt in her small hands. 'No. Please. Come in with me. Jesse's gone to Norwich and Mum's out to supper with our neighbours. And Dad's...away. I was supposed to be staying with Maddie Manning.'

And where, Ian wonders, is Mary? 'OK, just to the door, then.' Though by that time, if the guards know their business, it'll be too late, he'll have lost his advantage. He knows exactly what they'll conclude if they catch him with the girl, her wisps of wet clothes clinging to her in a way that makes her look somehow more naked than the day she was born. He knows exactly what they'll tell the reporters, in exchange for something to beef up their dwindling pensions. He knows better than most that explanations have no power over appearances. It would have been a fuck of a sight easier dealing with Mary.

She straightens up from delving beneath a tub of lettuces beside the back door in search of a key. All that security and they keep the back door key just where anyone else would. A dog begins to bark from somewhere deep within the recesses of the house. Ian tenses, then remembers the Dalmatian Mary had been walking. Not a lot of harm in a Dalmatian. She opens the back door and stand aside as the dog hurtles through it, a blur of black and white, pauses to give Ian a brief look over, then belts away across the carriage yard on business of its own.

'Come in with me,' she pleads, 'I hate it when the house is empty.' She's shivering, goose-pimpled, scratches all over her shins and forearms he notices now. He shouldn't. He shouldn't be there when Alice arrives home; if he wants to win her over, he should play Batman, swooping to the rescue then disappearing before he can be unmasked. Batman. Another stunted love; he's seen all the movies, but he never got to read the comics, doesn't remember Adam West and Burt Ward on the TV. But he finds himself smiling into those huge, anxious, shadowed eyes. Finds himself following her inside as she walks ahead of him switching on lights.

'We can both have a bath,' she says, flashing him a smile whose radiance entirely drowns out the low light from a sort of chandelier ornamented with blue glass flowers, suspended over the kitchen table. His internal organs seem to perform a synchronised backflip. 'We have six bathrooms.' She gives a charmingly embarrassed laugh and his insides settle back almost where they belong. He thinks of the shower block at the caravan site, its concrete walls streaked with green mould, the wooden drainage slats that feel as if they're coated in viscous saliva. He thinks of having to wait there, among the moths and spiders, while the asthmatic tumble drier goes about its business. Why not take a bath in one of Harry Theobald's six bathrooms? God knows, he deserves it. For so many reasons.

He follows the girl up a narrow, twisting flight of stairs immediately beyond the kitchen door, and along a galleried landing running the length of the south face of the house.

'Here,' she says, pushing open a door just to the left of the main staircase at the other end of the gallery. 'That's my mum and dad's room. There's a bathroom, and a dressing room. My dad's wardrobes are on the left. Just help yourself. He has all these clothes he never wears. Mum buys them for him, but he just likes his gardening clothes, and anyway...'

'What?'

She shrugs. Her gaze flicks away from him. 'Nothing. My room's along the landing. I'll see you downstairs.'

He steps across the threshold and closes the door behind him, waiting for a moment in the dark for the room to settle around him. It smells of furniture polish and expensive perfume, and linen dried in the open air. What had he expected? It was Craig Barnes who smelt of piss and vomit and dried blood, not Harry Theobald. Without turning on the lights, navigating by the moonlight which spills through the uncurtained windows, he finds his way to the bathroom, all green vitreous tiles and dark pink enamelware, and turns on the shower. He stands beneath the sluice of hot water until he feels his frozen muscles begin to relax, until his skin is stinging scarlet and the marrow of his bones has thawed. He shampoos his hair and washes his body with something lime-scented, and wraps himself in a white, fluffy bath sheet before making his way back into the bedroom and turning on the light.

The polished wooden floor, now bearing a trail of sandy footprints, is scattered with expensive-looking rugs and a lot of small, overstuffed chairs that don't invite you to sit in them. There are paintings on the walls. The bed is a four poster, though the posts support neither curtains nor canopy and poke, naked but elaborately carved, towards a decorated plaster ceiling. Looking at the plumped pillows and cloudy, quilted counterpane, he feels overwhelmed by tiredness and wants nothing more than to lie down and sleep. Just five minutes would do, five minutes to rest his head on goose down and close his eyes, to feel his aching spine sink into the gentle support of the thick mattress. He moves towards the bed as though his will is not his own. Five minutes to garner the energy to get dressed, go downstairs, feed the kid a story and get out of the house before her mother returns.

Then he notices the mobile phone lying on the bedside table beside a pile of glossy magazines and a book. Not just any book but *that* book, the one Craig had read to Jimmy Jones from. The cover is more faded now, but he recognises it from the way the gilding on the 's' at the end of 'Tales' is worn away and a tear in the fabric through the 'H' of 'Hans' that occurred when they were fighting over it, just before.

He picks up the phone. It's not password protected. He scrolls through the contacts. Harry at the top, so it must be Alice's phone, then Jesse and Polly. So that's the girl's name. Polly. He reads a few recent text messages. *forgot nets can u pick me up 6* from Jesse, and several others in a similar vein. Obscurely, one from Polly that just reads *vanilla* and two from Isabella about meeting for dinner. Perhaps Isabella is the neighbour Polly referred to. Then, *Love you. Miss you. Sweet dreams. Big hugs. Hxxxxx*, sent by Harry, about an hour before he had loomed out of the half-dark in the car-park at the Head of Etive and accosted Ian. He had probably been sitting in his Range Rover as he tapped it into his keypad. Thinking what? What lay behind those commonplace endearments? He's like some lovelorn teenager, Ian tells himself, returning to the homescreen, trying to analyse every letter of a message for some hidden, but conclusive, revelation of feeling. He'll be counting the kisses next. Five. He never wrote a single word to Orla. Wishes he had, now, wishes he had a package of letters done up in a ribbon, or even that his hand could carry the memory of words inscribed on paper, to add to the other good memories, to cancel out the final one.

He looks at the call log, and shivers, suddenly aware how cold the room is now. There's a fireplace, with a pretty surround of some kind of beaten metal, but it's full of flowers. The log shows a voicemail from Harry, received earlier today. At first, he stares blankly at the keypad, unable to see which key he needs to press to retrieve the message. Then, when he finds it, there's no signal, just a series of strident bleeps. He stands, moves about the room with the phone glowing in front of his face, until, beside the window, a couple of bars appear in the top left hand corner of the screen.

He listens to the message twice, because the first time, all he hears is the name Jimmy. The second time, he tries to focus on the background, to find something, anything, that will tell him where Craig was when he made the call, but all he picks up is an indeterminate rustling, anodyne, anonymous, the sound equivalent of magnolia paint. He slams the phone down on to the cushioned window seat. It bounces and almost slides to the floor, but Ian catches it. He runs the voicemail again. He really needs to know where Craig was when he made this call because, judging by the sound of his voice, he's probably still there. People who have spent less time around the dead and dying than Ian has might think Craig was just drunk, but Ian knows how hard he hit him, and Ian knows the kind of damage a blow like that will do. He'd believed Craig was dead by the time he abandoned the Range Rover at Southwaite. He's oddly disappointed in himself now to find he wasn't, and scared, if he's honest, that Craig might have succeeded in saying more to someone than he had to his wife. Mary, for example.

He finds a pen in the bedside table drawer, looks up Mary's number in Alice's list of contacts, and scribbles it on his forearm, on the smooth, hairless patch of skin where he had his regimental tattoo removed. Still dog tired (odd expression that; dogs, in his experience, are never as tired as people but always up for it, hopeful), but no longer relaxed, he drops the towel and opens another panelled door which leads into a dressing room.

There are more wardrobes on Harry's side, he notes, because Alice's are interrupted by a dressing table with bulbs strung around its mirror as if it's come from a theatrical dressing room. Curious, he slides open the wardrobe to the left of the mirror, and finds it almost empty. Perhaps half a dozen dark coloured evening dresses hang there, the fabric draped like the wings of roosting bats. He tries the one to the right, which is filled with shallow wooden drawers like the ones you used to find in old fashioned gentlemen's outfitters, and emits a scent of lavender. In the top drawer is a tangle of socks and tights, in the next her underwear. Removing a pair of pink silk camiknickers, he holds it out at arm's length and tries to imagine the body it fits. Boyish, he concludes, narrow hipped and flat chested. Is that what Harry Theobald goes for? Boy-women in pink silk lace? Phoney, like him? He thinks about Craig, pushing down the flimsy shoulder straps with the tips of his broad fingers, his scarred thumb. Ian rubs the silk between his own thumb and forefinger, feeling the ridge of scar tissue through the gauzy fabric. He wonders how Polly would look in a garment like this, and feels a shifting in his body as it adjusts to this new idea it has been presented with by his brain. Still holding the camiknickers, he touches himself, feels the cool glide of silk against his penis, the spring of his pubic hair, still damp, through the fine fabric. He props his buttocks against Alice's dressing table, closes his eyes and gives himself up to the fantasy.

Afterwards, cold, empty, disappointed, he shoves the soiled garment into the back of the drawer and slides open the first of Harry's wardrobes, releasing a scent of cedar to mingle with the lavender. He gazes at a row of suits, with shoe racks beneath them where pairs of brogues, hand stitched, no doubt, and probably made on Harry's personal last, are lined up, heels gleaming. He slides the door shut again, with a heavy, satisfying clunk, and opens the next. Shirts, trousers, more tailors' drawers stacked with rolled ties, sweaters and teeshirts. Ian grabs a pair of jeans at random from a row of about a dozen pairs, and a white teeshirt. Behind the next door he finds boxers, socks and a belt. He is so much thinner than Harry, he will need a belt.

There is a full-length mirror on the back wall of the dressing room. The clothes probably cost more than Ian would have earned in a month at the Head of Etive, but he still looks like a scarecrow in them. The jeans are too short; they skim his ankles, exposing socks decorated with images of *The Simpsons*. A present from one of Harry's children no doubt. Polly perhaps? Will she remark on them when he goes downstairs? The only footwear he can find to fit him is sandals; his feet are longer and narrower than Harry's and Harry's hand-lasted brogues crush his toes. As far as he can see, Harry only possesses proper men's hairbrushes, a pair of them, silver-backed and monogrammed in the same style as his ring.

His ring. Ian holds up his hand, but however long he looks at it, the ring is still not there. Fuck. Dashing back into the bathroom where he left his wet clothes, he goes through the pockets of his jeans. Nothing. Nothing but a sodden five pound note, looking more intact than he feels after everything they've been though together tonight. So far. The ring, he supposes, must be at the bottom of the sea. But not far enough out. It had been low tide when he plunged into the water after Polly; once the tide turns, surely it will wash the ring up on to the beach. The cops might blame the little shit for stealing it. Harry's gold, Harry's daughter. Same difference to a bloke like that. But Mary is a different matter. Where the fuck *is* Mary?

He returns to the dressing room and helps himself to a beige coloured sweater whose label tells him it's cashmere and dry clean only. He runs his fingers through his hair; the tips rest on the shoulders of the sweater, creating damp patches. He likes that. Without looking back, at *that* book or Alice's mobile, he leaves the room and makes his way downstairs. He uses the front stairs this time, grand and wide, and sweeping into a great hexagonal hall that contains a fireplace big enough to roast an ox in.

He finds Polly in the kitchen, to which he is guided by the smell of burning milk. She is swathed in a pink bathrobe (sugar pink, not the subtle shade of her mother's camiknickers), with pink satin bows on its pockets, frowning at a pan on the Aga. When she sees him, she bursts out laughing. Gazing at her flushed cheeks, her small hand in front of her mouth and the way her clean, flyaway hair catches the static in her sleeve, he feels privileged to be laughed at by her.

I'm making hot chocolate,' she announces, once she has recovered herself. As if on cue, boiling milk begins to rise above the lip of the saucepan. Ian lunges past her to remove the pan from the heat, knocking her aside as he does so. She stumbles on the step up to the Aga's plinth and grabs his free arm to steady herself, pulling herself into his embrace. He stares at the milk subsiding in the saucepan; she takes hold of his hand and coolly loosens its grip.

'You smell of my dad,' she says, as if that explains something. Stepping down from the Aga plinth, she moves to a kitchen counter, where she busies herself spooning chocolate powder into mugs. She counts – one...two...one...two – beneath her breath.

'Did you phone your mum?' he enquires, going to sit at the kitchen table.

Polly shrugs.

'You should,' says Ian, interpreting her shrug as a negative.

'Can't.'

'You only have to tell her as much as you want. Just something to explain the wet clothes and the not going home with Maddie.' And the scratches and bruises and everything torn to shreds, but, if she's worried about talking to her mother, perhaps it's best to take it in easy stages.

'Oh, it's not that. I've already decided what I'm going to say to her. It's that I can't phone. Our phones are all switched off and my mobile...well, I can't find it and even if I could it'd be screwed, wouldn't it?'

'Switched off?'

Yes, it's...er...' She pours the burnt milk. 'Ugh, skin,' she says, trying to fish it out with a teaspoon; by the time she has finished, half the drinking chocolate is puddled on the kitchen counter. The mug she places before him still contains gobbets of milk skin. He watches her in silence for a while, when she sits down across the table from him, his gaze drawn to the velvety shadow where the lapels of her dressing gown cross, to the promise of her breasts beneath the fluffy pink fabric. He clears his throat, as if by doing so he might also clear his head.

'So that guy,' he says, 'do you know him?' He doesn't need to ask why the phones are off.

She shudders and makes a moue of distaste identical to the one she previously directed at the skin in her drink. 'He works here,' she tells him, 'he's one of the security guys. Mum told him to go with us, to look out for us.'

'Christ.' That complicates things, if the little shit is dead.

'Yeah. Bad, n'est ce pas? That's why I had to think out what to say to Mum. She's got enough stuff going on right now, without...you know.'

'So what will you tell her?' Heart in his throat now.

'Just that I had a row with Maddie and came home early.'

'And the wet clothes and lost phone?'

She shrugs again. 'A dare. Swimming. I don't know. Doesn't matter. As long as she doesn't find out about...*that*.'

'While I drink this, then,' their eyes meet, she crumples her mouth in rueful distaste, he laughs, 'maybe I could put my clothes in the drier, so I can change before I go.' He glances at the kitchen clock; it's already after ten; he'll be leaving in damp clothes if he wants to be away before her mother comes home.

And as if this thought has conjured her, they both hear the crunch of wheels on gravel from beyond the back door. Polly's eyes widen, her mouth drops open. Ian bites back a string of expletives.

'Quick,' says Polly, 'this way.' She darts up from the table and leads him at a jog down a narrow, and surprisingly bare, passage to the hexagonal hall with the grand staircase and ox-swallowing fireplace. Opposite the fireplace is a pair of French windows giving on to the rear terrace. From there, he can find his way back the way they came, through the garden and down the cliff path to the beach.

'Go,' she commands, then, 'Wait...I don't know your name.'

'It's Ian.'

'And I'm Polly.'

There is a thudding of car doors, voices raised in farewells. He runs. Polly, he thinks. Polly.

The shift has changed by the time Basil's Jaguar draws up at the gate, and it is Chas who opens up and waves the car through, a heart-sinking reminder to Alice that she is going to have to find extra money to pay overtime to whichever of the Jedwards escorted Polly and Maddie to the party. Worrying about this, she is slow to realise, as Basil sweeps into the turning circle before the front door, that there are lights blazing from most of the downstairs windows.

'That's odd. It was still daylight when I left. I didn't leave any lights on in the house.'

'Shall I come in with you?' asks Basil. 'Do you want the police called?'

'God no! I've had enough of them for one evening, thank you. No, I shall be fine. You get off home.'

What if it's Harry? It must be Harry. Her heart is a kite, tugging at its strings. The back door is unlocked. Any moment now she will feel his arms around her and her senses will be full of him, his smell, his sandpapery evening jaw, his thumb, the one with the scar, tracing a fine line down her cheek, through her tears. He will have some explanation, but it won't matter. All that matters is that he's home, and this ghastly, tangled hiatus in her life is at an end.

'Harry..?' she's calling as she pushes open the door. 'Where's your master?' she asks Daisy, scratching the top of the dog's head as it bustles up against Alice's legs. 'Harry!' she calls again. Silence. She runs upstairs to her and Harry's room. Even though she can see it is in darkness, she peers around the edge of the door, hoping so hard to see the outline of his body beneath the bedclothes that she has to look for some time before her mind will believe what her eyes are seeing. The bed is undisturbed.

One of the children then, she tells herself, full of the bitter gall of disappointment, and then guilt that the thought of her children should make her feel like this. Jesse's bed is also empty, but when she cautiously pushes Polly's door ajar, she sees the counterpane heaped on the floor, and Polly's face above the duvet, serene, almost translucent in the bluish beam from her nightlight.

'Polly..?' No response. Polly is sound asleep. The party must have been too much for her so she came home. Sensible girl. Alice watches her sleeping daughter for a moment or two, and is about to set off down the back stairs and begin shutting the house down for the night when she hears the trill of her mobile phone from the opposite end of the landing.

Harry, she thinks again, telling herself she's beginning to sound like a stuck record. But who else could it be at this time of night? And he rang earlier, didn't he? She has the message, the police have the message. She didn't imagine it. She runs along the landing, racing the answerphone.

'Yes?

'Mo..?'

Alice freezes with the handset clamped to her ear. She dare not even breathe for fear of giving away her presence at the other end of the line. It's only once she has ended the call that, keeping her finger pressed against the power key for so long she actually switches the phone off, she realises it was on the window seat, not the bedside table where she left it. And that there is sand on the bedroom floor. Polly, she concludes. Polly always says their shower is better than the one she shares with Jesse.

She turns off the light and lies down on her side of the bed, in the dark, fully dressed. The night, the deep silence of the house, feel like a weight on her chest against which she struggles to breathe. She wishes she could give up. Nathan. Is he coming to snatch back the time she borrowed? Is it over, finally?

The party has moved up a gear by the time Ian finds himself back on the beach for the second time that evening, better dressed though uncertain, since realising he's lost Harry Theobald's ring, whether his circumstances are better or worse. The tide has turned and the breeze has swung to the east, making it noticeably colder than when he had dragged Polly out of the sea, though the partygoers seem oblivious. Not surprising, he thinks, as his Simpson-socked toes stub against empty bottles and cans. The unmistakable, decayed vegetation smell of skunk now pervades the scene, sweeping away the innocence of bonfire and burnt sausages. The music is loud enough to make the air shudder; it sets his teeth on edge and makes his ears hum; he's getting old, and yet...Polly.

As he passes out of the ring of firelight, towards the steps up to the caravan site, he keeps his gaze directed mainly to his left, trying to spot the place where he left the unconscious security guard. He's as certain as he can be the little shit will still be there, but, after hearing Craig's voicemail, wonders if he might be losing it. Eyesight, hearing, short term memory. The capacity to do comprehensive physical damage to another human being.

He's darkly, perversely reassured when his eye picks out a softer silhouette among the jags and angles of the tumbled breakwater. He averts his gaze and picks up his pace; he's seen all he needs to. More; the pale outline of the bare buttocks in the moonlight seems to have seared itself on to his retinas. He has a nasty feeling it won't go away in a hurry and sure enough, even after he's let himself into his caravan and pulled his sleeping bag right over his head, it remains, a sad impression of the utter foolishness and vulnerability of his fellow man. It talks to him as he falls into an uneasy sleep, in the fashionably estuarine tones of Polly Theobald, and skin becomes confused with pink silk, and the last thought he remembers has something to do with life and artifice and which is which.

DAY EIGHT

There are very small people hammering in his head, a vision of one of those carillons they have in the towers of churches in Bavaria, something plucked from before Orla, when the regiment had been given seven days' leave before deploying to Northern Ireland and he had no family to visit so had taken himself on a tour of the Black Forest. Not a bad preparation, in fact, because Ulster was a fairytale too, as unreal, in its way, as the gingerbread houses, and porcelain steins, and plump girls in dirndls. The wolves were in the streets there, though, they hadn't the decency to confine themselves to a picturesque slinking through pine forests. Bernadette and Bobby, Cinderella and Prince Charming. Half houses instead of half timbering, guns not roses.

The knocking continues, dragging him over the threshold of wakefulness, though, as he extricates himself from the sleeping bag and pads across to the door in Harry Theobald's Simpsons socks, the miasma of self pity stays with him, keeping his perceptions hazy.

Even so, it's clear to him that the woman at the door is Polly's mother. Same dead straight, sandy blonde hair, same brown eyes, same shaped face, a longish oval interrupted by fine, sharp cheekbones and a surprisingly strong jaw. As she says, 'Ian..?' he tries to stay focused on her face, so his mind doesn't stray towards thoughts of her in the pink silk camiknickers, to memories of the garment stuffed in the back of her underwear drawer. Has she found it? Can't have done. She wouldn't be here, with her polite, hesitant smile, if she had.

'I wasn't sure...these caravans...I'm not familiar...'

I bet you're not. Still, there's something about her accent, something flat and northern-sounding behind the posh. Familiar. Sheffield? Can't be. Just the thought of that level of coincidence makes his flesh crawl.

'That's me,' he says, raking his hand through his hair and trying to muster a reassuring smile, even though he can't remember when he last cleaned his teeth. 'You found me. Do you...er...want to come in?'

'No, no thank you.' Her reply comes a little too quickly, and she holds up her free hand, palm towards him, as though warding him off. There is a diamond on her wedding finger that looks as if it could save the economy if she donated it to the Treasury. 'I just brought you...' She holds out a hessian carrier, the sort that advertises the owner's material wealth as well as her concern for the environment. 'Your clothes, washed and dried. I even ironed them,' she adds, as though confessing to a weakness. 'And Polly baked you some cookies. I can't tell you...' she continues, as though the mention of Polly's name has broken down some barrier.

'Please,' he interrupts. Whatever Polly has told her mother, he has her good will, which is all he needs for now. 'Anyone would have done the same.'

'You were very brave. The sea...one never knows with nature, does one? I wonder, would you come to lunch? Proper roast, all the trimmings. It would give me a chance to thank you properly. Polly would like it,' she adds, as if fearful he might demur. *As if.*

'Thank you. I'd like that very much. I'll bring your husband's things back then, shall I?'

A slight flush colours her cheeks. He's aware of her appraising him, frankly, in Harry's clothes. 'I think you'll probably be more comfortable in your own,' she says. There is a dimple in her right cheek when she laughs. Does Polly share that? He doesn't think so. He's sure he would have noticed. So there, in that tiny variation in the working of their facial muscles, is what sets Polly apart from her mother, makes her purer, more perfect.

'I'll see you later, then,' he says, taking the hessian bag from her. 'What time?'

'About one?'

'I'll be there.'

He's slightly disappointed to find they're eating in the kitchen. He'd entertained visions of himself presiding over some vast dining table laden with cut glass and silver, offering to carve at the sideboard, fitting his hand to Harry Theobald's carving knife, serving food to Harry Theobald's family. As he walked through the village to Wildwood's front gate, and was buzzed through by the guard on duty, beneath the curious gaze of the loitering reporters, he wondered how Alice was going to explain her husband's absence.

In the event, she doesn't bother. Harry's name is not mentioned as she leads him from the front door into a small sitting room dominated by a TV screen the size of a football pitch and a tumbledown sofa covered with a crocheted blanket. The Dalmatian is taking up most of the sofa as they enter the room and, though she looks up and wags her tail, she makes no concessions to humans looking for seats.

'I thought we could have a drink in here as we're such a small party,' says Alice. 'I hope you don't mind. Get down,

Daisy.' The dog takes no notice. Alice shows Ian to a second sofa, a two seater upholstered in dark brown leather, scratched but less in danger of imminent collapse than the one occupied by Daisy. Above it is a painting of a girl in a straw hat and floral dress. She has her back to the artist and her face is visible only in a quarter profile. Ian wonders if it's a painting of Alice. 'I've told Jesse he can't have the TV on, or his Xbox. Beer? Wine? Something stronger?'

'A beer would be good, thanks.'

She lists an assortment of bottled beers and, when he has decided on a Corona, goes off to fetch it, calling to her children as she crosses the hall. Footsteps thud and clatter on the stairs, heralding the arrival of a dark boy in his early teens whose likeness to Craig Barnes is like a blow to Ian's solar plexus.

'I'm Jesse,' he announces, hurling himself into the large sofa next to the dog and picking up an Xbox controller from the arm. 'That's not my real name. I'm really called James but my dad doesn't like that so he called me Jesse. Jesse James.'

'Very funny,' says Ian, wondering why Craig had called his son James in the first place. 'I'm Ian.' He holds out a hand but Jesse is absorbed in his games controller and ignores it.

'Not very funny at all, really. Dad has an awful sense of humour. But Jesse's a cooler name than James so it's OK.'

'Good.'

Grand Theft Auto IV explodes into Technicolor life on the giant screen.

'I'll mute the sound,' says Jesse. Children should be seen and not heard, thinks Ian, mesmerised by a drive-by involving an off-roader with blacked out windows and a pink Cadillac with fins. 'The trick is not to kill the woman with the pram,' explains Jesse.

'No, you wouldn't want to do that.'

'Jesse!' exclaims Alice, returning with his beer and a large glass of white wine for herself. 'What did I tell you? Turn that off and go and find your sister.'

She arrives before he can do so, though he does at least switch off the game. Dressed in cropped jeans and an oversize sweater, thumbs hooked into her sleeves, she looks clean. Her hair is scraped off her face into a loose knot, held in place by a variety of coloured plastic clips. She is not wearing makeup, and looks porcelain pale. The backs of her hands are covered in scratches and her peacock blue nail varnish is peeling off. Clean, but damaged, like a chipped plate on a bric a brac stall. For a second she remains poised in the doorway, before plumping herself on the arm of the large sofa, then sliding down into it, nudging her brother out of the way. The dog holds her ground, Jesse fights to hold his, elbow in Polly's ribs, hip grinding against hers. Polly grabs his hair, her fingers hooked tight among his dark curls.

'Just remember who's the eldest here, yeah?'

'Just coz you got in a mess in the water and had to be rescued. Doesn't make you special, makes you stupid.' Jesse sounds on the verge of tears. Polly's knuckles have whitened; she's not playing, she's pulling his hair hard. For a second or two, her face carries a distant, glassy look, as though she has forgotten where she is, then Alice says,

'Apollonia, James, behave yourselves. We have a guest.' Apollonia? Jesse should be thankful he wasn't born first or Craig might have called him Apollo. No trace of the accent Ian had detected earlier but pure home counties drawl. Manners. Keeping up appearances. Shoring up the facade against the chaos that lies behind it. What made Britain great, and wrong, and no place for kids whose lives are the nightmares they re-live every night, alone in the dark with no-one to talk to. Apollonia, the golden girl. As he watches her return from wherever she was before her mother's telling off brought her back, he sees the sun begin to set in her eyes and recognises the gathering darkness there as though he's looking in a mirror. She lets go Jesse's hair and he rubs his head, and makes a great play of pushing the dog off the sofa in order to hide his embarrassment.

'So, Mr..?'

'Ian, just Ian will do.'

'Ian. What brings you to Aylsburgh?' Alice smiles, sips her wine, fixes her gaze on him as though unaware of the two teenagers shifting restlessly like small boats on choppy moorings. Who does she think she's talking to? The chairman of the parish council, some loyal servant of GardenMart being conferred with a long service award? All of them, he thinks, keeping up appearances.

'I'd never been here before,' he replies. 'It seemed like reason enough.'

'Did you, like, stick a pin in the map?' asks Polly, with intense curiosity, as if she's really asking him something else.

'Something like that.'

'Well, it's a good job you did,' says Alice, her warm heartiness at odds with the way she puts her glass down on a side table then picks it up again, like an alcoholic trying to resist her fix. He wonders if that's what she is, one of those rich women who pours drink into the empty stretch of her days. Not that different from people in prison, except it's more of a challenge to get the drink inside; you can't just pop down to Tesco's for a four pack of Strongbow.

'It is,' agrees Polly, mimicking her mother's tone. Again, that curious stare that seems almost to burn into the skin of his face. He runs a hand around the neck of his tee shirt, which suddenly feels tight, releasing a scent that recalls Alice and Harry's dressing room. Feeling his temperature rise another notch, he takes a long slug of beer.

Alice ploughs on. 'Will you be here for the summer?'

'I doubt it. Not much work to be had.'

'A pity my husband's away or he might be able to help you.' Though her voice doesn't falter, she does that picking up and putting down of her glass thing again. She is, he thinks, rather admirable, in the way of a French aristocrat going unflinching to the guillotine.

'Yes,' says Polly, 'my father has a lot of money.'

'Polly, really...'

'I'm sure he'd give you a handsome reward, if he was here.'

'I'm so sorry,' says Alice, blushing fiercely. This time she drains the glass.

'No need,' says Ian, 'she's had a nasty shock.'

'Nevertheless. I'm going to get some more wine. Would you like another beer?'

'Why not?'

'And while I'm getting it, Polly, I think you should apologise.'

'Why? What have I said? It's true, isn't it? If dad was here, he'd reward Ian for rescuing me. Wouldn't he?'

'He might let us have a pool now,' says Jesse brightly, 'if he thinks it's too dangerous for us to go in the sea.'

'No way. You know what he says about it spoiling the garden.'

'Way. We're more important than the garden.'

Polly gives a sceptical snort. How had Craig felt, Ian wonders, watching his kids grow up, seeing them pass the age at which Jimmy Jones stopped. Dead. Sixteen months old, he'd been, according to the prosecutor. It stuck in Ian's mind because it was the same age Danny had been the last time he'd seen him, sitting in the middle of the road, his landing cushioned by his nappy. A miracle, they'd said, and he'd thought about his mother, gold and virgin blue, her face turned from him and set towards heaven. He had been in two minds about miracles ever since.

'Lunch is almost ready,' announces Alice, returning from the kitchen and handing Ian his beer. He curls his fingers around the bottleneck, she wipes her hand down her thigh to dry the residual condensation. She brings with her the scent of roasting lamb, sharp herbs and hot sugar. He is, it dawns on him, very, very hungry. 'Polly, can you come and help me?'

'Why me? Why not Jesse? You're stereotyping me, Mum.'

'Oh for heaven's sake, alright, Jesse, then.'

'Can I make custard?'

'Yes, of course you can.' Alice ruffles her son's hair. He ducks out of the way, but the look of pleasure on his young face is heartbreaking. 'Excuse us,' she says to Ian, and she and Jesse head for the kitchen, followed by the dog.

'Good,' says Polly. 'I wanted to get them out of the way. I need to see you.'

His mouth goes dry; he takes a slug of beer, feels as if his head is about to float free of his shoulders, tells himself it's drinking on an empty stomach. To give himself something to do, he examines the label on the bottle to see what percentage of alcohol it contains. 'You're seeing me,' he says, aiming for nonchalance, ending up sounding brutal.

'Privately,' she insists, apparently unfazed. 'There's something I need to talk to you about.'

'I don't think so.'

'You will. I want to show you something.'

He's already seen more than she knows, and way more than is good for him, he reflects, remembering following her up the cliff path last night, her torn, skimpy dress, her bare arse. His struggle to formulate a reply is mercifully curtailed by the sound of the doorbell ringing, a deep clang that echoes through the hall, putting him in mind of the Addams Family.

Alice watches Jesse making custard. She prepares a roast every Sunday; last Sunday she had cooked a sirloin of beef larger than the three of them needed, so there would be cold for sandwiches for Harry when he arrived home; last Sunday she had not been aware she had to worry about buying more food than she needed. Today, the task of putting the finishing touches to the meal, of buttering vegetables and making gravy, seems impossibly complicated. It is easier just to watch Jesse as he measures and blends his ingredients, absorbed, single-minded, methodical, just as he is when he cleans and mounts skulls for the collection he keeps in the summer house on the island.

She has doubts about this obsession with the bones of dead animals, but Harry says she's being over-sensitive, that she should be grateful Jesse isn't toking behind the school bike shed or bunking off school to go on shoplifting sprees. Harry speaks about these things with an authority she finds fascinating, yet she has never asked him about his own schooldays in case he were to ask her about hers.

What would Harry think about the man she has invited to lunch? He has saved their daughter from drowning, must therefore be brave and honourable, yet somehow gives the impression he is neither. Why did she invite him? Out of a sense of obligation, or a compulsion? She found the sight of his lean, long-legged body in Harry's clothes shocking, even though it was merely sensible that he should have borrowed them when his own were soaking wet. When she asked herself why she had reacted as she had, she found it was herself she was shocked at, not him, at the lust that had thudded to the floor of her belly like a pornographic magazine falling through a letterbox. She was missing Harry, she told herself, her emotions were unbalanced by the worry and uncertainty.

Yet she felt lighter of heart than she had done for a week when he agreed to her invitation, and decided there would be no harm in putting on a dress and a little make-up. The second, however, she felt herself the victim of Polly's scrutiny, when Polly came down, her heart plunged once more and she knew herself for what she was: vain, foolish and disloyal. And now she had left them alone together, Polly and her rescuer, to prove to herself that she was none of these things, and that she trusted him as she should for dragging Polly out of the sea.

All done,' says Jesse, 'till it's ready for heating up. What is pudding anyway?'

Alice is about to say, rhubarb crumble, when the doorbell rings. Murmured conversation reaches her ears from the snug as she passes by, but she forces herself not to pause and listen. Even so, by the time she reaches the front door, the callers, whoever they are, have rung again. Such urgency on a Sunday lunchtime seems portentous. She feels gooseflesh rising on her bare arms and legs, and a sick lightheadedness, as if she is about to faint. Her hand seems to reach for the door knob in slow motion.

When she sees the boxy detective inspector and her elegant sergeant on the step, she has to clutch at the doorpost to keep herself from falling. The sergeant, seeing her distress, steps forward and grasps her arm.

'It's alright, Mrs. Theobald,' he says, 'we aren't here about your husband.' Relief washes through Alice, but it is tinged with guilt. Surely news of Harry is what she should be hoping for but then, no news is good news, or so they say.

'Actually, Mrs. Theobald,' says Detective Inspector Roberts, with a reproving glare at her sergeant, 'it's not alright. We're here about an unexplained death. Is your daughter at home?'

'My daughter..? Well...yes, but...I'm afraid she's not well, Inspector. She had...an accident at the party last night. Couldn't this wait until tomorrow? I can bring her in to see you after school.'

'I'm sorry, Mrs. Theobald. As I said, we're looking into a death.' She pauses, fixes her gaze on Alice. Her eyes, Alice observes, are the same mousy brown as her hair. 'A young man,' she adds, 'someone's son, no doubt.'

Alice stands aside to let them in, then leads them to the snug, where both Ian and Polly cast her quick, guilty looks before their attention focuses on the two police officers.

'This is my daughter, Inspector, and this is...a family friend, here for lunch.'

Roberts appraises Ian, his shabby clothes and hair down to his shoulders, the rough, undernourished look of him. It is clear to Alice she doesn't believe her explanation. Well to hell with it, it's her house and she can invite whomever she likes for Sunday lunch.

'Your name, sir?' asks Roberts, making the 'sir' sound like an insult.

'Slight,' he says, 'Ian Slight.'

Alice is unsure why, but she suddenly feels as if she has stepped through the looking-glass. The room is unchanged, the people in it disposed as they were seconds earlier, the police in the doorway, Jesse and Daisy now back on the large sofa, Polly and Ian, she noticed immediately, sitting together on the leather two-seater. Yesterday's newspaper headlines still read the right way, and the girl in the Vasnetsov above the small sofa still has her head turned away from the artist. Yet everything is different, as though Ian's recital of his name has cast a spell over them all.

'Is that a Vasnetsov?' asks the well-dressed sergeant, rather too loudly, walking over to give the painting a closer look. Alice is just about to congratulate him on his identification when Roberts asks,

'Is there anybody else in the house? Wasn't Mr. Theobald's aunt staying with you?'

'I told you yesterday, inspector, she was here but she's gone home.'

Ian twists in his seat and cranes his neck up at the painting. Though they are hidden from view by the sergeant, Alice imagines his and Polly's knees are almost touching.

'Ah yes, I remember now. Sorry. It's been a busy twenty four hours. Sergeant, perhaps you'd take this young man,' she nods in Jesse's direction.

'Jesse,' says Jesse, 'but that's not my real name...'

'Alright, Jesse, I don't think Inspector Roberts has time for all that now,' says Alice.

'Come on, then, Jesse, what about a kickabout?'

'I'd rather play cricket.'

'Good man. So would I. Do you bat or bowl?'

'And Mr. Slight,' says Roberts, 'perhaps you'd go with them.'

'I'd like him to stay,' says Polly.

Roberts looks as though she is about to object, but then thinks better of it. 'Very well,' she says, 'If that's alright with your mother.'

Alice nods, not trusting herself to speak. Polly's hand creeps across the brown leather cushions towards Ian's. Ian links his fingers in his lap. Polly's curl in on themselves, tighten into a fist.

'May I?' Roberts moves towards the chair where Alice had been sitting earlier.

'Of course.'

'Now, Polly,' Roberts begins. Alice half expects her to ask, are you sitting comfortably? 'I don't want you to be alarmed. We're talking to everyone who was at last night's beach party.'

'My daughter came home early, inspector.'

'The thing is, Polly, a young man's been found dead. I wonder, did you see anything? People fighting maybe?'

Polly shrugs. 'No, I didn't. But like mum said, I left early.' She stares at Roberts. Roberts stares back.

'Ah yes, because you had an accident. What sort of accident?'

'Just, you know, drank too much,' Polly mumbles, fiddling with her friendship bracelets. It's her tell, she always does it when she's lying. But why is she lying, Alice wonders?

'The thing is, Polly,' Roberts continues, 'although we don't yet have a formal identification, several people have told us the dead man worked here, as a security guard. Your friend, Madeleine Manning, told us he chaperoned you to the party.'

'Oh my god,' says Alice, frantically trying to remember which of the Jedwards had accompanied the girls. Was it Jack, or Dean? Or was his name Craig? For some reason, she always manages to muddle those two names up.

'Your accident couldn't have had anything to do with him, could it?'

'No,' says Polly, still now, leaning slightly forward, shoulders squared, staring, gimlet-eyed, at the detective, who seems to decide on a strategic withdrawal.

'Well, if there's nothing you can tell us,' she rises, 'I'll go and find my sergeant and we'll leave you to your lunch. Smells very good.' At the snug door, she pauses and adds, 'It was probably an accident anyway. Looks as though he tripped and hit his head on one of those concrete blocks. Probably drunk. You should be more careful who you employ, Mrs. Theobald.'

'I shall sack the firm,' says Alice. She will have to, she can no longer afford them. Only once Inspector Roberts has stumped off across the hall in search of her sergeant does Alice realise she said 'I'. 'I', not 'we'. She sends up a sort of silent prayer to Harry to forgive her.

She should ask Ian to leave, she thinks, returning to the snug. How can they all sit down to lunch in the shadow of that poor boy's death, even if neither Polly nor Ian knows anything about it? Yet she doesn't want to be alone with her children, to see the rest of the day stretching empty before her with nothing to occupy her but the routine of preparing for Monday; the ironing of shirts, the packing of school bags, the goading into homework; and all the while, the thorny entanglements that now beset her creeping closer, growing higher.

'Well,' she says, rather more briskly than she intends, 'we shouldn't let the food go to waste. What help would that be?' Sobs well in her throat, taking her unawares; she coughs to clear them; what help would tears be? 'And Jesse's already at the table so we'd better get a move on if we don't want to find everything's been eaten.' She forces a smile.

Lunch is a subdued affair. Only Jesse keeps up a barrage of conversation, about his custard-making skills, and Sergeant Belshaw being a good fast bowler, and George not having fixed the rowing boat yet, and needing his mother's help with his geometry homework. Nobody mentions the dead man.

Alice doesn't ask Ian to carve, but sets about the leg of lamb herself with a brutal competence that reminds him of sergeant majors he has known, men who inspired a comforting kind of fear. She takes her place at the head of the table, with her back to the Aga, and seats Ian to her right. The children sit next to each other on the other side of the table, Polly opposite him. Alice hands vegetables in an assortment of vividly decorated tureens with impractical handles. He feels as though he is being set some sort of test, a feeling which is reinforced by the intense, unblinking stare fixed on him by Polly as she pushes food around her plate. It's unlikely, he supposes, that she really is daring him to break a vegetable dish, but he prefers to imagine she is; it's easier than any of the alternatives.

'Have you finished with that?' Alice asks Polly eventually. She hasn't eaten more than a couple of mouthfuls, even though the food is delicious, the meat tender and delicately pink, seasoned with garlic and rosemary, the vegetables no doubt from the walled kitchen garden he has noticed stretching away from the southern wings of the house.

'Sorry, mum, not hungry. I think I might go and lie down, actually. D'you mind?' She appears to address the question to Ian, but he doesn't answer it; it's only because she's sitting directly opposite him that she seems to be speaking to him.

'Alright, darling.' An anxious expression creases Alice's grave, oval face as she looks after her daughter. 'Perhaps you'd better have tomorrow off.'

'Yeah, maybe.' She casts a wan smile over her shoulder as she exits the kitchen.

'Can I have hers?' asks Jesse, pulling the plate towards him. It looks congealed and unappetising, but that doesn't seem to bother Jesse. What is he? Twelve, thirteen? Ian remembers that hunger, the ravenous indiscriminateness of it, the way it became mixed up with a more general hunger for life. Jesse's lucky; he can fill his belly, he can find his body's limits on the sportsfield, he can probably assuage some of his curiosity about the mysteries between girls' legs in the piss- and salt-smelling shade of the wartime gun emplacements on the cliff. None of that had been possible where Ian was when he was thirteen, passing wakeful nights under spilled light from corridors with a griping belly and a well-thumbed copy of *Mayfair*, smuggled in by Badass Billy's cousin, stowed under his mattress.

Alice casts Ian an apologetic look, which she holds a fraction of a second too long. Is she coming on to him? No, more likely he's reading more into her look than is there because he'd been recalling his early sexual awakening, if you could call it that. All the same, despite growing up almost entirely among men and boys, his instincts are usually pretty sound where women are concerned. He experiments with a sympathetic smile. She turns her gaze abruptly to her plate, and seems absorbed in aligning her knife and fork.

'What about that custard?' she asks Jesse. 'D'you want me to finish it for you?'

'Almost done,' he mumbles through a mouthful of food.

'Really, Jesse, manners. We have a guest!'

'Don't mind me. Boys are always starving. That right, mate?'

Jesse gives him a grateful beam, only slightly marred by some specks of broccoli stuck to his front teeth.

He finishes the custard himself, with an absorption that makes him oblivious to the desultory conversation that is barely maintained between Alice and Ian. Watching his creepily familiar profile bent over the saucepan, Ian feels himself drawn away from the comfortable, well-appointed kitchen, through a dark wormhole at the end of which is Craig's den in the railway embankment, smelling of damp soil and diesel. Craig's profile bent over Jimmy Jones, quiet now, a bubble of froth at the corner of his mouth. He refuses dessert.

'Nothing against your custard, mate, honest, but I'm stuffed.' He pats his stomach.

'It's a bit close for rhubarb crumble, isn't it?' remarks Alice, fanning herself with her napkin. The kitchen is very warm, thanks to the Aga, but only now does Ian notice that the breeze from the open window behind him has died away and that the light has thickened, as if a premature dusk is descending. 'I'll have some, though.'

He watches her plough through most of Jesse's idea of a small helping, her colour rising, a sheen of sweat breaking on her upper lip. At one point, she raises her arm to sweep her hair back from her forehead and he catches the pungency of her underarm sweat, overlaid with a sweet, floral perfume. Jesse wolfs a mountainous island of crumble rising out of a high sea of custard, then excuses himself, racing away from the table with some garbled announcement that he is going to see if George has mended his boat yet.

'A man of many parts, your George,' Ian remarks, winning nothing in reply but a faint smile from Alice. Too much crumble, or something to do with George?

'Ian..?'

'Yes?'

'What did happen last night?'

Nothing to do with George or the crumble then. 'What's Polly told you?'

'Not much. Just that she got into trouble in the water and you brought her out.'

'Well then, that's about it.'

'And that boy dying like that?'

'I should think it's just like the cops said. He got drunk and fell. There was a lot of booze about, and drugs, I expect.'

'Was Polly..?'

'Drunk? Stoned? None of my business. You'd have to ask her.'

'You're very loyal,' she says, not sounding as though she means it as a compliment.

'Not me. I just like to stay out of other people's business, that's all.'

'If you save a life, though...doesn't that life become your business in some way?' She refills her wine glass; she has moved on to red over lunch and her lips, he notices now, are stained purple. Merlot. It's about the only thing he knows about grape varieties, that merlot stains the lips and teeth. He used to laugh about it with Tara, that come-on merlot smile that drunk girls would turn on equally drunk men at the end of an evening in the pub.

'Doesn't it?' Alice repeats when he makes no reply. The flat, northern vowels have crept back into her voice.

Lives taken, lives saved. Are they all his responsibility? Hasn't he got enough on just trying to drag his own basket case of a life from one day to the next?

'I'm sorry, love,' he says, 'but if your daughter's taking stuff she shouldn't be it's for you to sort out, not me. The Good Samaritan left a purse, he didn't hang about to mop up the other bloke's shit in person.'

'Oh, a religious man.' She sounds distinctly tipsy now. He wonders if he should take her glass away from her, but doesn't.

'Once.'

'What changed?'

'It's a long story.'

'I've got all the time in the world.' She flings out her arms; he snatches the wine bottle out of the way just in time.

'Well I've got just about time for a coffee, and it might be a good idea if you had one too.'

'I'm sorry,' she says, chastened, her vowels rounding out again, 'I'll put the kettle on.'

She stumbles as she rises from the table, putting her hand out to his shoulder to stop herself falling. He finds himself holding her by the waist, standing her up and steadying her as if she were a wobbling ornament, and then her arms are wound around his neck and she's trying to kiss him. He tastes second hand wine and tobacco; memories seep from his head to his loins, of willing girls and single beds, skimpy knickers lost down the backs of sofas along with empty vodka bottles. But it's not the sweet intimacy of kissing he wants to share with Alice Theobald.

Averting his head, he grazes the sinew between her neck and shoulder with his teeth, nips the skin until she cries out, with pain or pleasure, he neither knows nor cares. He runs his hand down her back, ignoring the zipper on her dress, pushes up under the hem, digs his fingers into the tender skin of her thighs, burrows into her panties, into her greedy little cunt. It's so easy he almost loses interest, until he reminds his flagging cock this is Craig's wife grappling with his flies, panting in his ear. Craig's life that he deserves since Craig took his own away from him.

He swats her hands away from his fly and bends her over the table. Her cheek slams against the waxed pine, upsetting the ashtray and sending a plate skittering to the floor. He holds her with one arm twisted behind her back, rips off her panties, unfastens himself and pushes into her. A throaty grunt escapes her, but she's not objecting. Far from it. She's slick as oil and arching her back to meet him, moving effortlessly into his rhythm.

Then suddenly, she stops. 'Polly,' she says, her voice deep and flat, weighted down with god knows what emotions. He's having enough trouble dealing with his own as his gaze flicks automatically towards the door from the hall and he sees her standing there, flushed and dishevelled from sleep, eyes saucered with shock. Within seconds he has pulled away from Alice and straightened his clothes, but Polly has already fled, leaving behind nothing of herself but the clatter of her feet on bare floorboards as she runs down the passage to the hall.

'Get out,' says Alice, pulling down her dress, looking, not at him, but at her discarded panties on the floor beneath the table. Her face is blotched with an angry flush and her mascara has run. He can see the beginnings of a bruise staining the cheekbone he slammed into the table. He grins; her shame is more than sufficient compensation for being caught by Polly. Being caught by Polly is, on reflection, the icing on the cake.

'Thanks for lunch,' he says. Despite the soupy thickness of the air, he moves lightly beneath the trees bordering the drive, and lets the sparse patter of raindrops among their leaves form a background to his thoughts. His grin broadens as he approaches the gatehouse, and the stand-off between press and security guards which has now developed the weary good humour of a longstanding picket line. He's walking away from another car crash, another bomb blast, but this time the catastrophe is one of his own making. He is not weighed down by grief or guilt or bewilderment as he slips through the gate with a jaunty wave at the assembled journalists. On the contrary, he seems almost to be carried on the current of the wind as he lopes down the sea-broken lane and across a stretch of sheep-bitten grass to the caravan site, and he's singing at the top of his voice. *Moonage Daydream.* Oh yeah. And it's like the words are forming in his mouth for the first time, like he was there when Ziggy Stardust burst into life. Free. Going into a record store with his pocket money, coming out lightning struck. Just like all the other kids of his generation.

Alice picks up her panties and steps back into them. She wonders about changing. Changing. It worked before, up to a point. The recollection of Nathan's voice on the phone, hesitant, querulous and then indignant, comes unbidden into her empty mind. She pushes it away; emptiness is preferable. She knows she should go and look for Polly, but she can't. Not yet. Not until she can think of something to say to her, but for now, she wants to take refuge in not thinking at all.

The remains of the meal scattered around the kitchen, the ash sprayed across the table, the shards of Susie Cooper on the floor, all seem to be pieces of a puzzle she can make no sense of. She starts moving pots and crockery about, but nothing she does appears to make any impression on the mess. Like rearranging the deckchairs on the *Titanic,* she thinks, oddly comforted by the familiar cliché. Then she realises, with blinding clarity, why it must have popped into her mind. It's telling her to go to her scrapbook. That's what she needs, to read the words and stare at the photos that have become so familiar to her they have succeeded in making order out of chaos.

She feels the quickening rain on her skin as if its outer layer has been peeled away. Her body cowers beneath the

battering of fat drops like tiny fists. Her bruises are beginning to ache, over her cheek and pelvic bones, on her wrist.
Walking sets up a sensation between her legs she calls pain,
but the definition sits uneasily on the empty floor of her
mind. It's too neat, too conscious. As she nears the studio,
she breaks into an awkward, shuffling run, bent over, hugging herself as though she has a gripe in her belly. She
fumbles the key in the lock in her haste, and feels tears
pricking behind her eyes. Her mind briefly entertains the
mad notion that her studio is refusing to admit her, punish-
ing her for what she has done. By the time she has managed
to open the door, the sobs are jostling in her throat, pressed
up against the barrier of her clenched teeth. It is not until
the scrapbook is in her hands, until she is thumbing the
familiar pages, releasing the crackle of old newspaper and
the dusty perfume of stale ink, that she feels calm again.

I lost track of time, she reads, curling herself into a corner of
the sofa under the skylight where she likes to sit and think, *You
start to hear this rumble. You hear this rumble. Everything is shaking.*
The dust covered the broken bodies on Vesey Street like a shroud.
More people appeared at upper storey windows crying soundlessly
for assistance.
New York City's medical examiners are still trying to identify 19,858
pieces smashed from the bodies of the 2,819 people who were slain.

Where are they all now, she wonders dreamily, thoughts and
images swimming through her mind, twisting and turning in
slow motion. Are they all bodies in the ground or ashes in the
air? How many of them walk among the ghosts she looks for,
every day, the ones whose eyes speak the same language as
hers, whose steps teeter on edges, whose fingertips brush fine,
dusty curtains that are forever threatening to disintegrate?

Day Nine

'**M**um.' Polly's voice is low and sullen, but it cuts easily through Alice's ragged sleep. She sits up, blinking in the light falling through the skylight, feeling her vertebrae grind together like small stones as she straightens them. Her mouth feels as though it is full of concrete dust and there seems to be a hammer pounding at the back of her right eye. She must have had more wine at lunch than she thought. Lunch. Polly. Oh god.

'Darling...' She tries a smile, feels her lips crack and a film of something on her teeth. She reaches out a hand towards Polly, who hovers in the studio doorway, ready for flight.

Polly shakes her head. 'Those detectives are here again.'

Suddenly, her head is as clear as if she has run it under a cold tap, and the cold is seeping along her veins as her mood adjusts from guilt and bewilderment to dread.

'They're waiting in the drawing room. They wouldn't tell me what they wanted.' Polly turns on her heel.

'Polly! Wait.'

She stops, but keeps her back to Alice, shoulders hunched. 'Don't, Mum.'

'Why are you in your uniform?'

'Because it's Monday?'

'Monday?'

'You were out here all night. I got Jesse up. He's having breakfast.'

'OK, thank you. I'll be in in a minute. I just need to...'

'Yeah,' says Polly, with a contemptuous glance over her shoulder, 'you'd do better not looking like some wrecked party animal.' She goes back to the house, slamming the studio door behind her, setting the dust dancing under the skylight.

Alice goes to the studio sink and sluices water over her face and neck. She gargles, and rubs her teeth with her finger, then pauses to check her reflection in a cheval glass she is restoring. She looks terrible, her linen dress crumpled, makeup smeared under her eyes, hair hanging in rats' tails. A bruise darkens her right cheek like purple blusher. Will they know, she wonders? Will surly Inspector Roberts and suave Sergeant Belshaw be able to read the clues?

Walking into the kitchen, where the remains of the children's breakfast has been added to the residue of yesterday's lunch, though someone has picked up the shards of broken plate and stacked them on the counter, she feels so sick she has to rush to the sink. She grips the counter edge, swallows down her bile and forces herself to take two or three deep breaths, drawing the cool morning air from the open window into her lungs. Her Camels and lighter are still on the table. She taps a cigarette out of the pack, puts it between her lips and lights it. As she contemplates the upturned ashtray, the bruise on her cheek begins to throb and an insistent physical memory makes itself known in a shifting and sharpening between her legs.

Roberts holds up a plastic evidence bag. It's exactly the same as the Ziploc bags into which Alice seals fruit and vegetables for freezing. Except that in this bag is not a pound of blueberries or runner beans but a gold cigarette lighter. 'I'm sorry, Mrs. Theobald,' the woman says, 'but if you can identify it, it may helps us to shed some light on your husband's disappearance.'

They are standing either side of the drawing room fireplace, in a drift of scent from the flowers in the grate. Peonies, heliotrope, lilac. Their combined perfumes are suffocating and sickly; Alice cannot now imagine why she believed they would work together. Roberts steps across the Voysey rug and holds up the bag again. Alice glances only briefly at the lighter, which she recognises immediately.

'Is this your husband's lighter?'

'Yes, inspector.'

'You're sure?'

'Of course I am. I gave it to him.' Her joke. A lighter with which to light her cigarettes. If Harry had ever smoked, he had stopped by the time he met Alice. 'How...I mean, where was it found?'

'Why don't you sit down, Mrs. Theobald?' asks the ever-solicitous Sergeant Belshaw. Roberts takes the lead, perching on the edge of one of the pair of Stickley Morris chairs flanking the fireplace. Alice follows suit, joining the sergeant on the chesterfield.

'Black Range Rover, registration...' There is a pause while Roberts unearths her police notebook from her handbag and flips through the pages. 'FH57XSJ. Registered to GardenMart plc.'

'That's my husband's, inspector, to save you having to ask.'

'Late last night some likely lad in Blackpool turned himself in for stealing it from a service station on the M6. Fancied giving his girlfriend a night out in a swish motor, apparently. Anyway, when they hopped over into the back seat so she could fully express her gratitude, they found they weren't alone. There was a body hidden under a load of clothes in the tailgate. No wallet, but a mobile phone registered to your husband. And Blackpool Police found the lighter on chummy when they arrested him.' Roberts stares expectantly at Alice but she has no idea what is expected of her so she just nods, her mind an exhausted blank.

'I'm afraid we shall need you to come to Inverness,' says Sergeant Belshaw.

'Inverness?' Why Inverness? Is there some mysterious bureaucratic process whereby all unidentified dead bodies are stored in Inverness, out on the far borders of the kingdom where they cannot pollute the lives of its citizens. She has a vision of giant filing cabinets, the dead stacked in their drawers, hugging clipboards to their chests with piously crossed arms. She sees Harry, feels the darkness pressing down on the membrane of his open eyes, filling his mouth and stopping his ears, the cold black of the inside of a fridge crushing his ribs.

She doubles over and draws her knees to her chest; if she makes herself the smallest possible target for the juggernaut of pain that is hurtling towards her, perhaps it will miss. She will pass between its wheels like a curled up hedgehog. Dimly, she is aware of the young sergeant leaning towards of her, of a calm voice asking if she would like a glass of water. Its utter professional indifference tells her how alone she is; no-one else can experience what is happening to her at this moment so what is the point of wasting her effort trying to communicate it. She will need all her strength for herself and her children in the coming days.

A glass of water is placed in her hand. She drinks from it.

'It seems that whatever...happened, happened in the Highland jurisdiction,' says Belshaw. As he explains that the trip to Inverness will involve an overnight stay because of flight times, she listens carefully and nods in all the right places, but all she really hears is Daisy scrabbling at the kitchen door, trying to escape.

The beach is deserted, a thin strip of greyish shingle between the crumbling cliffs and a sullen high tide. Half-submerged lumps of concrete stick out eerily from the water, looming through the steady mizzle to which the heavier rain of yesterday has given way. Ian walks the short distance to the water's edge and gazes out to sea. There is no wind and the sea stretches, pewter-dull and featureless to a blurred horizon. A couple of oil rigs loom, little more than concentrations of a denser grey, and a ghostly container ship moves across his field of vision from left to right. Its slow pace is hypnotic, keeping him there, in the grip of a lassitude that is more than the aftermath of yesterday's exultation. It's as though he's waiting for something. It's the way they all used to feel waiting to go into action, tense, yet inert, as though their lives had been suspended somehow.

He's shaken out of it by a voice calling his name, thin and high as the call of a gull. Turning towards it, he spies two small figures standing at the top of the steps leading to the caravan site. They are very still; they, too, are waiting. When you spend your life running, you notice stillness, you notice those who wait, in case it's you they want; even when they're smiling, you hope their smiles are directed over your shoulder, at someone else. You never want to be found. He stops a moment, assessing them, then the taller of them begins to wave. It's Polly. His stomach clenches. As he reaches the bottom of the steps, she runs down them to meet him, followed by Jesse, their feet clanging on the aluminium.

'It's Dad.' Polly is breathless, and will not look him in the eye. Just as well.

'What's happened?'

Jesse sidles up to him and noses his hand into Ian's. He feels Jesse's eyes on him, burning blue, as Polly tells him their mother has to go to Scotland to identify a body. 'But she says it might not be him,' she concludes, and suddenly looks straight at Ian. He feels ashamed. Her gaze pleads with him to make it not be her father, to save her. Again. Then her eyes slide away from his face and she adds, in a tone he cannot fathom, 'but they've found his lighter or something, so I suppose it must be.'

Harry's lighter? Fuck. How did he miss that? Still, it's a relief to think he won't be making any more phone calls about Jimmy Jones.

'Aunt Mary's coming back,' says Jesse, 'and Five-O are sending a...'

'Family support officer,' says Polly.

'Can we stay here with you?' Jesse pleads.

'I'm leaving today. I should be gone already really. You have to go home. Your mum needs to know you're at home. Safe.' He starts up the steps.

'We don't want to be left with a cop,' whines Jesse. Ian wonders how Polly feels about that; after what she saw yesterday, he wouldn't blame her if a cop was her preferred option.

'Your auntie'll be here soon.'

'Not before Mum has to go. She has to go straight away.'

At the top of the steps he turns on them. 'Then you have to go and say goodbye to her.' *Say goodnight to your mam, Arthur. No. No, he won't. He's fed up of his mam lying in a hospital bed. He wants her home, baking cakes, matching socks, telling him off for not tidying his room when she trips over his Dinky cars. And then, next day, the bed is empty, stripped, and the next time he sees her is when she's laid out in their front parlour, in her wedding dress, with her beads wound round her fingers, smelling of furniture polish and formaldehyde.* 'Christ!' he yells as the children hover, looking mutinous, 'Don't you think she's got enough to worry about without you two going AWOL? Why don't you bloody well try not thinking about yourselves for once and piss off back where you belong? I've got nothing for you. Nothing. D'you understand?'

They slink away, mute with shock, like a pair of whipped dogs, and as soon as he looks in the direction of his caravan, he wishes he'd kept them with him.

Bernard is lounging against one wheel arch. 'Not much of a morning for a stroll,' he remarks as Ian approaches the van, though he's watching the children trudge towards the gate rather than looking at Ian. 'I was thinking you'd probably already left when I got no reply at the door. But you've got less sense than I credited you with. And that wasn't much, frankly.' His tone is dangerously casual.

Ian lets himself into the van and begins to strip off his wet teeshirt. Bernard follows him and sits himself down at the table. He becomes aware the landlord is staring at the skin graft on his forearm, the one where he'd written down Mary's phone number, so long ago it seems now, yet it was only the day before yesterday.

'Suppose they let you out early, did they, on condition you joined up? They used to do that, didn't they?'

'Only in wartime.'

'Still, army's not fussy, is it? They want killers, don't they?'

'Look, mate, I've had a fuck of a day already and I haven't even had breakfast yet, so why don't you just get to the point and piss off?'

Bernard leans forward, resting his forearms on the table and linking his fingers. His movements are slow, deliberate; he's savouring his moment.

'Abigail Jones,' he says.

'Who's Abigail Jones?' asks Ian. Jones is a common name.

'Mrs. Jones? Had a kid called Jimmy. You remember Jimmy.'

Ian moves towards the table and stands opposite Bernard. He glares at the landlord for a few seconds; he figures that, if Bernard thinks he knows who he is, he'll be able to scare him off. But he quickly realises that isn't going to work. Bernard looks like a terrier with a rat.

'I remember Jimmy,' says Ian quietly, keeping his tone flat, emotionless. 'He was blond. He had chubby red cheeks. He was what they used to call bonny in them days.'

'Died young, though, eh?'

Ian folds his arms, then wishes he hadn't, then calculates that if he drops them to his sides again he will somehow have given himself away. 'Aye,' he says.

'Abigail Jones was his mother.'

'And what d'you think she's to do with me?'

'There's been something nagging away at the back of my mind since I took the pub here. Something about Harry Theobald. He always reminded me of someone, but I could never think who. Well, I didn't let it worry me. I was used to famous faces in my last line of work so I thought it was just that I must have seen his picture. Then, when the talk began about him not coming back from his trip to Scotland, I thought a bit more. I did a bit of digging in some of my old files, talked to a few people I used to know, and realised I'd actually never seen a picture of him. Not of Harry Theobald, at any rate.' He pauses, meaningfully.

'And what was your line of work, Bernard?'

'Private detective. Used to do a bit here and there for the tabloids. Standing up stories for them, that sort of thing.' He sounds proud of himself.

190

'Lucrative, I'd have thought. More money in it than running a village pub any road.'

Bernard looks shifty. 'Like I said,' he resumes, but his voice has lost some of its confidence, 'I realised I'd never seen a picture of Mr. Theobald, which I thought was odd enough in itself, given who he is. But that didn't explain why I thought I recognised him. Then you turned up.'

The irony of it. He wonders if Craig would have appreciated that, and thinks probably not. Earnest little shit was Craig. Intense. They'd probably have a label for him nowadays. They'd probably have a label for them both. 'So I did. Tell me, is this story going on much longer only I really haven't much time.' He gives his watch a theatrical glance; it hasn't worked since his wrestle in the sea with Polly.

'Asking about Wildwood. Too much of a coincidence in my book. Like you say, there isn't a lot of money in running a country pub these days, not unless you've got a fancy chef anyway. So I thought it might be worth my while having a little look round, see if I could turn up anything my old Fleet Street associates would be interested in. I found a post-it note in Harry's study.'

How the fuck had he got in there, Ian wonders, feeling a momentary, grudging respect for the man.

'It had Abigail Jones and a phone number written on it. When I rang the number, it was an old people's home near Sheffield. Jones. Sheffield. Penny dropping yet, is it?'

'Go on. Enlighten me.'

'Turns out Harry Theobald pays old Mrs. Jones' not inconsiderable fees for living out her twilight years at some place called Autumn Glade Therapeutic and Residential Complex in Wortley. And the minute I found that out, the rest slotted into place like a Rubik's fucking cube. He's not changed much, has he? And nor have you, Arthur, under all that bloody hair. Popped to the library in Holt. Quick trawl of the papers on the old microfiche and there you both were. 19th December 1967. Found guilty of the murder of Jimmy Jones, aged sixteen months. Indefinite detention.'

Ian manages a few rounds of slow applause; it covers him while he wonders what he's going to say. All his adult life he's feared this day would come, and now it has, he just feels blank, empty, wiped clean of thought, emotion, and anything in any way resembling a plan. He feels tears of frustration welling up in him and wrestles them down. The thought that he might cry now, in front of this cheapskate gumshoe, infuriates him. He's never cried, not since his dad said, here, lad, blow your nose, your mam wouldn't want to see you crying. You and me, he said, we've got to take care of little Danny now. Then his dad wrapped the car round a tree, and little Danny, baby Danny, unscathed by life, sat in the road after the crash without a mark on him, got himself a nice new family while he got Appsley House and fat Janet and Craig Barnes. What was the fucking use in crying?

He fights down the anger too. Save it, he tells himself, save it till you need it.

'Imagine,' says Bernard, taking a little bow, 'what some of my old contacts'd pay to know the sainted Harry Theobald was really Craig Barnes, notorious child killer.'

'And me?'

'Oh you, you're just collateral damage, mate. I could keep you out of it. No need for anyone to even know you were here, let alone taking midnight swims with his underage daughter.'

'That wasn't...'

'I don't give a shit what it was. I'm a practical man, Arthur, not a moral crusader. Live and let live, I say. Pity you don't feel the same. The mind of a killer, eh? What a mystery that is.'

Ready, steady, go, he says to himself, out loud, as if he's starting a race, and shoves the pushchair as hard as he can.

Letting the fury well up in him unchecked, Ian lunges across the table, grabs Bernard by his ears and slams his head several times into the table top. Bernard, with a nimbleness that takes Ian by surprise, tears himself free, clambers on to the table and hurls himself at Ian, knocking him to the floor. He's only winded for a second or two, but it's long enough for Bernard to straddle his chest, pinning down his arms with his knees, and land a stinging punch on his nose. He feels blood trickling into the back of his throat. The fear of choking surges through him, twisting him out from beneath Bernard's bulky form and back on to his feet. He delivers an upper cut to Bernard's cheek that would have made his army boxing coach proud, ducks and dodges a hook from Bernard whose momentum throws the bigger man off balance for a second. Ian hooks a foot around his ankle and Bernard goes sprawling, but he's quick for a big man and is back on his feet, his elbow in Ian's ribs, before Ian can take advantage of his fall.

Pain shoots through his chest, jarring his heart. He's dizzy, can't breathe. The bastard must have broken at least one rib. That thought makes him angry enough to focus, but it's too late. Bernard's meaty paw is clutching his throat as if he's about to use it to pull a pint. He really is seeing stars, blinding explosions that shoot across the black, empty sky of his brain. And die.

A police car awaits them on the tarmac as they disembark at Inverness Airport, a fact which seems to make DCI Roberts furious. But then, as Alice has learned during the journey, and the stopover at Edinburgh, where the grimy transit lounge windows gave on to a vista of the tram works, everything seems to make DI Roberts furious.

'Discreet,' she hears her mutter to Sergeant Belshaw as they pass under the wing of the aircraft into a sudden, buffeting wind. Alice is shocked by the cold and the greyness of the light. She doesn't want Harry to be dead here, in this bleak, liminal place, alone, here, so far from his bright and intricate garden, his children, his dog. She swallows tears, then finds herself smiling as a crumpled figure emerges from the police car and waits, leaning against it as if he's no more than a paper bag blown up against it by the wind. He has thick, curly hair, greying chestnut, whipping about his face and is swathed in a gabardine trenchcoat that looks several sizes too big. Colombo, she thinks, with a surge of nostalgic warmth. Colombo had been her dad's favourite, one of the few things that could erase the haunted look from his eyes and soften the bitter set of his mouth. Oh...ah...just one more thing, he'd say as he packed her off upstairs to bed, and she'd turn on the stair, and they'd laugh, and be a normal family for a few seconds. That reminds her...she reaches into her handbag to turn on her phone.

'Steyn,' he says, pushing himself away from the car and holding out a hand to Belshaw.

'This is DI Roberts,' says Belshaw, presenting Roberts as if she were a debutante being presented to the Queen, 'and Mrs. Theobald.' They all look at Alice as if she were an invalid.

'Pleased to meet you. I hope your flight was OK.' The Colombo spell is broken; his accent is South African. 'Shall we?' He takes Alice's overnight bag and puts it into the boot of the car. She sits in the back, between Belshaw and Roberts, thankful not to be near a window and prey to the curious looks of their fellow travellers as the car pulls away across the tarmac.

'We'll go straight to the hospital now,' says Steyn, turning to face them, one elbow crooked around the front passenger seat headrest, 'if that's alright with you, Mrs. Theobald.'

'Yes,' says Alice, feeling Roberts fuming beside her. 'I would like to get this over with as quickly as possible. The uncertainty...' Her voice fails her. Does she really want to know? Isn't the uncertainty in many ways kinder, even if it is merely a balm slicked over her pain like one of Isabella's anti-wrinkle creams.

The car is stuffy after the sharp wind racing across the tarmac, and Alice thinks she must have dozed off, because no sooner has the police driver pulled away from the airport than he is slowing up in front of the main entrance to Raigmore Hospital, under a broad porch where several patients in dressing gowns, hooked up to drips on wheeled stands, are smoking on benches. She panics; she needs more time; her mind has not yet shifted from the set of the docile, herded traveller into the place it needs to be to do this. What place is that anyway? She doesn't know.

Suddenly Nathan is in her thoughts. He knows. Perhaps she should call him. Before she goes in. He's left his number; when she turned the house phones back on before leaving, there was another message from him. He wants her to call. She could sit here, among the smokers, have a cigarette herself, maybe even blag a light off one of them, smile, exchange pleasantries, and call Nathan. If she can just hear his voice, knowing he has been through this and survived, it will be enough to make her calm and brave.

She mustn't break down, not in front of Harry. One of the things he had always loved about her, he said, was her self-possession. Her cool, he confided to her many months later, was what had decided him in her favour when she pitched for the contract to decorate display conservatories

for GardenMart. He had thought her design ideas deriva-
tive and unremarkable, if he was honest (they weren't hers,
she'd retaliated, as they were being honest), but he had liked
her presentation. There was an underlying detachment
which challenged him. Not the short skirt and tight blouse
then, she'd asked. I don't notice clothes, he'd quipped
back, just bodies, and there'd been a darkness behind those
blue, matinee idol eyes that spoke to something in her. She
has never understood quite what, still doesn't, but nor does
she believe love can be subjected to reasoning and analysis
and survive. She has tried to be what Harry wants. She has
a reputation, admittedly small, because she is first and fore-
most Harry's wife, for an original eye. She has kept alight
Harry's desire for her body, even though childbirth has left
her looser and thinner than before. She has maintained her
reserve, and she must do so now.

'Mrs. Theobald?' prompts Belshaw. Steyn and Roberts
are already through the sliding doors.

'Yes. Sorry,' says Alice and goes inside.

They enter a lift and descend to the hospital basement.
Facing them as the lift door opens are ladies and gents
cloakrooms.

'I must just...' says Alice, and dashes into the ladies. She
doesn't go into a cubicle but stands in front of the mirror
and assesses herself. Whatever Harry says, she does notice
clothes; he would notice if she didn't. She has on a flowered cotton dress with a scooped neck, button-through
bodice and calf length skirt. Over it she wears a yellow knitted jacket, under it a white cotton bra and panties. Safe.
Conservatively feminine.

The first time Harry fucked her, she was wearing cow-
girl boots. Cuban heels and silver toe caps. The first time
Harry fucked her he'd taken her to lunch at the Manoir

aux Quat' Saisons, where he'd overwhelmed her by chatting to Raymond Blanc about his herb garden as if they were old friends, and she'd worried about her nipples showing through her tight brown sweater. The first time Harry fucked her was in his Aston Martin DB5, in a lay-by on the A329. Who's fucking who, he'd asked, when she tried, halfheartedly to demur. You can't sit opposite a man all through lunch in a sweater like that and not expect to be ravished. Ravished. Hah. They've had jokes about ravishing lay-bys all their married life; even their children have adopted them, making up their own stories about what makes a lay-by ravishing, stories that have changed as they've grown. With a curdling of her guts, she wonders what stories Polly will tell now, after what she had witnessed the day before.

'Are you alright?' Roberts is standing behind her, her face dough-pale, puffy and cross.

'Yes, yes I'm fine.' Alice puts down her handbag between two washbasins, fishes out her make-up case and begins to apply lipstick. She sprays perfume on her wrists and throat and combs her hair. 'There,' she says, more to herself than Roberts, 'I'm ready now.'

The mortuary is behind swing doors made of heavy duty black rubber and scuffed by the corners of many metal trolleys. As soon as they have passed through these, Alice's eyes begin to smart. A smell like burning plastic mixed with disinfectant pervades the air. They are met by a young mortuary attendant who apologises as Steyn starts coughing.

'Formaldehyde,' apologises the mortuary attendant.

'Never get used to it,' says Steyn.

'You get a lot of suspicious deaths up here, do you?' asks Roberts, and Belshaw looks briefly as though he would like to add his boss to the list.

'I'm from Johannesburg,' says Steyn.

The mortuary attendant halts outside a door whose gold-lettered plaque informs them it is the chapel of rest.

'Mrs. Theobald,' says Steyn, 'this will be hard for you. Let me explain what you will see when we go inside.' Alice shakes her head but Steyn persists. 'it will be better for you to be prepared. The body will be covered when we enter...'

No need for you to accompany Mrs. Theobald, DI Steyn,' Roberts butts in. 'This is my case.'

'As you know, Inspector Roberts, we have witness evidence that suggests the fatal blow was probably inflicted in Glencoe. With respect, that makes it my case.'

'Please!' shouts Alice, patting at the air in front of her. Roberts and Steyn stare at her. 'This isn't some kind of pissing contest. This is my husband we're talking about. For god's sake have some respect.'

In the chastened silence that ensues, the mortuary attendant pushes open the chapel door.

'You need only look at the face,' Steyn persists. 'You need say nothing. I will ask you if it is your husband. You just nod or shake your head, that will be enough. This gentleman,' he indicates the mortuary attendant, a freckled, sandy haired young man with pronounced blue shadows beneath his eyes, 'will witness the exchange.' The mortuary attendant fixes wide, pale eyes on Alice and gives her a doubtful smile. She pities his youth; this isn't a job for a boy; already he looks as though working in this place is draining the life from him.

The body lies on a plain wooden catafalque in the middle of the room. An altar stands at one end, beneath a hideous stained glass window in an angular, abstract design and garish colours. The altar looks like a school dining table, improbably adorned with some silk flowers and a pair of electric candles which emit a flickering sodium glow. The room is cold and stinks of air freshener. Alice finds she would prefer the formaldehyde; at least that's honest.

She stares at the shroud, trying to puzzle out the meanings of its different protuberances. Feet, folded hands, raised chin, forehead. Nothing unexpected, nothing missing or bent out of shape. A blow to the back of the head, they had told her, yet she had worried. That he would be broken or twisted in some way. The attendant lays a hand on an upper corner of the shroud and casts her a questioning look. She nods. What has she to fear? She knows the dead. The crushed, the drowned, the blown to pieces. And the survivors' stories too, the relief, the exultation, the empty spaces and the guilt that rushes into them. She steps forward. She is prepared.

But she isn't. Not at all. It's like the difference between reading about childbirth and the real thing.

The face revealed as the orderly turns back the sheet is not Harry. It has Harry's features, but it is not Harry's face.

'Is this your husband, Mrs. Theobald?' asks Steyn, and she shakes her head.

'I mean...' she begins, catching sight of his expression. What she wants to say is that it is him, his body, but not *him*. His soul, if there is such a thing, is gone. What remains is a waxwork, a death mask. 'Yes,' she says, 'yes, this is my husband's body.'

And he has left her without saying goodbye.

And without giving her the chance to confess and be shriven. The bruises on her cheek and hips and wrist begin to throb, reminding her how alive she is.

'Thank you, Mrs. Theobald.' Steyn takes her arm to escort her from the chapel, but she cannot move. It is as though the link between her brain and the nerves in her legs has been severed. Though she knows, in her rational mind, that Harry is not here, her body clings to the catafalque, her hands clutching at the shroud in case he's hidden somewhere beneath it, if not in that dead face, in some other part of his body. He can't have simply vanished, without a word, without a sign. He wouldn't do that to her, not after nineteen years of marriage. He stayed with her after the miscarriage, didn't he? He didn't have to do that. And all the times she's been evasive, been unable to answer his questions, he showed no jealousy, no curiosity, merely stopped asking.

Perhaps he didn't love her after all. Perhaps, at that stage in his life, he had decided to acquire a wife, and now he needs a widow. Images crowd in on her: the faces of her children, wan and reproachful, bank statements covered in zeroes and minus signs; Abigail Jones fighting to keep a biscuit tin closed on a procession of tin soldiers, each bearing the same expressionless, waxy, handsome face. Anger flares in her like an icy fire. It's Harry's fault she did that... that *thing* with Ian. Snatching her arm from Steyn's grip, she pulls it back and slaps Harry's face with as much force as she is capable of. 'How could you?' she demands, 'How could you do this to me? Leave me like this? I don't even know what hymns you'd like at your funeral for god's sake.'

'Look, this has been tough for you. You should get some rest. We can talk about everything else tomorrow,' says Steyn.

'Everything else? If there's more, inspector, I want to hear it now, not tomorrow. Tomorrow, I want to make arrangements to take my husband home. I want to get back to my children. I don't imagine there's anything you have to tell me that can make things worse than they already are. My husband is dead, inspector.'

'Very well,' Steyn stands a little straighter, his tone loses the soft edge of sympathy, 'then we should go to the police station from here and complete the formalities.'

The mortuary attendant takes his cue and draws the shroud back over Harry's face. Alice turns away; it's not Harry; whatever story is written on that body lies in the past now.

At the police station, Steyn installs Alice, Roberts and Belshaw in a witness interview room. It has high, glass brick windows which admit very little of the grey outside light, furniture fastened to the floor and overhead lights guarded by steel mesh grilles. Alice imagines it is only distinguishable from the rooms where suspects are questioned by the livid prints of Highland scenery on the walls. Alice takes a chair, Belshaw waits beside the door and Roberts prowls in a hostile silence, her rubber soled shoes squeaking on the lino floor until Alice feels ready to tear them from her feet and batter her about the head with them.

Steyn returns with a slender manila folder which he places on the metal table before sitting down opposite Alice.

'Now,' he says, turning a little in his chair to include Roberts and Belshaw, 'the information we have that makes us think that whatever led to your husband's death began here in the Highlands, Mrs. Theobald.'

'What information?' Roberts looks hurt, as though she has just discovered a lover cheating on her.

'We have a witness statement that suggests Mr. Theobald may have been in a fight a few hours before his death.'

'A fight?' Harry involved in a physical fight is beyond Alice's imagining. All Harry fights with is recalcitrant weeds. Then a memory comes to her unbidden, of Harry beating a rat with the flat of a spade. He had the creature cornered in one of the greenhouses. Drawn by the unaccustomed movement she had paused in whatever she was doing to watch, and what she remembers now is not the savagery of the attack but the expression on Harry's face once the rat was dead. He had not looked disgusted, or even triumphant, at the wretched little heap of blood and fur on the tiled floor, but curious, the way Jesse is with his skulls.

'I take it Mr. Theobald wasn't in the habit of fighting,' says Steyn.

'Of course not.'

'Well, what do we know about other people? The longer I'm in this job, the more often I ask myself that question.' Roberts looks as though she is about to say something, but Steyn doesn't give her the chance. 'I'm afraid it means you can't take your husband home with you, Mrs. Theobald. The Fiscal will have to decide if there's evidence of criminal activity before he'll release Mr. Theobald for burial.'

'Mr. Steyn,' says Alice, 'please just explain everything to me. I'm confused. My husband's body is discovered in his car in Blackpool.' *A school trip in year nine. Riding the Revolution. Grabbing hold of Nathan's hand as they went into the loop. Telling herself this was love. The smell of hot oil and popcorn and* Rive Gauche *borrowed from her mum.* 'By this time the car has been stolen from a service station on the M6, and now you tell me the injury that killed him was probably inflicted in Glencoe.'

Steyn shuffles the papers in his file until he finds what he is looking for. Roberts plumps down in a chair beside Alice and even cool Sergeant Belshaw moves from his station by the door to look over Steyn's shoulder as he scans the witness statement. 'This is from a Tara Warwick, a barmaid at the Head of Etive. It's a walkers' pub up in the glen. A lot of casuals at this time of year. Anyway, she called in at the station in Fort William on the...17th to say her boyfriend had gone missing. She told them she'd last seen him talking to a man she didn't recognise in the pub car park just after closing on the Saturday night. He told her to go on to bed and he'd be with her shortly. She was staying in a staff chalet bordering the car park so, though she says she didn't see anything more, she heard raised voices, then sounds of a struggle, then a car driving at speed out of the car park. And she'd not seen her boyfriend since. She was able to give descriptions of the car, as it was the only one left in the car park by that time, and the man her boyfriend argued with, which fitted the details we'd had up from you.' Steyn nods at Roberts. 'She thought maybe her boyfriend had been hurt, but now it seems more likely it was the other way round.'

'Does this boyfriend have a name?' asks Roberts.

'Slight,' says Steyn. 'His name's Ian Slight.'

Stars. Exploding. Dying. Exploding. Insistent. Bang, bang, bang. Ian wishes they'd just shut the fuck up and leave him to sink back into the painless dark. But they won't. Blades of light are prising his eyelids apart, fists of air are pummelling his windpipe from the inside. There's a kind of rasping, gargling noise in his ears that he's afraid is coming from his own mouth, and with it the iron taste of blood. As he emerges grudgingly into consciousness, he realises the banging is not exploding stars but someone knocking on the caravan door. Light, rapid knocks that reverberate around his bruised brain like church bells too early on a hungover Sunday. He sits up and immediately wishes he hadn't. His nose throbs; he can see the swelling out of the inner corners of his eyes and wonders for a moment if the sockets have been somehow tilted towards the centre of his face. When he raises his hands to check, he sees his knuckles are grazed and swollen like those of an arthritic.

'OK, OK,' he says, 'I'm coming.' The knocking continues; his voice is so weak and hoarse he supposes the knocker hasn't heard it. He sits up, and almost faints from the pressure in his nose and the stabbing pain in his ribs. As he gathers himself for the effort of standing, he looks around the caravan. He's actually sitting on the edge of his own bed, he realises, which is almost as much a wonder to him as the fact that he's still alive. Most of the dolls' house kitchen cupboards appear to be smashed, as is the table in the bay window. Wedged between it and the window seat is...oh god.

'Ian! Let me in!' Polly Theobald. That's all he needs.

'Hang on a sec. I'm not decent.' Even he can hardly hear himself. As he finally manages to get to his feet, Polly bursts through the door as though she had expected it to be locked and found it open. Balanced on one foot she takes in the carnage, eyes slowly widening with a mixture of shock and a kind of glee.

'What..?' The question dies on her lips as she takes in the inert form of Bernard, lying face down between the table and the window seat, one arm hooked at an unnerving angle over the stretcher between the table legs. 'Is he dead?' she asks, coming to rest on both feet and closing the van door behind her.

'No,' says Ian, thankful for the shutting out of the daylight. The sun seems to have come out since he lost consciousness; he wonders how long ago that was. He's sure he can see the landlord breathing, and refuses to entertain the notion that the slight movement could be a trick of the light. The last thing he can remember is Bernard's hands around his throat; he feels the pressure again, every time he swallows. 'There was a bit of a fight, that's all. He'll wake up soon.' They both stare at Bernard.

'You're always fighting,' Polly accuses.

'Not always.' Their eyes meet; hers seem much older than the rest of her, yet the voice in which she asks him why is that of a little girl, high and plaintive.

'Who knows?' he says. 'People don't always see things clearly when they're upset.'

'My mum didn't look upset.'

'It's a fine line, Polly, don't be too hard on her.'

'Why not? She deserves it.' She steps closer to him, so close he can smell her. Shampoo, some cheap, marshmallow perfume.

'What do you want, Polly?'

'You,' she says, with devastating simplicity.

He laughs, a horrible, old man's wheeze that wracks his ribs and makes his nose throb. Then, realising she's serious, he says, 'Very flattering, an' all, but not now, right? As you can see, I'm busy here.'

'That's not what I meant.'

'So what did you mean?'

'There are police at our house again. Four of them, not in uniforms. They won't say why they're there, but they're just sitting around, like they're waiting for something. I think they're waiting for you.'

'Me?' He tries to sound incredulous; his voice cracks and squeaks as if he's an adolescent.

'You know, don't you? What happened to my dad?'

'Look, love, I don't know squat about your dad. Until this morning I'd just assumed he was away...plant hunting or something, if I'd thought about him at all. Now why don't you piss off home?'

'Don't get me wrong, I'm not going to dob you in,' she says, frowning at him in concern. 'You look pigging awful.' She goes to the sink and turns on the tap.

'Water in the fridge,' says Ian when nothing emerges from the tap. The fridge door is hanging off. As she bends down to take out the water bottle, the hem of her skirt skims her bare thighs

'Sit down,' she commands, advancing on him with the water, a bowl and a none-too-clean J-cloth which had been draped over the tap. He sits, thankfully, on the edge of the bed.

'So why are you here?' He watches as she kneels, sets the bowl on the floor and fills it with water. Her hair is bound in a French plait, which swings over one shoulder, revealing the nape of her neck, its outline softened by a fine down. Her skin seems almost to shimmer in the weak light from the dirty bay window at the other end of the van.

'All in good time.' The expression in her wise child's eyes tantalises and terrifies him. She kneels up, between his parted thighs, and begins to dab at the cuts on his face. A gap between her shirt buttons reveals a glimpse of her white cotton bra, decorated with pink hearts. Her breath is sweet. Her little breasts brush his naked chest, her hips flex against his inner thighs as she bends and straightens, dipping her cloth in the water and bringing it up to his wounds. He fights his lust, trying to concentrate on his pain, on the conversation with Bernard the night before, which is coming back to him now in snatches, catching him unawares the way his bad memories always do.

'I'm not going home. I hate it there.' She dabs at a cut on his cheek with excessive vehemence and he winces, sucking his breath in sharply between his teeth, which sends a stab of pain through his ribs. He hunches in an instinctive effort to protect them, and bumps foreheads with Polly. She pulls away, rubbing her head and laughing. The point of her tongue shines pink behind her teeth. Rich kid's teeth, white and even with tiny, perfect serrations visible along their sharp edges. He'd like to be bitten by those teeth, licked by that tongue. He'd like to...

A groan comes from the figure wedged behind the table and Ian and Polly spring apart. Bernard's shoulders heave, his legs kick convulsively; he is like some monstrous mer-man emerging from the sea.

'Go on, get out of here,' says Ian. 'You don't want him seeing you here with me.'

'That doesn't matter.' She fixes a gaze on him which seems to last a lifetime, which sees everything she wants him to be and reflects back at him all the yawning gaps between that and what he is. Bernard tries to roll over in the too-narrow space between table and window seat, groans again and falls slack.

'It does. Believe me.'

No. I'm not going back there. I can't bear it. Seeing *her* every day, baking cakes, doing all that *mummy* stuff, pretend-ing like she never... I'm staying with you, Ian. We can both go, get away from him...this...everything.'

'Look, love, you've got it all wrong. I travel light, and I certainly don't want the kind of attention running away with you would bring me. Go home. Forget all about me.'

But she doesn't move. 'No, Ian. I'm not going back, I'm going with you. You see...' She rummages in her skirt pocket and withdraws something small enough to remain concealed in her closed fist, 'I've got this.' Uncurling her fist she reveals, glinting on the flat of her palm, Harry Theobald's signet ring. 'You wouldn't want me to show that to the cops, would you?'

'How did you get it?' He feels calm, as if this latest twist in the path his life has taken since Craig turned up at the Head of Etive was inevitable.

'I don't know. It just dropped on the floor while I was getting undressed after you brought me home Saturday night.'

'So there's nothing to say I had it. Could have been the other bloke, the security man. Maybe he nicked it.'

'My dad never took it off.'

'He could have lost it, and the guy picked it up.'

'And hung on to it for nearly a week? In what way would that be worth his while exactly? Unless he wanted to get sacked from a pretty cushy, well paid job.'

'Whatever. There's nothing you could prove.'

'Not on its own, no, but you see, I overheard Aunt Mary on the phone. I think she was talking to Mum, and I heard her say your name. Ian Slight. That's you, isn't it?'

'So, say I agree to take you away with me. Seeing as you have all the answers, how do you see that one working out? Where will we go? Abroad? I don't suppose you brought a passport with you.' She shakes her head, but there is a defiant set to her jaw. 'How will we live? You going to wave me off to work every morning and have my tea on the table when I get home? Is that it? A nice cosy domestic setup? Or had you got something a little more risqué in mind? How do you suppose we'd even get away from Aylsburgh before the cops caught up with us?'

'We can take my mum's car. She always leaves the key in it. I could get it and be away before anyone in the house even noticed.'

'You can drive?'

She gives a stubborn shrug. 'I can drive the lawnmower. It can't be that different.'

He feels himself capitulating; it would be so easy, and enjoyable until she saw through him to the lies at his core. And underage pussy would be a new experience for him, as far as he knows anyway; new experiences are few and far between at his time of life. And he could get the ring off her easily enough at some point, so when he left her, whatever she said would sound like a pubescent kid's fantasy.

A series of bumps and grunts coming from under the table distracts him from this line of thought. Bernard is making a determined effort towards consciousness. He's managed to turn his head so he's facing Ian and Polly and his eyelids, swollen and purple, are flickering.

'Alright, then,' he says, 'you go and get the car. I have some unfinished business with Bernard. I'll meet you...outside the village, by that farm gate on the left, you know the one?'

'Peacock's,' she says. 'The white five bar one, with barley in the field.'

He nods. He has no idea what's growing in the field, but it doesn't matter. He's not sure yet what he's going to do, but the one thing he knows he's not going to do is keep his appointment with Polly. 'Go on now.'

At the door, she hesitates, her hand on the latch. 'You will come, won't you?'

''Course I will. What do you take me for? Besides, you've got the ring, haven't you?'

She turns, smiles at him, looks as though she is about to say something more.

And then it's too late.

Everything changes.

There is more knocking on the door, but heavy this time, not the rapid, light rat-tat of Polly's small fists.

'Mr. Slight? Are you in there?' Polly's smile dies, her eyes widen with shock. Her mouth forms a silent, questioning O. The racket has roused Bernard, who is now on all fours and shaking his head like an angry bull.

'Police, Ian. We're coming in anyway so you might as well open the door.'

He's hardly thinking now. Pure instinct drives him to grab a kitchen knife from one of the broken drawers. Lunging for Polly, he hooks one arm around her neck and presses the point of the knife between her ribs until he feels the resistance of her skin under her school shirt. The blood pounds through his broken nose, his heart batters his broken ribs. Part of him says, let go, give up, admit you're beaten, but there is another voice, visceral, elemental, howling in his ear about the need to escape, to stay away from locked doors because you can never be on the right side of them.

The van door opens inwards, which gives them the advantage, but it's flimsy and in poor repair, worth gambling on a single kick to give him the element of surprise. Dragging Polly with him, he charges the door and kicks out with all the force he can muster. It breaks free of its hinges and falls away down the outside steps. Though he cannot see clearly through his swollen eyelids, he has an impression of dark-clad figures staggering backwards, hears shouting, swearing, radio crackle, the clatter of the door on the steps. Grasping Polly around her waist, flailing the knife in his free hand, he bursts out of the caravan, jumps clear of the steps and the broken door and begins to run, his gait lopsided and ungainly from his injuries and dragging the kid with him. He doesn't look back, but he senses his pursuers, gaining ground then falling back as someone shouts, 'He's got a knife!'

His throat rasps, his ribs scream with every breath he draws. Sometime, soon, he's going to have to stop, make a stand, make it clear he'll stab the kid if they try to lay hands on him. Funny, he thinks, in a part of his brain that seems to have all the time in the world, how quickly your feelings can change. Sex and death. Just opposite sides of the same damn coin. Stars exploding in his eyes again now, so close, he wonders, briefly, madly, if he's running through the night sky, if he and Polly are following the moon path again, just like they did that night when he saved her from the sea.

Except this time he's not saving her, she's saving him. He blinks, draws air deep into his lungs, tells his cracked ribs to go fuck themselves. Yanking Polly with him, he whirls around to face his pursuers. Four of them that he can see. Just ordinary coppers. No guns. Young, whey faced blokes who waver to a halt as he confronts them, the knife once again rammed between Polly's ribs. He can feel her trembling, a pulse racing in her throat to match the one in his wrist as he holds her.

'Car keys,' he demands. The cops exchange fleeting glances. 'Or I kill the girl. If you know who I am, you know I mean it.' The first time he's ever played on his notoriety. It has a curiously exhilarating effect, like sitting at the top of a roller coaster waiting for the downward swoop to begin and hurl your guts up into your mouth. He gives the knife a dig for emphasis and hears Polly draw in a sharp, shaky breath.

One of the cops starts walking towards him, dangling a set of car keys at arm's length.

'That's far enough,' warns Ian. 'Don't try anything clever. Just chuck them over, right?' Another dig of the knife, another gasp from Polly. Though the morning is blustery and overcast, sweat pearls her upper lip. He's aware of her eyes flicking towards him, full of bewilderment and a kind of thin, questioning hope. As the police hesitate, he glances around quickly to orient himself, uncertain in which direction he ran from the caravan. He glimpses the site office, and the small car park beside it, over his left shoulder. There's the site van, and two police cars. 'Both sets,' he adds.

Two sets of keys are tossed towards him. Easy. Laughter is bubbling up from his guts like vomit.

'Pick them up,' he tells Polly, bending with her, keeping the knife to her side as she stoops to gather the keys. He can feel her trembling along the length of his body. Her fear jars his bruised and broken bones. For a second he thinks he will simply lie down, here, on the lumpy grass, holding her next to him, and close his eyes, and let the pain go.

Then the cops are yelling again, and he hikes Polly almost off her feet, and runs for the car park, forcing himself on with the last of his strength. Once he reaches a car, all he has to do is slump behind the wheel and drive. He anticipates it with the same longing with which he might imagine a hot bath or a comfortable bed. He can't, won't, think any further ahead.

He becomes aware of a shift in what is happening behind him, in the quality and direction of the voices of his pursuers and the pattern of sound made by their running feet. He daren't turn around, but he has the sense they are falling behind. He knows it's impossible, he hampered by his injuries and Polly, not quite a dead weight, stumbling at his side, the police young and strong. Perhaps it's the difference in what drives them, desperation versus duty. But he's not imagining it, this sense that he is no longer the focus of their interest. At the edge of the car park now, with only a few feet between him and the nearest of the two police cars, he steals a glance over his shoulder.

He would have laughed aloud if he'd had the breath for it. Charging blindly among the policemen, his brain still clearly not in full control of his body, is mad bull Bernard. Impossible to know whether he's resisting arrest or merely trying to attract their attention, but whatever his intentions, he's fighting a tremendous rearguard action on Ian's behalf. Suddenly he has all the time in the world to prise the car keys out of Polly's grasp and unlock the nearest car. He pushes Polly into the back seat, fits himself stiffly behind the wheel and starts the engine.

Glancing in his rear view mirror as he exits the car park, he sees one copper has managed to extricate himself from the chaos of Bernard and is running after him, head hunched awkwardly as he speaks into the radio on his shoulder. He wonders how long he's got, travelling in a squad car. They probably have some kind of tracker device in them these days, and even if not, they all have their numbers on their roofs so they can be easily spotted by helicopters. He'll have to ditch it as soon as he can for something less conspicuous. He should have acquiesced in Polly's plan to steal her mother's car while he still had the chance, he thinks, with a rueful glance at the gates of Wildwood as they race up the lane towards the road out of the village.

He'll find a farm, he thinks. There'll be loads of places around here, quiet yards where farmers leave their vehicles with the keys in. Intent on watching the roadside in case he misses a suitable spot, he fails to look in his rear view mirror so is surprised, and almost swerves off the road, when Polly clambers over into the front passenger seat and plumps down beside him.

'Wow,' she says, 'this is so cool.' She begins to fiddle with the dashboard controls. 'Which one turns on the blues and twos d'you suppose?'

'Stop it,' snaps Ian. 'We're enough of a fucking exhibition without lights and sirens.' When she ignores his command, he slaps her hand away from the dashboard. He'll ditch her and the car, he decides. Whatever yarn she decides to spin about Harry Theobald's ring, he doesn't need a kidnapping rap to add to the growing list of crimes he's committed since Craig Barnes reappeared in his life. As if playing up to the new impression he's forming of her as an irritating child, she begins to squirm about in the seat as though something is causing her discomfort.

'Aha!' she exclaims, producing the knife from behind her back and holding it up like a rabbit from a magician's hat.

Fuck. 'Give that to me,' he snarls, lunging for the knife with one hand while keeping the other on the wheel.

She leans away from him, holding the knife out of his reach. 'Shan't. Anyway, you don't need it half as much as you need me.'

He closes his eyes in momentary exasperation and has to make an emergency stop to avoid hitting a tiny deer that darts out in front of the car. 'What the fu...I mean, what's that?' Accustomed to the red deer on the Scottish moors, he thinks it looks like a fairy creature and, as it disappears into a beet field bordering the opposite side of the road, wonders if he actually saw it at all.

'Muntjac,' says Polly, and a reflective expression comes over her face. 'George used to shoot them, if he found them in the garden. He and Dad had an awful row about it. Ian..?'

The knife is lying in her lap. Making a swift lunge which sends pain shooting through his ribs, he grabs it, transfers it to his other hand and drops it into the storage well in the driver's door. 'Yes?' he says, once the knife is out of her reach.

'What did happen with you and my dad? You can tell me. I wouldn't dob you in, not after...Well, if my dad's dead and you, like, saved my life, then you're kind of my dad now.'

He pulls off the road and parks in a gateway which seems to lead nowhere. 'Get out, Polly,' he says. 'You can walk home from here. Get out and go home.'

She turns her bushbaby look on him, both candid and mutinous, and places a hand on his knee. He flinches. Bruises and broken bones he can bear, but her touch is in danger of overwhelming him. He grips the knife, to stiffen his resolve, but doesn't pull it out of the storage well. If she leaves now, unharmed, close to home, the worst they can charge him with is stealing the car. The damage he inflicted on Bernard was self defence, and his background as a private detective won't help his cause with the police. They don't like other people doing their job for them. And there'll never be enough evidence to pin the death of the security guard on him. And Craig...? He isn't going to listen to that nagging voice. Not now. Not yet.

'Go on,' he says.

'No. I'm staying with you. You needn't worry. If they catch up with us, I'll tell them I came of my own free will.'

'You're fifteen, you stupid little cow. In the eyes of the law you don't have any fucking free will. And the law has four sets of eyes saw me poke a knife in your ribs.' He pauses, then continues in a more persuasive tone. 'Look, I did you a favour with the guy on the beach. Now, if you want to do me one in return, you'll do as I say and piss off, and then we'll be quits. Yeah?'

With a theatrical flourish, she takes the ring out of her pocket. 'Tra-la! Don't forget this.' Then her triumphant smile freezes; her knuckles whiten as she clenches her fist around the ring. 'Oh shit,' she says. Following the direction of her gaze, he sees a woman dog walker approaching along the path that seems to go nowhere, a small brown and white dog skittering in front of her. 'Drive, Ian, just drive.'

The squad car has attracted the woman's interest; her demeanour is tense now, focused, her walk no longer the relaxed amble of a morning dog walker. Polly slides down in her seat and ducks her head. She takes off her school tie and flings it into the footwell. 'Come on, come *on*,' she urges, 'she mustn't see me.'

'You know her?' He puts the car in gear and releases the handbrake, but his foot still hovers over the accelerator as he weighs the consequences of Polly being recognised. Perhaps if he shoved her out of the car into the arms of some family friend it would go better with him when he's finally caught.

'*Ian!*' screams Polly. 'Go. NOW!' Her shouting, in the confined space of the car, sends sound waves jarring though his bruised and broken body. The walker is coming closer, inexorably closer. He can see her face now, wearing the eager, apprehensive smile that good people wear when they see policemen. Slamming his foot flat down on the accelerator, he roars out of the gateway and into the road, his rear wheels churning up dust so he can see next to nothing through his rear view mirror and hopes to god there's nothing coming along the road behind him.

'Yay!' exclaims Polly, raising both fists in the air as they speed down the lane, between the acres of grain and sugar beet, past scatterings of cottages and farm houses that blur in the tail of his eye. He's no longer looking for somewhere to ditch the squad car, he's running, he's back on the fire escape at Appsley House with the indifferent moon above him and the hard ground below, knowing he has to jump. His heart pounds in his throat, every pulse hammers blood through cuts and bruises. He is all pain, nothing but pain, and there are tears running down his cheeks, or sweat, or blood. It doesn't matter, it's all the same, it's all guilt, failure, and the ineffable solitude.

He glances at the kid, grinning like she's on some fairground ride, and notices, for the first time, a resemblance to her father. Her profile, as she looks out at the road ahead, shows a hard edge through the blurring of immaturity. If, he thinks, she had spent her childhood in places like Appsley House, underfed and under-loved, she'd look just like Craig used to, lying in bed and staring at the rocket in which three men burned to death.

'Apollonia,' he says.

'Don't.' She gives a theatrical shudder and flashes him a cute frown.

He laughs.

'You're crying,' she says.

'Don't be fucking ridiculous.'

She puts her fingers briefly to his cheek then licks them. 'You so are.'

'If you're so determined to stay with me, kid, you should be careful what you say.'

'"If you know who I am you know I mean it",' Polly quotes. 'Who are you, Ian? And what do you mean?'

Day Ten

They have driven back from Scotland overnight, after hearing the news about Polly, borrowing a car from the Highland police rather than waiting for the next day's flights. Roberts and Belshaw took turns to drive while Alice fell into a nightmarish doze on the back seat. She jerked awake as they pulled into a service station on the M6.

'This isn't..?' she asked Belshaw while Roberts was buying petrol and chocolate bars.

'No, Mrs. Theobald, don't worry. Even DI Roberts isn't that tactless.'

Now she sits in the stillness that follows the switching off of the engine. Her sleep deprived body feels as heavy as a dying star, sinking slowly through the car seat, through the chassis and the gravelled yard beneath it. Her mind is filled with collapsing walls, buildings silently concertina-ing themselves in clouds of white dust. She knows she's in the grip of a waking nightmare, almost a hallucination, but she hasn't the energy to shake it off. The familiar rear view of the house appears to her like a blurred photograph, what confronts her inside beyond her imagining.

There is a van marked J. D. TINKER, CHIMNEYSWEEP parked next to her Volvo. Surely she hadn't arranged to have the chimneys swept in June, and even if she had, surely the police would have sent the sweep packing. Besides, this isn't her regular man, whose name is Woods.

'Abduction Unit,' says Roberts, seeing her staring at the van. 'They don't like to draw attention to themselves.'

'I see.' Collecting herself, she walks towards the house. Mary meets her on the back doorstep. Daisy appears, uncharacteristically docile, at the heels of a burly man in ill-fitting jeans. The man scratches the dog companionably behind the ears as they approach. How quickly, thinks Alice, and it is the weight upon her of another misery, small but decisive, dogs shift their allegiance.

Though the man's demeanour is relaxed, when Mary looks to him to speak, he does so with efficiency.

'Sergeant Baxter, Mrs. Theobald.' He shakes her hand firmly in his great paw. 'Abduction Unit. We've set up everything we need to monitor phone calls, and we have a negotiator with us who can advise you how to respond when Slight calls. I'll introduce you to her in a moment. You probably noticed we'd cleared the press away from the gates. They're usually very co-operative in cases like this. They maintain a news blackout unless we ask them to do otherwise. We're assuming Slight's after a ransom, so we don't believe Polly's in any immediate danger.'

'But I can't pay a ransom,' Alice blurts out, casting a panic-stricken look at Mary. 'Oh god, d'you think that's what he was after all along? Money. For rescuing Polly?'

'No,' says Mary, 'I don't think it's that.'

'So..?'

'Don't worry, Mrs. Theobald,' cuts in Baxter, 'the last thing we want is for you to pay a ransom. Our aim is to get Polly back unharmed and arrest Slight at the same time. We can't have kidnappers thinking they can get away with it. We've got one big advantage in that he stole a police car. Pretty easy to track.'

'A police car?' Alice repeats.

'It's a long story,' says Baxter, looking both grim and embarrassed.

He explains what happened while Mary makes tea. What he does not explain is how Polly came to be in Ian's caravan instead of at school.

'Mary?' Alice queries. Mary has her back to Alice as she busies herself with mugs and teabags, but Alice sees her shoulders stiffen.

'I saw them off up the drive,' she says. 'I made sure they had everything they needed. I even helped Jesse with whitening his cricket pads.' She turns to face Alice. 'I'm sorry, dear. I should have foreseen this.'

Surprised, Alice says, 'No, of course you couldn't.' Mary knows nothing of the drama of the beach party, or what Alice has found out in Scotland.

'I'm sorry, Alice, I've let you down. I should have known better.'

'No, you couldn't be expected to. If you haven't got children you don't know what it's like. You're always on a tightrope, trying to watch out for them without them knowing you're doing it.' She manages a weak smile. 'To be honest, if you had tried walking them to the bus they'd probably have refused to go.' *And Polly would still be here.*

Restless, wanting to put some space between herself and Mary, Alice walks through to the staircase hall. Wires, laptops and other pieces of electronic arcana whose purposes she cannot imagine are everywhere. People with headsets hanging round their necks talk about phone tracking and helicopters, sniffer dogs and armed response, but no-one talks to Alice. She feels like an unwanted guest, perpetually in the way, an irritant barely tolerated by the seemingly endless flow of busy people who do not quite fill the empty spaces left by Harry. And now Polly.

She creeps away, up to Polly's bedroom. The room seems to swirl about her, as if it were the still centre of some bizarre fairground ride, a dizzying conveyor of her daughter's daily life. Trying to focus on her habitual muddle of discarded clothes, magazines, lidless lipsticks and dried out mascara wands, she finds it increasingly hard to believe Polly won't simply reappear. She can almost sense her, scuffing along the corridor in her school shoes with the downtrodden heels, mobile to her ear, chatting energetically to Maddie, or some other girl she had left only moments ago, when she climbed down from the school bus.

Her phone, thinks Alice, and the room stops spinning. She'll have her phone. They can ring her, make sure she's alright. She'll be able to tell them where she is, and they can go and fetch her. Slight can't have gone far, and he can't hold out against all these police. And yet...Four, Baxter had said, four of them who had been unable to save Polly because Slight was holding a knife to her side. Alice's legs give way and she sits, abruptly, on Polly's bed.

She picks up her daughter's teddy bear and holds it to her nose, inhaling the smell of fusty stuffing and talcum powder, remembering how Harry had arrived with it at her hospital bedside, a pink balloon tied to one of its paws. Somewhere inside the bear that moment of perfect joy remains, unchanged, her propped against her pillows, exhausted and exhilarated, her new baby in her arms. Harry with his radiant grin, and the yellow bear, and the pink balloon, and their laughter, silent yet wild, when the midwife couldn't spell Apollonia and asked them if it was a place they had visited on holiday, and then started talking to them about birth control when Harry said it was all to do with rockets. Which brings her thoughts back round to Ian and the swift efficiency with which he has smashed his way through the remains of her family.

There is a knock on the door.

'Can I come in, Mrs. Theobald?' A woman's voice, slightly estuarine. 'I'm Anita Shaw. I'm the negotiator.'

'Come in,' says Alice.

Anita Shaw is petite and dark. She has a cloud of wavy hair around a face shaped like a heart drawn with a ruler. Her mouth, wide in her pointed chin, is bracketed by lines which, rather than aging her, give her an air of competence, even wisdom.

'It's very untidy, I'm afraid,' says Alice.

Anita Shaw smiles, a smile which seems genuine to Alice, igniting small fires in her eyes. 'They always are, though, aren't they?'

'Do you have children?' How can she do this job if she has children of her own?

'Is that Polly's teddy bear?'

Alice nods meekly, understanding that she has been rebuked, that this is not about Anita Shaw but about Polly.

'What can you tell me about Polly?' asks Anita, sitting at Polly's desk and swivelling the chair to face Alice on the bed.

'What do you want to know?'

'Anything, really. Anything that might be useful. Is she likely to be frightened?'

'What a stupid question. Of course she'll be frightened.'

Anita Shaw makes no response to this, but she seems stiller than before, expectant. She fixes her gaze on Alice and waits; the silence is uncomfortable, it begs to be filled.

'Well,' says Alice, 'I mean...she's quite...headstrong. She's not a timid girl.' Then her gaze strays to the night-light, an opaque glass goose with a blue bulb in its crop.

'But she's scared of the dark. I noticed the nightlight. My son's got one just like it.' After a beat, Anita Shaw goes on, 'Do you have any idea why she was in Ian Slight's caravan this morning? According to the man we have in custody, she seemed to have been there for some time when he came round.'

'What man?'

'A Bernard Maitland. I expect you know him. Landlord of the village pub. It appears he and Slight had been fighting. He told us...she was tending to Slight's injuries when he noticed her.'

'Bernard?' Alice's mind feels sluggish and clouded. She cannot grasp how Bernard has entered the picture. As she struggles to think about it, she becomes aware of Anita Shaw's silence, the weight of its expectation pressing on her.

'Polly,' she prompts. 'What do you think was going on there?'

'I have no idea.' But even as she says it, an idea is forming, an idea which tumesces in her mind like an irresistible cancer. The image of Polly in the kitchen doorway that Sunday lunchtime replays itself, but it's as though it's differently lit, or shot from a different angle, so what she reads on Polly's face is not shock or revulsion, but jealousy. 'She went to a party last weekend. I let her...she was too young... it's my fault.' Anita Shaw's expression remains neutral. 'She got into trouble in the sea. Too much to drink, I suppose. Ian was on the beach at the time and he rescued her and brought her home. Ever since then she's...well, with her father disappearing. I suppose Ian filled an empty space for her, or so she believed.'

'Ian?'

Alice's face burns with mortification. 'I...invited him to Sunday lunch, to thank him.'

Anita Shaw nods; her impassiveness is almost worse than if she had told Alice to her face she was a negligent mother who was getting just what she deserved. 'Do you think she could have gone with him willingly?' she asks.

Alice feels nauseous. She puts down the teddy bear, suddenly sickened by the smell of baby powder. 'I don't know,' she admits miserably.

'I'm just trying to get a picture, you understand, so I can be ready when he makes contact. If we don't catch him first, that is.'

'The sergeant downstairs...'

'Baxter.'

'Baxter. He said Ian had a knife.'

'Of course. Well, I'm sure I'm wrong.' Anita turns back to the desk. 'And this is her laptop, I suppose?'

'Yes.'

'Do you mind if we take a look?'

'No, of course...'

'Do you know her passwords?'

'Passwords? I'm not sure she even has any.'

Again that neutral, yet condemnatory, smile. 'A lot of parents like to keep an eye on what their children are up to online. Not to worry. I'll let one of the tech guys downstairs have a play with it. Stop them getting bored while we're waiting, eh? And I'm afraid it will be a waiting game now, Alice. I can call you Alice? Obviously uniform are out in force on the ground, and there's aerial reconnaissance. There'll be a total news blackout and our lot won't be using a standard police radio frequency so Slight won't have any idea how the search is going. I imagine he'll ditch the squad car as soon as he can, but the silence might lull him into a false sense of security, make him careless. I have no sense that any of this was planned. So, we have to wait either until he's tracked down or until he calls here. What I'd like to do now is go through with you exactly what we want you to say if he calls. OK?'

'Why don't I try ringing Polly's phone? No-one seems to have thought of that.'

'I'm afraid her phone was in the caravan. She'd left her school bag there. The phone was in it. Maybe you could help us with the call list. Let us know if there are any numbers you don't recognise.'

'Why didn't you tell me?' By not telling her they had found the phone, they had allowed her that moment of hope, that now makes everything seem so much worse. 'Why didn't you tell me?' she repeats, shouting now.

'I'm sorry. We should have told you, but you'll appreciate, we have a lot to do, as quickly as we can. The first hour is crucial in these situations.' Although her words contain an apology, Anita Shaw's tone is as cool as glass; Alice can gain no purchase on it.

Anita Shaw stands, unplugs Polly's laptop and tucks it under her arm. Standing too, Alice says, 'I trust my children, Ms. Shaw. I trust their strength and intelligence and common sense, and I also know they have to find their own way in life. Life is a thing I can't protect them from. If I'd spent my time snooping around Polly's computer or noting down every number in her call register, she'd probably be in even more danger now than she actually is.'

'Good,' says Anita Shaw.

And then the phone rings.

Ian leans over Polly's inert form on the filthy mattress. He slips his hand into her skirt pocket and his fingers close over Harry's ring. He stands for a moment, looking down at her, tossing the ring from hand to hand, he's not sure why. There's nothing to keep him here now; it's time to hit the road.

By the time they had reached the Cromer road the previous afternoon, Ian knew where he was going. He'd cross the main road and keep heading west, sticking to the lanes and farm tracks until he hit the A17. All he had to do was follow the sun; he daren't use the car's satnav in case it triggered something that would make it easier for the police to track them. He had to ditch the jam sandwich as soon as possible.

The supermarket sign appeared at the roadside like the answer to a prayer. He pulled off the road, driving not into the supermarket's main car park but into some sort of service area round the side.

'Get out,' he told Polly. 'Quick.'

'What are we doing?'

'*We're* not doing anything. You're going to walk into the shop, find a call box and phone your mother. What I'm going to do is none of your business.'

'I'm not going home, I told you.' She watched as he pulled the keys out of the ignition and tossed them up on to the roof of a lorry parked beside a loading bay.

'Well you're not coming with me. You can say what you like about that bloody ring.' He set out in the direction of the customer car park, taking long strides, walking as fast as he could so she was unable to keep up. But he couldn't shake her off. She broke into a jog and grabbed hold of his sleeve. Eventually he had to stop, on an unmade verge on the edge of the supermarket access road. He was sure people driving past were staring at them, straight onto their mobiles, reporting the odd appearance of a tramp in blood-stained clothes arguing with a school girl. He walked on, looking for somewhere less exposed. The kid followed.

When they used to peer out of the barred window of his last place, at the glossy American wonder of the town's first supermarket, the plan they dreamed up had seemed easy. But then, they knew they were never going to actually try it, and if any of them had imagined having a fifteen year old girl in school uniform in tow, they wouldn't have been planning how to get rid of her.

Once in the car park, he found a spot some distance from the store, and the trolley parks, but not so far that there were no cars parked there. He leaned against a lighting pole to wait. He'd have given quite a lot for a cigarette, he remembers, and thinks he'll have a quick shufti round the farmhouse for tobacco.

'What are you doing now?' demanded Polly.

'Polly, just fuck off, will you?'

'No. And if you try and make me, I'll scream. I'll say you...you know...' She blushed and lowered her eyes so the sweep of her lashes shaded the thin skin below them. The top button of her was shirt undone, and a pulse fluttered like a trapped moth at the base of her throat. As he stared at her, a little smile caught at the corners of her mouth.

He grabbed her shoulders, pulled her to him and kissed her, forcing his tongue between her teeth, making her retch. He summoned everything he knows of darkness and violence into that kiss, the blown up cinema, the pram smashed against the front of the train, the eyes with nothing behind them but a wildernesses of loss. He bent her spine until he could see it snapping in his mind's eye, the vertebrae scattered like unstrung beads, the nerves frayed, springing apart like overstretched elastic bands. In that moment, he hated her with a passion. The more she struggled, the more murderous his grasp. He'd teach her all about sex, and death, and make sure she could never unlearn it.

Then, suddenly, she went limp in his arms. He stopped kissing her, exhilarated and terrified, raked his eyes over her pale face and bruised lips. The pulse was still there, fluttering in her throat. Tears oozed from the corners of her closed eyes and crawled down her cheeks.

'Isn't that what you want, you daft little bitch?'

Her eyes snapped open. 'Dickhead,' she muttered, 'I thought you said we had to be inconspicuous. Shall I scream or are you going to stop telling me to go home?'

In prison he learned that, to survive, you have to know when you're beaten and to start planning the next battle immediately, before regret or self-pity can cloud your judgement. Regret would be for her, not him, once she found herself in the dark and wet and grave-cold, but by then it would be too late. She'd blown her chance to escape. He let go of her. She stumbled, but quickly recovered herself, wiped her mouth, smoothed her hair, tucked in her shirt. He quite admired her for that.

'So? What are we doing?'

'Shut up and just do what I tell you, right?'

He turned away to scan the car park, which was filling up with mothers and kids fresh out of school. Trolleys rattled and tyres hissed. Children cried and adults shouted at them, making him wince. He was thirsty, hungry, bone weary. While he waited, his thoughts drifted to a hot bath, a soft bed and a breakfast tray loaded with bacon and eggs and croissants and hot, frothy coffee. He was just wondering if Polly figured in this dream when he saw what he was looking for and the dream dissolved.

A woman was struggling towards a blue people carrier. She had a baby seated in her trolley and another small child by the hand. The overloaded trolley was out of control, slewing sideways as she wrestled to keep it on course. As he watched and waited, the woman pushed the trolley up to the back of the car, went round to unlock the driver's door, put her handbag down on the seat and began to unload her shopping, hindered rather than helped by her toddler, who snatched items out of the carrier bags and flung them wildly into the rear of the car. Her keys remained dangling from the driver's door.

'Right,' he told Polly. 'See the blue people carrier? There, next to the mini with the Union Jack on the roof?' Polly nodded. 'As soon as the woman goes to put her trolley back, we make a run for it, right?'

'We're going to steal it?' Her voice was full of childlike glee.

'No, love, we're going to drive her home while she sits in the back and has a cocktail...now! Go, go, go!' Just like some bloody sergeant yelling at you to run out in front of a row of balaclava-ed Fenians brandishing Kalashnikovs. They ran, Polly in front, Ian limping and gasping from his broken ribs. The harassed mother had barely lifted her baby out of the trolley before he had shoved the keys in the ignition, gunned the engine and was swinging around the end of the line of parked cars, heading for the exit.

Polly laughed and bounced up and down beside him in the passenger seat. Not much more than a fucking toddler herself. 'That was so cool. I never...I mean, Mum does that all the time.' Sensing a sudden change in her mood, he glanced at her, saw a shadow in her eyes as she prodded at a cut in her bottom lip, opened by her laughter.

'Look in the handbag,' he said. 'See how much money there is.'

There were three front seats in the people carrier, one of those Fiats favoured by hippie types that always seem to be pale blue and decorated with flower decals, so Polly spread the contents of the bag on the middle seat, reciting each item as if she were playing Kim's game. Wet wipes, makeup bag ('really bad coral lipstick'), half a tube of fruit gums –

they had one each, hers was blackcurrant, which pleased her – mac-in-a-sac, some Duplo, chequebook, mobile, purse with credit cards, a library card, some store loyalty cards and £87.41p in cash. She counted out the money with meticulous care, sorting the coins into piles, extracting some fluff and a hair grip, which she threw out of the car window. He had hoped for more, but it would do, for now.

'Oh,' says Anita Shaw coming to an abrupt halt three steps up from the staircase hall so Alice almost collides with her. Mary stands at the foot of the stairs, offering up the handset. 'It's not him,' she says.

'You should have left it for Alice to answer,' says Anita Shaw, appearing, notes Alice, more ruffled by this breach of the rules than by any of the terrible things said and unsaid in Polly's bedroom.

'It's someone called Nathan Crowliffe,' says Mary, directing a mildly sheepish smile at Anita.

'I'll take it,' says Alice. 'I won't be long.'

She takes the handset up to her bedroom, carrying it pressed to her breast. She doesn't want Nathan to hear the commotion of the abduction team setting up their equipment; she doesn't want Nathan to hear Wildwood at all. Sitting on the edge of the bed, she hunches over the phone as if to contain her conversation with him in the space defined by the curve of her back and shoulders. 'Why are you doing this, Nathan? Why now? How did you find me?'

'And hello to you too, Mo.'

'Don't call me Mo. I'm Alice.'

'Not to me you're not. Whatever turned you into Alice Theobald, well, I wasn't around for that, was I? Look, I need to see you. Can't you understand that? All these years I think you're dead and suddenly you turn up as alive as me. You owe me an explanation.'

'And you owe me one. How did you find me? I've been... careful.'

'Not careful enough. You should have married someone less high profile.' He invests the word 'married' with deep sarcasm. 'You managed alright for twenty three years, I'll grant you that, but now the news has broken about Harry's death, there are photos of you all over the internet. Wearing a very fetching yellow hat.'

Chelsea. Two years ago. Harry turning away, affecting sudden interest in a garden full of thistles and dandelions planted in dustbins. The explosion of flashbulbs. The momentary blindness, followed by a nagging suspicion that had followed her for the rest of the day.

'There's no point in this, Nathan. I can't explain.'

'You can try.'

'There's too much stuff going on here. I can't. You have to let it go, Nathan. I have to go now. I'm...expecting another call. Don't ring me again.' She presses the button that cuts off the call. Before she is half way down the stairs the phone rings again, but the caller display shows her it is the same number as before so she cuts it off.

She cannot, however, cut off her thoughts which race, now, towards Nathan even though she should be focusing them on Polly. It is as though the dust of the earthquake is finally beginning to settle, and the figures on the other side of it are becoming clearer, sharper in her mind's eye. *I wept because I had been so afraid, and because I had survived...Tears are in my eyes again now.*

'We used to live near here when I was a baby,' Polly told him as they passed signs to Terrington St. Clement. 'I remember that silly name.'

'From when you were a baby?' His curiosity was irresistible.

'No, stupid. My dad has bulb fields here. He makes us come and look at the tulips. *Really* boring. Actually, I think Dad thinks so too, I thinks he likes all the twists and turns and surprises at Wildwood better than rows of tulips, but it's, like, a family ritual. Every spring, off we go and look at the tulips...well, we won't be doing that again, will we?'

He drove on in silence for a while, into gathering cloud and the sweet tang of ripening onions, and streams of optimistic holiday makers towing caravans towards the coast. He was going to have to risk stopping soon; the Fiat was almost out of gas. The best thing would be to nick another car; the Fiat's owner would have reported its theft by now, and it wouldn't take the plod long to put two and two together.

'I hate Mum,' she said. 'You know what she'll be doing now?'

'No.'

'Baking, or French polishing or something. That's what she does when anything needs talking about. Facing up to. She makes herself busy with stuff you couldn't criticise her for but which just isn't important. She doesn't care about me and Jess, you know, only Dad. We're like...accessories. You get married, you get a house, kids, all that crap. Dad's the only real thing in her life.'

He'd understood, then, something about Craig. He was always looking for that kind of exclusive attachment, that he didn't get from his own mother, who would send him to Appsley House whenever she had a new boyfriend, because he got in the way. It's what drove him to steal the baby.

- What d'you do that for, yer daft bugger?

- Dunno. It looked nice. Clean and tidy like.

He'd always remembered the words because they didn't seem like the kind of thing Craig would say. They seemed like words put in his mouth by someone else, an adult, someone like Fat Janet or one of the others. He can still see them, written on his statement, and hear the prosecution lawyer reciting them to the court in a voice that reminded him of church bells. But then he began to wonder if they were Craig's mother's words. Craig was never clean and tidy; his clothes were always wrong; he'd be wearing plimsolls in winter or some misshapen, hand-knitted sweater when it was hot; and he smelt, not bad like some of the kids, but noticeable, like a dog maybe.

'What was your dad like?' he asked, remembering the man in the car park at the Head of Etive, expensively dressed and accoutred, confident and articulate. Wondering how they could be one and the same.

Polly flashed him a pathetically grateful smile. 'Well, he was really boring about gardens.'

'Yeah, I suppose he would be.' She reached out to touch his knee, light and swift as the kiss of a butterfly. 'Stop it,' he'd snapped, making himself focus on the road ahead, and the petrol gauge, which was going down rapidly.

'He was cool mostly, and most of my mates said he was dishy, which was gross but quite cool too, you know? But he had, like, obsessions. If Jess or I was messing about, Mum'd scream at us but he'd just, like, retreat and go all narrow-minded about something. As if we were none of his business till we'd stopped doing whatever we were doing. Then he'd be normal again, though sometimes he'd give us some really lame lecture about the importance of family or something. Like he'd swallowed a parenting manual. So embarrassing.'

'What was he obsessed with?'

'Well, gardening, obviously. Ugly pottery, and the moon.'

'The moon?' He remembered the battered toy he had last seen in the den in the railway embankment, the lunar sheen of white plastic against the dark earth walls.

'Yeah. He's...was...' She hesitated; he glanced at her to see if she was upset; she was winding the end of her plait round and around her fingers but she was dry-eyed. 'He was hung up on those old guys who landed on it. He said it was "a defining moment of the twentieth century".' It was a creditable impression of her father's voice, the northern vowels almost, but not quite, rounded out. What was Craig's legend, he wondered? How odd to be bound to someone as he is bound to Craig and yet know nothing about him.

'People thought it was at the time.'

'Do you remember it?'

'Sure I do.'

'Did you have long hair then? Were you a hippie?'

He laughs. 'No, love, I'm not that old. I was a schoolboy.'

The governor of the place he was in then, the place with a swimming pool and bright painted walls and no locks on its internal doors, had rented a TV for the event. They'd been whispered awake in the middle of the night by an excited warden, and filed into the governor's sitting room in pyjamas to watch James Burke have a shave and eat a sandwich on live TV. There was a sense of unreality about it all, of being alone in the universe, in a bubble of electric light with this group of shooters, arsonists, rapists, knife-wielders and the men set over them, sadistic, sentimental and self-righteous. He had tried to imagine other people, in the world outside, gathered around TV sets, and the moon smiling down on them, as oblivious to its impending violation as Jimmy Jones was, or any of the victims of any of the boys lounging around on the governor's carpet. They sat on the floor; the staff took the chairs. The next night, he'd looked up at the moon to see if it had changed, if the treads of Armstrong and Aldrin's boots were visible on its face.

A petrol station appeared on their left, next door to a sprawling cafe with several coaches parked outside it. Good. Crowds were good. They could refuel and get away without being noticed. He pulled in.

'You go in and pay,' he told Polly when he'd filled up the car.

'Why me?'

'Because I've got blood all over my clothes.'

While she was in the shop, he'd gone into the customer toilets to clean himself up. He'd sluiced his face and neck with cold water, then confronted his reflection in the polished metal panel that served as a mirror. His face was as swollen and discoloured as a piece of rotten fruit. His tongue worried at a loose tooth somewhere in the back of his jaw as he splashed water on his clothes and tried to scrub away the bloodstains. Once he had done the best he could, he smoothed wet hands over his hair and went back out on to the forecourt.

And froze, so a woman who had been waiting to use the toilet almost collided with him as she moved towards the open door.

Polly was standing beside the Fiat talking to a cop. She had pulled her French plait over one shoulder and was twisting the end round and round her fingers. The set of her shoulders, the tilt of her chin, her shuffling feet and working fingers, every inch of her shouted 'guilty'. He slunk around the side of the toilets, pretending to examine a hose point that jutted through the tarmac there. His vision was blurred and his heart punched at his cracked ribs like a prize-fighter. There seemed to be no escape; there was a razor wire fence between the garage and the fields behind it and the fields themselves were flat to the horizon, full of low growing vegetable crops. No place for a running man to hide, except in plain sight. He'd simply to walk out on to the road and try to hitch a ride. No-one would notice him among all the comings and goings on the busy forecourt.

He began walking, slowly, struggling to keep his limp in check, towards the rear of the forecourt buildings, planning to make his way round behind them and back onto the road.

'Hey! Where are you going?' Polly plucked at the hem of his sweatshirt, bringing him to a halt. 'He's gone,' she announced, triumphant, a little breathless. She still saw their situation as no more than an adventure then, a harmless lark from a children's story. 'He was just one of those community police guys. Wanted to know what I was doing hanging round on my own.' She began to giggle. 'I said you'd got caught short by a dodgy prawn sandwich and were in the bog, so he wouldn't go looking for you.'

Ian closed his eyes for a second, hoping that Polly would have vanished when he opened them again. He wished he could go into the shop and buy some tobacco.

'I'm just going to the loo myself now, OK? Here.' She handed him the purse. 'It was £49.96. I got a receipt.'

'No. No time. And you've already drawn enough attention to us.'

'It wasn't my fault.'

'All the same, people will remember you now. And the car. We have to get going.'

Though her expression was mutinous, she followed him back to the car without demur, and sat in silence as he pulled away from the garage. The traffic was a steady stream, travelling at a monotonous forty five. He zoned out and tried to make plans.

They'd need clothes. They were too conspicuous, her in her uniform, him ripped and bloodstained. And they needed another car. Badly. Anyone who was on that forecourt and saw Polly talking to the CSO would remember the Fiat.

'I really do need the loo,' whined Polly as they passed a garden centre. 'Can't we stop?'

'We'll find a field.'

'Eurgh. That's gross. I'm not peeing in a *field*.'

'Other alternatives strike me as more gross. We're not stopping any place there are other people. End of.'

Polly folded her arms and looked sulky, but she didn't ask again. She switched on the car radio and channel surfed until she found something poppy he didn't recognise. Not the sort of music Tara would have listened to. She bopped up and down in her seat, waving her arms in time to the music; he was tempted to suggest that wasn't the best idea with a full bladder, but he didn't want her to start whining again.

'Nathan Crowliffe again,' says Mary.

'I really wish you'd let Alice answer the phone,' says Anita Shaw. Their duet is becoming a refrain. Alice glances at the clock. A little before ten. Not more than two hours since Nathan's first call, but since then he has rung four times, or is it five? Alice is uncertain, but it is clear to her by now that refusing to speak to him will not put him off. And that the police are beginning to wonder, more than idly, who he is.

'You really should try to keep the line clear,' says Anita Shaw.

'And how am I supposed to do that?' snaps Alice. 'I'm sorry,' she adds immediately. She wants to say that her nerves are strung so tight she can hear them sing, that each time the phone rings, and she gears herself up to act out Anita Shaw's instructions, it feels as though a layer has been shaved off her humanity with a sharp blade. But Anita Shaw already understands this; Alice can read it in her open, heart-shaped face, as well as a certain disappointment that Alice is failing in her role as the mother of a kidnap victim. She has attracted calls from the wrong man. Her love for Polly is not strong enough to draw Ian's demands through the radio crackle of Nathan's voice.

'I'm on my way to Norwich,' he's saying now. I'll be there in about an hour. I looked up a place. The Nelson Hotel. Know it?' She nods, and as if he has seen the sign of assent, he goes on, 'Meet me there at midday.'

'Alright,' she says, because it is easier than trying to explain why she cannot leave the house. 'Midday.' She ends the call. 'He won't call again now,' she says to Anita Shaw.

They had been drinking coke, discovered in the shopping bags in the back of the car. 'OK,' Polly conceded finally, 'a field. I don't care. I have to pee.' He pulled off the road almost immediately. Since they left the petrol station he had been scanning the country either side of them, looking out for remote farmhouses, isolated cars in laybys, busy car parks, anywhere he might be able to exchange the Fiat for another car. He had already heard the drone of a helicopter overhead, though when he looked up he could see nothing within the limited frame of the car windscreen. Polly put her head out of the side window, but he dragged her back in by the scruff of her neck, telling her they probably had powerful cameras on board to help them identify the car accurately. She giggled and said it was just like Jesse's computer games and stopped whining, briefly, about needing to piss. The drone faded away after that, so maybe it was a private flight, or the coastguard, or a military exercise. Maybe no-one was looking for them yet, but even as he thought that, he knew it couldn't be true.

He drove down a straight dirt track through a field full of something with crumpled, dark green leaves, towards an isolated stand of trees. He stopped in the shade of the trees, but kept the engine running, and told Polly to be quick. While he waited for her, he got out of the car and walked round to the back to see whether, by any improbable stroke of luck, there were any cigarettes in the shopping bags. He found half melted ice cream and a polystyrene tray of chops swamped in bloody water, and tossed both into the undergrowth. He found a packet of bourbon creams which he threw over into the front seats, but no cigarettes. As he straightened up he felt something dig into his spine, definitely something new, something coming from the outside, not one of the injuries he'd sustained during the fight with Bernard. He knew immediately what it was. He raised his arms slowly.

'You're trespassing,' growled a voice behind him. A second dig in the spine, and he realised it wasn't what he was expecting, not the double barrel of a farmer's shotgun but a single muzzle. The gun nudging his vertebrae was serious. The man holding it would shoot him if he didn't act fast to protect himself.

'Sorry, mate.' Words first, they used to say in training for Northern Ireland. *Me mam likes you. She'll talk them round. You'll see. They just want me to be happy.*

'Don't you sorry mate me. There's signs on the gate big as a barn door. Can't you read?'

'Like I said, I'm sorry. I was caught short and...'

'Littering an' all.' If the man with the gun was looking to where he threw the ice cream and the chops, maybe he had just the ghost of a chance to take him unawares and knock the gun out of his hand. And maybe he didn't. But he'd try, because it didn't matter. If he lived or died. Ended his journey here, in this wood, with the drizzle just beginning to murmur among the leaves, or there. Where he was going. Underground.

'I'm starving. Is there..? Oh...'

Ian whirled around as the gunman was thrown off-guard by Polly's return. More by luck than calculation, he landed a punch on the guy's jaw. He staggered, dropped the gun. As he stooped to retrieve it, Ian kicked it out of his reach, then flung himself on top of it, reaching beneath his cracked, jarred ribs to close his right hand surely around the butt. A Webley .38, wartime service issue. Bloke was a farmer, he decided, a man about his own age who'd kept his father's service revolver in a drawer in the kitchen, wrapped in an oil cloth, a few rounds of ammo left, probably in a tea caddy. The Webley wouldn't be loaded, he decided, other than with his father's disappointed hopes.

Training the gun on the farmer, who was rubbing his jaw with one hand and scrabbling his tweed cap back on to his head with the other, he said, 'We weren't doing any harm. My daughter here just needed a piss, right? We're going now.'

'You're going nowhere,' growled the farmer. 'I'm calling the police.'

'I really wouldn't do that if I were you.' Ian curled his finger around the Webley's trigger. The farmer reached into the inside pocket of his Barbour. Ian squeezed the trigger.

The recoil almost knocked him off his feet because he wasn't expecting it. The noise was tremendous, ricocheting off tree trunks, sending birds scattering into the air. Somewhere, as the sound of the shot died away, a dog began to bark. The farmer was lying on his back, a look of indignant surprise on his face, a ragged hole the size of Ian's fist in his chest.

'Is he..?' Polly sidled towards the farmer.

'Don't,' said Ian, holding up his free hand, palm outwards, to keep her away. To all intents and purposes the man was dead, though he kept blinking, and a pink froth advanced and receded over his lips as his punctured lungs continued to breathe and the remnant of his heart pumped blood up into the wound. Ian checked the chamber and found there were still five rounds in it. He cocked the hammer, squeezed the trigger and delivered the coup de grace to the farmer's head from a distance of about six feet. He didn't want to look at those bewildered, blinking eyes any more. He was briefly absorbed by the scatter of the man's teeth as his jaw disintegrated, but was brought back to reality by the sound of Polly retching.

His mind felt clear for the first time that day. There didn't seem to be a farmhouse anywhere near, so the farmer must have had a vehicle. 'Stay there,' he told Polly, 'I'll be back in a minute.' She had whimpered some objection or other but he took no notice. She'd do as she was told. Now.

The Land Rover, nearly as old as the Webley by the looks of it, was only a few yards from where Ian had parked the Fiat, but, grey-green and muddy, camouflaged in the drizzly light beneath the trees. The key was in the ignition, which he was glad of, as he didn't fancy having to go through the dead man's pockets. Climbing up into the Land Rover, he stowed the revolver in the glove box, started the engine and manoeuvred the Land Rover alongside the Fiat.

Polly was in the Fiat's driving seat. Its engine was running, but by the time Ian had jumped down from the Land Rover she had lurched forward a few feet and stalled. He yanked the driver's door open, leaned in and switched off the engine, and pocketed the keys.

'What d'you think you're doing, you stupid little bitch?'

'I want to go home.' Polly cowered away from him. Her face was dead white and sheened with sweat. Splashes of coke-coloured vomit adorned her clothes and her knees were stained with mud and grass.

'You had your chance. Now you don't. Start getting the food out of here and into the Land Rover.'

'You didn't have to shoot him.' She made a valiant effort to sound defiant, but he could see how scared she was as she began hauling carrier bags out of the back of the Fiat. She was shaking so much she kept dropping things, then darting him fearful glances like a dog anticipating a beating.

'Yes I did. He was going to call the cops...and I'm not going back to prison.'

'Prison?' That bush baby look again. 'What did you go to prison for?'

'A girl. A girl who was worth it. Now get on while I deal with that.' He jerked his chin in the direction of the dead man. 'And no pissing about, right?'

Before setting about concealing the farmer's body, he emptied out the Fiat owner's handbag and extracted her purse and mobile phone, aware of Polly watching his every move. He removed the Land Rover's ignition key and put that in his pocket too. Seizing the body by the ankles, he dragged it off the track and deeper into the copse. The farmer was a thickset man and Ian struggled with his dead weight, breaking into a sweat that felt more feverish than brought on by exertion. He wondered, briefly, if the injuries he knew about were masking anything more serious, but quickly put the thought to the back of his mind to be re-examined when everything that needed doing was done.

No time to bury the body, so he dumped it in a shallow depression and kicked detritus from the woodland floor over it. The confetti of twigs, dead leaves, empty seedpods and rabbit droppings was tinder dry. The slightest breeze would blow it all away. He just hoped the old man's hostility towards trespassers would keep dog walkers at bay and that there was no-one to miss him too soon. As he assessed his efforts, the notion crept up on him that he was being watched. He turned his head cautiously, cursing himself for leaving the gun in the Land Rover, but he could see only shadows between the trees. He knew they were cast by leaves and branches in the greenish sunlight, that he was watched only by small animals and insects, waiting to feast on the dead man's flesh and lay their eggs in his eye sockets. He even felt a certain reverence for that knowledge, but he was scared, breathless as a fish in air. Bright spots danced before his eyes and off between the trees like fairies. 'Fucking concentrate,' he muttered to himself.

He began to run, stumbling over treacherous roots and dead wood which flared into powdery spores as his feet kicked at it, and suddenly it was Arthur running as though only now, forty one years later, had the instinct to flee death awoken. It wasn't until he caught sight of the house that he realised he'd run the wrong way out of the clearing and emerged on a different part of the track to where the Fiat and the Land Rover were parked. Pausing just long enough to catch his breath and clear his mind of whatever momentary malignity had overtaken it, he jogged back along the track to find Polly.

Even if there was anyone in the house, he reasoned, arriving there in the Land Rover would give them the advantage of surprise because whoever was there would expect the farmer to emerge from the vehicle, not him and Polly. And he had the gun, though he would need to find more ammunition for it if it was to remain a credible deterrent. That, and clothes, and more food, and water, though water wasn't such a priority where they were going.

Polly had finished transferring the shopping bags from the Fiat to the Land Rover and was sitting in the Land Rover's passenger seat. Spooked by the woods, he thought, like him, needing to put sheet metal and glass between herself and the wild. They didn't exchange a word as he climbed behind the wheel, returned the key to the ignition and turned the Land Rover in the direction of the farmhouse. He was aware of her questioning look, but she didn't say anything so neither did he.

The farmyard appeared deserted except for a sheepdog tethered by a long chain to the wall beside the front door of the house. It set up a frenetic barking as they drive into the yard.

'Get down.' He pushed at the back of her head until she was doubled into the brace position. He took the Webley from the glove box, cocked it, and waited. If there was anyone in the house or outbuildings, the dog's racket was sure to bring them into the yard. A minute. Two minutes. The dog's barking faded to a few half-hearted yaps then it gave up completely and lay down with its head on its paws. Another thirty seconds. Nothing moved in the yard except some chickens scratching imperturbably in the earth and straw.

'Come on.' They climbed down from the vehicle and approached the house. The dog rose, wagging its tail, but as they drew closer it began to snarl.

'Good dog,' he said, but that just seemed to make the dog angrier. Slipping the safety back on to the revolver, he grasped it by the barrel and cracked the dog over the head with the stock; he wasn't wasting a bullet on a fucking dog. Polly whimpered and he was briefly tempted to do the same to her. He'd be long gone before anyone found her. But he rejected the idea; she already knew too much; if he wasn't going to kill her, he had to keep her with him.

The door was unlocked and opened on to a kitchen that looked like something out of a museum of rural life, but much filthier. The walls were the colour of cheddar cheese in the sparse light from a deep, dirty window above the sink. There was an ancient range with a dog blanket and a rocking chair in front of it, and a cut loaf and a pot of jam on the greasy deal table. There was even a meat safe, he noticed, because there'd been one in his childhood kitchen before his mum had it ripped out. A flitch of bacon hung, like a giant chrysalis in its muslin, from a hook in the ceiling. The room reeked of wet wool and sour milk, of man and beast living cheek by jowl for centuries. The reality behind the dream of Alice Theobald's farmhouse kitchen. He gave the room a short, savage smile.

'We might as well stop here the night,' he told Polly. 'Go and have a look around upstairs. Find yourself a change of clothes. Something warm.'

'But...'

'Just do as I fucking tell you,' he waved the gun at her, 'and bring me a sweater.'

As soon as she was out of the way, he put the gun down on the table and began his search for ammunition, riffling through drawers beneath the table and in a heavy, old fashioned sideboard which loomed along one wall, its surface covered with grimy lace doilies and a disorder of bills. Nothing but cutlery and the sort of bits and bobs that seem to breed in sideboards, rubber bands, dried-out ballpoint pens, empty matchboxes and pieces of paper, soft with age. A torch, but the battery was flat. He tried the meat safe, releasing several flies, and groped in the back of the cupboard under the sink, which contained nothing but a tin of Brasso. He was about to give up on the kitchen and begin exploring the rest of the house when he noticed a row of matching canisters, blue and cream striped, on a shelf beside the window. He took them down one by one, found teabags, sugar and salt solidified into lumps, flour. As his fingers sifted the flour, they came into contact with something smooth and metallic. He lifted it out, tossed it in the air and caught it.

'Gotcha.' A brass cartridge lying on the flat of his palm. He emptied the flour into the sink and found eight more, Smith and Wesson .38s, probably older than he was but at least the flour would have kept them dry. He stuffed them into the pockets of his jeans. Polly's footsteps were still thudding about the upper floor, so he decided to take a cursory look around the rest of the ground floor. Finding nothing of interest, he went back outside, past the dog slumped at the end of its tether, into a rundown barn which stood at right angles to the house. There was a sort of workshop at one end, where he found a jerry can full of petrol which he loaded into the Land Rover, then returned to the house. No sign of Polly.

'What are you doing?' he called. No reply. Fuck. Had the little cow done a runner? He jogged up the stairs smartish, his thumb on the Webley's safety.

Alice is lying on Polly's bed again. Both the house phone and her mobile are beside her on the pink patterned quilt. The bed is made, Polly's discarded clothes tidied into cupboards, drawers, the dirty linen basket on the landing outside her door. Alice has put the tops back on the lipsticks and returned the mascara wands to their tubes; she has taken care to match all of them up properly. She has neatly knotted the electric cables now bereft of Polly's laptop and placed them on the empty desk. The room waits as she waits, in the expectant calm of things put away, for Polly to come home. For now, the room, with the mark of her tidying upon it, is hers, her beleaguered space in the crime scene that was once her home. What Harry's death and Polly's disappearance have emptied out, the police have filled with their jargon and their paraphernalia.

She hears footsteps approaching along the gallery, then someone knocks on the door. She continues to stare at the ceiling, losing herself in the white paint, absorbed by brush marks, and the changing angles of shadows, and a small stain the shape of Africa in the corner above the bed. Damp, she thinks, then remembers, as the knocking continues, that she cannot think about damp because there is nothing she can do about it.

'Mrs. Theobald? Are you there?' If it had been Anita Shaw, she would have ignored her, as she has every other time she has come to the door, but it is a different voice, so she sits up, swings her legs over the side of the bed and calls, 'Come in.'

A very young man stands in the doorway. He looks scarcely older than Polly.

'There's a Mrs. Keats downstairs,' he says. 'Anita tried to tell her...well, she's standing her ground...and she's got a suitcase.'

Isabella is drunk. She sways a little in the front doorway and stumbles up the steps from the porch when Alice invites her in. Her makeup seems to have drifted, mascara smudged beneath her eyes and lipstick out of alignment in a way that reminds Alice of an Andy Warhol *Marilyn*. At the top of the steps she props herself against the extended handle of her case, which suddenly telescopes. Isabella pitches forward and only Alice's outstretched arms prevent her from falling.

'Some boy told me I couldn't come in,' she says, extricating herself from Alice's embrace, her tone sharpened by embarrassment. 'Well. I'm not going back there, I can tell you.' She gives the case a meaningful glare.

'Why? What's happened?' The Keats' marriage is famously stormy, but Alice has never taken their rows seriously. They are merely part of the pageant of village life, like Ellen in the Co-op who grumbles interminably about her bunions, or the five Mawson children who always miss the school bus, or the imponderable sulks of Bernard behind the bar of The Dog's Head. Or her and Harry, playing lord and lady of the manor up at the big house. Waiting for Isabella's reply, she feels the new, dark colours of the pageant enter her heart and settle there. Yet she is eager to hear what Isabella has to say because it offers some relief from the unbearable tension of waiting for news of Polly.

'Car's...' begins Isabella, but is interrupted by the same young constable as before coming towards them from the direction of the staircase hall.

'Mrs. Theobald?' Alice's heart freezes. She reaches out a hand to Isabella and squeezes her arm until Isabella gives a sharp gasp of pain. 'Your...guest's car. It's blocking the drive, I'm afraid. If she could let me have the key...'

'Dropped it,' says Isabella with the grin of a naughty child. 'Tha's why I couldn't move the car myself.'

'Perhaps just as well,' says the young constable. 'I'm afraid it's run over a flowerbed,' he adds, addressing Alice.

'Trying to park by the studio. Wanted to take a last look at my lovely drawing room.'

'A last look? Isabella, I promise I'll get back to work. As soon as...' But she finds she has not the energy to explain to Isabella what she is going through.

''S not that. I'm not going back to that house. Not ever. I've left him this time. Have you got a drink?'

'Darling, I think you've had enough. Come through to the kitchen. I'll make you a coffee.'

'D'you know what he's done?' she demands, trailing after Alice, while the young constable goes out of the front door in search of her car keys. 'I was getting his Hugo Boss suit ready for the dry cleaners and an earring fell out of his pocket. B'longs to his theatre sister. I know that coz I bought them for her last Christmas. He's fucking his theatre sister wearing my Christmas present. Tha's shitting in his own nest in my book. 'S breaking the rules.' She begins to cry with noisy theatricality. Anita Shaw appears from some-where, drawn by the commotion.

'This is Isabella,' says Alice, 'she'll be staying for a while.'

'I really don't think...'

'Look, why don't you go and do something useful instead of trying to tell me what I can and can't do in my own house? You've got Polly's computer, and her phone. Go and...look for clues or whatever.' Alice changes her mind about the coffee. What Isabella needs is sleep. Taking her by the hand, she leads her upstairs to the Morris room. Together with the Rose Room, where Mary is staying, and a shared bathroom, this makes up her regular guest suite and she keeps the beds made.

'A lie down for you,' she says, pushing Isabella firmly on to one of the twin beds.

''S not dark,' Isabella protests, but does not resist as Alice swings her legs up on to the bed and removes her gold leather trainers.

'We'll talk later.' Alice draws the curtains and leaves the room. The thought of Isabella there pleases her. It makes her feel strong, because Isabella knows nothing of what is going on at Wildwood; she does not even know for certain that Harry is dead. She is unspoilt, a part of the life before, and she feels to Alice like a talisman.

DAY ELEVEN

'Well?' asks Polly, stepping into the kitchen and giving Ian a little twirl, 'How do I look?' She's changed out of her school things into a flowered dress made of something fine and silky looking. Though the right length, it is far too wide for her and cinched with her school tie. She has a man's cardigan over the top of it, with leather patches on the elbows, though the sleeves are too long so the patches reach to her wrists and disappear into the rolled woollen cuffs. Her hair is bundled under a felt cloche hat that stabs Ian's heart with a sudden, shocking recollection of *The Great Gatsby*. He swallows, almost choking on the stale bread and jam to which he'd helped himself from the kitchen table while he was waiting for her.

After he'd found her, sound asleep on the bare, grubby mattress, in a back bedroom whose lugubrious furnishings were relieved only by a vase of garish plastic flowers on the dressing table, he'd slept himself for a couple of hours. He'd taken the room directly across the landing, leaving both doors ajar and resting the gun on his pillow. The bed was made up in this room, with bri-nylon sheets in a bilious green and a shiny purple eiderdown, which he dragged across the landing and used to cover Polly, so he supposed it must have belonged to the dead farmer. Birdsong awoke him; a squint at his watch told him it was three thirty.

'Well?' she repeats, throwing a sweater at him.

'Where did you find that stuff?' He catches the sweater, which feels both rough and oily against his palm. If there are women's clothes in the house, there must be a wife somewhere. Maybe she was just spending the night away and would be back later that morning, expecting to find her husband at home or around the farm. Polly leans across the table to cut herself a slice of bread. The neck of the dress swings away from her body, revealing the edge of her bra. One sleeve unrolls into the jam pot.

'Bollocks,' she says, the sleeve half way to her mouth before she thinks better of sucking it and goes to the sink, passing so close to him he catches the odour of mothballs and stale cologne that comes off the clothes. 'In that room where I was,' she says, in answer to his question, 'with the gross flowers. There's a whole wardrobe full of it. Brilliant.' She turns shining eyes on him. 'I love antique clothes. There's a really cool place on Saint Benedict's...' Her voice fades as she reads his expression. '...but you wouldn't know where that is,' she finishes and falls silent, her lower lip protruding in a pout.

'It means he's got a wife. Someone else who lives here. You should have told me instead of wasting time playing dressing up. This isn't a fucking game, Polly. There's a dead man in the woods and a bunch of cops who think I've kidnapped you. Come on, we have to go. Now.'

He grabs her elbow, but she shakes him off. 'I'm hungry,' she says, 'and besides, the stuff I found is ancient. It hasn't been worn for years. I think his wife must've died and he's kept her things to, like, keep her alive.' She looks like a wise child in her outsize clothes, her eyes shadowed by the brim of her hat.

'Alright,' he concedes, hanging the sweater over the back of a chair, 'if you're sure.'

'I'm sure. You've seen the room. I bet it's where she died. I bet I even slept on the same mattress.' Her voice is tense with excitement. She speaks, he thinks, as though death is her first love, its end kernelled in its beginning like a bitter promise.

'You could kiss me again, if you wanted.'

'What?'

'You were looking at me as if that's what you wanted.'

Was he? And how would she know? How can she read his face beneath all the masks he has been forced to put on over the years? 'Don't be daft.' He turns away from her and, with some misgivings, opens the fridge. He's staring at a wedge of cheese, cracked and dry as a neglected heel, when he feels her arms snaking around his waist, her breath hot between his shoulder blades.

'You have such cool hair,' she whispers, 'I love long hair.'

'Stop it.'

But she merely tightens her arms around him, the pressure on his damaged ribs making him gasp. What the hell? Why not? What difference can another half hour hiding out here make? He slams the fridge door and turns to face her, her shining eyes and parted lips, pulls the ridiculous hat from her head so her hair falls over her shoulders, longer than he thought it was, less neat. Taking her chin between thumb and forefinger, he tilts her face towards his and kisses her, gently this time, the sort of first kiss a girl deserves, even though he knows it's not her first and wonders if it is what the lover of death expects in a kiss. Her tongue works in his mouth with clumsy industry; her body squirms against his, an inept tangle of hips and knees and elbows, and breasts soft as kittens cradled against his chest. What does she feel of him? What does she know?

Almost as though responding to his question she shifts one hand from the small of his back, slides it over his buttocks and round into the taut space between their bodies. Perhaps it's her clumsy fumbling with his jeans, perhaps it's catching sight of the Gatsby hat lying on the sticky kitchen floor, but he's suddenly aware that the moment has passed and pulls away from her, disentangling himself from the grapple of her small fingers and her soft, unformed child's mouth. 'I know your game,' he says, his voice brutal with the desire that is slower to dissipate than he would like it to be, 'you're just trying to keep me here till the cops track us down.'

'I'm so not. You know how I feel about you.'

'Polly, Polly, this is real life, love, not one of your daft magazines.'

She draws herself up proudly before him, shining in her odd clothes, in this room that speaks of neglect and loneliness, in a way that thrills him in spite of himself. 'You think I can't tell the difference, Ian? My dad's dead, yesterday I watched you shoot someone. Nothing like being surrounded by dead people to teach you the meaning of life.'

'Yes, well, no time for philosophy. We're going. Now.'

'But...'

'There's food in the Land Rover. Remember? You put it there, stupid kid.'

She stoops to pick up the hat and crams it back on her head. It sits awkwardly, her hair sticking out straw-like beneath it. He wonders why he had ever thought it looked anything other than ridiculous. He picks up the gun from the table and the sweater she brought him from the chair back and goes to the kitchen door. 'You first,' he says, waving her forward.

'The dog's dead too,' she remarks, giving the furry corpse a brief, cool glance as she passes, raising a cloud of early flies from the wound in the back of its head.

Staying away from the motorways with their cameras, Ian takes the A15 towards Lincoln, planning to pick up the A57 there, then the A619 in Chesterfield. These are the roads he knows from hitchhiking; you can't hitch on motorways, not unless you're prepared to spend a long time waiting in the same place. He's tried it, ended up marooned in a service station, flipping burgers, met a girl who wanted to marry him, wanted to dig beneath his scars and feel his pain.

'So tell me about prison,' says Polly. They are bypassing Sleaford, the previously featureless horizon now beginning to be broken by the outlines of trees and rounded hills as they approach the edge of the Wolds. The sun is above them, highlighting every speck of dust and insect smear on the Land Rover's windscreen. The air smells of petrol and bourbon creams, which Polly is eating for breakfast. Ahead the sky is filled with blue-grey rainclouds, their bottom edges smudged with falling rain, and he can see half a rainbow off to his right. A sky of nothing and everything, undecided.

'Not much to tell. Prison's very dull.'

'Why were you there? Who was this girl? Why was she worth it?'

Curiosity killed the cat. 'I killed someone.'

Though he keeps his eyes on the road, he can feel her looking at him. He has a sense of her eyes, round and grave in the shadow of her stupid hat, of the thoughtful working of her jaw as she eats another biscuit. 'A crime of passion,' she announces. 'How romantic.' And reaches out to touch his knee with her fingertips.

It's simple to let her believe it and yet this blending of two truths to make a lie makes him feel oddly guilty. 'There's nothing romantic about killing someone. I'd have thought that would have been obvious to you by now.'

'But if the motive is noble.'

King fucking Arthur and the knights of the round table.

'Courts deal with motives that are either explicable or inexplicable. Judges, barristers and them. They're not very romantic people in my experience.'

'And your motive?'

'Never you mind.'

'Sorry. Is it still painful?'

'There are some things you don't want to get over, Polly. Not ever.'

'Ian?'

'Yes?'

'Did you kill my dad? Is that how come you had this?' She withdraws Harry's ring from somewhere within the folds of her dress, tosses it up and catches it a couple of times. So that's what she was doing when he thought she was planning to unzip his fly. He curses his vanity while admitting a grudging admiration for her cool.

'Every kiss has its price, eh?'

'Did you? Are you going to kill me?'

'Not unless I have to.'

'What would make you have to?'

He looks at her to see if her demeanour matches her tone. It does. It's as if she's making a purely hypothetical enquiry. 'You scare me, Polly, you're weird, you know that?'

She stares at the road ahead, smiling like a Sphinx. 'I swallowed too much sea water,' she says. 'The salt's pickled my brain.'

The finely wrought hands crawl across the face of the long case clock in the staircase hall; even the imperceptible motion of the clockwork planets seems to have grown slower.

Alice wanders about the house, keeping pace with the sun as its light shifts from one window to the next. Whenever the clock chimes, it seems to do so in slow motion, the sound drawn out to infinity in the still, expectant air. She feels entirely alone and separate, as if she is moving inside a glass box, able to see and hear the world beyond its confines but not part of it.

Isabella emerges from the Morris room, makeup restored, hair re-arranged, sheepish but immoveable. To Alice's surprise, she takes charge. She makes tea and sandwiches for the kidnap team, finds a lasagne in the freezer for Jesse's evening meal. When Basil calls to say he is playing golf and will be late home, she tells him he will find the house empty and not to bother trying to contact her, and turns off her mobile phone. She accompanies Alice to meet Jesse off the school bus, and updates him, even though there is precious little to tell, in succinct and businesslike tones. She suggests a game of cricket and, watching them through the garden room windows, Alice discovers Isabella is quite a hand with a bat. Words form in her mind – gratitude, friendship, loyalty, practicality – and hang there, meaning nothing. She tells herself she will sort them out later, into the right feelings, the right phrases. Later she will be able to contemplate Jesse without the sense of loss and unfairness that overpowers her whenever she conjures the image of him walking up the drive on his own, without Polly. For now, however, it seems right, in a way she cannot readily describe to herself, to leave him in Isabella's care.

Polly's asleep when he pulls into the car park beside the tourist office, choosing a spot obscured by the recycling bins where the Land Rover is unlikely to attract immediate attention. As the engine stutters to a halt she awakes, stretches and looks around. 'Are we there?' she asks. He's touched by the childish question. *Are we there yet, Dad? Are we nearly there? Seconds before the car slewed off the road and hit a tree.*

'Almost.'

Wriggling upright in her seat, Polly gazes through the windscreen. 'This is it?' Her tone suggests she wants an explanation.

'We walk from here.'

She makes a face. 'Is there a loo? I need a pee.'

'Come on, then.' He leads the way towards the toilet block next to the tourist information office, and notices there's a shop there now, the sort of place that sells that odd mixture of hiking boots and commemorative mugs, maps, fleeces and greetings cards you only find in holiday towns. 'I'm going in there,' he tells Polly. 'There might be some useful stuff. I can trust you, right? You're not going to wander off?'

'Are you going to hold the shop up? The gun's still in the Land Rover.'

'Don't be daft. And don't get any stupid ideas about that gun. The wisest thing you can do is keep quiet and behave yourself.'

She smiles, touches his arm. 'Why would I do anything else?' Her changes of mood unsettle him, but when she's like this, he can dream a possible future with her, far beyond the reach of the real world, seeing her growing to woman-hood and himself growing young again in her company. He watches her until she disappears into the shadow of the ladies' room doorway, the wisps of bright hair escaping from her hat, the flex of muscle in her bare, brown calves, then makes his way to the shop, thinking he'll buy her a sleeping bag if he has the money, to soften the coming hardship. Even a short time down there and they'll be freezing.

It isn't until he delves into his pocket for his wallet at the checkout that he realises he no longer has Fiat woman's phone. So it wasn't just Harry's ring she took. The boy behind the till is saying something. He's holding out his hand. But Ian cannot move. His mind is filled with the memory of kissing Polly in the dead farmer's kitchen, of her hand sliding between their bodies, of his expectation. His hope. Hope is surely the dumbest of emotions. Furious with himself, he flings the cash across the counter and leaves without waiting for his change. If he's lucky, the phone's battery will be flat, if not...

Anita Shaw is holding out the handset, at arm's length as though it is a ticking bomb. It will be Nathan again, Alice tells herself, or Inspector Steyn, who had promised to let her know immediately the outcome of the Fiscal's inquest into Harry's death, or some village worthy wanting to borrow Wildwood for a charitable function. She glances at the caller display; it is not a number she recognises.

'Alice Theobald,' she says, hearing, in the silence that follows, the hollow hiss that tells her the police are listening in. Her voice sounds querulous, as though she has aged twenty years since the last time she spoke on the phone.

'Mum?'

'Polly?' Suddenly, she feels unsure. She had expected tears, terror, remorse, pleading, yet the voice sounds cool and self-possessed, as though Polly, too, has aged since morning. 'Polly! Talk to me. Where are you? Are you alright?'

'I haven't got long, Mum, so listen to me, please.' Alice folds her lips together over everything she is longing to say. She waits. She feels the police waiting too, all of them straining to catch the slightest clue to Polly's whereabouts.

'I think I know what happened to Dad.'

'Dad? What do you mean?'

'I can't explain now, there's no time. But I know, and I'm dealing with it.'

'Dealing with it..?'

'Chrissake, Mum, you sound like an echo. Please, stop talking and listen to me. D'you remember Peony?'

Peony? *Peony.* Of course. 'Your doll. You lost her. In Castleton. Is that where you are?'

'That's it. I couldn't remember the name of it but I recognised it.'

'Stay on the line, Polly, while I speak to someone. The police are here. I'll tell them what you've said. It'll be alright, darling. You'll be safe, very soon. Anita..? Sergeant Baxter...?'

'I'm going now, I'm sorry.'

'Polly? Polly!' White noise. A click. Silence.

'It's OK, Alice, we heard everything. Don Baxter's on the phone to Derbyshire now.'

Alice becomes aware that she has been holding herself rigid, and with awareness comes a sudden slackening. Anita Shaw has to help her to a window seat in the staircase hall, where they sit in silence for a moment as the hall bursts into activity around them. People pace back and forth muttering into mobiles and radios. Disjointed phrases drift into Alice's hearing, sounding as if they have strayed from the script of a TV drama. Tactical firearms unit. Golden hour. News blackout. Public safety. Triangulation.

'Can't get the exact location,' calls someone from the dining room. 'Hilly round there. Inconsistent signal.'

'It doesn't look like a very big place,' says someone else then returns to the conversation he is having on his mobile. 'Can you tell if the landlord found out anything?' The landlord? Bernard? Alice's brain clicks slowly back into gear.

'What's Bernard got to do with anything?' she demands of Anita Shaw. Without replying, Anita Shaw glances up from the window seat. Following her gaze, Alice sees Mary standing in front of them. She and Anita Shaw exchange a look which seems to Alice to have some significance, but the nature of it eludes her, as though they are speaking a language of which she knows only a few, disconnected words.

Frustrated, angry, she turns on Anita Shaw. 'You said he'd make a ransom demand,' she shouts. 'You never said anything about her phoning instead of him. About her "dealing with it". What does she mean? What's happening?' One or two of the people pacing about the hall pause and look at her but most take no notice.

'I was afraid something like this would happen,' mutters Mary. 'I told you...' she says to Anita Shaw.

'There are procedures we have to go through.' Anita Shaw is imperturbable. 'Things have changed since your day.'

'Not Arthur,' says Mary bitterly. 'Always had an eye to the main chance, that one.'

'Who's Arthur?' demands Alice. 'Will someone please tell me what's going on?'

'Alice, dear, why don't you go and make everyone a cup of tea?'

Alice stands up, but makes no move towards the kitchen. 'Oh I see, I'm in the way am I? It's only my daughter who's been kidnapped and you want me to go and make tea. Maybe you'd like me to bake a cake while I'm at it.'

Anita Shaw rises also. She places a calming hand on Alice's arm but Alice shakes it off. Though Anita Shaw's features remain composed, something flares briefly in her dark eyes. 'It's more important than ever now that you let us do our job, Alice. These people,' she embraces the people in the hall with a gesture of her arm, 'are experts. This situation is familiar to them...'

'In Norfolk?' Alice manages a scathing laugh. 'This is hardly Chelsea. There isn't a Russian oligarch round every corner. How many kidnaps do you see in a month? A year even? None of you has the faintest idea what you're doing and in the meantime...' Feeling tears about to overwhelm her, she falls silent.

'Right,' says Mary, with the air of a woman who has come to a decision, 'come with me.' She grasps Alice's elbow; Alice feels as though Mary and Anita Shaw are tussling with her like two dogs after the same bone.

'Why?' she demands, standing her ground. 'Where?'

'Miss Canter...'

'Ms. Shaw, I know a great deal more about this situation than you do. Come on, Alice, somewhere quiet. We'll go into the garden.'

'No. What if Polly calls again?'

'Take the phone with you. We'll stay within signal range.' Though she speaks with resignation, as though she thinks it unlikely they will hear from Polly again.

As they step out on to the terrace, into a late afternoon of stale, accumulated heat, the crack of bat on ball reaches them, a cry of triumph from Jesse and a shout of, 'Six. Well done!' from Isabella.

'Let's go the other way,' says Mary, grasping Alice's elbow again and leading her out of the sunken garden in an easterly direction, towards the hydrangea walks and the lake. 'Alice,' she resumes, as they arrive at a concrete arch set with a tapestry of brick and flint, framing a view of the turning circle in front of the house and Alice's studio on the far side of it. The pantiled roof glows against a mass of steel blue thunderheads as though the sun is imprisoned in the building. The women stop beneath the arch, Alice with her back against one of its pillars, her face turned away from Mary towards the drama of light playing out around her studio. That is what she wants to think about, the living colour, not the dead and the lost. But Mary is speaking again and she must drag her attention back.

Yet before she can begin to sort out in her overburdened mind what Mary is saying, her attention is distracted by the sound of a car approaching up the drive. A silver Porsche sweeps up to the front door with much skidding and spraying of gravel. Alice does not recognise it, but she knows the man who climbs out of it immediately, even though she has not seen him for over twenty years, even though he is heavier now, his large jaw padded with fat, and his Viking hair is faded and thinned from the forehead.

Her mind clears suddenly. Pushing herself free of the column, disregarding a thorn of Rosa Rugosa Hansa which snags at the loose-knit cotton sweater she is wearing, she hurries through the arch into the drive. 'Nathan,' she calls and waits, aware of Mary looking curiously over her shoulder yet knowing it doesn't matter. As Nathan turns away from the front door and walks across the drive towards her, the planet begins to spin a little faster for her than it does for Mary, or Jesse and Isabella, or Anita Shaw, or the surveillance officers who have cleared the De Morgan lustreware vases from her dining room table to make room for the arcane paraphernalia of their trade. It begins to spin with purpose.

'Hello Mo,' he says. 'I waited at The Nelson and you didn't show so...'

'You can't be here,' she says. He can't. He belongs in a life other than this one; there is no more place for him at Wildwood than there is for the laptops and cables and headsets littering its dining room. 'Come on.' She opens the Porsche's passenger door and slides into the low, red leather seat.

'Where are we going?' he asks, climbing in beside her.

'Castleton,' she says, aware of the look he gives her as she stares at an insect smashed against the windscreen. He sighs and starts the engine, but they are scarcely half way down the drive before he has to brake to avoid a confrontation with the post van, no longer intercepted at the now empty gatehouse. He is about to pull over on to the verge when the postman emerges from the van, brandishing some letters and a package, which he thrusts through the passenger window of the Porsche as Alice buzzes it open. She throws them all on to the narrow back seat without looking at them. 'Come on,' she urges Nathan as soon as the postman has turned his van around and driven back towards the gate. 'We have to go. Now.'

'What's up?' he asks as they pull away from the village and gather speed, but Alice makes no reply. For the moment, she feels capable of no more than remaining still and silent, cradled in the deep leather seat, in the car's closed space, bounded by engine hum and the countryside rushing by outside the windows.

'Aren't you going to look at your post?' tries Nathan.

'Do you have a cigarette?' If she could smoke, she feels, she would be able to explain. The nicotine hit would clear her mind sufficiently for her to be able to set her thoughts and feelings in some kind of order.

'Sorry. I haven't smoked for years. I had to give up on medical advice. Blood pressure.'

She steals a glance at his profile, noting his high colour and the thickness of his neck above his open collar and the jacquard V neck sweater she can imagine him wearing on the golf course. She feels an incipient panic; there's no time to stop, but she cannot imagine making the entire journey without a cigarette. Even if she asked him to stop, perhaps he would refuse to buy her any. She has come away without anything but the clothes she is wearing, no money, no phone, nothing. A memory comes to her, unbidden, of a series of classes she once attended that were supposed to make her give up. Whenever you crave a cigarette, the therapist said, take a deep breath. Visualise the clean air as a bubble of infinite peace, floating in your chest just as the blue earth floats in the seething chaos of space. Alice tries it now and, to her astonishment, it works; as she lets the breath out, the words come with it, a little ragged, but in order.

'A man took my daughter,' she says.

'Shit.'

'Let me finish. I think he knew Harry. I think there are things Harry didn't tell me.' Things Mary knows, she suddenly realises, things Mary was about to tell her when Nathan arrived.

'You were well suited then.'

She feels Nathan's sarcasm scathing her like sunburn. She is not forgiven. He has not come after her in search of reconciliation. 'The police...they just tell you to do nothing and wait.' She stares out at the road, at the black tarmac and the white lines rolling up beneath the Porsche's wheels like ribbons around bobbins. Not fast enough. Never fast enough. A green road sign whips past: King's Lynn 10 miles. 'How can they? What do they know about it? How it feels to have your child snatched away by some... by some...'

'Perhaps it's better they don't. You don't want a kidnap negotiator who's an emotional wreck, do you? I remember...'

'Don't, Nathan. Not now. Just drive.'

Polly's leaning against the Land Rover when he comes out of the shop, all innocence in her old fashioned dress and her outsize cardigan. She has worked holes in the cuffs with her thumbs and pushed them through, so the cuffs now double up as mittens. She is no longer wearing the hat. She looks cold, he thinks, with spiteful satisfaction, her skin beneath its rich girl's tan grey and tired. Well, she'll be a damn sight colder where he's taking her now.

'You stupid little cow,' he mutters, flinging his purchases to the ground beside the Land Rover. 'You've phoned the fucking cops, haven't you?'

She shakes her head vehemently. 'No, I phoned my mum. I just wanted to let her know I was OK, that's all.'

'And what do you suppose she'll have done?'

'I didn't tell her where we were.' She looks him in the eye, but picks at the frayed cuffs of her cardigan.

'They can trace mobile phone calls. Where's the phone now?'

'I chucked it down the loo.'

'What did you do it for? You told me you hated your mum. I thought you were glad to be away from her.'

She pouts, shrugs, continues to pick at her sleeve. 'Don't know.' She stares at him, something unfathomable in her expression. 'Maybe I wanted to make sure she was suffering,' she says, as if her motive has just become clear to her. 'Yes, that's it. I suppose that's why you're angry with me. Because I've made her unhappy. You must care about her, after all.' She seems to issue that last statement as a challenge.

'Jesus, Polly.' He shudders, as if he's there already, in the cold and dark. Just...start getting the food into that rucksack while I think.' He unlocks the Land Rover from the passenger side and, after glancing around the car park to make sure they aren't being watched, removes the Webley from the glove box and shoves it into the waistband of his jeans. The spare ammunition is still in his pockets. Polly has only taken the phone. And Harry's ring, of course which she is now wearing openly on the middle finger of her left hand. He should have checked if anything else was missing when she showed him the ring. She's messing with his head. He should dump her and fuck off out of there before whatever mayhem she has unleashed with her call overwhelms him. But she knows too much.

At the sight of the gun, Polly gives a little shiver. He hopes it's induced by fear; if she's afraid of him, he can control her. But there's a gleam in her eye that says more to him about the thrill of transgression than the fear of its consequences. She's her father's bloody daughter alright, he thinks, ruefully. When she's finished loading up the rucksack, he locks the Land Rover and tosses the key into the bottle bank.

'Come on,' he says, shrugging the rucksack on to his shoulders. He touches his right hand briefly to the bulge of the Webley's stock protruding beneath his sweatshirt. 'You first. You can take that sleeping bag. I bought it for you in any case.'

'Where are we going?'

'You'll see when we get there. Now shut up and move.' He wonders why he's bothering, what perverse hope or nostalgia compels him to lug a back pack full of food and a sleeping bag up the pass when he knows, now, they won't be needed.

'Why am I doing this?' Nathan changes down and accelerates past a lorry loaded with carrots.

'You tell me. I told you not to come.' Alice is desperate for a cigarette; she has no patience with stupid questions.

'I had to. Surely you can understand that. Seeing you again, seeing you alive, it's turned the whole of my life into a lie.' He snaps his fingers in front of her face. 'Just like that.'

Suddenly she remembers them going to see Tommy Cooper together, at the Fiesta, and starts to laugh.

'What?'

She plans to tell him, but then shies away from it. No going back. That was what she told herself as she scrambled out of the collapsed restaurant, blinded by the dusty sun. That is what she has been telling herself ever since. Newark (A1), she reads as another sign flashes by, 13 miles. No going back. 'Nothing. Are you sure you don't smoke?'

'Oh for Chrissake, I'll stop at the next pub and get you some. Five minutes won't make any difference.'

But it might, she thinks, it might. But she's desperate now, now the possibility of a cigarette has taken shape in her mind.

'D'you still smoke Bensons?'

'Camels. Full strength if possible.'

'You're never worried about killing yourself?'

'I'm dead already, remember?'

As the sides of the pass rear up either side of them the last light of the day seems to intensify, funnelled between cliffs of millstone grit and sheep-bitten grass. Though he has no idea why, Ian finds himself compelled to check his stride and look up, into the broad, jagged strip of robin's egg blue, fading to a fragile yellow towards the head of the pass, and wraithed with silver-pink cloud. Last breaths of the no longer visible sun. He feels tears prick behind his eyes and tells himself not to be idiotic. There'll be other sunsets, at the end of better days than this.

'What now?' Polly complains, scrambling in his wake.

They have spent most of the day in the shepherd's hut he remembered from before, a dry stone hovel, with its roof long gone, built into the side of the hill with a clear view of the cavern entrance several hundred feet below. Worn out by the climb, Polly had grown fretful, had whined about the sheep pellets littering the hut's gritty floor, and the fact there was nothing to eat except cheese strings, and the Coke was warm. After about an hour of it, he'd pulled the gun and told her to shut the fuck up.

After about another half hour, her mood had mellowed, and she'd shuffled up close to him, in the patch of sunlight where he was sitting, trying to recall the exact way the sun feels on your skin when you have just come up from eight hours underground, and laid her head on his shoulder.

'It's OK,' she said, in response to the wary stiffening of his body, 'I'm not going to try anything. I'm just tired.' He put his arm around her and drew her into his side, and was content to let her sleep, even though his arm developed pins and needles and he needed a piss. Sheep conversed with their lambs as the sun traversed the pass, swinging the shadows of the rocks from west to east. Breathing deeply and evenly, he stored up the scents of warm stone and bracken and Polly's hair in his lungs. Once he was tempted to wake her, to look at a kestrel hanging miles up in the blue air, suspended, as they were, between one possibility and another, but he didn't, and the bird dropped, and time began to move again.

At five o'clock, the last party of visitors exited the cavern, moving hesitantly into the light. A figure emerged from the gift shop and began to rattle down the shutters. They were new, he'd thought, uneasily. He woke Polly and told her it was time to move.

But now, coming up beside him, she stops too, as if his voice is a brake. He watches her tilt her face up briefly towards the brightness and then they move on. A further ten minutes' scramble brings them to the gift shop at the head of the cavern. He glances at his watch: coming up to a quarter to six. If nothing's changed since the days when he worked here, everyone will have gone by now, down to the village, to the pubs and cafes and the cheap apartments up by the youth hostel where most of the seasonal workers stay, bed-hopping their way through the summer. No-one stays up here any longer than they have to; no-one wants to be here after dark, when you can feel the dank breath of the cavern on the back of your neck as the hill sighs itself to sleep.

Dragging Polly with him, he walks round to the back of the shop in the desperate hope they still keep the keys in the same place. How many years has it been? Enough for them to have replaced a broken key cabinet.

But they haven't. It's still there, the wooden box nailed to the back wall with its warped door painted dark green. It's had a new coat of paint, he guesses, but no-one has thought to replace the damaged wood; it's still an easy matter to prise the cabinet open and unhook the keys to the turnstile and the steel-plated door behind it.

'Where are we going?' Polly looks at the big, old fashioned keys and shudders; though her tone is that of a frightened child, her features, drawn and grey in the gathering dusk, look freakishly ancient. The cavern is working its malign magic; its black water is already running in his veins, chilling his bones.

Nathan parks in the town centre. The evening is mild, and the little tourist town still lively. As Alice climbs out of the car and stretches, she is overcome by a sense of dislocation. How can these crowds of people drift past bright shop windows, in and out of pubs and cafes, laughing and chatting? How can they remain unaffected by the drama which is being played out somewhere among them, between a desperate man and a girl missing from home. And where are the police, she wonders, scanning the throng for dark blue uniforms, straining her ears for the stutter of radios among the gentle babble of holiday voices. She turns away from the town and looks up at the hills, half expecting to see armed men lining their summits, silhouetted against the luminous night sky. But all she sees is the ruined castle which gives the town its name, a Don Quixote of a castle, tilting in vain against the unremitting landscape.

'I'm not sure where the police station is,' says Nathan, coming round to her side of the car.

'Someone'll tell us. I thought we'd see the police, you know, making enquiries, asking people if they've seen them. It all looks so...normal.'

'Of course it does. The last thing they'd want would be for the guy who's got Polly to realise they were on to him. That might...well...send him over the edge. They have to be discreet.'

'So maybe we should do some investigating ourselves. No-one would mistake us for police.'

'We should just tell them we're here and leave them to get on with their job.'

'I can't just do nothing, Nathan! You can't imagine what it's like.'

'Mo...Alice,' the name sits uncomfortably in his mouth and he looks embarrassed, 'I've got four daughters of my own.'

'Oh...I never thought...'

'It wasn't my life that ended in Kalamata. What did you think? That I'd spend the rest of my days weeping over your

271

grave like the hero of some bloody romance? I got married again, Mo, it's what people do. They move on.'

She stares at him, seeing him, she feels, for the first time, understanding that he was never real to her before. You have to grow away from people, she supposes, in order to see them in perspective, and wonders if she will ever grow away from Harry, if she will ever move on. She dismisses the prospect. She will never regard Harry with the same dispassionate curiosity with which she is now looking at Nathan, trying to imagine him with a wife and children. 'Well, if it was one of your daughters, what would you do?' she demands, fishing in the pocket of her trousers for the cigarettes and matches Nathan bought her.

'I'd let the police deal with it,' he says, with a slightly overstated decisiveness.

'No you wouldn't. I know you. You're like a bull in a bloody china shop.'

'I'll tell you one thing I wouldn't do. I wouldn't stand around in a car park arguing about it. Look, it's,' he glances at his Rolex, 'nearly eight. What I suggest is, we find a place to stay and we can phone the police from there.' Without waiting for her reply, he takes out his iPhone and starts busily thumbing the screen.

'Oh for god's sake!' She starts to walk away from him, towards the main street, which is growing quieter now as the late opening shops lock their doors and people settle on places to eat. The weight of the hills presses between her shoulder blades, walling off the valley, veined with the bones of the men who have died in them, questing for lead or the rare Blue John stone. She struggles, and fails, to ignite a cigarette, and almost collides with a man standing in the pavement outside a pub, who offers her his lighter. She thanks him then asks if he knows where the police station is.

'There i'nt one 'ere, love. You've to go to Chapel, but they shut at five an' all.'

'Chapel en le Frith?' she queries, aghast. 'So what do I do if I want to contact the police now?'

The man shrugs. 'Call 999, I s'pose.' He turns away from her, accosted by a remark from someone else. He has no wish to get dragged into her problems; he just wants to enjoy his beer and a smoke. A sudden, terrible surge of envy makes Alice want to hit him.

'Did you hear that?' she yells instead at Nathan, who has followed her out of the car park.

'So we go back to my original plan,' he says, with a calm that makes her even angrier. 'We find a place to stay, and some dinner, and we call Chapel. There's bound to be some out of hours number.'

'But...'

He grasps her firmly beneath her elbow, discreetly frog marching her away from the smokers outside the pub. 'Come on.'

'I can't, Nathan. I can't leave her all night. She might not have a bed, or any light, or...' Her throat swells with sobs; tears roll down her cheeks into the corners of her mouth. 'She hasn't even got a toothbrush, Nathan. And she's scared of the dark. She still has a nightlight at home.' She slumps against him, and for a second the wish is there. To turn back time till before the earthquake, to face her life instead of running away from it, to not have to pay this unendurable price.

They have no luck with any of the town's main hotels. Despite the conspicuous trappings of Nathan's affluence, Alice suspects they want to have nothing to do with a man who has no luggage and a bedraggled and tear-stained woman who looks as if she would rather be anywhere but standing in their cosy reception areas, an affront to the well-heeled couples making their way in to dinner. The thought gives her a perverse joy because it seems to locate her in the same twilight world as Polly. She sees, as if in a fever dream, Polly, invisible in plain sight, sad and frightened, struck dumb by the consequences of her actions. Someone here must have noticed her surely, the memory of such an ill-assorted pair as her and Ian must have lodged in someone's memory. At the next place, she will go up to the desk too, and ask.

The next place, the only place left after nearly an hour of tramping around the town is, with the inevitable logic of the nightmare she is in, The Chalet.

'Still here, then,' says Nathan as they stand in front of the red brick Victorian villa which looks no more like a chalet now than it had twenty five years earlier. 'You still got that little ring?' Alice casts him a look of scornful desperation. 'No, I suppose not.'

Alice runs up the front steps and pushes open the door with the air of someone jumping off the edge of a cliff because there is nowhere else to go. Nathan follows her. A surprised desk clerk, a man with leonine hair and a beard and a lumberjack's shirt, tells them he has one double room left, but it is too late for dinner.

'We're looking for...some friends,' says Alice. She describes Ian and Polly, aware of Nathan staring at her in furious mystification but not caring. The clerk listens to her with more than polite interest. When she has finished, he says,

'Odd, that. Someone was in here earlier asking about a couple who sound exactly like your friends.' He pauses, leans across the desk towards her, an interrogative lift to his eyebrows. 'If you want my opinion,' he says, 'the bloke was a cop.'

'We'll take the room,' says Nathan, handing over a credit card.

'Nathan Crowliffe,' says the clerk, examining the card. 'Are you the same as has the deli up How Lane? The manager there said he'd had someone asking about that couple an' all. We buy our cakes and croissants there,' he adds, beaming at Nathan. 'Very good quality.'

'Glad to hear it. Quality's the thing in our market sector.'

'So have either you or the manager at the deli seen them?' Alice interrupts.

'Sorry, love.' The clerk shakes his head; his leonine locks follow the movement with a slight time lag. 'Mind you, Lawrence at the deli said the man sounded like someone he used to know.' Alice's heart lurches; she stops breathing, stops anything that might dilute the concentration with which she is willing this to be a clue, a lead. 'Chap that worked up at Speedwell a few years back. Lawrence remembered him because he used to go out with one of the girls that worked for him. They both left after he got caught breaking in after hours. Funny place to take a girl courting if you ask me but still, takes all sorts, doesn't it?'

'Speedwell,' Alice repeats.

'Thanks,' says Nathan, 'we'll go out and find something to eat now.'

'Doors locked at eleven.'

'Don't be stupid,' says Alice, as soon as they are back out on the street, 'we have to go up there now. That must be where he's hiding her. Speedwell. It's ideal. There's a whole maze of caves beyond the stretch that's open to the public.'

'Exactly. Even if they are there – and the evidence is hardly conclusive – the police'll have to call in caving experts. There's nothing we can do now except phone the police and make sure they have the information.'

'Christ, Nathan! How can you be so calm? What would you do if it was one of your kids down there?'

'I don't know,' he admits, 'but I'd like to think I might have someone around who could keep a cool head for me.' He seizes Alice by her upper arms, pinning them to her sides, and juts his face close to hers. His florid cheeks look almost purple in the light of the sodium streetlamps. 'Mo, listen to me. If you try to do anything now, on your own, in the middle of the night, at best, they'll probably have to waste resources rescuing you as well, at worst, you could make the guy panic.'

She struggles, mutters a protest, but he holds on to her; her skin burns in his grasp as she twists her arms.

'Let me think for you, Mo, let me help you for once.'

The urgency and pathos of his appeal seems to break something inside her. A longing to give up overwhelms her, an urge to lie down and sleep and not wake up until Polly has been found. If she could close her eyes now and open them to see her daughter's face, everything else – Harry's death, the threat of losing Wildwood, the excruciating humiliation of her sexual encounter with Ian, the sudden reappearance of Nathan in her life – would find its place in the scheme of things and become bearable. But she can't; she must keep thinking for herself; if she cannot keep Polly alive in her thoughts, how can she possibly save her from Ian? As this notion crystallises in her mind, it brings with it a realisation of the sense of Nathan's plan. She knows well enough from her work that to coax life back into a piece which has been deadened by neglect or abuse is a long and delicate process. She knows from her scrapbook that it takes many years to become truly lost and that Polly, wherever she is, is not lost.

'Alright,' she says.

THE LAST DAY

The cold in the cavern is absolute. It's the dictionary definition of cold, pushing wet, black thumbs into his eyeballs, making his skin stick to his bones like wet clothes. Polly's whimpering the whole time, stripped of her bravado now, just a little girl afraid of the dark. He'd taken as many torches as he could carry from the store at the head of the cavern, but several had already gone out, so he had turned off the rest to conserve battery power for when he'd need it. It would be daylight outside by then; there was no point in trying to find his way out by the old mine shaft during the hours of darkness; even if he made it to open air, he'd likely as not lose his footing on the hillside and end up dead, or in hospital under police guard, neither of which options figures in his plans.

In the madness of pitch dark he fancies he can see Polly's disembodied voice as a wavering line of light, a firefly shivering with cold and fear. Or perhaps it's his eyes that are shivering, blurring his vision. He wonders if he should attempt to comfort her, but sees no point. Her state of mind no longer matters; she's completely in his power now, in this domain that was once his and that he has reclaimed. Besides, he's in no mood to comfort anyone.

Polly's sobs, monotonous and smothered, as though she's crying into the sleeping bag, get on his nerves. He'd hoped the sleeping bag would shut her up, that maybe she'd go to sleep again. He shouldn't have let her sleep so long in the shepherd's hut. He tries to assess what time it is; he doesn't want to turn on a torch to look at his watch because he doesn't want to attract another barrage of questions from Polly about how long they have to stay in the cavern and what his plans are come morning.

Maybe he should do it now, then at least he'd have some peace. He could take back the sleeping bag, set his alarm for first light and get some rest. But he knows he wouldn't, knows he couldn't pass the rest of the night down here, in the dark and dank, with nothing for company but the drip of water from the cavern roof and the metallic clang of the boat's hull against stone summoning him to wakefulness every time he turned over. The water here, in the mine workings, has no current; it is still, ancient and monstrous; even if he heaved the body over the side it would stay with him; even if he pushed it under the surface, the water in the channels is scarcely deep enough to cover it. You have to be able to put some distance between yourself and the dead; that's what he learnt during the hours he was trapped in the blown-up cinema, whispering to Orla that Gatsby struck him as a man of honour who deserved to get the girl. *He sees her truly, with his heart, just like I see you.* And he'd waited for her reply in the low rumble of settling masonry and the tick of cooling metal.

'Shut the fuck up, will you?' he shouts at Polly, hearing his voice bounce off the rock walls with mounting petulance. Coming here has been his plan from the outset, so why does he feel so out of control?

'I'm scared,' she says, again. 'Why did you bring me down here? What are you going to do?'

'I've told you, we have to lie low till morning. Won't be long now.' He should do it. What's he waiting for? He can just dump her and walk the boat deeper into the Far Canal. He needs to go that way anyway, if he's to find his way into Pilkington's Series and out through the old shaft which is officially blocked. He's trusting to luck that the official blockage hasn't become actual in the years since he was last here. He'll do it now. He withdraws the Webley from his waistband and breaks it as quietly as he can in order to check the alignment of the remaining cartridges.

'What's that?'

'What?' Fuck. Not quietly enough. He can't afford to awaken her suspicions, can't risk a struggle in here where a bullet fired by accident might ricochet in any direction.

'Not sure. I thought I heard something.'

'You're imagining it, kid. Go to sleep.'

'Can't. It's too cold. Ian..?'

'What?'

'Tell me a story.'

'I don't know any.'

'Yes, you do. Tell me about my dad. Tell me why you killed him.'

And perhaps it's a miracle, or perhaps it's the fear of being dragged down by the weight of all his stories, so deep into the black water bowels of these ancient hills he'll never escape, but the moving lips of the wooden Virgin with his mother's face appear to him out of the darkness and her voice says, *Tell her. Why not? You've done your time, you've a right to be rid of your burden.* Why not, he asks himself. After all, whatever he tells her won't be going any further.

Alice lies between waking and sleeping. She falls into a doze, then is jolted awake by Nathan snoring, or adjusting his position in the creaky armchair. Suddenly cold, she pulls the duvet closer around herself, until she is too hot, and throws it off again. The waistband of her trousers feels tight and the loose knit fabric of her sweater digs into her flesh like rings of chain mail. Visions of Polly scroll through her mind in a grim slideshow. Polly screaming, crying, pleading. Worse still, Polly smiling, holding out her arms, Polly acquiescing. All in a remembered half-light, in the gleam of torch beams deflected by water and the wayward glitter of lead or quartz running through the deep, dark rock. Polly's face, a pale, oval stone, sinking, hair golden for a moment in the wavering light, then gone.

Needing the bathroom, she slips out of the bed and pads across the room in her bare feet, skirting the chair where Nathan seems to be asleep. Closing the bathroom door as quietly as she can, she pulls the light cord over the mirror and stands, immobilised by the sight of herself in the sudden, white glare. She looks dirty, crumpled. There are mascara shadows under her eyes and a red indentation down one cheek, from a crease in the pillow, that looks like the weal of a whip. She raises her arms to rake her hair back from her face and smells sweat and stale deodorant. Maybe she'll take a shower; somehow, that seems like a better use of her enforced idleness than some vain attempt to sleep. It will be better, tomorrow, when she is reunited with Polly, for her to look herself. If Polly were to see her like this, dishevelled, out of control, it would scare her.

Sliding the bolt across the door, she turns on the shower. Mothers, Alice believes, should be steadfast, unalterable. She begins to strip off her clothes, folding them neatly on the closed lavatory seat. They should be constants in their children's lives, dependable, predictable. She holds her wrist under the shower jet to test the temperature, then steps in.

And remembers, as the hot water needles her scalp and shoulders, that she has not spoken to Jesse since her abrupt and unexplained departure with Nathan. How many hours ago? He and Isabella must have seen her climb into Nathan's car and disappear down the drive. He would have had only Isabella or Mary, or the police, to turn to for an explanation, and none of them would have had one to offer. Will anyone have told him about Polly's call, or Ian's gun? Will anyone have guessed where Alice has gone?

She will call him now. It doesn't matter that it is the early hours of the morning, she will find Nathan's phone and call him immediately. Better to wake him in the middle of the night than let him continue to sleep on the festering suspicion that he is being ignored, neglected. Mothers do not neglect their children. Mothers must maintain a balance, even when the needs of one appear to outweigh those of another. Stepping back out of the shower, she wraps herself in a towel and returns to the bedroom. She forgets to switch off the bathroom light, whose beam now falls square on Nathan's face. His eyes snap open.

'What now?' He throws off his blanket and rises from the chair. He has removed his chinos and hung them in the wardrobe, and looks vulnerable in his shirt and boxer shorts, a plump middle-aged man with spindly legs and thinning hair. She recognises nervousness and lust in the look that flickers over her body in the bath towel and feels, for a moment, powerful, until Nathan's inviolable ordinariness strikes her with the double force of a thought both new and remembered.

'I need your phone.'

'Now? Why? Who are you going to call at this time? It's...' he picks up his watch from the chair arm, 'nearly three in the morning.'

'Jesse. My son,' she adds, in answer to his raised eyebrows. 'That's not his real name, though. I called him James, but

Harry never liked it so he nicknamed him Jesse. Jesse James. He had such a stupid sense of humour.'

'Your dad would have been pleased, I'm sure.'

'Don't be sarcastic, it doesn't suit you. Phone.' Alice holds out her hand. Nathan looks briefly as though he is going to argue with her, but changes his mind and begins to hunt for his phone. He goes through the pockets of his jacket and trousers, hanging in the wardrobe, sweeps the wardrobe floor with the flat of his hand but gathers only dust and an old dry cleaning ticket, probes down the back of the chair and shakes out the bed clothes.

'Must have left it in the car,' he concludes, pulling on trousers and shoes, and picking up the car keys from the bedside table.

When he returns with the phone, he is also carrying the post Alice had left on the Porsche's back seat. 'Look,' he says, 'if you can't sleep, why not open your parcel. That might help to pass the time. And you can ring Jesse when he gets up.'

Alice, dressed again now, with her damp hair fastened in a pony tail, shakes her head. 'We'll be on our way by then.'

'On our way where? You don't know that. Face facts, Mo, we could be hanging around for hours yet.'

'No. No, we won't. We know Polly's at Speedwell. We'll be going there at first light.'

'Alright, text him then. That way you won't wake the poor kid up in the middle of the night. I'm going to make a cup of tea. Want one?'

She says yes, more to show her appreciation of his kindness than because she wants anything other than to find Polly and go home. While he fusses about with the tea things, she does as he suggests and sends Jesse a text to say she is sorry for not being in touch sooner, but that she has gone to fetch Polly and will be home later in the day. She says he should be polite to Mary and Isabella, and work hard at school, and be careful taking the boat out to the island, and that she loves him. She signs off with four kisses.

Still wide awake, she sips lukewarm tea that tastes of UHT milk and turns her attention to her parcel. The handwriting on the address label is neat, but made with a painstaking rigidity which suggests a writer who lacks confidence. The postmark is too smudged for her to make it out. Intrigued, now, despite herself, she tears away the layers of brown wrapping paper to reveal Abigail Jones' royal wedding biscuit tin. A note is taped to the lid, in the same hand as the address label, on a sheet of lined paper torn from a child's exercise book.

Dear Mrs. Theobald, Alice reads, hope and dread curdling together in her stomach

I am sorry but Abigail die yesterday.

Alice scans the letter for a date but there is none.

As home have no record of relatives, I decide send this to you. I hope is not wrong thing to do. I have not looked inside. Is not my place. In my home country we say a noisy cow give no milk. Abigail have nothing else but old clothes I send to charity shop and, forgive me, little brooch which I keep. Is not diamonds, only glass and will remind me of her. She was sad lady, I think, but not bad.

Yours respectful
Stefanya Spandler
Care Assistant

Alice lifts the lid from the tin, which seems to contain nothing but newspaper cuttings, thinned and yellowed by time and handling. Their smell is familiar; it reminds her of her scrapbook. Most of the cuttings are small, single columns or half columns, but one is a full page, folded many times to fit the tin, and fragile along the folds so Alice has to open it with care to prevent it falling into pieces. She smooths it out on the bed. There is a banner headline in thick black lettering, and several photographs, but it is only the largest of these, in the middle of the page, that she notices, with a mixture of recognition and total incomprehension.

When I was five, both my parents died and I was sent to a home. No, that's not the place to begin, it makes him sound as though he's looking for pity. *When I was eleven I killed a little kid.* Nor that either, because it's not true. And what is the point of a confession if it isn't true?

'Your dad and me were best friends once.' His words fall into silence as he pauses to gather himself. The boat lies motionless in the still, black water. He can't even hear Polly breathing. 'Are you listening?'

'Yes.'

'Nathan, come here. Look at this.'

He stands beside the bed and peers over her shoulder. 'That's your dad,' he says.

'It is, isn't it? I wondered...I mean, it's so long since I've seen him. But it is.'

'He looks young.'

'This was...' Alice hunts for a date at the top of the page. '...1967. The year before I was born. He'd have been...'

'What?' demands Nathan as her voice trails away. 'What is it?'

'The woman. No, not that one, the one standing just behind him, looks as if she's trying to shield her eyes from flashbulbs. That's Abigail Jones.'

'That name rings a bell...wait a minute...'

'What's she doing with my dad?' Suddenly unable to look at the picture any more, she rises, crosses to the window and opens the curtains. The irregular patch of sky visible beyond the jagged outline of Mam Tor and the ruined castle is a deep, luminous lilac. 'Nathan..?' Though she says his name, she feels as if she is talking to the fading and indifferent stars. 'Did anything funny ever happen?'

He gives a nervous laugh. 'What do you mean?'

'I'm not sure. When you...got married, maybe. How were my parents about that?'

'Gracious. Generous. They always give my kids Christmas and birthday presents. Pauline takes your mum out shopping sometimes.'

Though his tone is accusatory, she feels relieved, then ashamed, then horribly as though everything that is happening is no more than she deserves. But it is not what Polly deserves, nor Harry. 'The thing is, Abigail Jones. Harry used to pay her care home fees. I found out when he disappeared. I went to see her, but she was in a pretty bad state and I couldn't find anything out. But if she knew my dad, and Harry knew her, well...it must add up to something, mustn't it?'

'But what? Come on, let's read the article. That's sure to tell us something.'

'A place called Appsley House,' says Ian to the listening dark. 'Your dad and I both lived there...well, I lived there all the time, he was only there some of the time.'

'Was that before my grandparents died? Were you, like, a servant's son or something?'

The arrogance of her assumption infuriates him but it's also so preposterous he finds he's able to laugh at it, and his laughter gentles the silence of the cave.

'Not sure your dad ever had a father,' he says, 'but his mother was still very much alive when I knew him.' *At the front of the public gallery, backcombed, catching theatrical sobs in a crumpled lace hankie, mascara panda'd round her eyes.*

'No,' says Polly. 'His parents were killed when he was little. Like Bruce Wayne's, only not murdered. A train crash.'

So like Craig to find the strand of truth and twist it, like the sad old perv that used to do Appsley House Christmas parties, twisting balloons into poodles.

'Whose story is this, kid?' His hand tenses on the butt of the gun.

She says nothing, but a rustle of the sleeping bag and a knocking of the boat's hull against the cavern wall tells him she's shifted her position, feels herself to be on uncertain ground. He relaxes his grip on the gun, strokes the barrel with his fingertips as he speaks.

'Appsley House was a children's home, Polly, in Sheffield. Your dad and I lived there, for a while. Well, I lived there for quite a long time. Your dad came and went. It depended on his mother's love life as far as I could understand it. New boyfriend, Craig came to Appsley House, no boyfriend, he stayed at home. You get my drift?'

'Craig?'

'Harry Theobald wasn't his real name, love. His real name was Craig Barnes. I'm getting to why he changed it.'

Only now, as she finishes reading the article and looks back at the main photograph, does Alice notice that her father and Abigail Jones are holding hands. 'Jones,' she says, and the word feels different in her mouth, though she is not sure whether it is she or the name that has been changed by what she now knows. 'I never thought...I mean, it's such a common name and I'd been Alice Theobald nee Walker for so long. Didn't you know any of this, Nathan? Has my dad never said anything, all those nights you take him to the pub?'

'You think..?'

'What?' she snaps, whipping round to face him where he sits beside her on the bed. 'Do I think you'd have married me if you'd known there was...*this*,' she stabs at the newspaper article with her finger, 'in my family? Well? Would you?'

'Mo, I swear, I hadn't an inkling. All I've ever known is that there was you and your mum and dad. I had no idea your dad had been married before and certainly no idea... about Jimmy. I mean, I was only two when it happened, and god knows, there've been plenty of other cases like it since to overshadow the memory.'

'Not his memory, I imagine.' *Not Abigail's.* 'It was his son... my brother.' She waits, for the meaning of her words to take shape in her, but nothing happens. The words hang in the air like a frosted breath. Perhaps she is in shock, or perhaps the true heart of herself has been trapped for so long beneath the layers of invention that the life, the feeling, has been smothered out of it.

'Half brother,' says Nathan, as if that makes any difference, 'and he died before you were born.'

'But not in Dad's memory, or Mum's. No wonder she used to tiptoe around him so when he had his moods. Imagine living with a secret like that, never knowing when he might lose it and say something to me. I always knew there was some barrier, something that stopped him loving me, both of them, really. I suppose that's why I let myself marry you. A combination of wanting to please them, and wanting to find a relationship that was...complete.'

'What happened, Mo, after the earthquake?' Nathan's expectant stillness burns at her side. She stands up, stretches, and goes back to the window. A milkfloat rattles past on the road below and somewhere, a cock crows. She hopes Jesse isn't having a nightmare, that, if he does, he will wake up, and see the light returning, and read her text, and be consoled. She can see her own reflection in the glass, ghostly and blurred by the effect of the double glazing, one self superimposed upon another. Suddenly furious with herself, she realises she would be able to be stronger for her children if she were not so worn out with maintaining the subterfuge of her own life. She takes a deep breath and begins.

'We used to bunk off school quite a bit, me and your dad. To be honest, he was a bit of a goody two shoes at the outset, took a bit of persuading. Said education was important and how his mum was always going on about wishing she'd stayed on at school.'

'I can just hear him,' says Polly, and he fancies he can hear her smiling, 'the bit about education being important, not about his mother, obviously.'

'Well, I reminded him his mum had left him at Appsley House while she had it away with some bloke so what the fuck did she know and after that we hardly went to school at all. He showed me this den he had, like a little cave dug into a railway siding. It was about fifteen minutes walk from the school the Appsley House kids were supposed to go to. There was some shops on the way, including an offy, and we'd hang around outside there till we could find an adult who'd buy us half a dozen barley wines and ten Number Six...'

'I'm sorry but I have, like, no idea what you're talking about?'

'Shut up. Doesn't matter. Then one day your dad just grabbed this pram some woman had left outside the greengrocers and wheeled it away, baby inside an' all. He said he meant to leave it at the next shop, that he thought it'd be a laugh to hide and watch the mother come out of the grocer's and run around squawking like a headless chicken till she saw where the baby was. But the thing is, all the time he was saying that, he had a look in his eye, like that wasn't what he was intending at all. He started running with the pram, and I followed him. I was a bit scared, I suppose, but mostly I was excited, and pleased with myself, because your dad had started out such a goody goody and it was me persuading him to wag that had turned him into this bloke who'd steal a baby. We didn't stop till we got to the den.

'It was alright for a bit. We played with the baby, hidey-boo, stuff like that, and it laughed, but then it began screaming and we couldn't shut it up. We had some gin and orange, and we tried getting some of that down it coz I remembered me own mum giving gripe water to our Daniel and she said it had a dash of alcohol in it that'd help him sleep. But the baby was sick, and then it smelt as well as screaming and the whole thing was a nightmare. Craig said he was going to take it back up to the road and leave it, but I said what if someone saw him and that we ought to wait till it got dark.

'We hung on for a bit, but the kid went on bawling. I couldn't stand it after a while and I went out onto the embankment to have a fag and wait for the London train to go by. Diesels were new then, exciting. Cutting fucking edge technology. I honestly don't know to this day exactly what happened, but when the roar of the train died away, I realised it was quiet. I mean, quiet. No crying baby. I was getting cold so I went back into the den. I asked Craig if it was asleep but he didn't answer. I looked at the baby. Its eyes were shut and it looked sort of peaceful, except its lips and eyelids was blue and its head was at a funny angle to the rest of it. Craig's face was the whitest thing I'd ever seen, and horrible. Haunts my dreams does that face, even after all the other stuff that's happened in my life. You know what, Polly..?'

'What?' Her voice has shrunk almost to nothing.

'That'll be what he looks like in his coffin. White and horrible, and ten years old. You can lie all you like while you're alive, but it all stops when you're dead.'

'Noooo! *You're* the one that's lying!' Her cry reverberates around the cavern, each echo more anguished than the last. The boat begins a crazy rocking as she lunges for him. Water splashes his leg; it burns him, it's rotting his skin with the heat of decay. His fist curls once more around the butt of the revolver, his finger caresses the trigger. He lifts the gun high, well clear of the rocking boat and the hellish black water. It shines, in his mind's eye, it shows him the girl, foundering, grasping, the sobs forcing themselves out of her warm lungs and dying on the fire-cold air.

'When I woke up, came round, whatever,' says Alice, 'to begin with I was just thirsty. I kept calling for you to bring me a glass of water but you didn't reply. It was so quiet, I remember that, how very quiet it was, and I knew it wasn't right but I couldn't work out why. After that, it's a bit vague. I feel as if I fell asleep, but maybe I lost consciousness. The next thing I knew I was falling, and there was a lot of noise, roaring and grinding. I remember thinking it sounded a bit like a train. And then I was lying on my back staring at the night sky.'

'The building where the restaurant was collapsed,' says Nathan. 'I thought you'd been buried underneath it. I thought...I kept running over and over in my head that only two days before I'd been standing beside you in church promising God I'd stand beside you for the rest of our lives and that I'd failed already. You were under a mound of concrete and I was safe. See this..?' He pauses, but she continues to stare out of the window. 'I have this deformed thumb nail. I ripped out the nail bed digging in the rubble with my bare hands and it grew back more like a claw than a nail. You could walk off without a care in the world, but not me. I could never forget.'

The lilac sky is giving way to a luminous citrus yellow. Alice keeps her eyes fixed on it; her mind runs along a track of colour charts, the names like poetry, keeping at bay the texts she has by heart from her scrapbook, the dreadful and fascinating smell of newsprint coming from the bed.

'I looked for you for days, Mo.'

Pale citrus. Lunar Falls.

'Queued in the sun for the consul, useless twat. Flies gathering round my injured hand. Some Greek nurse with some Dettol and a pack of paracetomol.'

Wild primrose. Yellow weld.

'Maureen Crowliffe, I kept saying, my wife. We've only been married two days. Then I remembered you hadn't changed your passport yet.'

Rose ochre. Light Gamboge.

'So I joined the end of the queue again and asked about Maureen Jones.'

Aconite yellow. 'I did go to the consul. In a striped gazebo, like it was a garden party. It took me a long time to find him, walking in the sun, stepping over cracks. Some dead cats. A perfect tray of *galatoboureko* iced in concrete dust.' *I'd forgotten that, till now.* 'And while I was walking, something that had always been a bit out of kilter suddenly slotted into place. I'd made a mistake. I'd let myself be pushed into things. You know what it was like, us being neighbours, our parents going down the Miners' Club,' at this she gives a bit-terly ironic laugh, and hears it echoed by Nathan, 'together, every Saturday night. We were thrown together, we never had a chance to make up our own minds.

'I kept thinking it would be OK. I thought...you know... the first time you brought me here...I thought maybe sex just took practice, that I'd learn to like it. After all, I had learned to like Def Leppard,' she smiles, almost turns to face him, but lets her smile die in the window glass instead, 'well, sort of. When we got engaged it seemed so inevitable I wondered if that was why I wasn't as excited as people seemed to expect me to be.' She hears the rustle of bed-clothes and newspaper, a deep sigh from Nathan. The skin between her shoulder blades crawls in anticipation of his coming up behind her, touching her, but he doesn't, so she continues.

'I didn't know exactly what I was going to do, but then, when I got to the head of the queue and was asked for my name, I said, Alice Walker. It just popped into my head, I had no idea why. It was only later I remembered there'd been a girl in front of me with a copy of *The Colour Purple* sticking out of the top of her backpack. I said I'd lost my passport, which was true.'

'They sent that back to your parents, with some official letter explaining how long you have to wait before you can presume a missing person dead and what paperwork has to be done. No mention of me. It was like we'd never been married.'

'I'm sorry...no, that's crap. Actually, I'm not. It's a good thing. We never should have been married. I'm glad they made me out a temporary passport in the name of Alice Walker, I'm glad I became her and married Harry. And look... it's light out now. We should be going.'

'It's a quarter to five, Mo. We've told the police all we can, and they told us to stay put until they contacted us. Just let them do their job; that's the best way to get Polly back safe. Come back and lie down for a bit.'

'God, Nathan! How can you be so reasonable, so...*nice?* Why can't you just leave me alone?'

'You were the one got in my car and asked...no, *ordered* me to drive you up here.'

'Just go home. Go home and let me do this my way.'

'No. You fucked up my life once already, you're not doing it again. I'm not having your kid's death on my conscience, not after everything you've just told me. We're starting again, Mo, and this time it's going to be on my terms.'

'Fuck you, Nathan.' Alice storms away from the window towards the door, but Nathan, though not quick, has less ground to cover to bar it. She flings herself at him, she kicks, she claws at his face, but she is small and weak and exhausted, and her bitten nails make no impression on his skin. She collapses against him in tears, and weeps until she no longer knows whether it is fresh tears wetting her face or the ones that have already soaked into his shirt. With his arm around her shoulders and one hand hooked beneath her armpit, he draws her towards the bed, sweeping Abigail's newspaper cuttings aside with his free hand.

INGLISS CHANGES PLEA

she reads, as the sheet flutters to the floor like a sere leaf.

'I'm not listening any more. I've got my hands over my ears.' It had been the matter of a moment to overpower Polly and fling her back to the stern of the boat where she landed with a muffled thud and a whump of expelled air that told him she had at least not gone overboard. The force of his relief when she speaks, so he knows she's conscious, shakes him. He hadn't realised how desperate he was, having begun his story, to finish it. He will consign it to Polly's hearing and then, by severing her senses forever from this world, he will be rid of it.

'Well,' he resumes, his tone conversational yet shot through with the determination of the bore at a party who won't be deflected from what he has to say by any amount of interruptions, 'there's the baby, dead, and Craig gibbering with shock.' Polly begins to sing, loudly and tunelessly. He ignores her, knowing she'll give up if he just keeps going. 'D'you know, it was more than forty years till I heard him say another intelligible word. What to do? I figured we couldn't just leave it there, in the den. Even though no-one except me really went there with Craig, its existence was an open secret. It wouldn't take long for them to put two and two together once they found it. So I thought the best thing'd be to make it look like an accident. So I wheeled the pram out of the den and shoved it down the embankment on to the track. As the train to Leeds had just been, I knew the London train'd be along in a few minutes, and it'd hit the pram and the driver might not even notice, up there in his cab, in charge of that great speeding, roaring heap of metal. Then I gave Craig a good shaking, and I told him that if anyone asked, he was to keep his mouth shut and I'd do the talking. He kept rambling on about some fuckin' tin soldier. *The tin soldier didn't say a word.* That was what he said, over and over, till I thought he'd wear the words out. So I give him a good slap across the face and he shut up.'

'*The Steadfast Tin Soldier,*' says Polly. It's by Hans Christian Andersen. My dad used to read it to us when we were little. He falls in love with a paper dancer and...'

'That's as maybe. All that matters is, once the shit hit the fan, and the cops came round Appsley House, saying they'd found fibres from the baby's blanket or some such in the den, I just told Craig to remember he was the tin soldier and let me do the talking. But...well, I was shit scared and they weren't...clever, exactly, but they were patient, wearing away at us. Like the sea at your place. You know it'll get it in the end, that you can only trick it for so long with sea walls and netting the cliffs. And they got me muddled. They kept saying they knew me, boys like me, that were bad lots through and through, always doing wicked things then lying about it. They wore me down.'

Alice leans down from the bed to pick up the stray cutting. Immediately below the headline are twin school photographs of two boys, scrubbed and neat, grinning big-toothed grins into the camera lens. One has an ungainly, angular face whose bones seem somehow too big for it. His eyes are pale, and too close together, and his hair is long enough to push behind his ears. The other is handsome, his features regular, his hair dark and crisply curling. His gaze, fringed with long, dark, almost girlish lashes, makes Alice feel as though he is in love with her. Harry. It's Harry. So certain is she of this that, when she reads the name Craig Barnes beneath the photo, her first instinct is to believe the reporter has made a mistake. Bewildered, she looks at the other boy's name: Arthur Ingliss. But, looking back at his photograph, she realises she knows him as Ian Slight, and all his actions since he had turned up in Aylsburgh and rescued Polly from drowning take on a new and horrible significance.

He, then, is the one in the headline, the one who has 'changed his plea.' Plea to what, she asks herself, but the question is rhetorical, and constituted only to put off the point at which she has to confront the answer.

'Here, let me,' says Nathan, seeing her hesitation, and takes the cutting from her, and begins to read.

'Read it out to me,' she commands, after watching the back-and-forth flick of his eyes for a few seconds.

'Sure?'

She nods.

'"It was a momentous day today in the trial of Craig Barnes and Arthur Ingliss, accused of the murder of sixteen month old Jimmy Jones, when Ingliss suddenly decided to change his plea to guilty. As all the evidence for the prosecution had been heard, and counsel for Barnes explained that he could mount no defence for his client as Barnes had refused to speak, even to confirm his name for the court, the judge, Mr. Justice Rutherford, dismissed the jury. He thanked them for the fortitude with which they had listened to the very distressing evidence in the case. Mitigations on behalf of both boys were then heard before sentence was handed down.

'"Mr. Justice Rutherford told the court the task before him was both simple and challenging, simple in that the boys had committed murder, for which only one sentence was possible in English law, even for children as young as these. They must be sentenced to life imprisonment. However, because of the mercifully unique nature of their crime and their extreme youth, he wished to spend some time considering the best way to dispose of them, bearing in mind Ingliss' acceptance of his guilt and Barnes' continued, and troubling, silence in the face of overwhelming evidence of his complicity. The court would therefore reconvene in a week's time, and Barnes and Ingliss would, in the meantime, continue to be held in the remand homes where they have been since their arrest."' Nathan returns the paper to the bed. 'Little bastards,' he says. 'I can never understand kids doing that sort of thing...Mo..?'

She is staring once more at the photo of the boy called Craig Barnes, the boy who is Harry. She hopes, if she looks long enough and hard enough, she will see it isn't him, discern some fundamental variation between Harry's features and those of the boy in the photograph. But the longer she looks, the more unmistakable the likeness becomes, reinforced by the evidence of Harry's financial support for Abigail Jones, his payment of Craig Barnes' blood debt.

She's back on her first date with Harry, in a restaurant where she feels underdressed and exposed beneath the pathologically attentive gaze of their personal waiter whose name, she suddenly remembers, was Gino. Leaning in to her across the table, as though unaware of the hovering Gino, Harry says, 'There's something between us, isn't there? Can't you feel it? The moment I first saw you, I recognised you.' She must have given away her alarm in her face, because he immediately sits back, raises his hands as if to show he is unarmed, and explains what he means by 'recognised'.

At the time, she thought it was no more than a pick-up line; now, staring at that same searchlight smile on the face of a schoolboy called Craig Barnes, she knows exactly what he meant, and that she felt it too. It was just that she had had less practice than him at dealing with it. She had only been Alice Walker for three years, whereas he...

'I wonder how long they went to prison for.' She turns back to the papers spread out on the bed and begins to riffle through them. 'It might say somewhere. I should think my...Jimmy's...Abigail would have wanted to know when they came out.'

'If I had my way, they'd still be there now.'

'Well, they're not.' She pushes the court report towards Nathan. 'Look,' she says, stabbing the picture of Barnes with her finger. 'Recognise him?' There are photos of Harry around, though she now understands why he, like her, was always reluctant to be photographed, and Nathan would very likely have come across some while tracking her down.

'Oh my god,' he says, after a few seconds of stunned silence. 'It's...oh shit.'

'Shall I say it for you? Craig Barnes is Harry Theobald, the man I married. I married the man who murdered my baby half-brother.'

'Can't be. Coincidences like that don't happen.'

'It's true. Why else would he have been paying for Abigail's care? If I had a photo of my son on me, I'd show you. They're identical. Jesse's thirteen, only a couple of years older than... Barnes in this picture. No wonder Harry didn't like me calling him James...It makes me wonder if he knew who I was all along, if marrying me was another part of his atonement.'

'That's just sick.'

'It's plausible, though, isn't it? If he kept tabs on Abigail, what's to say he didn't do the same with Dad? And then it wouldn't have taken much effort to identify me, not for someone with his resources and his...insight into the whole business of being someone else.'

'You must hate him.'

She hesitates before replying, but more from a courtesy for the convention Nathan represents than because she needs time to consider her answer. 'No,' she says, 'that's not the way love works, is it?'

'But how can you love him?' demands Nathan, after a beat which lasts a fraction of a second, but is not lost on her. 'For one thing, the man you married didn't even exist. He was just some alias thought up by a probation officer somewhere to protect him from what he had coming if anyone found out who he really was.'

'By that reckoning, Nathan, he married a woman who didn't exist either. But the marriage was real enough. The children are real enough.' She feels the ache of them, deep in her womb, Polly and Jesse as lost to her, at this moment, as the baby she miscarried. That, she had believed, was her punishment, and Polly was her absolution. She had never, until now, given a thought to her parents. To her father, who mourns the loss of both his children. She is overwhelmed with shame and the need to atone for what she has done. Turning to Nathan, clasping both her hands around his, which curl into fists at her touch, she says, 'It doesn't matter. Nathan, nothing matters now except getting Polly back. If you won't come with me, just give me the car keys and I'll go up to Speedwell on my own. There must be something I can do.'

Pulling his hands from hers, Nathan rises from the bed. 'Right, then. I'll go. You stay here and I'll ring you. You're in no condition...'

'No. That's no better than waiting for the police. I'm coming with you.'

They glare at each other, and Alice feels illuminated by a certainty, a wave of light sweeping through her, scouring, setting things in order. She was right to do what she did, right not to acquiesce in her marriage to Nathan. Perhaps, she thinks, taking in Nathan's air of stubborn decency, you can only define love by what it is not, like looking at a photographic negative. 'Look, just drive me up there and leave me. Go home. This isn't your problem.'

'Jesus! Were you always like this? Have I just gone through the past twenty one years conscientiously refusing to think ill of the dead? Don't you see? You've made it my problem, you daft cow.' He shoves his arms into the sleeves of his jacket and grabs his keys from among the newspaper cuttings strewn about the bed. 'And you'd better not leave that lot lying about, unless you want to find yourself in the eye of a tabloid storm.'

As she sweeps the cuttings back into Abigail's biscuit tin, a small headline catches her eye. It is from the *Ludgate Courier* and dated May 21st, 1973.

HOSPITAL GARDEN WINS TOP PRIZE

First prize in the Ludgate Garden Festival went to St. Helier Hospital inmate, Craig Barnes, 16, for a design entitled *The Steadfast Tin Soldier.* The garden will be shown at Chelsea as part of a larger entry from HM Prison Service.

It is the final link in the chain that binds Harry Theobald to Craig Barnes. She stuffs it into the tin and pushes on the lid.

Silence. Ian has no more to say. The rest of it, the trial, the sanctimonious judge, the implacable piety of the jurors, Craig's mother with her lace hankies and no-one crying for him, is a matter of public record. Polly can read it in the papers if she wants to...correction, she could, if he let her out of here alive. But he can't do that. Not now. He's going out alone, a clean sheet. He'll be wanted, the way Danny was. His last memory of Danny is when the ambulance man picked him out of his, Arthur's, lap so his partner could see if Arthur was hurt. His last memory of Danny is mixed up with their dad, bowed over the steering wheel as if in prayer, and the scream of the car horn, the hiss of escaping steam, the manic jangle of bells on emergency vehicles. His last memory of Danny comes back to him sometimes, in dreams, smelling of boiled sweets and baby piss. Danny doesn't know he exists, doesn't know he pushed a baby on to a railway track to even the score.

He adjusts his grip on the Webley and cocks it.

'What are you doing?' Polly's voice is querulous and fearful; she sounds like some old lady afraid of a mugging.

'Nothing. Shut up.'

'I heard something.'

Dropping from the helmsman's thwart to his knees, he begins to crawl along the hull. 'Just looking for something to eat,' he reassures Polly, because he can't prevent the boat rocking as he moves. 'Hungry work, telling one's life story,' he adds, with a joviality so false it almost becomes real.

'I'm thirsty,' Polly complains. He pretends to be look-ing for a bottle of Coke. His free hand, groping ahead of him, makes contact with her leg under the sleeping bag. She gasps, pulls her leg up, leaving him with nothing but a handful of slippery, padded fabric. He lunges forward, flailing in the darkness for a hold on any part of her body. He can hear her whimpering, voicing half formed questions and pleadings, scrabbling in the dark like a rat. She knows. It's an instinct. He'd seen it in the army, and before, at the place with the swimming pool, on the face of a boy who throttled himself with an electric cable. They were stopped having desk lamps after that. He can't see it this time, of course, but he can smell it, rank and bestial, and not the way a pretty fifteen year old girl should smell at all.

Then suddenly, his nostrils are filled with the scent of Bronnley Lily of the Valley soap. Light fizzes and crackles around him, coalesces into the perfect, bland features of Robert Redford which blister and blacken before his horri-fied gaze. 'Don't worry, I've got you!' he shouts, or thinks he does, but his mouth is full of brackish water, bitter as bile, so perhaps nothing comes out of it but a gargle. The water booms and moans in his ears. There are words wrapped in the sounds it makes, but they elude him; they are eel words, slippery and cold. They are around his wrists and ankles, dragging him down, and eating their way into his brain. If he can only decipher them, everything will be alright. If he can only get free of the water, and breathe the lily of the valley scented air, everything will make sense. He inhales deeply, reaching for the remembered perfume, and hears Orla speaking to him in her sassy, streetwise Belfast that hides the sweetness of her like the tart shell of a sherbet lemon. *Let go, Ian,* she says, *just let go and I'll catch you.* Her arms are stretched out towards him, the mood ring shimmering all the colours of the rainbow on her wedding finger.

There is no sign of activity around the cavern entrance, and the car park is empty except for Nathan's Porsche. As Alice climbs out of the car, nothing reaches her ears but the sounds of birdsong and bleating lambs, and the song of a light wind among the rocks. She flexes her fingers, stiff from gripping the biscuit tin, and hammers her fist into the car roof.

'Hey!' shouts Nathan.

'Where is everybody? You see, I told you we shouldn't leave it to them. We should have...'

'Morning.' The voice sounds like something out of *Wallace and Gromit.* Its owner, as he saunters towards them across the car park, has a pervasive air of brownness. Brown hair, brown eyes, brown cord trousers and a brown waxed jacket. Alice shivers, suddenly aware of the absurdity of her cropped trousers and flimsy sandals. The brown man fishes a warrant card out of one of his jacket pockets. 'I know it doesn't look like it,' he says, 'but there's a police operation going on here so I'm going to have to ask you to leave.'

'I'm Alice Theobald,' says Alice. A surge of adrenalin squares her shoulders and banishes the cold. 'It's my daughter down there.'

'D. I. Bill Grandage.' His brown eyebrows draw into a frown. 'I must still ask you to leave, Mrs. Theobald. Your being here could cause all sorts of bother. This is a situation for the specialists.'

'Where are they?' Alice's eyes hunt the surrounding moor, the rocks and mounds of sheep-bitten grass, the dark cavern entrance and the gaudy little shop beside it.

'Where they need to be,' says Grandage, imperturbable.

'Come on, Alice.' Nathan tries to take her hand, but she twists it out of his grasp and moves away from the car in the direction of the cavern.

'I'm not going anywhere,' she says, her voice sounding weak and plaintive on the wind that swirls around the head of the pass. The sky is blue now, with a scrim of white cloud, and she can hear skylarks. A memory comes to her, of lying up on the top of Kinder Scout with Nathan, her back arched over the uneven ground, nothing but the fine layer of her teenage skin between her ribs and the sky. You could never spot the larks because they flew so high, but the rising bubble of song was everywhere. She loves this landscape, she realises, with a surge of conviction that Polly can come to no harm here. She has an acute sense of the ground beneath her feet, and beneath that, the cavern where Polly waits like Persephone to return to her mother. 'I'm not going anywhere,' she repeats, but softly this time, in a strong whisper Polly will be able to hear through the thin crust of lead-veined rock.

All she has to do is stay focused on Polly. She walks on towards the cave entrance. Though her gaze remains fixed on the dark shelter where visitors wait to be loaded on to the boats, her nerve-ends tingle with the awareness of Grandage's team hidden all around her. If she were to look hard enough, she would see them, armed men, frogmen,

men with metal detectors and loudhailers and GPS radios, hidden among the rocks. They would emerge into view like Wally in the books Jesse used to love when he was little. It is her will that holds them all together in their web of purposeful synchronicity. She steps out of the car park, into the narrow road which separates it from the cavern entrance before winding on up the pass.

She is vaguely aware of sheep droppings adhering to her soles, of the crackle of a radio somewhere off to her right. The steel door to the cavern glimmers in the shadow of the waiting area like a distant star, long dead, its last light marking a portal to other worlds. There are voices behind her, stentorian, barking like dogs, and further bursts of radio crackle. She stretches out her hand towards the door, and it begins to open. She feels blest.

But now her progress towards Polly is impeded. Hands grasp her arms and shoulders. The radio crackle is louder and shouting surrounds her, too close, too bewildering for her to know what is being said. A scream cuts through the shouting, then a thunderous explosion silences it, or perhaps it is the other way round. Afterwards, everything happens in slow motion, as if the explosion has happened in a film and not here, half way up the Winnats Pass, outside Speedwell Cavern. Uniformed men scatter in slow motion, then reform, as if performing a circle dance of which she is the centre. Slowly, Alice falls, slowly her head bounces twice against the tarmac, but it doesn't hurt. Her head is cushioned by the bubblewrap of skylark song.

She is lying on her back, though she has no idea why, trying to shield her eyes from the sun, though she cannot remember how. Somehow, closing her eyes and breathing at the same time has become too complicated for her, and when she tries to raise a hand to cover her eyes, it floats away from her, quite independent of her will. Her view is suddenly cluttered with faces, but they are all in the wrong place, and the sun still strikes between them, stabbing through her eye sockets into the back of her head. She sees herself nailed to the ground by sunbeams. She tries to tell the faces to go away, to stop using up her air, but all they do is talk; they don't listen to her.

Their words come to her at random, and with echoes attached. She must be in the cavern, where the boatmen play games with the echo effect, to tame it for the tourists. But where is Polly? Someone says, 'ambulance.' Polly. She must find out where Polly is, if she's safe, if she is the one in the ambulance, but although she concentrates very hard on forming the question, the voice that comes out of her mouth is her mother's, telling her she must always wear clean knickers in case she was run over by a bus and had to be taken to hospital.

Then everything inside her is pushed out of place by a ballooning, aggressive embarrassment that hurls hot blood into her cheeks and shrivels her guts as if they wish they could disappear. She left home without packing; she is wearing the same underwear she had on yesterday. Please...if she can just explain to the ambulance staff. She's not a dirty girl, she just had to find her daughter. They'll understand, they'll sympathise...

But nobody is listening. They have moved on to other conversations.

Six Years Later
Persephone

Today is my twenty first birthday, today, in even the most cautious parts of the world I travel, I have become an adult. I lift my left hand in front of my face to admire the gift I have given myself, which weds me to my past the way my mother's scrapbook, or the bills my father paid for an old woman's care wedded them to theirs. The past must be objectified, set outside oneself; if you do not do this, you will become warped by it, as my Hades was.

My gift, my past, is a ring. The ring is set with an opal. The opal contains the last sunset I saw before I went underground. Before Polly became Persephone, before her heart was petrified by the steady, poisonous drip of things she didn't want to know. An opal with a sunset trapped in it, and not just any sunset, but that particular sunset, is neither cheap nor easy to find. But I charge highly for my professional services, and my work gives me the opportunity to travel. I scoured the opal fields of Australia and Nevada for this stone, of Brazil and Nicaragua, Turkey and Ethiopia, though I found it closer to home, in a back street in Budapest. I will not tell you what I paid for it. It is worth any price, and none.

Today I plan to tie up the remaining loose ends of Apollonia Theobald's life and to smash to dust the brittle stone that is the heart of Persephone. Tomorrow, Polly Barnes, a young, wealthy and eminently respectable widow, will emerge from the chrysalis of her mourning and take possession of her house in Chile, overlooking the Pacific Ocean. The paperwork is in order. The house has been a year in the building, but it is finished now. Of all the places in the world I could have settled, this was the only one for Polly Barnes, whose tastes are particular, refined in fires which are beyond most imaginings.

Today I will make my last visit to Wildwood, where I have slipped from time to time, unnoticed, willing myself out of darkness, as the Moon turns herself from darkness to light, from nothingness to being. I make myself anew as she does. I vomited up Apollonia in a wood in Lincolnshire and left her there. For a few days, in darkness, I did not know who I was, not until my Hades told me, reformed me from words and the dark. When I emerged once more into the light I was Persephone, with a gun in my hand and my head full of things I was never supposed to know.

On my secret visits to our old home, I have watched my brother, as anxious for him as the mother he believes he has lost. Jesse has the skin of a waning moon, like a parchment lampshade. He is thin and his hair is greasy. Isabella Keats has not taken proper care of him, she has exploited him as both free labour and a tourist attraction. I have watched Wildwood, whenever I have been able, for the past six years, and have witnessed its transformation from my father's dream to my brother's prison. A prison which is shrinking year on year as the sea gnaws at its edges, and Jesse, I fear, is shrinking to fit it.

But he is loyal to Isabella, who was there when he needed her and who did not turn out, like the rest of us, to be someone else. I respect his loyalty. A code of honour is essential to my profession; that is almost the first thing you learn.

This morning I am waiting for him on the edge of the village, in a gateway where I could once have made a different decision, in our father's Aston Martin. (When I heard it was up for sale, I had my agents ensure mine would be the highest bid.) I am not certain he will come, though I am certain he got my message, despite the subterfuge I had to employ to deliver it without Isabella's knowledge. The scrapbook was delivered to the boathouse on the island, where his collection of small skulls moulders under a gauzy blanket of dust. My note was succinct:

Read this. Understand. Meet me at the gate to Peacock's field tomorrow morning at nine.

I obtained the scrapbook on one of my earliest visits, giving my 'school party' the slip and picking the lock to my mother's studio, where the same fine dust covered her plans and scale models and pieces of half-restored furniture as coated Jesse's skulls. I had caught her out once, curled in the corner of her old sofa, leafing through the crackling pages of the scrapbook when she was supposed to be working. She told me it contained design ideas, but I could see it was full of newspaper cuttings. The memory had snagged at my mind ever since, and remained stubbornly in place despite the mass of memories, tumbled, broken and disorderly, washed into me by the tide of revelation my Hades unleashed while I was underground. So I found it, and took it, before all my mother's unfinished projects finished up in a skip when Isabella transformed the studio into a gift shop.

At first it made no sense to me. All these accounts of disasters linked by no common thread, it seemed, other than the scale of their casualties. To me, with my professional interest in the artistry of the individual death, mass slaughter seems banal, the language in which it is described clichéd and meaningless. But when I found the cutting slipped into the paper wallet inside the back cover of the scrapbook, in which a brief account was given of the tragic disappearance, and presumed death, in an earthquake, of new bride, Maureen Jones, when I recognised the photograph of Maureen Jones, in her veil and circlet of orange blossom, as my mother, I began to understand. It wasn't the dead who obsessed her, nor the survivors, but the ones who, like her, like my father, like my Hades, like me, had been transformed.

At three and a half minutes past nine, Jesse appears. Though he says nothing, I detect the flicker of recognition in his blue eyes. I am adept at reading faces quickly and accurately. My life often depends upon it. I am unsure, however, whether his expression is meant for me or the car. He slips into the passenger seat like a hand into a well-worn glove and we set off. I have allowed three hours for the journey, though it may take less; my calculations are based on memories of a Land Rover with the weight of a dead man dragging at it. Your first death always weighs heaviest.

I have visited our mother before, of course, though no-one knows it. An ability to blend into one's surroundings is fundamental to what I do. I donned a white coat, I carried a chart, I hung a stethoscope about my neck. I wore glasses to make me look older and my hair, of course, has not been blonde for a long time. Discreetly, I watched them, the pieta they formed around my mother, Nathan, my grandparents, Nathan's wife, Pauline, sometimes, and her children, whom I think of as my sisters, even though they are not. I have seen my mother graduate from bed to chair, from tubes to bowls and spoons and those feeder cups toddlers use. I have seen the rest straighten from grief-stricken stoops to careful tending to a slightly shame-faced ease in bodies which know how to stand and walk and open tin cans and fall in love. All of which knowledge, and so much more, was wiped from my mother's body, if not her mind, by the third bullet from the Webley .38, the one that was meant for me.

Human beings do not mourn for ever; it is not our nature. We either die of grief or we shrug it off. Sometimes, those who wish to die, like my Hades, need a little help. I killed him because I loved him. I have, perhaps, loved all those whom I have killed.

I considered revealing myself today, dreamed, for a moment, of walking into my mother's room alongside Jesse, without my white coat and glasses, and embracing my grandparents. But it is impossible, it is not my destiny. Mine is the legacy of Alice Walker and Harry Theobald, and Ian Slight, mine the burden of lies and deceit, the privilege of make-believe, of dressing up and being someone else.

So, as we sit in the car park, waiting to go in, I explain to Jesse that he must say goodbye to me here, because he is about to begin a new chapter of his life as himself, as James, while I go on with the old story. I will, I say, as I thrust the scrapbook into his hands, go with him as far as the door to our mother's room. I will, I promise, watch him, and listen as he recites the words I have given him. I remind him to show our mother the new pages in the book, the ones which give accounts of unexplained shootings in hotel rooms the world over, outside the back doors of bars from Mumbai to Rio, and one in a sauna in Athens, Georgia, of which I am particularly proud.

But I myself will be like the Moon on a cloudy night, just a breath of luminescence, transient and unnoticed, and then the world will turn and I shall be gone. He nods. There are tears in his eyes but his thin frame is taut with expectation, with the yearning towards new beginnings. He will not disappoint me. I will not need the Bersa in the glove compartment. I kiss his cheek, and we go in.

I keep my gaze fixed on my mother for as long as I can look through the small viewing-pane in her door without attracting attention. I see only Jesse's hands as he places the book in her lap, and Nathan's as he lifts it out again. And I see my mother's locked-in eyes, staring endlessly off to her left. She does not comprehend the book, she does not even notice it. All that is in her eyes, all that has been in them for the past six years, is the image of me, running towards her from the cavern door, firing the Webley. I came at her from her left.

When Nathan opens the book, the first new cutting he will find comes from the *Sheffield Telegraph* and it tells how Detective Inspector William Grandage was suspended from duty pending a full enquiry after the failure of the operation to rescue Polly Theobald, daughter of the GardenMart magnate, Harry Theobald, from her kidnapper, Arthur Ingliss, the notorious child murderer. During the bungled operation, Ingliss drowned, the girl's mother, Alice Theobald, was shot and seriously injured, and Polly herself vanished. Ballistics reports confirmed that Mrs. Theobald was shot using a gun belonging to murdered Lincolnshire farmer, Reginald Openshaw. No armed response officers were implicated in the shooting.

The article goes on to say that it seems the gun went off by accident and that I must be presumed to be wandering somewhere in a state of shock, perhaps amnesia. I was not shocked, and the memories I have lost I have put aside deliberately, not mislaid. I knocked my Hades unconscious when he came for me and hauled him into the water because I realised he could not let me live with what he had told me, and that he had told me his story in the full knowledge that

I would kill him for it. I, on the other hand, realised I could live with it, in ways more fascinating than I had hitherto believed possible. I shot my mother because I knew it was the only way to stop her looking for me and trying to bring me home. I could not risk her wearing me down. I wanted to kill them both because of the way they betrayed me, coupling like dogs at the kitchen table at Wildwood, where Isabella's staff now make sandwiches and assemble cream teas. The gun did not go off by accident, though, knowing what I now know about firearms, I realise it is a miracle it didn't, a gun as old and uncared for as that.

The only accident was that I failed to kill her and yet even that may have been intentional, on the dark side of my consciousness, because I do not love her. True, she taught me the art of deceit, but only by deceiving me. She taught me self-reliance, but only by also teaching me the dual possibility of existing and not existing. She was the path of moonlight on water, lovely and treacherous, and I do not love her, and could not kill her, because, perhaps, I am her.

I turn to leave, letting the muffled exclamations of surprise and delight on the other side of my mother's door fade from hearing. The keys to the Aston are in Jesse's jacket pocket, where I slipped them as we crossed the car park. I am being picked up in town by a man who has a job for me. It will be my last. My value as a professional assassin has lain not so much in my skill, which anyone can learn, but in my invisibility. No-one expects a schoolgirl to pull out a gun and shoot them.

After today, I will be Polly Barnes. I will live quietly in my house atop its cliff, waiting for earthquakes and whiling away my time in charitable works with lost children. And Persephone? What is Persephone but a myth?

ACKNOWLEDGEMENTS

My thanks are due to Stephanie Thwaites and Emma Herdman at Curtis Brown, to Kathryn Skoyles for introducing me to the special magic of East Ruston Old Vicarage Gardens and to Alan Gray for showing me round, to Indra Strong at Voewood House, and Jill Pompa and Teena Vallerine for the photos. Thanks also for their wisdom to Ruth Dugdall, Martin Figura and Chris Hobley, to Guy Bower for his observations on the pathology of strangulation, Hugh Bower for fight choreography and Siân Bunn for lateral thinking about mobile phones. And to Michael, Sue and Libby Tunbridge for warm hospitality after a cold day in Speedwell Cavern.

Thank you to Jane Dixon-Smith for her beautiful and atmospheric cover design.

Thanks also to Glyn Crews, Claire Gough, Kate Griffin, Jenny Knight, Sarah-Jane Page, Kate Worsley and Luke Wright.

Special thanks, as ever, to Mary-Jane Riley and Sue Fletcher, and to the Dark Knight for helping me make the best of my mortal powers.

S. A. HEMMINGS

I would like to acknowledge the London Library and the Oppenheim John Downes Trust for their generous support in the writing of this novel.

30593660R00181

Made in the USA
Charleston, SC
20 June 2014